E N D

O F L

I N E

adam byfield

Anna,
If you liked THC you'll
probably like this too, hope so! :)

First published 2019

Copyright © adam byfield 2014

All rights reserved

ISBN: 978-1-9162920-1-7

www.adambyfield.com

For Catherine,
for Terry, for Sabbath
and for Mary.

Endings were always difficult.

I'd had plenty of practice, loving relationships, best laid plans, shook sworn deals between friends, I'd ruined them all in my time. The quick break tantrum, the dithering linger, the slow burn fade out, I was adept in all the techniques to kick a thing over and yet endings just never got any easier.

And this was to be no exception.

I stopped pacing in the gloom and dropped onto the battered wooden chair by the table. My legs jiggled, restless still, while I drove my weary eyes over the familiar shadows one more time. My basement bedsit in darkness, approaching midnight again in silence.

Beneath the yellow gloom from the streetlights outside lay the detritus of my life. Clothes, crockery, rubbish and menus, an incredible volume of takeaway menus, covered the floor and lay heaped all around me. Some of it had been here when I'd moved in but I'd added my share over time.

It didn't look as bad in the dark I realised. Painted with shadows the drifts of crap lost their texture and appeared organic, almost homely. The mess irritated me vaguely, ate at me slow, but as ever I let the frustration wash through me, just another tooth on the saw.

The motionless meter out in the hall said no cash, no lights, no power, but the darkness was ok by me. A squat candle spluttered valiantly amid the chaos of the table, just about managing to push back the black and quiver yellow on a clearing in the clutter.

I drummed my fingers in the limited light, legs still twitching, eyes not looking, my hand skipping rhythmic in the tabletop glow. There'd been hours of this, possibly even days by this point, round and round, up and down, still not able to just end it.

Finally, I sighed and turned to face the arrangement full on, grim concentration tightening my jaw. To my left was a large spliff, pale, plump, eagerly awaiting the lick of a flame. Smoking it would mean carrying on. Endless possibilities rolled within that paper, such curiosity as to what tomorrow might bring as to put pay to any ending tonight.

I left the spliff where it was and peered back out into the gloom. Just a few feet away sat the comfortable bulk of my armchair. Gradually easing through slow collapse, the chair was battered and broken in all the right places. It made drinking and thinking an easy way to kill time, a cradle and a key to soft focused memories worn thin with use. I felt myself smile just a little.

Clenching my eyes shut tight however, I shook my gritted teeth. Sitting in that chair meant doing nothing at all as the sitting itself had no ending. Sitting there just meant staring and remembering and doing nothing and nothing and nothing. That's all it ever led to.

So I stayed where I was, eyes closed, jaw locked in the darkness, while my body pawed at me for attention. My throat barked thorns, the price of too many pale, plump promises, while my lower back ached, groaning from too much sitting and staring. Even my hand on the table moaned its sharp little pains, the joints stiff and spiking.

My body felt old now, older than it should be though no more than I deserved. I'd long since spent my life's allotment of righteous vigour, used it up quick and loud then spent as many years again mortgaging more against a future I never expected to see. Yet here I was, spent up and worn out with a lifetime of dues to pay.

Opening my eyes again, I shook away all the petty pangs and relaxed a little, focusing firmly now on the other object painted real by the candle. The crisp, black lines of the revolver cut the yellow light hard so that everything around it was vague and smoke smudged.

I lifted the weight from the table, the handle felt cool in my palm. Turning it back and forth I soaked up its details, its angles and curves.

This was the one thing.

2

Not everything tomorrow, not nothing forever, just one thing, right here, right now.

This was my ending.

Tilting the barrel to the ceiling, I eased back the hammer with my thumb. The click cut straight through the gloom to shiver quick up my spine. I moved with slow and deliberate care to rest my chin on the upturned muzzle, adjusted the angle to my satisfaction and settled. My finger curled over the trigger and I licked my lips, steadying myself until I felt calm and ready.

To take your last breath, knowing that it is your last, is an incredibly powerful experience. I took four. Eventually however, I finally knew it was on and so closed my eyes and began to tighten my finger. I felt the trigger begin to give under my pressure and my face begin to flinch

noise!

A sound.

I jumped violently and then clenched, suddenly frozen in mortal terror of pulling that very same trigger by accident. The harsh, electronic noise continued while my eyes bulged and my brain locked into a silent loop, just the gonging absence of a gunshot over and over again.

A few, pounding, heartbeats, later, the engine finally turned over and I realised that my phone was ringing. And that I hadn't shot myself. Lungs burning, I noticed I wasn't breathing and so gasped loudly before starting to wheeze and gingerly lowering the quivering revolver to the table. I twisted in the chair and straightened my leg to retrieve the phone from my pocket.

I had to blink a couple of times before I could read the familiar name flashing up at me. I let a couple more curse laden breaths rattle in and out of me before raising the quivering phone to my ear and answering.

"..kin hell, o. Hello? I mean hey, how're, how're you doing?" I stumbled.

The reply was so panicked and gasping I couldn't take it in at first.

"Hang on, hang on," I had to interrupt, my heart rate dropping as I tuned back in to what the guy's

3

hysterical voice was saying. "Start again mate, nice and slow."

The flurry of words came again but this time I caught most of them and a sequence of events began to line up before my mind's eye. Waiving the standard practice of breathing between sentences, his story built to a desperate, breathless finale in the form of a question. I thought about how to respond for a few seconds, even though the answer was immediately clear.

"Yes mate," I said, deciding on blunt honesty. "You know what he's like. He'll kill you, and he'll be a right shit about it too."

A low groan and whimper crawled out of the phone.

More seconds ticked by. Why should I care? What did it matter? It wasn't like I was going to be around long enough to feel guilty. I tried to think of something different to say, something other than what I knew I was going to say.

Nothing came. I cursed, silently this time, and sighed while shaking my head.

"When's it all happening?" I asked, nodding at the babbled reply. "Alright, so that's nine hours to find it yeah? That's plenty. If I find it and get it back there by 9:00am then he'll never know what happened will he? It'll be fine, ok?"

More babbling, mostly tearful thanks this time but again ending with a question.

"No, no," I replied, looking at the revolver still seething on the table, "nothing that can't wait. Seriously, I'll sort it, no worries."

I disentangled myself from the call and just sat, adjusting to the sudden change of pace. Slipping my phone back into my pocket, I suddenly realised how tired was. As the adrenalin had ebbed away during the call a deep fatigue had settled through me.

The thought of setting out into that night felt like more than I could bear. Plunging back into all the old craziness, another almost certainly impossible task, pushing my luck just a little bit further, it was more than my nerves could bear.

I'd do it anyway though, I'd hate myself and curse

myself for it but I'd do it for him, of course I would. How could I not?

I snapped out of the funk and stood abruptly from the chair so that it teetered back into the shadows for a moment before rattling to stand. I scooped the spliff up into my mouth, gently uncocked the revolver, nudged the safety back on and then blew out the candle. Moving easily through the domestic twilight, I returned the gun to its home deep in the guts of the broken down, fire trap armchair.

Finally, I retrieved my jacket from one of the piles of debris nearer the door and slipped it on before fishing a lighter from the pocket. Pausing briefly to eye my charcoal self seriously in the smudged mirror on the wall, I lit the spliff and strode out into the hallway, pulling the door closed behind me.

I took remembered steps through pitch black to the door then stone steps up to ground level and suddenly I was under the streetlights. I hunched my shoulders against the cold and began throwing long, quick strides up the hill.

It felt strange to be out in the world again. The vast emptiness hanging overhead, the cold, endless shapes crowded all around, the scale and the chill of it all made the previous hours of dramatic indoor tension seem dreamlike, indulgent and fanciful.

The street was deserted and I took quick hard drags of the joint in time with my feet. As the crest of the hill came into view I could hear voices and traffic from the main road up ahead, albeit slightly fogged now by the familiar thick blanket of the gear already settling upon me. It fuzzed the streetlights overhead to make them twinkle and the night seemed just a little less cold.

The tarmac pavement rolled on under my feet, occasionally patched a different shade of cornered grey or spotted ugly with pale, rounded gum. I didn't want to be out and tried to resent it, wondered if there had been any way I could have said no on the phone. In my guts I knew there hadn't been but now I was out here I realised I had no clue how I was going to keep the promise I had made.

Recoiling from the thought, I turned to the lad

5

instead. I'd known him for a while now and he was sound enough, dependable and earnest with it, bit of a dreamer really. In a way it was refreshing, seeing that kind of hope and vigour in a scene as grim as this, but ultimately he was too soft for it and he'd already paid for it, heavy.

I had to give it to the him though, he'd never once bitched about what had happened and he hadn't let it change him. Despite what it had cost him, he'd just kept on keeping on, just as he was, a good lad. Not exactly honest, but as straight as bent gets. Of course none of that mattered really and it certainly wasn't why I'd agreed to help him.

I was nowhere nearer a plan but was closing on the corner, lost in thought and taking distracted drags on the joint. I'd just bested the hill and turned left into thin strings of people alongside the main road that circled the park when a great screeching suddenly tore through the night. I jumped violently, wide eyed panicked, before quickly composing myself and wondering if anyone among the already gathering crowd had noticed.

A catastrophically drunk young lass had stumbled out into the road just as a large, family car was sweeping majestically by. Somehow the guy had managed to stop what looked like an inch from disaster but her response had been to pound on his bonnet and hurl insults at his windscreen. In seconds the driver was out on the road, albeit still behind his car door, attempting to respond with a verbal assault of his own.

"You jump in front of my car.." he roared but was quickly drowned out by the screeching, deathwish drunk. I relaxed again and paused, smoking slow and enjoying the show.

The guy was clearly used to being in charge. At home, at work, he was obviously a boss, a big man, king of his own particular hill. It clearly hadn't occurred to him though, when jumping out of his ride full of self righteous outrage, that he wasn't on his hill anymore. Out here with the rest of us, out of his bubble, that car, that job, that pay packet all of that stuff he stood on to feel taller, it didn't count for shit down here.

Realising he was out of his depth the driver fell back, trying to take the path of sense and reason to higher ground, getting all paternal with the lass though she was having none of it. As she slurred through an increasingly hilarious tirade of abuse, smirks and chuckles among the audience grew to open laughter, whistles and calls of encouragement.

The driver gave up trying to respond and just grew redder and redder as he squirmed instead. His pride had pushed him out of the car and into this scene, in front of his wife and his kids and a slowly growing number of strangers and until he swallowed it he was stuck there.

I moved past them with a smile and continued along the pavement as the lass's voice sank beneath the crowd's chatter before fading altogether. The last time I looked over my shoulder I saw that the driver was back in his car but that the drunk was now refusing to move out of the way. The traffic behind was backed up and honking in a bizarre Tienanmen parody, tottering high heels of drunken rebellion before the might of the establishment's family saloon.

With the distraction behind me, my train of thought rerailed, though not along the lines I wanted. The sound the lad's voice on the phone had put me on a track back to memories of what had come before before him and of what had led up to him taking his fall, memories I usually avoided.

I followed the pavement with its patches and spots to where it plunged down the far side of the hill. Over the street, off to my right the void of the park loomed dark in the corner of my eye. Stretching back from the road, the park was an enclave of the ancient night amid the modern bulb lit streets and it yawned at me to look.

Despite the tug however I didn't turn my head, hoping to avoid its bottomless gaze and the memory I knew would follow. Not looking didn't help though and as I quickened my pace the chilled night caught me and dragged me back by contrast .

The relentless heat of that summer's sun. I'm laid out flat on the very same welcoming grass that's hiding over there in the blackness, stoned as a bastard and thinking of nothing but the perfect

warmth seeping over and through my skin.

Then a shadow falls across me I am reborn to the world, blinking and confused. I don't know it now of course, but this is the beginning of the end. Things weren't great at this point but this is the moment when the slide begins and it all starts going to shit.

The skinny kid standing over me is all scowls and slouching. His face looks mean but he stands desperate and moves unsure.

"Get up," he spits at me. "There's someone you need to talk to."

I sit up blinking, rubbing my head and looking around blearily, still drunk on the bliss of a moment before.

"What?" I say eventually.

"Don't fuck about man, you heard me," he tries to growl. "You've been called, so get up and follow me."

I lean back on my elbows and take a look around us. The park is busy with pockets of people lounging about stretching off in all directions. A warm and gentle breeze carries the tinny parts of a song from some far off car radio and all the world seems soft and easy.

I turn my attention back to the kid, squinting up at him and yawning. From the lines of his clothes and the hang of his hands I'm pretty sure he's not tooled up.

"Called?" I ask. He fidgets his irritation before looking around quickly.

"Yeah. Called. And when he calls you you come fucking running." He pauses, licking his lips before dropping to one knee so as to lower his voice. "Or are you going to make me do something?"

I meet and hold his eyes for a second but don't find what I'm looking for so put my hands behind my head and lie back down.

"Do what you like lad," I say, closing my eyes once more to the mighty glare.

There's a long pause. The chimes of an ice

cream van drift lazily over the chatter of the park and somewhere distant dogs are barking.

"Ok look," the kid's voice is softer now, betraying defeat. "Tall James wants to see you, he's waiting for us down the street." Another pause and then almost a whimper. "Don't make me go back without you man."

I take another long, deep drag of summer and then sit back up. I can smell barbeque.

"Fair enough, let's go."

The scene faded as I began to descend the hill, leaving the park to the night behind me but carrying the memory still. Alone with my footsteps I tried not to resume. Picking over all that old shit wouldn't help me with the task ahead. As the familiar sign of the pub came into view, tiny and distant at the foot of the hill, I reflected that I needed to focus if this job was going to get done.

I docked the joint and slipped it carefully into my jacket before shouldering through the heavy, narrow doors and pushing into the low lit heat. There was a fair crowd in but the place wasn't heaving, by this time of night people had either called it a night or gone on into town.

Approaching the bar I was pleased to spot barmaid rather than the landlord serving the drinks. I needed a drink and a chat, not hassle about my tab. Dropping onto the vacant stool, I fished around for some change and then fiddled with it on the bar as I waited to start the night's work.

Eventually she came over, all soft curves and kind eyes, smiling her greeting.

"Alright Kaz, usual?" she asked, already reaching for a glass.

"Cheers," I replied, scooping up the coins and returning the smile.

"Haven't seen you in here for a while," she said, managing to sound genuinely interested as she pulled the pint.

"Yeah, I've been..." I thought about it, "...busy," I decided.

Seconds of comfortable pubhubbub rolled by. She

placed the pint in front of me and I passed her the change, her soft, clean fingers briefly brushing my own.

"Ta," I said, taking a quick sip. "So what's this I hear about some nasty shit happening in here a while back?" I glanced to an empty spot down at the other end of the bar. A flicker of sadness pinched her face over the till so that guilt flushed my cheeks. I dropped the subject and looked down into my pint instead.

"Sorry," I said quietly as she returned with my change but she shook her head.

"The old guy who used to read the paper," she said, glancing to the same empty spot at the far end of the bar. "He was stabbed in the gents, bled to death before the ambulance could get here."

"Shit," I winced, sipping at my pint so as to avoid her eyes. "You didn't find him did you?" I asked. She shook her head again.

"No, John found him later on," she explained.

I nodded but, "Shit." was all I could think of to say again as we both stared past one another.

Tuning back in, it occurred to me to ask. "So do they know who...?"

"I know," she interrupted, suddenly back too and angrily animated with it. "Fucking bastard," she hissed with venom and I felt my eyebrows jump. The lass had been pulling my pints for a couple of years and I'd never heard her say a bad word about anyone. The tangible spite in her voice was a bit of a shock.

"Someone we know?" I asked carefully, professional interest cooling my embarrassment now.

"Don't know if you ever met him," she began, glancing about but finding no-one else waiting.

"He used to come in in the afternoons mostly, was always really rude, I never liked him." She leaned across the bar a little and lowered her voice even further while her perfume danced all about me.

"He had something against the old guy, kicked off with him a few times. John had always put up with it before but then the idiot threw a glass at him for no reason. John gave him a bit of a kicking and barred him." Her eyes slipped off beyond me again.

"I know he came back and stabbed him, I just

10

know he did. And now every time I hear the door to gents go I half expect to see that cheeky old sod coming back to the bar, asking if he can have just one more half on his tab..."

I set my pint down and rested my hand gently on hers. "I'm sorry about that love, that's really shitty." She smiled then took her hand back, shaking herself back to smiles. "So what do you want then?"

For a moment I feigned offence but her stare broke me down almost immediately. I hid behind my pint while she drummed her fingers on the bar until I wiped my mouth on the back of my hand.

"Ok," I started, leaning in.

It was on.

"Don't suppose any of my friends have been in tonight have they?"

"Friends?" she asked sarcastically, waving goodnight to someone leaving behind me. "Plural?"

"Yeah, yeah," I nodded, smiling sourly as she giggled. "You know who I mean."

"Yeah your friend," a wicked grin underlined the singular, "the lad with the eye, he was in. He was with a few other lads actually, bit lairy but they were ok." I nodded, tilting my glass a little further.

"That lad worships you you know," she added in a sterner tone.

I swallowed before nodding some more. "I know," I said.

"God knows why. You owe him though, after what happened..." her words hung over me, the unspoken heaviest of all.

"I know that too," I said quietly, remembering the panic in his voice on the phone and picturing his face. The lad with the eye she'd called him. It was a better description than it sounded. I imagined that eye, wide and wet with panic as he'd blurted all his terrors into his phone.

"So who else," I shook myself. "Anyone new?"

"It's been a busy night," she said, gathering a few glasses from along the gradually emptying bar. I waited until she was standing right in front of me again.

"C'mon," I said in a low voice. "Who's been in that

I might want to know about?"

She looked along the bar both ways again before leaning forward and I almost managed not to glance down her top.

"A couple of lads, 'bout the same age as your friend. They came in just after him and his mates but didn't stay very long, just a couple of shots each, lots of heavy talking. They were really wound up and way out of it." She glanced about again before her expression turned little more serious. "Looked like Dutch courage to me. A pre match party, full works."

I thought about this while she moved away to serve someone else. Already possible next steps were lining up to audition before my mind's eye. The bottom of my glass began to wink at me as I relished the middle of my pint. A thoughtful moment more and she was back.

"So what did these lads look like then?" I asked.

"Well they were both dressed pretty low key. One had kind of sandy hair, bit on the short side, bit chunky. The other was taller and skinny, dark hair and mean looking. Big gold ring on his little finger." Before I could respond she'd moved away again to supply another demand.

I stared through what was left of my pint and let the pieces fall together. A pre match party she'd said, one last romp of earthly pleasures before a job that might put them inside or worse. They sounded like professional improvisers, or at least habitually unprepared, and reckless. Just what I was looking for.

I glanced across at her pulling more pints and chatting bullshit. She wore dizzy smiles and golden curls but she was as sharp as pin and plugged right in behind those big blue eyes. If she thought those guys were preparing for something big then that was fact as far I was concerned. If they'd been partying hard then that meant gear and girls, neither of which they'd find in here. They'd come here for their last round, for a bit Dutch courage and most likely for something else as well.

Things were starting to make sense.

It occurred to me that I was now hooked, well and

truly into it. I shrugged and drained my glass, placed it back on the bar and pondered. Gear or girls, which way to go? I had options either way but found it hard to weigh one against the other.

I sank into the choice, which was quicker? riskier? more likely to yield results? I was frowning my concentration when suddenly and from nowhere, the gear and beer seemed to get right up on top of me and I zoned out. A weird head rush took me and just for a moment everything was bright white silence until, with a start, I was back in the pub, on the way off the back of my stool.

I snatched at the bar and managed to steady myself, quickly glancing around to see if she, or anyone else, had noticed. Shaking the fuzz from my brow I focused. Gear was the way, at some point I seemed to have decided that and so now knew who I had to see next.

I rose from my stool as the barmaid returned. I smiled as she took my glass.

"Mind how you go won't you," she said, a stock phrase but now with additional meaning, genuine concern peeking from behind her professional smile. For a moment I thought how great she was but then just said goodnight and turned away.

Back out on the street, I rubbed my hands together and thought about the next stop on my trip. Turning left I set off briskly, planning the rest of my route as I went. I reflected on how lucky I'd been to catch fire on my first go but cautioned myself against too much optimism, the night was young and I was bound to encounter at least a couple of dead ends.

All immediate decisions made I dropped into a steady rhythm up the dark and quiet street, but while my body was all purpose and direction my mind began to wander once more. Try as I might to resist, the moment my mind's eye drifted the images rolled and there I was, following that skinny kid out of the park again.

We're heading over the road, away from happy park sounds, down one sunbaked back street then into the cool shade of another. Finally a

13

huge, black SUV comes into view. Every window is tinted blind. I can feel the bass and smell the gear from ten feet away.

"For fuck's sake," I mutter as we approach. "Why not just paint a sign on the side?"

The kid opens the back door so that waves of bass and smoke spill out all about us. He ushers me inside before jogging away to stand lookout at the end of the street. The door slams shut and I'm immediately drowning in relentless sonic pounding. A conditioned chill seizes me and despite myself I shiver.

Still stoned, the sudden change is jarring and I work hard to keep straight as I adjust to this new world. Squinting through the smoky gloom I find that both the driver and front passenger seats are full to overflowing with two almost comically huge guys, both of whom have just about managed to twist round in their seats to glare at me.

Next to me sits Tall James, all of five feet and change. He's smoking a blunt like a baby's arm and scowling his best gangster scowl. I hate this guy and have to work hard to keep it from showing. Everything he wears, says and does is lifted straight from an album cover or music video, there's nothing of him in any of it.

He likes to bang on about being 'ghetto' and 'coming up from nothing', as if he cut his teeth on the mean streets of some hellhole slum, but I remember his parents. His dad was an accountant for a local manufacturing firm, his mum a receptionist at the doctor's I think. They weren't exactly minted but they had a nice house and were a solid, straight, respectable family.

I also remember James as a shitty arse little kid, cute enough with his little fro but never wanting for anything and yet always wanting more. His parents had retired and moved away in the end, heartbroken that he hadn't gone to university and increasingly shamed by his increasingly dark behaviour.

"I got a job for you," he glowers then nods

14

grimly in silence. His meat puppets are nodding too. I watch James take a deep, heavy drag and the end of the blunt glows vicious. Seconds tick by and by, counted off by the pounding bass that ripples relentless through us.

The novelty of contrast is fading quick and as moments pass the try-hard bad vibes begin to piss me off. I feel irritation rising up through my buzz. Eventually I draw breath to speak but James, apparently waiting for this as his cue, cuts me off.

"It's this bitch," he snaps, his voice barely breaking the surface of sound so that I have to focus hard through the rhythm to catch his words.

"Thinks she can walk away from me? From me!" The stereo thugs shake their heads slow as I wait for the next verse to fall. I take a cool and smoky breath and work hard to remember, I'm supposed to be looking intimidated .

"She's got my kid man," it comes finally, "and she's got the pigs on with it too. Got a fucking restraining order and everything." I nod as if I get it but still can't get a handle on where this is going.

"I can't get anywhere near him and the pigs know all my boys..." he leaves this hanging with the smoke as he takes another drag, revelling in the needless tension.

"So you're going to watch him for me," he says, eyes narrowing. "You're going to follow them, see where she takes him, what he does and when, and then you're going to tell me all about it." He nods to the slab in the passenger seat who shifts himself awkwardly then shoves a small bundle of cash and a photo at me.

"That's an advance," James explains. "Expenses and shit. You get the same again next time I see you, long as you have something for me."

I pocket the cash and glance at the photo before doing the same with that too. Some little kid riding a tricycle, an address scribbled on the back in childish scrawl as if the kid had written it himself.

"Got it?" James studies me severely.

"Got it," I reply, calm and smooth.

"Right, fuck off then." James and the rest all turn to face front while he brings out a mobile. He inspects it with well practised nonchalance and I apparently cease to exist.

I slip out of the smoky, bass blasted twilight and back into the summer shade.

"Wanker," I hiss to the cool crumbling brickwork as I stride away from the car.

I give the young lookout a nod as I pass him and step back into the glorious blaze, my body relishing the sudden return to pervasive heat. Ambling back towards the park, I finger the notes in my pocket and ponder the texture of the niggle they carry.

The sun is still high and in theory so am I but even with the grass back under my feet I can't quite find that bliss from before. I look all about the park again, soaking up the colours, the shapes and the sounds but somewhere deep in the back of my mind I know there's a piece of this thing I'm not seeing.

The subtle sour feeling lingered as the cool night air breathed me back to the present. I was staring at the pavement, all old, well worn slabs round here, occasional absences filled in with tar to look like missing teeth.

Then I remembered the joint in my jacket. Relieved by the distraction, I retrieved it carefully with a happy smile and then fished out a lighter to match. I was just about to flick the flint however, when I paused to listen instead.

Up ahead was the narrow left turn into the long, dark alley that would shave a good twenty minutes off my journey. The alley itself however, was firing ugly sounds out onto the desolate street, sounds of brutal violence.

I lowered my hands and their respective burdens and took a few more cautious steps forward. I craned my neck to find the source of the ugly so that an oblong of streetlit street at the far end of the alley came into view. It framed a silhouette of a bloated man swaying over a body on the floor and panting heavily. A few seconds more and he recovered his breath.

"You. Fucking. Bitch!" He roared, each word emphasised by way of a brutal stamping motion, down into the figure at his feet. The resultant squeals made me cringe. More insults and kicks rained down until the guy even kneeled to land vicious punches instead when his legs gave way.

I looked at the nasty tangle that blocked me and then past it to the street beyond. Glancing off to my right I eyed the long way round but really didn't fancy the extra distance. Paralysed by indecision I dithered. The squealing stopped leaving only wet crunching sounds in its wake.

This really wasn't my bag at all and besides, wasn't I already in the middle of helping somebody out? I could never be described as a knight in shining armour after all but before I could get any closer to a decision the guy noticed me and straightened up to meet my eye.

When I didn't look or move away he stepped out into the light and came over. Despite the chill of the night he was wearing a horrific Hawaiian shirt, his chest pushing out the gaudy pattern to compete with his gut as he glared.

"Who are you then?" he growled, his breath thick with booze and cut sharp into lines by telltale sniffing. "Her knight in shining armour? Eh?"

I smiled at the coincidence.

"It's funny..." I began but was cut short as one of his huge ham fists landed smack in the centre of my face.

"Ok," I conceded, staggering back and blinking the blood from eyes. "It's not."

"You need to fuck off mate," the guy took another step forward. "While you still can."

I coughed and spat and stared around, still recovering from the blow. The street seemed to ripple beneath me while the streetlights had painted everything fuzzy.

"Are you fucking deaf?" he roared, his anger now almost everything in him.

17

With a sigh I raised the joint to my sticky lips then brought the swaying lighter up to meet it. It took me a few squinting seconds to line the two up and light it, but I got there and took a good long drag.

"I said..." the guy lost patience and moved in again but this time I replied.

"I'm no hero mate," I croaked.

He paused, confused but still ready to explode.

"Ask anyone." I continued. "Tell you what I am though, what I've been told I'm very good at being..." I paused for another drag, still coughing and spitting blood onto the pavement, black on yellow.

The guy stepped in again to come within arm's reach.

"Yeah?" he hissed, ready to strike. "What's that that then?"

" A distraction," I said calmly, raising my hand to shield my eyes.

For a moment I think the guy must have just stared his confusion at the lighter in my palm, but then the bottle exploded over the back of his head, showering me with glass and dropping him to the kerb.

As I shook the glass from my jacket and carefully stepped past them, the battered girl from the alley fell onto his groaning form. She was a skinny little thing, all straight lines, sharp angles, hissing her curses through swollen lips and plunging what was left of the bottle into him again and again.

The glass flesh skitch sounds followed me down the alley, fading slow while I gingerly wiped my face between slowly soothing drags. My next stop was just round the corner but I knew he rattled easy and wouldn't appreciate a bloodied face or jangling nerves. I concentrated on composing myself and leaving the sticky shocks behind.

I had just finished the joint and flicked the roach to the road when I saw myself in a darkened shop window. I spent a minute or two moving spit from my mouth to my thumb to my face to clear away the black that I knew to be red. It hurt like hell but eventually I reckoned I looked ok and pressed on, hands deep in my pockets now.

I was putting plenty of distance between myself and the ugly happenings in the alley but my mind was dragging behind, my stomach turning over and over as I replayed it all again and again. Suddenly that summer appeared a lesser evil and this time I fell back gladly.

Billy is under a car when I find him, as always.

He's been running this garage for as long as I can remember, mostly straight but always willing to help a friend. He's known me since I was a kid and every so often I do some legit driving for him when he's busy.

It's another seething hot summer day. I step off the not-quite-shimmering street into the cool gloom of the garage. The shade feels good. I blink for a moment as my eyes unscrunch and adjust to fix on a familiar pair of legs emerging from beneath another old banger. A drowsy wave of fuzzed radio chatter is spluttering out from the back of the place. It fills the oily space around us and stumbles out into the street to be consumed by the sun.

"Now then lad," comes a familiar voice from below. "I suppose you'll be after a favour won't you."

I frown and look left and right round the edges of the car. The legs still haven't moved.

"You sneaky old bastard," I laugh. "How d'you know it was me?"

Billy emerges from under the car, filthy and grinning.

"When was the last time you bought a new pair of shoes eh?" He moves through stages to standing, a little stiffer and slower than I remember. I suppose we're all getting older while he wipes his dirty hands on a dirtier rag.

"I wouldn't have survived long round here if I couldn't spot a wrong 'un coming from under a chassis now would I?" Billy says, heading for the office.

"Get fucked," I grin and follow him to the doorway but no further.

19

Billy's office is actually more of a storage cupboard with a small, fetid sink clinging to the back wall. Somehow he's managed to stuff in a small desk, a filing cabinet and a chair leaving just enough room for him.

Add in the mounds of paperwork heaped on the desk, pinned to the walls and in drifts on the floor and the overall impression is that the administrative hub of the business has always been here and that they built the garage around it.

"Brew?" he offers, rummaging through curling invoices to retrieve two dubious looking mugs.

"Aye go on then," I reply.

Billy digs out the kettle while I eye the familiar faded curves of the old calendar pinned to the wall next to a board of keys on hooks. We're all getting older but for her it will always be December 1993. Bad hair, nice smile, tits forever firm.

We sip insanely sweet coffee and catch up. Who's gone down, who's out, who's copped it, who's had kids. We even reshare a couple of tales from years back. Eventually though, in its own time and way, the conversation makes its way round to business.

"So what d'you need?" Billy asks, draining the dregs of his brew.

"Mixed transport. Couple of weeks." I reply, my own mug now hanging from my fingers, just slow crystal sludge remaining.

"Aye that's no bother," says Billy. "You can start with that 'un," he adds, nodding to a small red Ford parked on the street just outside.

Turning to rinse his mug Billy reaches over to the board on the wall and retrieves a set of keys without looking. He turns back to face me and I swap him my mug for the keys then slap him on the shoulder for good measure.

"Good man," I say and head back out into the glare.

There was no glare on the street though as I

paused in a shadow to look up at the flats looming ahead. Back in the moment and soon I was making my way up the stone stairway, hard, dark and cold, pushing through the echoes of my footsteps to the third floor. Strolling along the landing, I held my chin to my chest against the unrestrained chill and listened hard for sounds of company but found nothing more than distant TV mumbles.

Pausing at a familiar door, I knocked and tried the handle. To my surprise the door was locked. I frowned, confused and knocked again, checking back and forth along the landing as I waited. If this guy wasn't in I was going to have to try a less friendly source of information and no doubt pay a much higher price for it too.

Absently I pushed my hand into the base of my back which was still complaining bitterly, aching face for attention. I pressed my fingers against the pain while waiting, shifting my weight slightly and grimacing. Just as I was beginning to give up however, I heard movement just inside. The lock clicked and a thin crack of black appeared down the edge of the door.

"Who is it?" hissed a voice, dripping with paranoia.

"It's me." I sighed. "What're you doing man?"

Although we hadn't spoken for a few weeks I needed this guy's help tonight and really didn't want to have to deal with one of his rare but legendary freak outs. A heavy stoner by trade, the guy was plagued by an occasional desire to mix things up with a binge of pills and powders. A few of the subsequent comedowns had scuppered my plans in the past while I'd had to wait for him to ride out the paranoia and psychosis. If knew if he was on one then he'd be useless to me for a least a couple of days.

The door slammed back through the fraction it had opened and there came the sound of a chain being shakily unhooked. A moment more and the door retreated again, further this time though still not all the way.

I slipped through the gap into the murky hallway just quickly enough to avoid being caught as the door was slammed shut and the chain and lock both quickly reapplied. He bustled past me down the hall and through

21

into the front room where he settled back onto the sofa. He was wrapped in a large blanket and shakily trying to roll a joint on a DVD case.

"What the fuck man?" I asked, concern overriding irritation as I noticed for the first time the heavy bruising down the left hand side of his gaunt face. He was painfully skinny white guy with a large nose and slightly sunken eyes.

The thin ratty dreads fitted the rest of him, all gangling bones and lolloping strides and which served to made him look younger than he was. In all the time I'd known him I'd never seen him wear anything but a holey, stretched out rainbow jumper and torn baggy jeans.

Usually though, his eyes were bright and the harsh angles of his face would be softened by a knowing grin, signs of his relentless cheer. It was clear that something dark had happened in the last few hours.

"It's, it's all gone to shit man," he stammered, the embryonic joint twitching from his fingers into his lap, spilling its precious cargo. I sat down gently beside him and retrieved the DVD case from his lap, along with the paper, roach and scattering of gear.

"Alright mate," I said as I began to put the joint back together. "Start at the start. What's going on?"

He raised his long fingers to his purple face carefully, wincing at his own touch.

"Haven't you heard man?" his voice cracked. "Haven't you heard?"

"Heard what? C'mon mate, seriously, take a breath. What's.." I paused to run my tongue along the edge of the paper, "..happened?"

"It's bad man, really fucking bad. You really haven't heard?"

I twisted off the business end of the joint, lit it and passed it to him. His hands were shaking as he took it.

"For fuck's sake man, no I haven't heard! You going to catch me up or what?" The guy nodded as he took several hungry drags on the joint.

"You know about that new, Southern lot in town?" he began, pausing to exhale a great plume of smoke. "How they went after his daughter then when that got fucked up they offed his son?"

I nodded, of course I knew about that, everyone did. No-one ever used his name, you didn't need to. He owned everything worth owning, ran everything worth running, had been untouchable until a bunch of Southerners had rocked up and started messing with his kids. A tiny cold spot appeared in the pit of my stomach at the possibility of some crossover between this thing and my own.

"Well," he struggled on, burning through the joint at record speed. "There was supposed to be a sit down tonight, his lot and their lot, settling up so they say."

"Ok," I said slowly, the cold spot growing as my mind trotted ahead. I was pretty sure I knew what was coming.

"Someone hit it," he said. "Hard."

My stomach turned.

Fuck.

"Who..." I began but he was in a full flow freak out now.

"No-one knows man!" He turned to face me full on, eyes wild amid the bruising and still dragging hard only now blowing the smoke in my face.

"No-one fucking knows! Was it his lot? Was is their lot? All people know is that it was a total fucking slaughter, proper bloodbath and now both sides are out putting the squeeze on anyone who knows anything. It's fucking chaos man, it's fucking war!"

He went to bury his face in his hands but cursed and pulled back before carefully fingering his bruises. The cold spot exploded to chill clarity all through me as adrenalin shouldered past the gear and the booze.

I took a breath and asked the inevitable. "So what happened to you?"

"They fucking happened to me man!" he shrieked. "Those Southern bastards." He looked at the dead roach between his fingers blankly for a second or two before flicking it away and reaching for more papers and gear.

"What did they want?" I had to ask.

"They were looking for the guys they think did it weren't they. They thought they might have come here to score earlier on." His hands were still trembling but less so as years of practice began to show through the shakes. He laid out another paper.

"And you held out?" I couldn't keep the surprise from my voice.

"Did I fuck," came his bitter reply. "I told them everything straight away."

"So why..." I couldn't see it.

"Just because man!" he snapped. "To make sure I wasn't holding anything back yeah? I told you, it's all out war and everyone in between is getting stomped just in case. It's fucking crazy!"

Lighting the new joint he finally collapsed back against the sofa and looked to the ceiling before closing his eyes. We sat in silence while I tried not to be sick. This road I'd agreed to walk had just twisted to run smack through the middle of a long awaited, apocalyptic gang war. Eventually my host sighed and sat forward, suddenly looking more like his usual self.

"Sorry man," he croaked, back to his usual, sleepy tone. "It's been a heavy night and I'm a bit rattled. Did you come to score?" He began to reach under the couch as he spoke but then noticed my reddened nose for the first time and paused.

"Shit man. You been dancing yourself tonight?" he said, returning to his reaching.

"Misunderstanding," I mumbled, brushing it aside and pushing on ahead. "Actually," I said, already finding the words bitter. "I was after some information."

He froze then straightened slow.

"Like what?" he asked quietly.

"I'm trying to trace a couple of young guys. They'll have been out to score earlier tonight. One was kind of short and chunky with sandy coloured hair..." but he'd already erupted from the blanket, up and away from the sofa.

"No, no, no, no," he was saying, shaking his head. "This is bad man, way too bad. No, no, no.." I stood as he began to pace back and forth.

"Look, mate, it's fine. It's nowt to do with any of that and it's not the lads I'm after, I just need to talk to them about something." I explained in my most reasonable tone.

24

"No fucking way man," he continued, even wagging a finger at me from amid his building frenzy. "I like you man," he gibbered. "You always pay up front, you never dick me about, you're ok. I'm not sending you the same place I sent them man, no way. They will fuck you up."

"Seriously, I have to find those lads tonight. It's a favour for a friend mate, I've no choice and I need your help. C'mon man, help me out." I laid it all out there and rolled the dice.

He stopped pacing, took a drag and thought about it.

"Some friend man," he muttered and sat back down. "Like I said to those bastards before, those lads didn't score from me. If they're not local and they're asking around to score heavy they'd probably have been pointed at Dick's."

"Dick?" I asked, returning the name and accepting the joint.

"Yeah, Dick." He spat the name as if it tasted sour. "Some little rich cunt, turned up a couple of weeks ago. He's barely out of school but, get this, his parents have gone abroad somewhere for a few months so he's pawned everything in the house and spent it on gear.

"He's set himself up out of some flash apartment and thinks he can turn a profit then buy all mummy and daddy's shit back before they get home. Plus he gets to play at being a drug dealer for a couple of weeks. Idiot's been telling anyone and everyone where he is and what he's got, it's a fucking miracle he hasn't been turned over already."

I passed the joint back and he paused for smoky breath.

"Anyway," he continued, "as I say, if they weren't local and were they asking around, Dick's the guy they'll've been told about, that's where they'll've gone."

He told me where the apartment block was, I knew it, it wasn't far, and he even gave me the number but while I was taking it in I wasn't really listening. A crew of vicious thugs had battered the hell out of my dealer friend as thanks for his complete co-operation. Those same thugs were now most likely waiting for me at my next logical stop and I really wasn't looking forward to meeting them.

He launched into another round of advice against heading over to Dick's but was almost immediately silenced by heavy pounding on the front door. The colour drained from his face so that the livid purple of his bruising stood out ugly against the grey. His eyes were glassy with fear and he wobbled ever so slightly.

I pulled in a hard breath against my pounding heart, then another, then stood.

"You're alright mate, I'll go." I heard myself say.

Leaving his trembling stares behind, I moved quietly into the darkness of the hall and approached the vague grey shape of the door. Half way there another round of pounding sent my heart to my mouth. I swallowed hard and pressed on.

Reaching the door I moved slowly against it, pressing my ear to the cool wood. I was sure there was still someone out there, as if I could sense a sound just beyond hearing from the other side of the door. Suddenly I thought I heard movement, even footsteps, but then nothing.

And then nothing more for seconds, and then minutes.

Finally I sipped my fingers around the door handle and began to ease it down. Planting my feet carefully, I prepared to brace myself and pulled the door open just a couple of inches. I cringed as the shock didn't come and then gradually opened the door all the way.

The landing was empty.

Whoever had been knocking had left and as the relief washed over me, I knew it was time for me to get out of there too.

"It's ok," I called back into the flat. "They've gone mate."

I made my way back through the darkness and into the front room. He was standing just where I'd left him. He'd picked up the heavy glass ashtray from the table, apparently as a weapon and had spilled grey all down the front of him as he'd done so. I looked from the ash to the tray to the grey of his face.

"It's ok," I repeated. "It'll've just been someone

looking to score. You are usually on at this time." He nodded silently, knuckles still white on the glass.

"What were you going to do with that?" I asked him, nodding at the ashtray. He looked down.

"Ah shite!" he exclaimed, seeing the ash for the first time and returning fully to the room in the process.

"Right, I'm going to get off mate," I said as he placed the ashtray back on the table and began to frantically pat himself down. I headed back to the front door but he hobbled after me, still trying to brush away the grey.

"Do you even have a piece on you?" he asked as I reached and opened the door.

"You know that's not my thing," I replied. He shook his head.

"That's some friend man," he said.

"I guess so," I replied, almost to myself as I headed back out on to the landing and off towards the stairs. Trotting back down to street level I tried to ignore the way the cold stung my aching face while it occurred to me that the mysterious heavy knocker from before could be lurking in any one of the shadows all around me. I quickly decided however that the definite dangers ahead were enough to be going on with without inventing new ones as well.

Back on the street I found I had to work hard to force my stride to quicken, as if part of me didn't want to get to where I was going. Ignoring my turning stomach and whinging back, I played with different approaches to the problem, including just walking the hell away from the guaranteed shitstorm ahead.

I checked my phone. I was only an hour and a half in, there was still plenty of time to start again, to find and follow a different, perhaps longer but definitely safer, path to my ultimate goal. The problem was I'd been lucky so far, I was two for two in fact, and that was something I couldn't quite bring myself to walk away from.

I dithered for a moment, my gut telling me that this really wasn't the way to go. As ever however, the feeling of compulsion, of being driven back from something was all it took. Irritation quick dried my resolve and set me to it. Hands back in pockets I set off towards the more affluent end of town and tried to ignore the niggling.

Instinct was all well and good, but sometimes you just had to face the practical facts.

On the face of it this is a practical concern.

Hanging about out in the open makes it more likely that I'll be spotted. Also, seeing as the target is a toddler, someone noticing my persistent presence is likely to get exactly the wrong impression and involve exactly the wrong kind of people. Beyond this however, I'm simply not getting paid enough to tramp about all day after some woman and her kid, not in this heat. I can't be arsed.

So Billy's deal is working out well for me.

He often gives himself extra time when telling customers how long work will take. "Just in case," he always says to me. This means that if he finds something worse than first thought or had to wait for a part then he can usually still get it back on time. Equally, if everything goes smoothly then he just returns the car 'early' and so incurs the gratitude of the desperate owner.

Of course this also means that if a friend such as myself needs a ready and varied supply of cars, say so as to be able to follow someone in a different but ordinary-looking car each day, then Billy can accommodate that as well.

Best of all, if the pigs or by some amazing chance the actual owner of the car, see me out and about in it and start asking questions, I just say I'm test driving it for Billy, checking it's running ok after the repairs. It's perfect. Cheeky, but perfect.

And so that's how it begins. I know the address on the back of the photo and the day after my visit to Billy I'm sat in the battered little red Ford. I'm across and down the terraced street from the kid's house reading the paper and cursing the car for its lack of air con.

By the time the front door opens my back is stuck slick to the seat through my T-shirt. Almost

immediately the little lad appears, dashing out into the scrappy excuse for a front garden but stopping at the front gate, clearly well trained.

Leaving the mop of hair and chubby fingers, my eyes move back to the door to watch mum, skinny and haggered, catching up. She's juggling a brightly coloured rucksack with her own blander handbag and her keys as she locks the door.

Absently, I fold the newspaper and drop it onto the seat next to me, shift into driving position and gently turn the key in the ignition. I close my eyes in a grimace as the engine coughs loudly to life, barking the length of the street. Peeking however I find that the pair have made it through the gate and don't seemed to have noticed me at all.

I let them get a fair distance ahead of me before pulling away from the curb and rolling along well behind them. The kid is carrying his backpack now, dashing ahead then pausing to look back as if on an invisible leash. Mum is on her mobile but ever vigilant, every so often calling out warnings or waving him back to her side.

They turn the corner and as I suspected they would, pause at the bus stop. I drive straight past and take the next right. I lose sight of them but I'm confident they're not going any further on foot. I make a long and lazy U-turn at the end of the street then head back to park up on the corner.

A few other people have joined them at the bus stop, including another mother and child. The women are chatting while the kids make their own entertainment and everyone else just loiters, doing the standard bus stop stare.

Looking her up and down I'm surprised that this woman has ever been with Tall James. Flash in all things, James is known for his pathological preference for gratuitously gaudy packaging, regardless of content. I can't see how this lass could have ever fitted that bill,

I think on though as the bus queue lengthens. I can't see James having being a

29

**particularly involved father, even before she'd
split. I suppose then that if I'd given birth and
then spent the last few years raising a kid single
handed I'd probably have lost my own killer good
looks as well.**

**Finally the bus pulls up, obscuring my target,
his mate and their mothers. I restart my wheezy
little engine and wait until the double decker pulls
away again. Seeing the bus stop empty I pull out
into the low level traffic, a couple of cars behind
the bus, and toddle along behind it towards town.**

That was enough, I couldn't follow that road any
further right now so I paused to look up the hill instead.
The two matching apartment blocks stood tall at the
brow, looking down at the city, all irregular eyes and gap
teeth with their occasional windows lit yellow. I climbed
the hill towards them, temporarily leaving both
memories and choices behind me and scowling at the
buildings ahead.

Even from a distance, the difference between the
flats of people like my dealer friend and the apartments
of the likes of Dick was obvious. In theory they were the
same of course, both just a small collection of rooms
copied across a floor a few times and then stacked one
on another to form a block. Both had lifts and views and
that weird dynamic of having neighbours above and
below as well as either side.

It only took a glance however to see that the
apartments were intended for a very different type of
person than lived in the flats. The pavement outside was
smoother, less patched and better lit while the road
beside it bore fresher painted markings and far fewer
potholes.

The residents here would never tolerate litter and
dog shit and broken glass, piss in the lift and stolen cars
or occasional casual arson. The letters of complaint they
wrote would be read and even acted upon because
ultimately the value of the pad and of the person within
it, what made it an apartment and never a flat, was the
amount of rent you paid.

By the time I reached the tall glass doors of the
block I knew what I was going to do. There was a

reception desk in the lobby but it was unoccupied save for a lone, beaming lamp. I assumed the guard had sneaked off for a smoke or a shit and counted myself lucky at the fact. As I moved past the desk however, something else caught my eye. I paused at the bottom of the stairs to stare.

Just behind the desk, laid on its side, was a man's shoe, shiny and black. I felt a bitter little smile pull at the corners of my mouth. It was almost but not quite funny, how an empty desk could briefly appear so fortunate then so quickly be outed as anything by the presence of an empty shoe. I stared at the lonely shoe and tried to tell myself that luck can be deceiving. Shaking away these reflections, I focused on what lay above instead and beyond and began to to climb the immaculate stairs.

By the time I reached Dick's floor I was practising lines. I'm just a guy looking to score, everyone knows Dick and someone told me he could sort me out. Only a complete fucking idiot would knowingly stroll right into the middle of such a shitstorm so my ignorance had to be legit, right? I'd just walk into it all behind some bare faced bullshit and then talk my way out again, preferably with a lead or two for my trouble.

Padding round the long curve of the stylishly carpeted corridor, I swallowed hard and tried to get myself looking lost and stupid. As Dick's door came into view I had the expression set right though it occurred to me that it was probably only half a deception.

I landed a couple of overenthusiastic but not alarming knocks on the door was just bracing myself to begin when I noticed the door swing inwards a little from the force of my blows. Glancing back and forth along the corridor I carefully stepped forward and pushed the door a little further. After a couple more cautious pauses I stepped into a large, lushly furnished lounge made to look all the more spacious by being empty of people.

I listened hard.

I couldn't hear anyone else moving about but I had no idea how big the apartment was. If they'd already taken him and gone I was screwed, though if they were still in here with him things weren't exactly

31

going to be great. Of course they might not have even arrived yet, perhaps they'd gone somewhere else first and he was here on his own. I shook my head, enough with the maybes, time to work.

Relaxing a little, I began to look around. The lad was definitely not shy about flashing his cash and it occurred to me that despite having encountered a good few pimps and dealers over the years, I had never seen quite so much expensive, gaudy shite in the same place at the same time. This kid made that prick Tall James look downright reserved.

Every wall of the room was lined with sleek, trendy shelving units, all of which bustled with novelty, kitsch and attempted irony. The only exception was a flat screen television, far too large for the apartment, which clung to the wall, limpet-like, directly opposite a deep, white leather sofa.

The shitstorm of overpriced tat actually began to hurt my eyes and I immediately began to share my dealer friend's dislike of this lad. He was the only lead I had at the moment however and so for now I needed him. I moved past the enormous sofa, my reflection in the vast, dead TV screen catching my eye just for a moment.

The continued silence was making me wonder if ·I'd missed the thug army after all when something on the thick, cream carpet snatched my eye.

A bloodstain.

A fucking massive bloodstain.

And now that I looked at it, a bunch of smaller ones leading off towards one of the heavy wooden doors across the room.

Shit.

I stared at the impassive surface of the door, smooth and polished and strained my ears. Just for a moment I thought I could sense movement beyond the door when suddenly it began to open!

As I gaped, the door swung inwards and a great lump of a man backed through it awkwardly, talking to someone beyond. Shaven headed he wore a couple of thin gold chains around his neck and was clad in a coat made from acres of black leather, he pulled the door closed before finally turning and noticing me.

His right hand was in a cast and sling but this made him look no less of a monster. His face was a slab, except for a small, vivid scar. It curled from his left cheek around, up to and then through an ugly pinch of skin where his eye had once been. His brow furrowed at the sight of me, actually managing to make him look even more intimidating.

For a moment we just stared at one another but in a moment more he was an unstoppable force bearing down on me.

"Hey dude," I started my script, struggling to deliver the lines cooly while frantically backing away. "So like, I'm looking to score and this guy told me Dick could sort me out?"

"Who the fuck are you?" he growled, a thick Southern accent dripping from each word.

"I'm Kaz," I said, swallowing hard but maintaining the grin.

"Kaz who?" he rumbled.

"Just Kaz," I said. "So if you could hook me up that'd be great," I tried, almost tumbling backwards over the arm of the sofa but keeping my eyes on the incoming man mountain.

"I could hang around and skin one up if you like, we could maybe chill out a bit?" I felt the wall against my back.

"Or not. Erm..." The guy was right on top of me now and I realised I had nowhere to go. I'd run out of ideas instead of the door.

"Dick?" I asked, forcing a grin.

"Nah mate," he said before delivering a catastrophic left hook that turned up to down and everything black.

Nearly every time I have been knocked out, I have returned to consciousness in exactly the same way. First an image of the world appears amid darkness, very dim and far away. Gradually it grows and brightens around me until I remember who I am and start to wonder where. I force my eyes open wider and drag myself into sitting, then I shake my head. Every time. I shake my head to be rid of the spiky grey fuzz and every time I instantly stop and curse my habitual stupidity.

I was nursing the splitting pain in my head and explaining to myself just how stupid a twat I was, when the significance of my surroundings finally dawned on me. The one armed Goliath had apparently left me were I'd fallen and I noticed I'd added a new bloodstain to the carpet.

From the cut I found on the back of my head I guessed he'd knocked me out on my feet and I'd cracked it again on my way down as I'd fallen deadweight to the floor. The right hand side of my jaw was swollen and aching and my teeth on that side were loose. The pain linked up with the bruising around my nose so that my whole face throbbed. I knew I couldn't take another one of those tonight and so whatever I did next I decided it was vitally important that it didn't include getting hit by that colossal bastard again.

Doing something next overtook rubbing my jaw as priority one.

I was alone in the room again, just me and an uncomfortable, brooding silence. My eyes fell onto the front door and in a heartbeat the notion of escape chimed through me. I began to lift myself from the floor, ignoring the complaints form my back, but just then I heard the jawbreaker's heavy door begin to open across the room.

Without thinking I dropped back to my prone state, closing my eyes and slackening my jaw while clenching everything else. Dreadful, ugly sounds were now spilling out of the room beyond now. A shrill, panting voice was begging and pleading but being overridden by thick, hoarse chuckles.

"What's that? You say, you don't mind a little pain?" came a deep, mocking voice. "Proper hard man you aren't you?" There was more but it quickly disappeared beneath screams that turned my blood cold and made my neck sweat.

Heavy footsteps approached me, rumbling through the floor. It took everything I had not to flinch as they paused what felt like inches from my face. Seconds ticked by with nothing but the sounds of the sadist's soap opera washing over me but I was certain that the father of those footsteps was there, standing over me, looking down at me, deciding whether or not to just stomp me to death where I lay.

I strained my ears to pick out the sound of nearby breathing under the background horror show but could find nothing, nothing but an intangible sensation of proximity. Eventually I felt my eyes pulling to open, desperate just to know, to confirm whether there was someone there or not. I had to fight hard to hold the lids fast but not squeeze them, to maintain the pretence of sparko oblivion. Just as I felt myself losing the fight the footsteps erupted once more, however ebbed this time as the figure moved back across the room towards the sickening sounds.

Slowly I allowed one eye to flicker open just a little and was immediately flooded by a cool sense of relief at finding the room empty once more. The far door had been left ajar this time and I could still hear the voices beyond.

"Nah," rumbled the voice I recognised from before. "Still out cold. Do you want to do him now?"

My eyebrows leapt and my mouth shrank to a tiny o as I waited for the response.

"In a bit, let's finish with this one first." This

second voice was just as low, Southern and menacing as the first but with a slightly light camber, as if emerging from a smile.

More cool, liquid relief flowed over me except this time it froze almost immediately back into hideous, sweaty chills as another desperate, anguished scream tore through the softly furnished flat. Paralysed with fear but also more than a little grotesque curiosity, I listened hard to catch the voice under the laughter.

"But I've told you, I've told you!" Screeched the thin reedy voice which I assumed must belong to Dick. "No, don't, don't, I geeyarghh..." His words twisted themselves into a broken, primal howl as the ugly sounds became muffled and somehow wet.

"Woah!" This was the second voice again, now racked with laughter.

"Fucking hell!" added my assailant, now also laughing, I could almost see him wiping a tear from the laughter lines around his good eye. "Did you see it go? Fucking hell.."

Their chuckled banter was underlined by low moans and then the sound of weeping. "What have you.. what have you done?" the words were panted and frail. There were some sounds of motion and then a cry of utter dismay as Dick was apparently shown the fruits of the their labours.

"Oh no! No!" Dick screeched before collapsing back into anguished whimpers beneath the rumbling cackles. Unable to prise my eyes from the door, I tried to get to my feet but found I was shaking so hard I couldn't. It was as if the terrible sounds and the images they conjured in my mind's eye had turned all my joints to water.

"But I've told you, I've told you," Dick kept insisting. "They said they were staying in Suite 213, the George Hotel. Suite 213! 213! I've told you..."

"I know you did and I believe you, I just don't like you, you Northern cunt.." and with this last Dick upped the volume once more, all the time accompanied by hysterical whoops and cackles.

This was finally enough to get me up, as the adrenalin kicked in and firmed up my limbs. I ploughed through the headrush straight to the door only to find it locked. I cursed and turned to take in the room. The many floors beneath me meant the windows were out. That left the locked door as the only escape route and taking on One-Eyed-Jack and the as yet unseen, Maim-For-Laughs-Bastard as the only alternative option.

Fuck.

Breaths tore in and out of me as my brain dashed off into the realms of possibility, any possibility. My hands flexed in and out of fists impulsively as I scoured the room for an idea, or failing that, a weapon. There had to be something, there was always something. I began to rip through previous dilemmas, mental page after mental page of close scrapes and near misses, desperate to find a reusable solution.

Nothing.

Fuck, fuck, fuck!

Back to searching the room, wincing as I didn't quite ignore the sound of the horror show next door. My mind took a moment to boggle at the fact that, despite the room being awash with gadgets, trinkets and ornaments, all of it vastly expensive, every single piece of it was utterly fucking useless. How was that possible?

For example, sitting on a small and irritatingly over designed table just next to the front door was a hideously tacky ornament shaped like an open topped human skull. It held some change and a bunch of keys and looked pretty solid. If it was ceramic I could probably do some serious damage with it, though it would be pretty awkward to swing and not exactly subtle. On the other hand if it was plastic it would be completely

a bunch of keys?

My eyebrows leapt for joy as an idea finally occurred. I seized upon my new found plan and snatched the keys roughly from the bowl, spilling some of the change into the plush carpet below. There were four keys on the ring and I bullied my shaking hands into forcing the first one into the door lock.

It didn't fit.

The second key was too small for the lock so I skipped to the third. I noticed the bad noise from next door had stopped.

It didn't fit.

A noise from behind snapped my head round to look. There at the far door stood the one eyed, sling wearing behemoth from before. His good eye widened at seeing me on my feet and for a moment we both froze, a no action replay of our first encounter. Then, just as before, he was bearing down on me like a juggernaut.

I found I couldn't turn my head away but luckily my hands weren't prepared to wait. Entirely of their own accord, my fingers slipped the fourth key into the lock and twisted it. The lock gave and just as that huge left arm lunged at me I whipped the door open, slipped through and slammed it shut behind me.

Instantly I could feel pressure on the handle from beyond but this time my nimble fingers and I were as one, slipping the key back into the lock and twisting it once more before stepping back. Sounds of thunderous rage came through the door as the handle thrashed up and down. A grin grated against the sore in my jaw as I eyed the hanging keys.

For a second I thought of Dick. We'd never met and I was pretty sure that if we had he would have lived up to his name perfectly. Even so I still felt guilty about what I was going to do next. I tried to reassure myself that he was already proper fucked and that there was nothing I could do for him that wouldn't just result in my becoming proper fucked too.

While the monster within continued to pound on the door, I raised my left leg and stomped hard at the bunch of keys and then again and again. Finally the key broke and the bunch fell to the floor. Quickly, I retrieved the bunch and then fished in my pocket to swap them for a lighter. I moved down the corridor towards the nearest of the round, white plastic devices attached periodically to the ceiling.

Standing right up onto my toes I stretched up and clicked the flame into being. I wobbled for a second or two before a piercing, electronic alarm began to honk violently throughout the building. I returned to the door and gripped the handle, pretending to lean my weight into it. A few seconds more and doors began to open

39

along the corridor. Across the way a bewildered looking little old lady in curlers and a dressing gown was peering out at me.

"Help!" I cried in what felt like a convincingly urgent tone. "Call 999! My friends are inside but the door's stuck!" I barged my shoulder into the door half heartedly a couple of times for extra effect. Wide eyed the old lady nodded and disappeared back into her flat.

The moment she turned her back I walked away, quickly but calmly, joining the growing throng of residents now crowding the hall. Most had clearly been roused from their beds and I let myself be carried along on the grumbling pyjama tide, all the way down to the street.

By the time we spilled out onto the pavement I could already hear a distant siren. Moving away from the cold and irritated crowd I glanced up at the face of the building, eyeing what I thought were the windows of Dick's apartment.

"There you go fuckers," I said to myself, absently touching my fingertips to my aching jaw. "Deal with that." I turned away from the building and crossed the street, heading off in the direction of the George Hotel. It would be a fair walk I knew, but time to recover was just what I needed.

Taking a deep breath of cold night air I felt my shoulders sag with relief as the adrenalin began to fade. I dropped the keys through a drain cover then patted through my pockets in faintest hope of discovering a forgotten joint. I knew my pockets were empty but still felt disappointed when I didn't find one.

The disappointment was heavy and seemed to push me down into the pavement so that more dark feelings tumbled down from above. My back and my nose and my jaw all grumbled and bit at me while I plunged my hands in my pockets and drew my shoulders up to my ears and it all closed in around me.

That had been close, even for me. If I had been just a little bit slower I wouldn't have got out of there and by this point it would have been me, half mad with pain, begging to see what they'd done to me. I shivered at the thought and suddenly the night was full of menace. The darkness between the cones of streetlight seemed hard edged now and the empty wind of the early hours carried a bitter edge.

I'd lived my whole life this way, I thought as I squinted against the wind, pushing my luck to breaking point, taking it to the edge on a whim and surviving by the skin of my teeth. I'd never questioned it before, never looked at it too hard until now. Grudgingly, I had to admit I didn't heal as quickly as I used to any more and for the first time ever I wondered how many near misses I had left in me.

Suddenly I felt tired, that deep fatigue again only this time with the volume turned right up. The wind chilled the aches in my face into shrill spikes, my nose and jaw now competing to turn my stomach. The rest of my body felt leaden, my brain worn thin and flat. All I could think of was stopping, sitting and maybe never moving again. The pavement stretched on ahead however, long, straight and empty and despite it all my legs kept doing their thing.

I thought about going home, about smoking in the dark and ignoring his calls as the time ticked down to zero. Who would ever know I'd cut him loose? It'd just be another one of those ugly things that happen every single night. Law of the jungle, way of the world, and all those other guilty clichés. What did I really owe him anyway? He'd lost the thing, wasn't it on him to find it again? No-one in the world would expect me to risk everything like this for him, even after what had happened back then. There was only so much one man could do.

This last thought tasted bitter though and suddenly irritation flared somewhere deep inside me, a spark under a stone at the bottom of a hole. I clenched my fists in my pockets until the embers glowed and the fire caught. A furious heat began to build through me.

"Fuck it," I said out loud.

Enough whinging and bitching. Of course I was going to see it through, whatever the cost, because well, in the end what else did I have? If I didn't do this I wouldn't do anything, wouldn't be anything. This was all that I was and could be and on occasion I was pretty fucking good at it too.

My stride quickened.

I'd escaped Dick's more or less in one piece and even slowed the competition down in the process. Now I had a lead to the George Hotel where I just happened to have a contact or two. I was on form and on track and that was bad news for anyone looking to get in my way.

I ignored the trails of lingering doubt and puffed out my chest. Walking tall now, I continued in the direction of the centre of town and in particular towards the train station next to which sat my new destination. A few dozen steps and the ritual commenced once more, each stride lulling me back to those memories.

I knew where following those thoughts would eventually get me, just as sure as I knew where each of these streets would lead. Despite the horror that loomed on the horizon however, I ploughed right on into them.

Bring it.

A couple of weeks in and I pretty much have the little guy's routine down. He emerges from the front door of their little terrace each morning to play in the tiny scrub garden. His hair is combed neat, clothes clean and straight and for a good five or even ten minutes they stay that way. By the time mum appears however he has invariably scuffed or muddied something and the mop of hair never stays down.

Then it's off to start the endless rotation of nursery, then shopping, then home for tea, then playing out in the garden, then in to bed. Every so often there might be a trip to a friend's house or the swimming baths, and so far I've also seen one of the fortnightly trips to the dole office. They seem pretty skint but she takes good care of him anyway. He always looks well fed and happy.

Not that Tall James seems particularly interested. I've reported back to him once so far and all he was bothered about was what his son had been doing, the where and the when of it all, and above all whether there were any other blokes on the scene. I'd eyed James coolly, pocketing a second small bundle of cash. He wasn't interested

in being a father to this kid, he just wanted to make sure no-one else was either.

I'm reflecting on just how much of a cock the guy really is when the familiar pair emerge onto the street behind me. I've been parked up down the street from the kid's nursery for about twenty minutes. Today is a dull grey Honda with no radio, but at least it has air con.

I slide down a little further into my seat and watch them carefully in the far wing. Mum looks as knackered and put upon as ever but looking at her now, hand in hand with the kid in the vibrant sunshine, I realise I've started to see her differently over the last few days.

Initially she was just been some bint who'd fallen for James's bullshit and let him knock her up. Seeing how she lived however, everything for the kid, all day every day, I've found that tag to be unfair and something like respect had taken its place.

They pass me by and carry on away from me down the road. I wait a little longer before starting the engine and pulling out into the slow moving, school run traffic. Even for this time of day though the traffic is snarled, something is blocking the road up ahead.

I crawl along, still a little way behind them, watching them make their way. As I let my eye fall to mum's soft, rolling arse, it occurs to me that the new found respect makes her a little more attractive too. Perhaps I can imagine what James had seen the first time they'd met after all.

Turning my attention back to the traffic ahead the source of the jam comes into view. A fire engine is parked up ahead cutting the already busy and double parked street down to just one lane. The cars ahead of me grind to yet another complete halt as the traffic coming the other way makes it through the gap to move past us.

For a moment I lose sight of the pair and I realise I'm hemmed in front and back. I tap the wheel and my feet in irritation until my unspoken

curses gain voice. Eventually the traffic starts to move my way again and I roll bumper to bumper with the car in front, desperate to make up the distance.

I needn't have bothered. The two come back into view just as soon as I make it past the fire engine. Expecting them to have covered more ground, I roll past them in a moment so that I have to park up further along and wait for them to catch up.

That moment sticks with me however, a snapshot of the two that I've never quite be able to shake since. The kid's eyes are so wide, goggling at the huge red engine, the mighty reach of it's ladders, the deafening potential of its sirens.

They'd paused to look while I'd been cursing the bottleneck but now mum is determined to move on, literally dragging him along behind her. As I roll past his left arm is following mum, an umbilical cord pulled taut, while his right strains back to the fire engine so that there he stands, crucified by his enthusiasm.

Then I'm past them and looking for a space when I suddenly realise I'm grinning.

An echo of that grin flickered across my face as the front of the George Hotel came into view. It was lit up as usual, pushing back the night from its frontage. I eyed the grand front doors from across the street before checking the time on my phone. The lad I'd usually talk to had gone travelling with his girlfriend which only left me one other choice but I was a bit too early for her. I could wait but I needed to stay sharp, I still wouldn't be the only person out looking for the mysterious pair.

I ran my tongue over my teeth as I dithered, considering moving round the back to wait in the alley. Just then however a large car with tinted windows swept onto the carpet of gravel laid out before the hotel. It crunched to halt right in front of the doors and two guys in sharp grey suits emerged. One was wearing a neck collar and he moved awkwardly as he opened the rear passenger door to allow a third suit to emerge.

The three strode purposefully up the stairs to the

front door, leaving the car behind them as if they owned the place. The one at the back had floppy hair and paused before they entered, scanning the street with a scowl. They looked like they meant business.

I backed away from the kerb absently, soaking up the details of the suits and the car. I didn't recognise them but something told me they were on the same clock as me. I sat down in a shop doorway, pausing half way at the insistence of my back, before making it to the floor and hugged my knees to my chest against the cold while I pondered.

Surely the guys wouldn't have gone back to their hotel after hitting the meet, they couldn't be that dense. No, the hotel was just another step along the way. Somebody in that building knew something about those lads but I was confident enough in my contacts to let the suits have a front door crack at finding them first.

As I settled into the doorway and the wait, various hungers began to rise inside me. I stared down at the pavement and considered them. If I had time to kill then maybe there was somewhere I could get a drink or perhaps even score in the meantime.

The thought of another joint made me smile and I pictured myself back at my dealer's. I imagined the night under other circumstances, free of horror and commitments, rolling and toking and talking and rolling and giggling until the sun came up.

Suddenly there was a jangle of metal and something tiny but hard was hitting my hands. I jumped and looked around me only to see a shadowy figure moving quickly away down the pavement. Down in my lap I saw the glint of a coin, and then another. The guy had dropped a handful of change onto me apparently assuming I was homeless. For a moment I felt a desperate need to dash after him and correct him, to push the change back into his hand and inform him of his mistake.

I don't know where that feeling came from but it faded as quickly as it came. I had a perfect vantage of the front of the hotel, was apparently ideally camouflaged and now probably had enough cash to get another drink somewhere later on.

What was there to complain about?

Smiling to myself I pocketed the change and checked my phone once more. As ever I was startled to find how much time I had spent daydreaming but at least that meant it was nearly time to move. My face still ached but the pain had become familiar now and that made it easier to ignore. I stretched out my arms, yawned and made ready to stand.

Just as I'd got to my feet however a splash of motion drew my eye back to hotel. The suits had reappeared but this time were not alone. The one with the neck collar and his mate with the hair were marching a young lad in a hotel uniform down the stairs to their car while the third suit followed behind at a casual pace.

I frowned as I wondered who these guys were that they could calmly abduct a uniformed employee if not in broad daylight at least in plain sight and just walk him out the front door without any fear of interference or consequences.

I moved across the pavement to stare from the kerb as they reached the car and the lad began to struggle. The flanking suits grappled with him and just before they managed to bundle him into the back I caught a glimpse of his face.

Danny's face.

My friend Danny's face.

It looked like travelling with his girlfriend had fallen through but that he was about to go on the journey of a lifetime after all. In that flashbulb moment our eyes had met and I'd seen wide eyed surprise turn to desperate pleading. But then he was gone. The car doors slammed with expensive subtlety and a high performance growl had seen the car ooze form the forecourt and off up the street, leaving just two red eyes fading into the dark.

I stood still while my mind raced after. I hadn't known, I hadn't known he was there, now what could I do for him? I didn't know who those guys were or have any clue as to where they might take him and even if I did, what could I do? And why had he looked so surprised to see me?

I cursed at the night and looked back and forth

hopelessly appearing for all the world like someone who'd missed the last train home. After a few more seconds of flapping I finally acknowledged that there was nothing else for it. He was just another casualty of this brutal night. There was nothing to do but take the next step.

Hands back in pockets, I stomped the long way round to the alley at the back of the hotel, kicking my frustration at any litter I happened to encounter. The air was heavy with the stink of piss and there was a good scattering of broken glass but the shadows to the side of an overflowing skip meant I could wait more or less out of sight. Thankfully I didn't have to wait too long before the employee's entrance opened.

A small crowd of weary looking people in cleaners' tabards bustled out into the alley, several lighting fags as they did so. I stepped out of the shadows and nodded to a couple of the girls I knew and to the young Iraqi guy who's name I could never remember. He gave me a big friendly smile like always and like I always I returned it while scouring both his face and my memory for his name.

Finally she appeared, tiny and shrivelled, cackling with her workmates as always. Her bright eyes fell on me instantly but looked away again just as quickly without a hint of recognition. She continued her banter and repeated whatever the joke of the shift was one last time before saying her goodbyes and pausing to delve into her bag.

After just enough fumbling for her workmates to have left the alley, off to their beds or more likely another cleaning job, she retrieved and lit the thinnest rollie I'd ever seen. I stood away from the wall as she took her first drag and eyed me hard.

"Thought I might be seeing you tonight," came her ragged old voice. She coughed, spat and then took another drag.

"Not just a pretty face are you?" I chuckled, enjoying the familiar routine.

"Cheeky little shit, I should crack your head," she croaked, raising an impossibly spindly arm to illustrate.

We made our way out of the alley in comfortable

silence and began to move along the street. I could hear her breathing through the dark, frail and laboured and yet there was something incredibly solid about her miniature form. She'd still be around long after I'd bought it, somehow I was certain of that.

Suddenly she paused by a small, battered excuse for a car. More bag delving and a jangle and she was opening the car door, motioning for me to move round to the other side. Once inside she continued to smoke while I looked around the interior of the car. I seriously doubted if it would even start.

"Well," I broke the silence. "This is a right piece of shit you've got yourself here innit?" I didn't even see her hand move, just felt it's tiny bones as she cuffed me on my swollen jaw.

"Fuck!" I cried, putting my hand to my face and leaning away from her.

"You soft ha'peth," she snapped in the darkness. "I warned you about cheek didn't I? This is Gladys and you'll show her the same respect you show me."

"Alright, alright. Christ!" I conceded. "It's not a piece of shit, it's Gladys, fine."

"Better," she said, suddenly erupting into frantic motion as she wound her window down just enough to gently slip the dog end of her fag outside.

"So..." she left the silence for me to fill.

"I'm looking for a couple of lads," I started.

"Bet you are," she interrupted almost immediately. I genuinely couldn't tell whether she was taking the piss or not and so just waited to see if there was more.

"There's a lot of unsavoury characters looking for them lads," she continued eventually. "Did you know young Danny got gripped?" I nodded.

"Yeah I saw," I said.

"Wasn't 'owt to do with you was it?" I could feel her dark little eyes burning into me from the shadows.

"Not me," I said honestly. "I thought he was off round the world with his mrs." The look in his eyes just before they'd got him into the car came back to me.

"Oh her," she said sternly. "She went off travelling alright, just took some other lad with her. Poor Danny, he's heartbroken over it all. I'll tell you what, if I were ten years younger I'd knock seven shades of shite out of that girl."

We sat in silence for a few seconds more before she sighed and rustled her bag into her lap before sliding something from it.

"There you are then," said said, thrusting the sheet of paper at me while still peering into the bag. "Silly sods tried to burn it in the bin."

I squinted in the dark but could just about make out what was left of a credit card statement. It was a big bill and the kind of thing she'd collect but for the life of me I couldn't see why I'd be interested. I read it over and over but got no further until she sighed, gently frustrated by my silence.

"It was a pre-match party love," she tried again, still nothing. I was beginning to feel genuinely thick.

"They thought tonight was going to be the answer to all their problems..." she nudged me along.

Suddenly the pieces began to fall into place and I felt heat flood my cheeks as I realised how slow I'd been.

"They checked in under false names," I thought out loud while she murmured her encouragement. "And paid in cash, no ID, no trace..."

"Yeah..." she added patiently.

"Then had a party in their room, got all messed up and had a bonfire. Getting rid of all the shit from their old lives like bills and..."

"...credit card debts," she finished the sentence for me.

I focussed on the bill again, in particular the details at the top.

"So this is..." I asked.

"Exactly," she said, looking expectant.

I dragged my racing mind back to the present and offered her the paper. She took it and returned it to a bundle of papers and receipts in her bag.

"Got to get these to our Denise's lad straight away," she said, patting the bag on her lap. "He's a computer genius that child you know, don't know where he gets it from but with the graft he's doing on these credit cards I'll be going to Florida for my jollies this year. Go on then."

"I owe you one for this love," I said, clambering out of the car and stepping back out on to the road. She turned the spluttering engine over and I was surprised to hear it catch and rumble.

"You owe me a lot more than one," she called after me as I closed the door.

Moving back to pavement I shook my head and grinned as the tortured little engine dragged itself off up the road. My funk from before seemed to evaporate into the chill of the night and I felt a familiar giddiness rising, making my head spin just a little. I got a grip on it and focused on what came next, one step a time.

Another address to track down, somewhere else to walk to. I was well on my way to keeping to my promise and saving the day. Somehow that made it seem ok to think just a little further along that same old track.

The last time I follow the kid for money he doesn't go anywhere at all.

It's a Saturday and he spends the whole day in and out of the house, in and out of the imaginary world he's made for himself in that shitty little garden. I'm too far away to be able to hear but I can see him chattering away to himself as great events and crises are played out all around him, invisible to anyone tall enough to reach a light switch.

I shift my weight in the well worn driver's seat of the car of the day, some little Japanese thing. It's tiny and stupid looking but it has both a radio and air con and so it's ok by me. Despite the gentle summer heat my old war wounds still ache, my back, my throat, my hand, yet somehow they all seem a little further away today. Half dozing in the sun, watching the kid do his thing, I find a different ache instead.

I've never really thought about having kids, who needs the hassle? Plus my lifestyle doesn't exactly cater for heavy responsibility and early years development. I've never even managed a proper long term relationship, not for more than a few months anyway.

Even when my old man had been on his way out, whining at me about grandkids, about my being the only one left to carry on the family name, all that shite, it isn't something that has ever bothered me. Hell, I could get dropped tomorrow. Wrong place, wrong time, I've pissed off enough people over the years that the chances of sudden, random payback are now relatively high. So what? That'll be that.

At least that's what I've always told myself.

Mum's sat on the doorstep now, talking into a mobile while the kid rummages around in the dirt, below the fence and out of my sight. Suddenly he stands, a chubby fistful of yellow glowing beneath a grin. Dashing to his mother's side he thrusts the colour at her, a few dirty dandelions now transformed to vibrant bouquet.

I glance at the empty seat next to me and wonder. Maybe it wouldn't have been all bad, some snot nosed little bastard following me about, talking shit and making me laugh. Maybe that would have been ok.

I sit up straight and kick the air con up another notch, welcoming the distraction of goosebumps and a shiver. That kind of life lies down a different road, a road I forked right off a long time before. I think about what I'm doing here, about the money in my pocket.

There's no going back now.

And I hadn't, I'd gone on, and on and on, ever deeper into that shit. I got back on track as the street sign I'd been looking for finally came into view. Actually seeing the street in the dark however, I cursed and set my jaw.

Cul-de-sacs make me nervous and this one was no exception. I hesitated on the corner, checking back and forth up the silent residential street once last time.

Silence.

Nothing but parked cars and dark houses.

Glancing at my phone I found it'd been nearly three hours since I'd got frantic call from my friend. I took a moment to enjoy just a little pride at being practically on one of the guys' doorsteps already but then decide enough was enough and headed in.

Despite the early hour I immediately felt exposed, walking carefully up the well lit street, each lamppost seeming to bear a screaming spotlight. There was no anonymity in a cul-de-sac, no just-passing-through, only the feeble I-must-be-lost bit which was invariably met with suspicion and mental note taking.

The lawns beyond the spotlit pavement sat dark while the homes beyond were smudged black. I desperately squinted through the night to find a house number, a reference point. The closer I looked however the worse I felt.

The lawns were too neat, the cars too mid range. There was no way the scumbag thug-thief I was looking for lived down here. Cursing silently I was just beginning to doubt the old woman's tip when two white painted numbers glowed subtle through the darkness.

I paused and looked around as casually as my nerves would allow before taking a couple of nimble steps onto the lawn and squinting harder at the house number. It matched the address I'd seen on the bill but nothing else matched up at all.

I was about to take another step towards the front door when I froze. Sat in the shadows above the front door was a small but powerful looking lamp. I was prepared to put money on it being a motion sensor security light and I'd double up that one more step would trigger it.

Trapped on the grass I licked my lips and scanned the darkness for inspiration. Nothing came forth. The lawn itself was neatly trimmed but broad and empty with nowhere to hide. Beyond the lawn however, off to my left, towered a privet hedge. Also clipped to unnaturally straight lines, it separated the garden around me from the previous one.

An idea hastily assembled itself for inspection. Without any other options I leapt at it and scampered across the carpet-like grass before inserting myself into the hedge in a crouch. My eyes peered through the leaves and swung from the curtains of the house and then across the street and back again, searching for any sign of movement. Meanwhile my hands were scrabbling blind in the dirt at my feet, finally landing upon a large enough rock.

This was going to be tight.

I closed my eyes, took a deep breath and steadied myself, as best I could while crouched in a hedge in a cul-de-sac anyway, then launched myself back out onto the lawn. With one quick, fluid motion, I hurled the rock high into the air, sending it sailing across the street and then dove back into my hiding place to curse my back and watch it land.

I'd had my eye on one car in particular across the way which I was certain would be alarmed. This was the vehicle I'd fixed on as I waited for the impact and subsequent distraction to come. And it did, almost immediately in fact, it just wasn't what or where I'd expected.

Instead of a heavy thunk and a warning wail, the sharp sounds of crashing glass hissed out into the street from the shadows that lay beyond the car. It took me a moment or two of staring stupid into the farside gloom to realise that one of the windows of the house behind that particular car now looked somehow different than the rest.

I winced at the error but prepared myself to seize the homemade opportunity regardless. Sure enough one of the non-broken windows upstairs suddenly glowed yellow. And then the glow began to flow, window after window lighting up in sequence.

Soon all the lights were on over the road and the front door was open too, a figure moving about on the lawn. Lights were coming on elsewhere too as the cul-de-sac slowly yawned to life. After what seemed like a leg twitching forever, the door across the lawn from me opened as well and out stepped a guy. Sure enough, the moment he stepped out the security light above him clicked on and lit him up in perfect detail.

He was neither of the guys I was looking for.

He was pretty tall but that was where any similarity with my targets ended. Well into in his fifties, the guy's cotton pyjamas fluttered about his shins from below a tightly tied dressing gown as he made his way down the drive to the street, carpet slippers flapping all the way.

Ever more doubtful I waited until he had made it across the street and joined the small but growing neighbourhood crowd. Then, never taking my eyes from the distant figures, I loped back across the lawn and in through the door he'd left ajar.

The light was on inside and I found myself in an immaculate hallway with thick carpet and tasteful trinkets aplenty. No sound came from the stairs that rose to my left but I was certain there'd be somebody up there, somebody who could just as easily be down here at any moment.

I stepped off the hall and into a shadowy front room. Huge four piece suite, modest sized TV and photos, an incredible number of framed photos all across the opposite wall. The room ran right through the house to a dining area at the back where a pair of large french windows framed a second, perfectly manicured lawn.

My heart pounded out the clock, the unknown number of seconds before this window of opportunity would close. When it did I'd need another window to bolt through and so I moved quickly across the room to open the French ones.

Exit in place, I breathed a little easier and returned to the front of the house. Frantically I began to scowl at each photo in turn, desperate for something, anything to make this mad gamble worthwhile. A heartwarming family scene from years past, a school photograph, another school photograph, another family scene, some incredibly old woman in a chair and on and on.

This was taking too long, I knew I had to leave and actually began to turn to head for the back garden when one last image hooked my eye and reeled me in. It was just a standard university graduation photograph, generic background, gown, scroll, silly hat, but the face behind the tassel, that's what had me.

The lad was tall, that was one, and skinny was another. His hair was dark which gave him a third, plus he definitely looked mean which was four. The final piece that made him my very own five star bastard however was the big gold ring on his little finger, nestling in next to that precious scroll he was holding so proudly.

"Got you you little shit," I said under my breath.

This was the kind of kid who might not have to pay off his own credit cards, though if that was the case why burn them in some celebration of freedom? Either way it was now clear to me that his credit card bill hadn't been addressed to his own house but rather to his

I got no further along that track however as the lights came on and I was suddenly very aware that there was someone standing behind me.

Shit.

Standing in the doorway was the guy from before, still wearing his hilarious dressing gown and carpet slipper combo. Finishing his Englishman's cliche however, he was now also carrying a far less amusing cricket bat.

"If you're looking for Bradley he isn't here." The man's voice was firm but sounded weary, not up-in-middle-of-the-night weary but rather years-of-this-shit tired.

"Ok," I replied slowly, my eyes flicking from his face to the bat. I wondered how fast the old guy could move.

"And if it's money you want we don't keep it in the house," he continued. "Not any more."

"Right," I nodded, turning ever so slowly so as to be able to back towards the dining area.

"So?!" he barked, taking a step towards me and raising the bat.

My silence and expression of confusion seemed to infuriate him even more.

"What has he done this time? Why are you in my house?!" This last was almost screamed and I heard movement upstairs.

This was very bad.

"Nothing, it's fine, he's fine, it's ok. I just need to talk to him." I took another step back but he matched me and kept distance. Apparently this wasn't enough.

"He doesn't owe me money. I'm not here to hurt him or.." I looked at the bat again, "..you. I just need to ask him some questions." As I spoke we continued our slow motion dance back towards the dining table, like two quivering insects, one about strike.

"Who are you?" he growled.

"Ok mate, look." As much as I knew I had to get out of there, the bat in my face was getting my blood up and I could hear my voice hardening.

"A friend of mine, a very good friend, is in a lot of trouble tonight and I'm going to pull him out of it." I encountered the first chair at the table behind me and began to move sideways, my eyes now fixed on his and pushing back hard.

"The only way I can do that, is by talking to Bradley. He's not involved, he just knows something that will help. I was given this address but clearly he's not here so why don't you tell me where he is, then I can leave." I could see his former fury dampening.

"I'm not going to hurt him, I swear," I added in a slightly softer tone.

The bat came down but his guard was still up.

"I don't know where he spends his time," he snapped. "He only comes here when he needs money and last time he tried that I sent him packing." His eyes seemed to cloud at the memory.

"It's his bloody mother, bless her," he continued, more to himself than to me now. He glanced over his shoulder, back towards the doorway into the hall.

I had a clear run to the back garden now, in fact looking at the guy, I could probably just walk away but where was I going to go?

"Anything you know that could help..." I tried again.

"The Oakwood Estate," he said hoarsely.

"What?" I asked.

"The last time he was arrested, that's where they found him, holed up in some grotty little flat on the Oakwood Estate. Now get out of my house!" His vigour had returned and as the bat came back up I nodded my thanks and headed back out into the night.

Across the back lawn and over the back fence and I was back to a nice dark alley way. I straightened up slow then set off, moving silently through the anonymous safety of the pitch in the direction of the more familiar turf of the rundown highrises of the infamous Oakwood Estate.

Just like any other rough estate, the majority of people who lived there were ordinary and respectable, living their lives as best they could same as everyone else in the city. There was also the minority however who lived on the other side of the line and made the estate what it was. Funnily enough, I happened to know one or two of them pretty well.

This time I didn't want to slip in the reverie, I knew I'd already gone too far and was nearly at that unspeakable place. Try as I might however, the journey was in motion and now had to run its course. I found my chest already aching in anticipation of what was to come and yet before I could even take a breath, the images were up and on me.

I meet with Tall James one last time, answer his questions, take his money. The job's done, time to move on. Heading home though his questions gnaw at me, sharp little tendrils that tangle about my heels, trying to pull me back.

As ever the twat hadn't given a shit about the kid, just wanted to know his routine, who else was in the kid's life. No matter how many times I tell him it's just her and the kid though his suspicions won't fade. What really bugged me though was his last. Where would the kid be at half three tomorrow? Where exactly? Who would be with him?

I told him everything of course, that's what I was getting paid for after all, I didn't even have to think about it. Half past three? On a Thursday? He'll be just getting off the bus on his way home from nursery, obviously. Probably proudly clutching some unrecognisable painting in one of his chubby little hands or maybe wearing some god awful paper hat he's made, though I keep these final details to myself.

I don't want to know what James is planning, I want to walk away. I didn't ask for this job and even if I had, it's done now, it's finished. I do know though, it's so blindingly fucking obvious

that I can't help but look at it.

He's going to snatch the kid.

Why? Who knows, who even cares. Probably just to hurt the kid's mum, to show he's still in charge despite the restraining order. What a cunt. Of course it isn't my problem, it has nothing to do with me and even if it does, what can I do?

Tell her? It'll be pretty obvious who's tipped her off and she might not even believe me. Even assuming she does, what's she going to do? Short of round the clock police protection, and there's no way the pigs will stump up for that, if James really wants the kid he'll take him. Plus I'll end up dead, probably real slow and sticky like.

So stop them myself? Yeah, me against Tall James's whole crew. That just ends up the same way except that if the snatch turns into a ruck there's a chance the kid might catch one in the crossfire. No, there's nothing I can do and I know it.

This being the case I find it hard to explain, even to myself, why I borrow another car from Billy and get myself down to that bus stop at around quarter past three that Thursday. With no payment pending I'm now just a stalker but I don't care as I watch the minutes tick down and wait for the bus.

After what seems like forever it trundles into view and I sit up ready for I didn't know what. The bus pulls away and sure enough there they are. Today he's pirate. As the bus disappears round the corner I look back up the street, hoping for nothing but finding a chill instead.

A large black SUV with tinted windows is creeping along the street, slowly closing on the pair from behind. Unsure why, I start my engine and squirm. The kid is chattering away, his mum listening and nodding as ever while all the time the shitstorm I've helped create is bearing down on them.

I realise I'm holding my breath but still no ideas come. I grit my teeth and growl my

**frustration as the dark heavy shape glides past me
and slows even more as it reaches them. My heart
rattles about my chest and my hands drip cold as
the SUV pulls up alongside them.**

This is it.

Yeah, that was that but fuck it, this was this.

Walking onto the estate I managed to put the
breaks to my train of thought just in time and tuned
back in to my latest destination. Unlike the deathly,
middle class quiet of the cul-de-sac, the Oakwood estate
never really slept and even at this early hour there was
plenty going on.

I stood at the base of the three mighty towers and
looked up as the sounds of hundreds of lives and their
secrets tumbled down on me from the myriad windows
above. Faint hints of music, maybe a too loud TV, the
odd scream, the odd bark, the atmosphere was thick,
dirty and alive.

Somewhere distant a siren wailed but was
suddenly muffled as I slipped into the ground floor
entrance of the nearest block and the heavy doors
swung closed behind me. Of course technically the doors
were locked, a resident's keycard or buzzer being the
only ways through. Luckily for me though, one of the
Estate Management Officers liked a jar or two in my local
and was an occasional drinking partner of mine.

A master keycard was a handy thing and as I
slipped mine back into my pocket I considered the lift.
Not being a fan of the stink of piss however I headed for
the stairs instead and began my climb, catching a
glimpse of each landing as I passed.

Each glance through each set of windowed doors
showed the same four door scene, except that each one
was different. One floor was mostly immaculate, three
well painted or even uPVC doors, with actual flowers in
pots outside one. The fourth door however was flimsy
timber, kicked in by the pigs and who knows who else
too often to warrant a proper replacement.

The next was more ordinary, standard council
doors but all neat and clean. Another floor another
version, this time a fancy door, two normal doors and
heavy steel sheeting on the fourth, scorch marks around

the edges.

The higher you went the dirtier the stairs and landings became so that by the time I reached the double figured floors even the neatly kept frontages were tainted by litter and grime. The small interior windows in and around the communal doors became increasingly broken, it was as if the building was dying from the top down, it's healthy entrance roots as yet unaware of the terminal cancer seeping down from above.

Thirteen never sounded like a very big number but by the time I reached that floor it was looming fucking huge. I paused for a second or two to catch my breath and compose myself before approaching the familiar door.

From across the hall the door appeared normal enough but once you were close enough to knock it became obvious that under the paint this was a different beast. Reinforced hinges, heavy plate across the lock, it was almost vault like, its heft becoming even more apparent as I landed a few firm blows on its steely surface.

Glancing about the other three doors, all sleepy and quiet still, I waited and listened hard. Other than the faint strains of the estate's permanent soundtrack from outside I couldn't hear a thing. My hand slipped into my jacket to land on my phone, pondering an alternative approach but emerged again to try one last knock.

Just as the blow was about to land however the door was suddenly torn inwards and in a scuffling second of chaos I was dragged roughly inside. I was vaguely aware of hearing the heavy door slam shut again before finding my vision filled with ancient wallpaper.

Someone was behind me, pushing me first face into the wall hard and after a bit more of a struggle a blade slid into view between my face and the wall, waving around to attract attention before the point settled in just below my right eye.

I felt a smile play across my face as I marvelled at the adrenalin suddenly rushing through me again. The gleaming point, so close to my eye as to lose focus, sent a thrill right through me. It seemed strange how this life that I was ready to end myself suddenly felt so much more precious when someone else wanted to take it away.

"Who the fuck are you?" The lad's voice was pumped fierce but brittle with fear. I took a breath and considered my options.

"I said.." the tip of the blade pushed in just a little further, pushing the skin just below my eyelid in against the bone now, "..who the fuck are you? What are you doing here?!"

I let the moment hang just a little longer, relishing the rush before replying.

"You'd best run this past your boss lad," I said, slow, low and firm.

The blade twisted a little more but each second I kept my eye told me this tiny sabre was just for rattling. Suddenly the blade was gone and a punch exploded into my kidneys instead.

"Oh for fuck's sake!" The female voice from deeper within the flat was thick with wearied fury. "Haven't you done enough tonight? Get off him!"

I found myself free to move, turn and wince, my fingers touching my face and then my back of their own accord. Facing my would be blinder I found myself looking up at a kid. A good few inches taller than me he looked barely into his twenties and for all his aggro vibes, his eyes were shiny with fear. I held his gaze as I cracked my neck before turning to meet my host.

"Lindsay P," I said with an appreciative grin. "Been a while."

"Kaz," she said, briefly returning the smile. "Much as I'd love to sit down and compare scrapbooks, catch up on old times, we're kind of in the middle of something so unless this is urgent..."

She was talking to me but glaring at the lad beside me, still slinky cool as ever though looking a little older than I remembered. The lad couldn't take more than a few seconds of it and quickly dropped his head and made to move past her back into the depths of the flat.

"Oi!" She barked. "This is Kaz, an old friend of mine and you've just nearly had his eye out. You got anything to say about that?" He couldn't quite bring himself to meet her blazing eyes but instead turned back to look at my shoes before mumbling something about a phonecall.

"You what?" Her arms were folded now, eyebrows up, lips pursed. He caved and just about met my gaze.

"Sorry about.." he tried again, "..that."

"No bother," I nodded, suddenly feeling distinctly sorry for the guy who had just almost cut my eye from my head.

"Yeah you are," was Lindsay's response. The lad moved deeper into the flat, not daring to look back. "Anyway," she said, watching him go, "like I said, unless this is urgent, we're kind of busy."

"It is I'm afraid love," I replied. "Shouldn't take a minute though, just need a quick chat."

"Yeah alright then," she sighed, turning to lead me into the living room.

I followed her in to find a few more kids, mostly lads hanging around. All of them eyed me hard but I guessed that my presence wasn't their main concern. Lindsay gestured towards the couch before settling into the large leather armchair that dominated the room.

Lindsay was small and slender with long straight hair and pretty face pulled tight. Creases around the eyes and lips were just beginning to show her years but she still had those wild teenage eyes. Back in the day when she and her mates had been kids they'd been a force to be reckoned with on the estate and I'd known her almost as long. Of all her friends however she was only the one still around.

There were several reasons for this that I knew of, not least her lack of greed. She'd never been a big player, always happy to just hold her corner and take her cut. She had the standard reputation for brutal retribution that her trade required but her continued life, freedom and success came from something else entirely.

If she'd been born a couple of miles up the road Lindsay P would have been a top politician, a millionaire business leader or a chess grand master, maybe all three. She knew how to play the game, when to bribe, when to beat and how keep the people that mattered sweet.

Old folks and the straights didn't get hit on her turf and in return they turned a blind eye to her business. That also meant that the pigs who gave a shit had worse people to prioritise and those that didn't were paid off as usual. Then there was her creative streak.

People didn't fear Lindsay P for what she would do to them, they feared her because they didn't know what she'd do to them. When people crossed her bad things tended to happen. Sometimes they'd just get straight up jumped but other times the bad things would come out of nowhere. Accidents, cases of mistaken identity, unfortunate coincidences.

They never never knew the how, just the who.

"So, you want a drink? Something to smoke?" Lindsay offered, lighting a fag. I thought about it.

"Actually a joint would be good, cheers." I said. Lindsay glanced at one of the lads to her left who immediately moved across the room between us to disappear into one of the bedrooms.

"So what can I do for you?" asked Lindsay, smoking with effortless cool.

I told her about the lads I was looking for, not too much mind, she didn't need the whole story, just the descriptions. Meanwhile the lad returned to his post, dropping a decent sized bag of weed into my lap on his way.

"Yeah," Lindsay began thoughtfully as I fished some skins form my jacket and started to roll. "Think I know who you mean. We don't know them though and they're not from round here."

It seemed that was that.

Dead end.

I focused on skinning up to avoid my disappointment, even if just for a few seconds. These seconds gone however, I held the finished article loosely between two fingers and stared at nothing for a moment, considering my options. My hands took it upon themselves to begin searching my pockets for a lighter while I continued to think.

All the while Lindsay smoked slow, eyeing me shrewd. Eventually she nodded again and a hand with a lighter swung into view, the flame clicking to life just before me. I leaned into it and dragged the joint to life before looking up at this latest attendant to nod my thanks. I leaned back into the sofa, meeting Lindsay's gaze through the smoke.

"The short one though," she said eventually, shifting in her great leather throne to lean forward. "I seem to recall he was screwing a girl off the estate, might be able to give you a name, maybe even an address..." she left this hanging amid all the grey curling between us.

"Go on," I said, still holding her eye.

"Well as I say," she sat back again, all casual. Here it came. "We're a bit busy tonight, had a little hiccup, needs dealing with. Of course if that went away then my lads would have nothing else on tonight. They'd probably even have time to take you over to that lass's flat personally."

There didn't seem to be any other option but I played dumb anyway. "Ok," I said. "I'm on the clock myself tonight but maybe we can work something out. What's the hiccup?" Lindsay smiled, just a little, before raising her voice.

"Leo! Get in here you little shit."

The lad who'd made me feel so welcome just before now emerged from the bathroom and shambled into the living room, still shamed, head down.

"Show our friend what you did," she said. He looked up at her, startled, glancing at me and then back to her, his eyes all questions. Lindsay just raised her eyebrows in response. Apparently this was enough. Beckoning me to follow, Leo turned and headed back to the bathroom, shoulders sloped, feet dragged.

As soon as the lad's back was turned Lindsay's face softened into a wicked grin and she threw me a wink. The lad to her side produced an ashtray and held it before her. She stubbed out her fag lazily and then rose. I extracted myself from the sofa and moved ahead of her as we followed the lad back down the short corridor to turn off into the bathroom.

Leo turned to face me, leaning against sink. He was still carrying a heavy weight on his brow and pointedly not looking to his left. I stepped into the

64

bathroom and peered round to the right where the bathtub came into view.

"Oh," I said, nodding and taking another drag on the joint.

Laid out in the bath, fully clothed and dry as a bone, was a hefty looking bloke, looking for all the world as if he were fast asleep. All the world that is except for the ugly gash torn right through his throat and the subsequent heavy dark stains that had spread to cover his chest.

"I see," I said.

Don't get me wrong. I've seen my fair share of corpses and I've never shied away from helping out a friend, especially when it meant helping myself, but if I'd enjoyed heavy lifting I'd've got myself a day job.

Still, looking through the frosted glass of Lindsay's bathroom window I noticed the sky was starting to lighten, just a little, so it looked like I didn't have much choice. Of course Lindsay didn't need to know that so I continued to smoke and look thoughtful as we stood, the three of us crowded into her bathroom staring down at the body bloody.

"So who is he?" I asked, my eyes roving over the awkward corpse, trying to tease out a clue.

"Oh I don't think we need to get into that," said Lindsay calmly, arms folded. "He's here and he needs not to be. Simple as that."

"Ok," I tried again. "Is anyone likely to be looking for him? Anyone we should avoid?"

"No." Still evasive, still enjoying it. This time I tore my gaze away from the stains and looked her right in the eye, lowering my voice.

"This anything to do with anything else that's going on tonight?" I could feel her looking right through my eyes, trying to work out what I knew until eventually I nodded slowly. She looked mildly surprised and even a little impressed before moving slowly to close the bathroom door so that it was just the three of us.

"Indirectly," was her attempt to continue playing it cool but when I didn't look impressed she relented. "Oh alright."

She leaned back to perch herself on the radiator, and waved for the joint. Leo sat down on the toilet next to her, still looking miserable. I passed it over and she took a long drag before sighing in grey and coming clean.

"We heard about what went down earlier, course we did. Then we get an anonymous call saying someone's asking after me and the next thing this random comes knocking on the door," she gestured at the bath with the joint leaving trails to hang between us.

"I think he was just looking to do some business but this dickhead," the 'ick was underlined by a hefty slap to the back of Leo's head, "answers the door, doesn't recognise him, panics and slashes his throat."

"I thought he was going to..." Leo began to whine but another cuffing cut him back to silent sulking.

"Sounds familiar," I said, accepting the joint back and sharing a brief, wicked smile with Lindsay while Leo stared miserably at the floor. "So I help you ditch," I looked down into the bath once more, "this, and in return your lads point me at the girl's flat."

"That's the deal," she replied. I pretended to think about it some more.

"Why d'you need me? You're set up well enough to deal with something like this aren't you?" Lindsay eyed me hard, trying to guess my game but after a second or two came back with it anyway.

"Of course," she said, "but I don't want people to know this happened here, sends out the wrong message, bad for business. Farming it out puts some distance between me and this fuck up." She paused and we both looked at Leo again.

"Speaking of which," she continued, "Leo here is going to be doing the grunt work, least he can do, but obviously I can't trust him to do it alone so..." and there we were. I nodded, a good replica of being just about convinced.

"Throw in the rest of the weed?" I said.

Lindsay thought about it, I could almost see the numbers floating before her eyes as she balanced her books.

"Done," she said.

"Alright," I said, taking the last drag of the joint before thrusting the all-but-dead roach at Leo. He looked to Lindsay first but then took it and looked up at me, waiting.

"Big car. Small plastic bag. Big rug. Spray paint. Go." Leo nodded and left in silence.

"Camera's?" I asked Lindsay.

"No, we're off rotation at the moment, thank fuck," she said, standing away from the radiator and looking down into the bath one last time.

"Cool," I said absently. For a moment we stood in silence, pondering the dead guy.

It was a well known fact that the council couldn't afford to actually run all cameras hanging from lampposts and doorways. Only about a third of them were ever on at any one time, the trick was finding out which and when and of course Lindsay knew just who to ask and how. She shook herself and moved to the door.

"Oh and when it's done," she said, pausing on the threshold with her back to me. I turned to hear the rest of it.

"Don't come around here for a while. No offence, it's just.." she trailed off.

"..business," I finished for her, turning back to the ugly. "I know, that's fine."

I knelt down next to bath, steeling myself for what was to come.

"Sorry buddy," I said to the pale but peaceful face below me. "Just not your night."

With that I carefully began to search his pockets while simultaneously trying to touch him as little as possible.

Blank staring eyes can be freaky, believe me, but I found I'd rather that than sleep shut. Despite the horrific tear through the guy's throat and the dark sticky blood that had painted his frontage, I couldn't shake the feeling that at any moment those eyes were going to open, probably just as I had my hand on his wallet too. It never happened though and by the time Leo half emerged round the door and mumbled his readiness I had all the guy's jewellery and the contents of his pockets in a neat little pile.

"Put those in the bag then bring the rug in here," I said, pointing at the dead guy's stuff.

I've always worked alone, preferring to stay under the radar and in control, but as I watched Leo bag up the watch and the wallet, the change and scraps of paper, I began to see the appeal of having a crew. As he left to retrieve the rug however I looked at the bath again and at the mess he'd made and realised that company also had its drawbacks. Swings and roundabouts.

The rug he'd found was plenty big enough but damn did it honk. To fit it on the bathroom floor we had to keep it mostly rolled with just a few feet of flat to initially take the load. I neither needed nor wanted to know where he'd found the rug but I was pretty certain it was a long time since it had sat under a coffee table. I made Leo take the bloody end, head and shoulders, while I gripped under the knees which had been left relatively unstained.

Never underestimate the weight of the dead.

I swear the guy weighed half a ton and after the second time of dropping him back into the bath, panting and cursing, I honestly began to wonder if this was going to work. The third time was a charm however as we managed to roll him over the edge of the bath so that he fell onto the unrolled section of the rug, dull and hefty.

Leo and I stood for a second or two, catching our breath, until I nodded and waved at the waiting roll of rug. Gradually we managed to turn him over, again and again, unrolling one tube to form another around the body, like some hellish reel to reel tape recorder, all spastic, sticky jerks.

Eventually it was done and other than a couple of dubious looking stains in the bath, and the increasingly horrendous stench, the bathroom now appeared to contain nothing more sinister than two guys and a roll of carpet.

I sat on the edge of the bath, breathing hard and ignoring my back. I noticed there was sweat on my brow but then looked at my hands thought twice about touching my face. After a moment's hesitation I dragged my jacket sleeve across my forehead instead. Leo was sat in a similar pose on the toilet, now looking at me for the next instruction. After a few more unpleasant but necessary deep breaths I stood and headed out the door.

"Come on then," I called back to Leo. Not hearing motion I looked back to find an expression of confusion on his sad little face. He looked at the end of the heavy roll nearest my feet and then back up at me.

"Not likely," I said. "You grab the end," I pointed, "and you drag it."

I stepped out into the hallway and glanced into the living room. Lindsay was back on her throne, holding court. We exchanged nods and the minion nearest too me handed my bag of weed. I slipped it into my jacket and headed for the front door.

After leaning out and scanning the landing, I stepped through the door and held it wide, waiting as the sounds of grunting and carpet dragging came closer. Gradually Leo dragged his load through the door turning around to lean backwards and put his full weight into the heaving. I pulled the door closed behind us and looked at his stance.

"Don't worry mate," I said, grinning and slapping him on the shoulder as I moved past him. "We all have our crosses to bear."

I approached the lifts and pressed the call button, purposefully ignoring its sticky surface while Leo caught up. Somewhere deep below us the lift mechanism rumbled into life. Glancing up I noticed the neat little box and lens the hung from the ceiling and recalled Lindsay's assurances from before.

The lift arrived and once the doors had stuttered opened I stepped inside the piss box and held them while Leo huffed and cursed his burden in there with me. As the lift began to descend I looked at the massive tube, propped against the wall of steel and bent awkwardly about half way down. I couldn't help but wonder what that kink was doing to body within but quickly moved my mind on to other things.

We hit the ground floor and I braced myself, this was the riskiest part of the whole thing. The doors shuddered apart but revealed nothing more than empty space. Nodding my relief I gave Leo the nod and held the doors open once more. By the time he'd lugged the rug out into the car park the lad was looking genuinely knackered so I let him drop it and catch his breath.

"Bag?" I asked.

Doubled over and unable to speak Leo simply patted his jacket.

"Car?" I asked.

A thumb over the shoulder and then wheezing. "Round. By the. Bins."

"Paint?" I asked.

He straightened up, starting to breathe a little easier. "Int' car," he gasped and swallowed.

"Alright, go bring it round then," I said gently.

It was true that dragging the body round to the car might have made the loading less conspicuous but it would have taken longer plus I wasn't sure the kid had it in him. Leo nodded his relief and moved away into the shadows.

Of course this left me standing next to a corpse in a pre dawn car park under a thousand windows. My eyes and ears were on full alert but somehow the urgency couldn't touch me inside. What did it matter really? This was just another scrape, just another fucked up mess I'd found myself in, one or another of these would do for me eventually.

My mind drifted back to the phonecall that had started all this, or rather to the moment just before it. I knew I was high but even so, everything felt permanently smudged now, tainted and terminally uncertain. The clarity of that moment called to me, everything had been so sharp and right, cool and controlled.

Suddenly the shadows about me seemed darker, despite the gradually lightening sky. My face began to hurt again, my back complained as ever. From the depths, from the black, an unthinkable scene that I'd usually managed to dodge before emerged from memory and grew until it was bloated and unmissable. I didn't want it, I couldn't face it, here it came.

The battered old estate lurched to a halt in front of me. I looked around desperately, suddenly remembering the dead man at my feet and the exposed car park all around. Then Leo was standing there, frowning.

"Are you..." he began.

"Just get the fuck on with it," I snapped, taking one last look around before climbing into the passenger seat.

I sat low in the seat and seethed at myself for the lapse. Fists clenching in and out, jaw set, I composed myself and resisted the urge to skin up again. I felt the car dip at the back and heard the boot slam shut before Leo appeared at the driver's window and slipped in beside me.

"Where we going?" asked Leo, starting the rickety old engine.

"Blackroyd industrial estate," I replied, flat end empty, scanning the car park all around us.

"But what're..." he tried.

"For fuck's sake man," I growled, shaking my head but still not looking at him.

It was enough. We drove across the car park and pulled out on the road, rolling along the empty street in silence. Leo had sense enough to keep it under the speed limit, under the radar, and on we went. Each second that passed, each lamppost and shuttered shop that slipped by, put more distance between Leo's mistake and his mistress and brought me closer to finally ending this hideous, fucked up night.

We slowed approaching a red light before coming to a gentle halt, the engine rumbling away, hungry to take us further. Suddenly I noticed Leo tense up, gripping the wheel tight and shifting in his seat. A second more and I saw why as the police car pulled up alongside us.

"Ok man," I said carefully, moving back to sit casual, now looking straight ahead only.

"Take it easy. Just watch the lights. We're fine, we're good." I could see the terror clenched in his jaw but to his credit he kept it together.

He kept his eyes front and when the green light finally came, after what seemed like an insanely long time, he pulled us away nice and smooth while the pigs turned off behind us. I twisted in my seat to watch them go before half turning back to look at my driver. Leo

73

visibly sagged in his seat while I let out a relieved sigh.

" 'fuck for that," I said. The lad could only nod his agreement.

A few uneventful miles more and the buildings about us began to thin until there was nothing but a few boarded up husks and the odd scrawny tree. Up ahead we could make out large low buildings, huddled in the gloom and soon after came the right turn we'd been waiting for.

I directed Leo deep into the estate, through twists and turns between warehouses and old factories before finally telling him to pull up. Stepping out into the cold I looked over to the Eastern horizon and frowned. The black of the night had now paled through blue and was even starting to tinge pink. I was running out of time.

"Ok, this'll do. Put him over there, sat against the wall." I pointed to the back wall of a derelict warehouse before moving away, listening hard and looking back and forth along the thin strip of road we'd just travelled. Behind me I heard the boot open and then struggling sounds of motion. More grunts and curses came but I filtered them out, casting my ear further afield for threats.

"He won't sit," came Leo's voice. I turned to find Leo stood beside our mutual friend who was leaning perfectly straight against the wall I'd pointed to. The dead man was out of the rug, has face against the brickwork.

"What?" I asked, not understanding.

"He's all stiff," said Leo and poked gingerly at the dead guy to illustrate.

"So bend him then," I replied irritably, turning back to look out.

"What?" Leo whined. I turned back and took a couple of steps towards the pair.

"Turn him round, fucking bend him over then sit him down!" I hissed and then, "for fuck's sake," more to myself than to them as I turned away once more.

As much as I stared and strained to hear, the gloomy street offered nothing to fear and eventually, after a lot of scraping and shuffling, Leo called over that he was done. I turned to find the guy from the bath now sat on his arse, back against the wall.

"Good. Paint?" I said, approaching the body. I heard the car door open and then close before a spray can appeared in my outstretched hand. Leaning over the body I carefully sprayed the letters, "g R a $ $" across the wall immediately above his head before adding a long horizontal line below that broke briefly from the wall to run across the dead man's eyes. I took a couple of steps back to assess my work.

"Ok," I said to myself, nodding. That would probably muddy the waters sufficiently to keep Lindsay and the estate out of it.

"Bag?" Leo delved into his jacket before holding the carrier bag out in front of me. I dropped the spray can into the bag and headed back to the car. Leo made to follow me but I called over my shoulder. "Roll the bag up in the rug and get it back in the boot."

I got back into the car and wondered if I should call the lad with the eye, whose phonecall had put all of this in motion in the first place, with an update. It wasn't as if I had anything important to tell him, not yet. He only had a couple of hours left now however and by this point was probably a gibbering wreck.

Before I could make a decision Leo was back in beside me. I supposed the rug was a lot lighter now while he started the engine. I gave him an address in the centre of town and put my fingers to my phone in thought. I decided straight after this would be soon enough and watched the outskirts slide by.

The roads were no longer ours with a few early commuters now making their bleary way through the ever thickening dawn light. As the buildings grew and huddled the traffic thickened a little too and by the time I was pointing out the alley down the back of the George Hotel Leo was getting jumpy.

"A fucking skip?" he hissed at me as he opened the boot to retrieve the rug one last time. "A fucking skip in the fucking city centre?! Are you mental?"

"Just get it up here will you," I said and turned to walk further into the alley, towards the same skip I'd waited by just a few hours before. There were far fewer shadows now however and a much clearer view of the

75

rising tangle of crap twisted up into a heap above the scuffed metal brim. Leo shut the boot and then scurried over with the rug over his shoulder.

"Jam it in there," I said, pointing to a gap in the jumble. "Deep as you can."

Leo looked back down the alley towards the car before taking the rolled rug up in two hands and plunging it spear like into the heart of the skip. To give him credit he did put his back into and fairly shoved it in until most of the rug was submerged.

"But what if somebody takes it out again?" Leo whined as we walked back out to the car.

"Listen mate," I said, opening the passenger door. "No one is going to touch that thing, let alone nick it. For one thing it's filthy beyond repair and for another," we climbed in the car. "It fucking reeks. It'll go straight to landfill and take the bag with it. Done."

"It doesn't smell that bad." Leo didn't seem convinced, but then he'd been hugging the thing for most of the last hour or so.

"Yeah not to you mate because now you reek too, you're used to it," I smiled.

"I don't!" he cried, indignant but then lowering his face a little and trying to smell himself.

"You do mate. Sorry, you just do." I managed a second of twisting my lips before the laugh coughed out.

"Fuck off!" Leo tried to snap but I saw a smile twist his snarl at the last second.

He started the car and got us back on the road. We both chuckled a bit and the atmosphere in the car seemed to brighten with the sky. My shit to do was still there but for the duration of this short car journey it was ok to just sit and do nothing, think nothing.

Everything seemed a little more manageable in the light of day, especially when there weren't too many people about like now. We rounded a corner and the towers of the estate came into view. I glanced over at Leo to find him gazing at them obvious relief, relief to be home. I wondered how that must feel as we pulled into the carpark and stepped out onto the concrete.

"So should I take you over to Jenny's now?" Leo asked across the roof of the car.

"No you're ok," I said. "Just give me the address."

"Lindsay said.." he started.

"I know, but it's fine. You did alright tonight lad, I'll let her know that." I smiled at him and meant it.

"Yeah?" His eyes brighter than I'd seen them all night. I walked round to meet him next to the front doors of the block.

"Yeah. I mean don't get me wrong, you fucked up and I reckon you're going to have to take a lot more shit for that." I said, watching him sag a little. "But you made it right," I added, "and you kept your cool while we were out. You did alright."

"Cheers man. Jenny's is number 44, that block over there." He pointed across the car park.

"Good man," I said and we shook hands.

I waited until Leo had entered the block behind me before I set off across the carpark and reached for my phone. I tried out a few versions of the impending conversation before raising my thumb to make call, only to freeze at the sound of screeching car tires.

Inches before me was a familiar looking car. Sleek and very expensive looking, all the windows were tinted. I'd managed to put my phone away and step back when both front doors erupted and guys in grey suits emerged from either side.

The guy on the far side was clean cut but sported a neck collar above his yellow tie. Meanwhile the one practically standing on my toes was all designer stubble and shoulder length locks, eyeing me hard as he straightened his green tie carefully.

Shit.

"Morning gents," I opened brightly. "Up early or up still?" I grinned but really I was wondering what had happened to Danny when he'd taken a ride with these guys earlier.

"Up yours," said Green Tie and lunged at me.

"What the..." I think I said, trying to dodge what I thought was a gut punch. I didn't realise he had a stun gun until a stiffening cage of pain was running through every last bit of me. Then I was on the concrete and there were just far away feet, all fuzzed like on an old TV. Then there were hands on me, lifting me and then impact, a slam, and everything was dark.

I got confused in the dark and wasn't sure where I was. All I could remember was that something bad was going to happen and that I had to try and stop it. But what was the bad thing? I tried to think harder but everything felt soft and unreal.

Then came images, reminders, memories of the bad thing.

A kid and his mum on a late summer Thursday, half past three. A big black car, dark windows pulls up. I know they're going to take him but I don't do anything. I can't think of anything to do.

Then a sound, a spatter of dull cracks, gone as soon as they start but heavy enough to linger. Now screeching, engine and tires. The big car dashes away revealing them, revealing her, revealing him. She's kneeling there, she's screaming. He's in her arms, he's full of holes. There's a lot of blood, it's running off the edge of the kerb into the street.

Other people are screaming, crowding round. She hugs him to her as she howls and in the swing, just before he disappears into her breast and then behind the crowd, I catch the briefest glimpse of his face. Still round and open, his eyes are wide but too dull. Two dark, ugly little holes stain his forehead and cheek.

I leave. I flee. I drive and I drive.

I can't escape the images, the feelings, the hot shame and guilt. Lost in the dark I see it over and over until I feel sick. A desperate clenching tears at me, an unbearable need to go back, to change it, to stop it from being true. Each wanting spasm ends however, with a heavy blow of certainty, the knowledge that it will be true forever.

Each repetition runs faster, crushing the tragedy in on itself, making the pain denser and denser, until eventually it is a continual strobe image of his dead little face swinging through the air and my mind fills with silent screaming.

What have I done?

Suddenly there was light again and hands again and lifting. Another impact, harder this time, and then stillness. I had a go at opening my eyes. Same feet different concrete. I managed to get a hand to my face as a cough racked through me.

" 'kin hell," I wheezed, gradually pushing myself up into sitting. Fading snapshots from before still played through me and as menacing as the scene now before me clearly was, it didn't feel real, not quite, not yet.

There were three of them now, Yellow Tie and Green Tie had been joined by an older guy wearing a purple tie. Balding and skinny he looked almost bird like, particularly looming over me as he now was.

The expression on his face, the way he moved and especially the way he looked at me, a kind of amused disdain, all screamed high class. The soft looking hands and immaculate nail job were a dead give away too. This guy was someone important, or at least he liked to think he was. Apparently satisfied he moved away from me and let Yellow Tie and Green Tie come back to the fore.

"On your feet please," he said, he words clipped and precise.

I frowned my incredulity at the idea of my being able to stand and rubbed my head instead. He stared at me for a second or two before nodding towards the Green Tie. The floppy haired suit lunged in once more and I cringed in preparation for another shock.

This time however he simply snatched up my arm and dragged me up with it. I tottered back and forth a couple of times before settling, after which he dropped my arm and stepped back into line. I blinked and tried to focus.

Somewhere out there through the spiky grey fuzz, I was pretty sure that the apocalyptic gang war I'd been hoping so much to avoid tonight had finally caught right up with me. I wasn't really sure what to do about it either since all my plans so far had been based on this never happening.

"You evaded us at the hotel," came the same plum trimmed voice. "But as you can see, you can never truly escape us."

"The fuck?" I began, genuinely confused but he cut me dead.

"Where are they?" he snapped.

"What? Who? No idea what you're talking about." I croaked and staggered but looked him right in the eye. He nodded to Green Tie again who in turn took the stun gun back out of his pocket.

"Alright!" I said, raising my palms as he took a step forward. "Hang on, hang on."

The stubbly git glanced back to Purple Tie who nodded for him to hang back. Green Tie looked disappointed. He really seemed to hate me which I felt was unfair given that we'd never met.

"I do know who you mean and I have been looking for them," I said to Purple Tie, eyeing the vicious little stun gun still nestling in Green Tie's eager hand. "But I haven't found them, they've disappeared, they've gone."

"Really," came the response, not a hint of belief about it.

"Seriously!" I continued, keen to stay Green Tie's hand. "I've spent all fucking night running all over the place, getting into all sorts of shit trying track those two down and I've found nothing. No-one's seen them, hell, no-one I know even knows them."

Purple Tie squinted at me as if to better spy the lie.

"If that is indeed the case," he said slowly. "Then what was the purpose of your car journey with that young man?"

I licked my lips as my limbs began to feel solid again and my head began to clear. Standing a little taller I cracked my neck and sighed.

"That was something else, a favour for a friend," I said.

"In return for information perhaps?" His voice rose from suspicion to triumph and Green Tie looked keener than ever, especially as I reached into my jacket.

"No," I said producing the bag of weed. "In return for this. I've had a very long and unsuccessful night and all I want to now is go home and get fucked up."

The old sod sucked on his teeth at the sight of the gear before apparently accepting defeat.

"Fine," said Purple Tie visibly annoyed.

I pocketed the weed and wondered what time it was.

"Regardless of that, we know who you're working for," he began again. This one threw me and I think I showed it though he just took this as another attempt to feign ignorance.

"Oh it's no use trying to play dumb I'm afraid. Why on earth would anyone else be so desperate to find those two?" He began to inspect his nails as he spoke to me, the epitome of reason and grace.

"You see they are visitors to our city, these people with whom we are having," he paused to think. "Our little disagreement. They lack local knowledge and so should they wish to locate say, two individuals who would rather not be found, then they are forced to rely on the, apparently somewhat mediocre services of people such as yourself."

I could see which end of the stick Purple Tie had grabbed at here, though to be fair to him neither end was right. What I wasn't so clear on was exactly what he was intending to do with the stick now that he had hold of it.

"Alright mate, look," I said. "I'm not on anyone's payroll tonight ok? I've reasons of my own to want to speak to those guys. I know about the ruck with that lot from down South, everyone does, what they did to your..." Something dark flashed across Purple Tie's face and it occurred to me that raising the subject of his kidnapped daughter and murdered son probably wasn't in my interests.

"And I was sorry to hear about that by the way," I said quickly. "But I'm not involved in any of that and I've no connection to them whatsoever." I folded my arms. He stared at me for what felt like a long time. When he spoke his voice was hushed, almost choked.

"Listen to me you filth! The only reason," he hissed, "that I have allowed your life to continue is that it is within your power to deliver a message to your masters." He was actually shaking a little bit.

"If you are to insist that this is in fact not the case however..." His eyes were wide and wild now so that the threat needed no voice.

I swallowed and had a think. Yellow Tie's neck collar surely ruled him out as any serious threat while even if old Purple Tie was capable I doubted he'd dirty his hands. That just left Green Tie, stun gun bastard that he was. My thoughts raced ahead as the silence piled on. Even if I could break away form this right now, it'd just catch me up again later. I needed to talk my way out of this if I was going to get clear long enough to finish what I'd started.

"Ok," I started slow, literally making it up as I went.

"Well, just because I don't.." somehow the tension stepped up even further, "..work for those guys." Green Tie tensed, ready to pounce.

"Doesn't!" I held him back with a raised finger. "Doesn't mean that I can't get a message to them. If that's what you need."

Purple Tie's face broke into the coldest, most bitter little smile I'd ever seen amid a look of total contempt. I thought curses but grinned without.

"Hell," I said with a shrug. "I'll even do it for free, common courtesy and all that."

Yellow Tie and Green Tie both fell back to their master and cocked their heads to receive his whispered words. I slipped my hands in pockets and smiled, pretending to enjoy being all carefree as I could see how much it infuriated the old git.

All of sudden something had been decided and things were happening. Purple Tie and Yellow Tie were getting back in the car while Green Tie strode up to grab a handful of my jacket, pulling me into his breath.

"You tell those Southern cunts," he snarled, "that those lads weren't working for us and that we know they weren't working for them. They were small time independents. They didn't know who they were hitting."

I nodded, working hard to look interested but unruffled.

"This is our city," he continued, still seething, "we'll find those two ourselves and when we do.." he paused, apparently for effect as if this was the really important bit. "You tell them that they're welcome to come and watch what we do to them. After that if they still want to get round the table then he'll listen. Right?!" He released my jacket and glared.

"Sure," I said, straightening my clothes. "Indies, coincidence, you make them go away to make it right and then you all get back to talking."

Glaring all the way and still brandishing the stun gun, Green Tie backed away until he reached the car. As his arse met the door he gave me one last death stare before turning, stepping round the door, climbing in and starting the engine.

"Yeah and I'll get right on with delivering that message for you too, you twat," I said to the morning as the sleek machine slipped across the concrete and away, leaving me to thank fuck and wonder where the hell I was.

First things first however, I snatched my phone from my pocket and stared at the clock. Just over an hour to go. I looked about me frantically but found the tower blocks still close at hand, the suits hadn't taken me far. That was a relief and hopefully this would be too. I made the call as I strode quickly across yet more grey to park cars on, heading for the block Leo had pointed out earlier.

"H-hello?" came the lad's trembling greeting.

"Alright mate, it's me. How're you doing?" I tried to keep it light.

"How am I doing?" he almost squealed. "Fuck that, how're you doing? Have you found it yet?"

"Not yet mate," I said hearing him instantly groan in reply. "But I've got an address and I'm on my way there now. There's still time, just be ready when I call yeah?" I could hear him breathing hard.

"Yeah ok, I will be, I'll be ready and thank you Kaz, I really mean it, thank you for sorting this out. I don't know what I'd do..." he gushed.

"Yeah yeah yeah," I interrupted. "Thank me later, I have to go." The desperate thanks and pleas were still bleeding from my phone as I cut the call.

I pushed myself to walk a little faster as the blocks loomed ever larger ahead. Just one hour left now, sixty little minutes before my friend's time ran out and really bad things would begin to happen to him. Even for me, this felt a bit tight.

I glanced up at the stack of windows ahead, stretching all the way up to the sky. Behind one of those windows had to be the answer to this particular problem. Had to be because if Flat 44 didn't contain the answer then it was too late, my friend was fucked and I was... what would I be?

There people coming out of the block now, off to work and I had to wait an infuriating second or two before I could actually get into the place, going against the flow as I was. What would I be if this didn't work out?

Alone was the first word that sprang to mind. It wasn't as if I spent a lot of time with the lad, but I realised I'd come to count on his existence as my one actual friend, as opposed to all the contacts and business acquaintances. Somehow, having at least one real mate made my life seem less empty. It was like he was a badge I wore to prove I was still human.

I walked past the lifts, too busy at this time in the morning, and started on the stairs, ignoring the dizzy deja-vu as I drove my already aching legs upwards. Trying to ignore my body's complaints I thought on and knew there was more to my desperation then just the fear of solitude.

If this didn't work out, if the answer was not at the top of all these fucking stairs, then that lad was going to die. Another innocent kid, life brutally torn away from him, his future wiped out and all because I hadn't been smart enough to work it out, hadn't pushed hard enough to stop it happening.

Those dreaded images from the car boot threatened to come back, I could smell them and began to take the stairs two at a time as if to escape them. I wouldn't be able to take it, I realised as sweat broke out on my forehead. I couldn't take another one of those, it would break me.

My shoes squeaked on the smooth, hard floor as I turned to face another flight. Racing up them my thoughts fell back down to that moment before the phonecall, the cool of muzzle metal against my face flesh, the rising tension and impending oblivion.

Even that would be tainted now, if I fucked this up. That way out would no longer be a free lifestyle choice, it would become an just another shamefaced escape, just me scuttling off this mortal coil with my tail between my legs.

My lungs called a halt to my progress and I doubled up to gasp at their command. That's what this was about, it was now cold and clear, riding the back of my adrenalin. This desperation, I couldn't let it happen again, I just couldn't. No matter what it took I had to save the lad this time, I had to.

Reaching out to the handrail I noticed my hand was actually shaking a little but frowned it back to still control. Resuming my ascent I took the steps at a brisk but less frantic pace, the chill of my internal revelation still with me, focusing me completely on the task above and ahead.

Finally the eleventh floor came into view and I stepped onto the landing, my eyes immediately locking onto the door with two fours. I let a few more heavy breaths roll in and then out again before cracking my neck and stepping to.

I delivered three sharp knocks and waited, my ears straining to reach over, under and around the edges of the door and probe within. Nothing and nothing and nothing and then, that was a footstep, that was another. I braced myself, helplessly speculating about who stood on the other side of the door, who I was about to face and what I would say to them.

But nothing.

I leaned a little closer, listening extra hard. I had definitely heard movement just moments before, someone had approached the door, but now nothing. I didn't dare check my phone for the time now, I knew whatever it told me would be too little. I stared at the peeling paint disguising cheap timber and supposed that if I were either of the guys I was looking for, I probably wouldn't answer the door either.

Fuck it, desperate times etc. I took a step back and a deep breath, preparing the stomp the door open when an alternative thought presented itself and instantly won me over. Slowly, carefully, as if it might booby trapped, I moved my hand towards the door handle. Might as well try it first.

The metal was cool as I gripped it, still listening for clues from beyond. A little pressure and then a little more and to my surprise the handle began to yield. I paused to glance about the landing and then slowly started to open the door.

The hallway beyond was dark, the flat strangely silent and still, as if holding its breath. I stepped inside and closed the door behind me carefully, all the while peering into the gloom ahead. I could make out an empty, broken down sofa in the living room up front but the curtains must have been closed through there as low light smudged all the details.

There was still no movement, no signs of life.

I crept in, landing each footstep lightly, prowling further into the twilight. This was tricky now, someone was in here, I'd heard them, but apparently they weren't in the mood to receive company. If it was one or both of my guys then they would no doubt assume I was here to do them damage. If that was the case then they'd now be lying in wait, holding their breaths, ready to jack-in-the-box and hit me, almost certainly with weapons, probably guns.

The thought put me on hold, staying tight and still on the threshold of the living room. They had the advantage here and if I let them get the jump on me then I'd be down and quite possibly out before I had time to explain.

I wondered if they were looking at me right now.

I straightened up from my vampiric creep and cracked my neck again. Best to just get it all out in the open, declare my intentions and nullify the tension. It was a gamble but what else did I have? I peered about and glanced over my shoulder one last time before drawing breath to speak.

Just as my mouth began to form the words however, a flashbulb image from a second ago hung before my mind's eye. Time froze as I interrogated the image. The glance I'd cast back over my shoulder towards the front door, hadn't there been a shape in the shadows? A tiny figure stood right by the door, as if they'd been hiding behind it when I came in?

I span round and just managed to get my arm up in time to meet the incoming bat. The wood-on-bone impact turned my stomach and knocked me backwards a couple of steps into the living room. The bat was already swinging again but as I watched, still stunned, my body leaned and stepped itself back to avoid further blows.

Then the adrenaline kicked in and I was back, trembling with defensive fury.

Everything became sharper and I focused through the gloom. Each swing of the bat was accompanied by a sharp, feminine grunt and for the first time I managed to look beyond the blows and see the rampant swinger.

The girl was just about five feet tall, with long sandy hair and a slender frame. From a distance she could have passed for a child but if I'd had to guess, in between dodging her brutal blows, I'd have said she was probably in her twenties.

"Hey!" I tried but she kept on swinging. I felt the sofa against the back of my knees and lunged to my left so as to continue my retreat.

"Wait!" I tried again, backing towards the window now, the bat missing my jaw by less than an inch. "Look," I managed to redirect the bat on its next swing with a slap that left my palm stinging.

"Fuck!" I cursed the pain. "Will you just," swing "fucking," swing "stop, please!"

We paused. I held up my palms, ready to duck and or dive while she stood before me, bat ready to strike. She was trembling with fury and glaring at me through her now crazy hair with one murderous eye.

"You stay away from him!" she screeched, her voice unsteady with rage. I licked my lips and tried to ignore my pounding heart.

"Look, Jenny right?" No response just quivering fury which I chose to take as a yes. "I'm not here to hurt anyone and I'm not working for anyone either. I just need to talk to..." but another howl drowned my plea.

She came at me hard, putting everything she had behind the bat. I was just able to catch it with both hands so that we clashed and tumbled backwards towards the window, colliding heavily with the wall beneath.

Amidst the tangle of hair and grunting I managed to wrench the bat from her small but determined hands and throw it blindly away from us. Suddenly she was all points and sharp edges, scratching and biting.

"For fuck's sake!" I managed as I tried to push her off me but she was too nimble and twisty.

We thrashed about a bit until I somehow ended up on my back with her straddling me, raining down sharp little blows, only some of which I was able to slap away, death by a thousand cuts. I'd catch one slender wrist only to find her biting mine until I had to let go and on it went.

Finally something in me snapped and everything became fuzzy.

I twisted onto my back and exploded up onto my knees sending her hurtling away behind me. The very instant I made it to my feet however she was back on me, riding my back this time, trying to get her sharp little fingers into my eyes.

We swung round a few times as I staggered this way and that, reaching up and over my head, trying to get hold of her. Finally I could feel firm flesh in each of my hands and with a roar I lunged forward, tearing her from my back and hurling her across the room.

She hit the wall upside down before slamming down into the threadbare carpet in a crumpled, broken heap. I stood there gasping and shaking, staring at the tangle of slender limbs on the far side of the room. If I'd had the time I would have probably puked.

"Ah shite," I said to the empty room as I moved to stand over her, rubbing my hand back and forth over my head as if that would make everything better. Licking my lips I continued to hover, my eyes roving over her form. She wasn't moving.

"Ok, ok," I said to myself. I had to get back on the clock, back in the game.

I rubbed my face with both hands and then crouched down next to her. Slowly, gently, I reached through all the hair and found her throat with two fingers. Feeling her pounding heartbeat at my fingertips slowed my own just a little. I shifted to my knees and leant in close, she was breathing ok too. Sitting back on my haunches I let out a good long breath of my own as sweet relief cooled the sweat under my clothes.

She was bent in an awkward tangle but nothing was obviously broken. With great care I managed to scoop her up into my arms and carry her across to the sofa where I laid her out flat. I stood back and looked down at her. Out cold she appeared tiny and helpless and I found it hard to reconcile this fragile little form with the homicidal banshee of just a few minutes earlier.

"Never judge a book by..." I began to myself but was interrupted.

"Jen?" The voice was weak and wavering, only just making it round the half closed bedroom door. "Jen baby, are you ok?"

I stared at the door, or rather at the gap to its side, and began to creep across the carpet towards it. Almost at the threshold and I could hear laboured breathing now. I could see sunlight on the floor in the bedroom but paused before stepping into it.

"Jen?" came the feeble voice once more.

I pushed the door inwards. It swung slow with a creak, revealing the foot of a bed. I pondered my options but knew I only really had one and so stepped into the room, braced for impact.

It didn't come.

Laid in the bed, covers up to his chin, head propped up on pillows, was a stocky young guy with sandy hair. At least I assumed it that was its usual colour. Most of his head was lost to dark stains, old blood in the hair and livid purple across his features. One eye was swollen shut, literally ballooning out of his face, while his jaw on the other side was also too large too and almost black with bruising.

The way he was laid, perfectly still and wheezing weakly in pain, I guessed he didn't look much better under the covers and had more than couple of broken ribs. His good eye was locked on me, wet with fear but determined. I winced at the very sight of him but a threatening bulge in the covers, just about where his right hand would be, overrode my immediate sympathy.

"Jen?!" he called past me, desperation cracking his voice. "What have you," he aimed this at me but paused for pain. "What have you done to her? If you've hurt her I'll fucking..."

Eyes fixed on the bulge I took another step into the room.

"She's fine man, take it easy," I cooed.

"You're lying," he croaked. "Jen! I swear to god man, one more step and I'll plug you. Jen!"

"We just had a little misunderstanding but she's fine," I said, staying put for the moment. "She thought I was here to hurt you but I just need to talk, that's all."

"Bullshit!" he spluttered. "Jenny! What have done to her? You fucking bastard, you fucking bastards..." this last was lost in a whimper. I thought he might be crying but it was hard tell what with all the purple. I cocked my head to one side, considering the bulge one last time, before putting both my eyes into his one.

I took another step.

His eyes widened and I saw him tense up but nothing happened. A couple more easy steps and I was at his side, pulling back the covers to reveal nothing more than a pointing index finger. His hand relaxed in defeat and I dropped the covers back over him.

Sobbing openly now he turned away from me. "Jenny," he burbled to himself before shifting back to face me with a snarl. "Well go on then!" he spat. "Fucking do it! Just get it over with you cunt." he closed his eyes and waited.

I sighed and backed off a little before sitting on the end of the bed and retrieving the bag of weed from my jacket. I fished out some skins and set about skinning one up. After a minute or two his one good eye reopened, fixed on me and then narrowed.

"Look mate," I said kindly. "Your mrs is safe alright? I'm not here to hurt her, or you."

He looked confused but knew he had no choice but to listen.

"To be fair to her though, that was a reasonable assumption she just made, after what you and your mate got up last night eh?" I dropped my eyes from him to the joint as I rolled it up with well practiced precision.

"He's not my mate," he muttered quietly.

"Fallen out have we. I suppose this was him was it?" I gestured up and down his broken form. He just nodded, best he could, in reply. I nodded too, before running my tongue along the paper.

"Yeah," I said, twisting off the top. "All told, this Bradley sounds like a bit of a cunt." He licked his lips and eyed the joint.

"I didn't know," he said.

I asked the question with my eyes.

"I didn't know who we were hitting," he explained. "Brad told me it was a local poker game, reckoned he'd heard about if from his mate Dick. Nothing huge but enough cash for me and Jen to get out of here, go start again somewhere else." I lit the joint and made an understanding noise.

"Then we get in there and there's no game, just all these mean looking bastards and two huge bags of cash on the table." The smoke from the joint caught the sunlight and tumbled over him in rolls. I took a couple more tokes and then rose from the bed, stepping up to stand beside him.

"Before I know what's happening Brad's fucking shot two of them, grabbed the bags and we're legging it. Crazy bastard." I held the business end of the joint just in front of his face. He looked up at me sulkily, still suspicious but then raised his chin and strained forward a little to take one toke then another.

"Then he stomped you and took it all for himself?" I filled in the gaps as he shakily blew plumes and nodded.

"Jen got me back here and ever since we've been waiting for..." he tried to shrug and fell silent. I fed him a couple more blasts.

"Tell me about the bonfire," I said. It wasn't strictly relevant but it had been bugging me.

"What do you mean?" he wheezed, threatening to cough. I took the joint back.

"You burnt some bills and stuff in the hotel room," I said.

"How d'you know about that?" he asked. I just looked at him. "It was supposed to be a celebration," he said. "Getting out of all that debt."

"Him too?" I asked, in an even tone.

"Yeah," he answered, not getting it yet. "He's just as skint as me, grew up on an estate like this over on the other side of town." I nodded but didn't meet his eye.

"That's not true is it?" he moaned, the penny finally dropping.

"Not so much, no," I said gently.

"Fucking bastard," he whispered to himself, actually seeming to sink deeper into the bed.

"Tell you what mate," I said brightly in an attempt to draw him back up. "How about I get you a car and little bit of cash so you and Jenny can do one? I'll even help get you downstairs, how's that?"

His good eye narrowed again. "Why? Why would you do that, and who the fuck are you anyway?"

"I just need to know one thing," I continued, ignoring both his questions. It was time to get right down to it. "Where's the car?"

His suspicion melted into confusion. Trying to keep it smooth and gentle I answered the question before he asked it.

"Last night you guys stole a car from outside a pub, the car you used to hit the meet. I don't care about the money or the meeting or any of that shit. I just need that car back." I took a hard little toke and waited.

"The car?" he said, catching up slow. "I don't know..."

"Look," I said, a little harder than before. "I need that car back man, it's really fucking important."

"I don't know!" he snapped up at me. "Brad took it didn't he, after he did," he jiggled himself just a little under the covers, "this. Then he fucked off in it, left me for dead."

I dragged my palm down my face to sit over my mouth as I stared down at him.

"Alright," I tried again, dropping my hand to my side. "Where would he go? He's not going to keep it is he. Where would he dump it?"

"I don't, fucking, know!" he spluttered.

"You have to man," I said, feeling the panic

turning me mean. "You fucking have to know because if I don't get that car back in.." I fought angrily with my jacket until it released my phone, "..twenty fucking minutes then bad things are going to happen. Really bad. Worse than this." I gestured wildly at his broken body.

I jammed my phone back into my pocket violently and we froze into silence, my desperate eyes boring down into his wet one while the joint in my hand burned away to itself. Curls of smoke crept between us, twisting their way to dissolving.

"Where's the car?" I asked in a low voice, shaking my head slowly.

"I don't know, I don't know, I don't know!" he screamed at me. "Why aren't you listening to me? Why is this.." he paused to pant raggedly before pushing on, "..so hard to get through to you? I. Don't. Know."

"Fuck," I whispered.

"Fuck!" I roared, kicking bed causing him to jump and then groan.

I looked at him one last time, his pain and his bruises, his wet eye and his broken bones, before shaking my head and storming out of the room. What had I done? What the fuck had I done? There was no choice now, no time left and no choice. The lad would have to run.

I crossed the empty living room, passing the bare, knackered sofa without a second glance on my way to the door. I had to tell him, tell him to get out right now. I was almost at the front door, one hand reaching out to it, the other fumbling my phone back out of my jacket, when the image of the empty sofa returned to my mind's eye with a chilled echo of deja-vu.

Before I even had chance to turn around I felt the blow to my back, low down on the right, heavy and weird. I staggered forward, still clutching my phone, scrambling at the door. I think she got me a couple of more times before I made it out on the landing, heaving the door shut behind me.

Dashing to the top of the stairs I found myself struggling against a weird fog. It wasn't the gear, that was there too, this was something else, something I

93

couldn't quite get. My foot dropped onto the first step but my leg above wouldn't have it and crumpled under me useless.

I flailed wildly trying to catch myself but I was already tumbling down, the sharp edges of the stairs biting into me hard as I went. Blow after blow with no up or down and then just as suddenly I wasn't moving at all. The sickening spinning slowed and I found myself on the landing between the two flights of stairs.

I started to get up but knew immediately that at least one of my legs was broken, badly too. Fighting back the puke I managed to get sat, back to the wall and then I noticed the wet. At first I just couldn't work it out, had I landed in a puddle?

There was liquid, warm liquid, seeping through the seat of my pants. Had I pissed myself? Still bleary I reached down gingerly until my palm found the wet. Utterly confused I raised my hand once more and stared down at it, stared into the red.

That fucking bitch!

I'd assumed she'd caught me with the bat again but she must have had a blade. I reached back, pushed my fingers up under my jacket, under my shirt to touch my lower back as carefully as I could. Christ! I winced and cursed the worse. Yeah there were holes back there, at least three, all running free with more red stuff.

She's killed me, I realised, the truth cold and clear through the ever heavier drowsiness, she's fucking killed me. I stared blankly at the phone in my clean hand. Somehow I'd managed to cling to it all the way through the fall.

He could still get out.

The thought staggered through the fog, fuzzed out but there. If I could just warn him he could still make it, still run. I watched as my thumb moved uncertain across the keypad, as if never having used a phone before. Eventually I could hear ringing and slowly, through a series of jerks, I raised the handset to the side of my face.

"Hello?" came the familiar voice, the mortal desperation now familiar too.

My mouth opened but there came no sound. It

was as if my voice had leaked out onto the floor along with all the blood.

"Hello?!" the voice continued but all of a sudden the phone and my arm seemed way too heavy and both fell into my lap. Looking down I noticed the darkness, spreading out around me across the floor. Then the stairwell around me began to slide and turn and then I was on my side, my face wet with the warm.

Everything was dimming, as if the sun were already setting. I knew that wasn't right though, wasn't it only just morning? I lay there, feeling nothing but cold now and reflecting in the dark sticky pool that in the end I hadn't been a very good friend to the lad after all.

I thought about the little kid and wondered what he might have gone on to do if things had been different. Finally I wondered what it would have been like to have a kid like that of my own and felt sad that I'd never find out.

Then a weird head rush took me and just for a moment everything was bright white silence

On the way off the back of my stool.

I snatched at the bar and managed to steady myself, quickly glancing around to see if she, or anyone else, had noticed. Shaking the fuzz from my brow I focussed. Girls were the way, at some point I seemed to have decided that and so now knew who I had to see next.

The barmaid returned and smiled as she took my glass. "Another?" she asked brightly.

"Aye go on then," I returned the smile. "Just a short."

After depositing my pint glass into a tray beneath the bar, she turned her back to me to catch up a smaller, cleaner glass as she went. My face frowned down at the bar with the thinking as I absently ran my tongue around the inside of my teeth. Despite tantalising wisps of plans and chances however, my eyes quickly flicked back up and over to land on the small of her back.

I followed the pleasing lines of her waist, hips and arse as she worked the optic. Her gentle curves reminded me of another body I once knew well and made me wonder how those lines were looking these days. The measure made, she began to turn so that I quickly dropped my gaze back to the bar and made a pretence of distraction, fumbling to retrieve a banknote from my wallet.

"There you go love," she said, placing the small glass in front of me and accepting the note before moving away again, all in one fluid motion. She returned a moment later with a handful of coins.

"Sorry, no fivers," she said.

I thanked her anyway and smiled, cradling the glass in my hand for a moment and watching the light shift and melt through the colour within. Even though it had always been my usual short, it had been a while since I'd drunk bourbon and the smell carried with it a whole other time and place. Looking at it I wondered why I'd ordered it in the first place, maybe part of me wanted to remember.

Not this part though.

I shook myself. Time to check on those old time curves I decided and slipped off my stool to stand. I necked the shot without thinking about it too much, placed the glass back on the bar, then wiped my mouth with the back of my hand as the nettling warmth seeped down through my chest. Turning to leave I heard her voice from behind.

"Mind how you go won't you," she said, a stock phrase but now with additional meaning, genuine concern beneath her professional tone. For a moment I thought how great she was, half turning back to face her.

"Anyone ever tell you how smoking hot you are?" I asked, grinning like a fool.

Her face stiffened ever so slightly before twisting into kind but weary disapproval.

"Yeah," she said. "Most of you do once you've had enough." She rolled the blue in her eyes and turned to serve someone else. I realised my mouth was open so I closed it, feeling a different kind of heat rise to my cheeks. I shook myself and headed for the door, keen to move on.

Back out on the street, I rubbed my hands together and thought about the next stop on my trip. Turning left I headed briskly down the street, planning the rest of my route as I went. I reflected on how lucky

I'd been to catch fire on my first go but cautioned myself against too much optimism, the night was young and I was bound to encounter at least a couple of dead ends.

The first step of my plan decided, I began to plant some decisive steps on the pavement. Getting up to a good solid pace, I thrust my hands deep into my jacket pockets, pulling it to me, and buried my chin into my chest.

So, these lads looked like the guys I was after. They'd had themselves one last blow out then twocked the lad's car from outside the pub and gone off to do their thing, landing him, and themselves, in very deep shit in the process.

Now if I was very lucky, and occasionally I was, then I should be able to track down the company they'd kept earlier tonight with relative ease. After that it should just be a case of the right kind of words and the right number of notes and I'd be on their trail.

Find them, find the car. Piece of piss.

That was the end of the road as far as the plan was concerned but there was a lot more actual road to walk yet. I tried running through it all again but there was nothing to keep my interest so I watched the real road roll under my feet instead. It was all old, well worn slabs round here, occasional absences filled in with tar to look like missing teeth. Occasionally I'd glance up at the posters for gigs or club nights that bustled on fences and walls beside, all trying to catch the eye before their neighbour.

Under the streetlights their colours were all washed out and tainted lending them a weird and sickly glow. With each step I took I could feel my mind wandering further. Now devoid of novelty and ready occupation, I could feel those other, familiar things waiting in the wings, eager to rush forth and fill the void.

Of course the instant I'd stepped out of the pub the thoughts had returned, the lad in the park, Tall James' summons, it was all chasing me along the dark road, trying to drag me off to an even darker place. I'd flinched at the prospect of recalling what had come after that first meeting though and tried desperately to leave it alone. I didn't need that shit tonight and it would still be waiting for me back at the flat. It always was.

Without getting into the detail, it was safe to say that it hadn't gone well, that thing with Tall James, in fact it had turned out really bad. I kept putting one foot in front of the other, striding on but never quite outrunning those memories. I felt my heart quicken at the idea of returning to that place, that first dark place, but the smell from the pub sent me somewhere else, skipping ahead instead to the slightly lesser evil of the aftermath.

I'm in the flat and I'm drinking. It's been nothing but whisky and weed for days now and although my body's all stumbles and puke, in my head I'm still stone cold sober. Nothing works. I can't stop seeing it, it's on the back of my eyelids, in my heartbeat, in all of me.

Sometimes I rage for a bit, stagger about and punch the walls, roar, curse, brutalise the furniture. Then I fall on the floor and my face gets all wet, my body shudders around me and I'm at the mercy of those pictures, the memories of that afternoon.

The images rip through every part of me, over and over until my shaking hands can force more booze and smoke into me. These two will hold me still for a bit but I can feel the anger building all the while. I know eventually it'll drag me to my feet again and that the cycle will run on and on. The window brightens and darkens seemingly at random. I don't know day from night anymore but it seems like a long time since I was outside.

And now a new thought arrives.

It's so simple, so obvious, so right. My fingers feel thick and clumsy and the floor just will not stay level but after who knows how long, I manage to find my gun and and my jacket. The sleeves of my jacket don't work right anymore and it takes me a long time to get it on but now I'm in front of the mirror and the gun's in my hand.

My reflection sways left and right, distracting me as I fumble the gun under the back of my belt.

I find myself sat on the floor a couple of times and getting up is a struggle but I eventually make it and now I'm heading for the door.

Outside is very bright and loud and the people on the street look weird. I think some of them talk to me but their voices are all mangled and I forget what they say almost instantly. I'm not really sure how I got here but I'm in the park, the grass feels so soft under my shoes it's like walking through a swamp. I keep stumbling.

I'm heading across the park in one particular direction. I can't remember where it is I'm going but I seem to know my way. There's a road now and I'm crossing it but there's a car here, right here at my knees, the horn hurts my head.

I turn to face the car, leaning forward so that I have to put my right hand on the bonnet, peering in at the driver. The horn is still hurting me and now I'm reaching for my gun but the road lurches sideways beneath me and I'm suddenly sprawled out on the floor, most of me on the pavement. The car drives away and I hear the driver shouting something, I don't know what.

After several exhausting attempts I make it back up onto my feet. Everything's spinning but each time it comes round I see the end of an alleyway and something in me says that's where I'm meant to be. The alley way comes closer, bit by lurching bit until I'm in it, leaning against the wall.

I'm being sick I realise, that's just happening apparently. But now I'm done and there's another corner I need to get to. The alley seems narrow but when I reach for the walls to steady myself they're not always there so that I fall again.

There's something wet on my face, it's warm and sticky and I try to brush it out of my eyes. There have been some more corners I think and I'm finally where I'm meant to be, but something's missing. There should be a car, a big black car.

I look back and forth along the alley, I can't work out what's wrong, why there isn't a big black car here, but I need to sit down now so I'm moving towards a pile of comfy looking black bean bags piled against one of the high, dirty walls.

It takes a lot of effort and concentration to sit down slowly and the beanbags aren't as comfortable as they look. I'm in them now though and it's better than standing up, I could even sleep here I reckon.

Have I been asleep? I can't tell. I can't remember what was happening before. I'm here though, I'm at this place where I'm meant to be. It smells really bad but now there's noise, a car! It's rumbling along the alley towards me. It's weird but even though it's a sunny day I can't really see the car very well, it's a blurry car and much smaller than it should be.

I can't think about that though, I have to get my gun out of the back of my pants. My jacket is in the way and won't move and the uncomfortable black bean bags all around me are poking at me as I try to shift it. Here it is! My gun is in my hand. I'm here and I've got my gun and now I'm going to do what has to be done. But where's the car?

The alley is empty again, even though the car was right here. I can't work it out and now my head's hurting really bad. I'm pointing my gun but there's nothing except the blank wall opposite. The gun's very heavy and my arm keeps drooping but I'm holding it straight and now I'm pulling the trigger.

I've closed my eyes but nothing happens. The gun's right in front of my face now, I'm trying to bring it into focus. "What's your problem you fucking..." my voice sounds weird, all thick and soft. There's a little button on the side of the gun and now that I've jabbed at it it's moved, moved to reveal a little red dot.

The gun's turning back and forth in my hand now, showing me one of its sides and then the other. It's pointed up at the sky, all black and heavy and.. fuck! What the fuck? A noise, a very loud noise that made me jump and now I'm sat

back down again. The gun jumped too but it must be tired now because it's in my lap. I'm quite tired as well I think. These beanbags are shit.

I cringed at the memories, not my proudest, and shook my head to clear them. I swallowed hard and noticed that the thorns in my throat had grown sharper. The red brick ends of half a dozen terraced streets were sliding into view round a lazy corner now. Great expanses of brick, the same terrace ends towered overhead again and again, only their antique road signs and occasional graffiti distinguishing one from another.

Down between two of these great drab slabs was one particular door and I began to plan out what I'd say when it opened. It had been a while and though I was pretty confident she'd still be there I wasn't at all sure how she'd feel about seeing me. I just hoped she wasn't working, I didn't feel like hanging about downstairs, trying not listen while the guy did his thing. I'd always hated that.

I backed out of that particular cul-de-sac and went back to planning my opening lines, slowing a little to give myself more time. Before I could get any further however, a faint but building sound invaded my space.

Footsteps, rapid and pounding, beat their way through the still of the night. The rhythm grew ever closer, ever louder, ploughing on through its own echo so that it was impossible to tell from which street the runner was about to emerge. I straightened up a little, removing my hands from my pockets just in case and eyeing the next two corners in particular.

Sure enough in a moment more the perfect stillness was shattered as a young asian lad burst from the end of the next street along. Eyes wide and wild he came to a stumbling halt, doubled up panting. I stopped still and looked at him while he wheezed.

He was medium height but slender with it, all wrapped up in a heavy winter coat. The white fabric of his kameez flowed out below the hem of his coat to flap about his knees as if panting along with him. I'd caught a glimpse of his face as he'd exploded round the corner but once he'd folded himself in two to breath all I could see was the white, patterned top of his taqiyah. As I

103

watched his breathing gradually slowed and he straightened up, wiping his brow and adjusting his taqiyah as he composed himself.

Suddenly he spotted me and for a heartbeat he recoiled, flinching before apparently realising I wasn't who he'd feared I might be. Casting a desperate glance back down the street behind him he moved towards me, still breathing heavy. As he came closer I noticed he was shaking a little too.

"P-please, please," he gasped. "You've got to help me. They're going to..."

He reached out and grasped my jacket sleeve, bending forward again to breathe.

"...get me," he eventually managed.

His accent told me he was a local but otherwise I was still in the dark as to who he was or what was happening. Now I'm no knight in shining armour at the best of times and I was already on the clock as it was so the last thing I had time for was to get tangled up in someone else's bullshit. That said though, he still had hold of my jacket.

"Alright mate, what's..." I began but paused again almost immediately to listen to a new, decreasingly distant sound. More footsteps pounding closer, lots of them this time. My gut told me this was bad, really bad and the guy's goggling face, eyes even wider, mouth working silently, seemed to agree.

He let go of my arm and looked back and forth between the corner he'd just rounded and the frown he'd put on my face, eye's pleading. My mouth twisted towards a repeat of the question but I was cut short once more as a half a dozen young guys burst onto the street, the last couple crashing into the backs of their forward friends.

The lads were all black, white or somewhere in between. They were all short sleeved despite the cold, displaying toughness and inks all generic. Their exertions had made them manic and their eyes gleamed as they locked onto the lad at my side before running up and down the length of me, weighing me up.

I felt my jaw tighten and my chest puff, my eyes hardening despite myself. The group approached slow, the one at the front, tall and skinny, eyeing me hard before he spoke through a vicious grin.

"Oh aye, so who are you then?" was his opener, all shoulders and brow.

"Please..." quavered a small voice next to me.

"Shut it you paki cunt!" This from a stocky one, further back in the knot of bodies. He underlined his point with a stubby finger and left his mouth hanging wide as a challenge beneath his flat nose and knotted eyebrows.

"I said.." the first one started again but this time I cut him off.

"I heard what you said," I replied, low and steady, shrugging off the clinging fingers to stand free.

"Yeah?" was the guy's emphatic if senseless response as he took another step forward, stretching his neck and almost bouncing in anticipation.

"So who are you then, his boyfriend? Like a bit of brown up you do you?" The group spread out now, spilling onto the road, all trying to get within striking distance at once. I was aware that the young lad had taken a step back to stand just over my shoulder.

I smiled without humour and held his gaze while dragging my right palm down over over my mouth in irritation.

"No mate," I said, still keeping a level tone despite the guy now being toe to toe. "I'm not his boyfriend, I'm.."

I didn't get any further however as the stocky one's fist cut me short, coming in from the right to land a hefty blow to the very centre of my face. The punch caught me by surprise and off balance and before I knew what was happening I was on the pavement, my arms around my head with shoes coming down and in from all directions.

From somewhere beyond came the sound of screeching tires and a blaring horn. For a moment I hoped for an interruption but none came. Then, the shoeing stopped as quickly as it had begun and just like that they were gone, sprinting off up the street. I realised the lad behind me must have bolted the moment the first punch was thrown.

".. a distraction, apparently," I said, managing to sit up. Through winces and groans I got to my feet, trying to blink away the pain in my face.

The kicking would leave some bastard bruises but there didn't seem to be any real harm done. That first punch though, that had really hit the mark and from the amount of blood my hand lifted from my face I guessed I must look a right mess. I wiped at my face a bit longer until my hand began to come away clean.

I swayed back and forth for a second then carefully shook my head, planted my hands back in my pockets and resuming my journey. There'd be time to rest and pity myself tomorrow, right now I had a job to do and as I returned to thinking about opening lines it occurred to me that my bloodied nose might actually come in handy.

A couple more streets along and I turned, making my way past front doors and windows, all dark and closed to the night. Occasionally I'd pass a window that flashed the colours of a TV inside or maybe let slip the sounds of post pub drinking, but for the most part the street was dead.

Shards of pain ran up from my nose and my throat to spike my brain but I reflected that at least they kept those unwanted thoughts at bay. I focused on the pain until I'd made it about two thirds of the way along the street and reached a familiar, peeling front door. I cursed under my breath.

The house was dark and silent, upstairs windows too.

If she was working there'd be some lights on and if she wasn't working she'd surely be out. There was no way she'd be tucked up in bed at this hour. I knocked on the door anyway, it was something to do while I thought of an alternative at least. I probably could track her down, check the same old haunts, but that would take time, possibly a lot of time, and this was only supposed to be step one.

I knocked once more then stepped back out on to the street, peering up at the two sash window eyes above, still closed and sleeping. Just as I was about to turn away however, the right eye blinked to yellow life.

106

Relief overwhelmed my confusion as I waited and sure enough, moments later, the lights came on downstairs as well. I stepped back to the door at the sounds of a key in the lock and watched the door retreat to be replaced by a familiar figure.

"What the f.." she began to snap, clutching a robe to herself and squinting. Seeing my face however she caught herself.

"What have you done to yourself?!" she cried, her tired eyes suddenly widening. "Come on, come on, get in here,"

I moved past her into small front room and glanced about while she locked the door. I didn't recognise anything. She'd had it all redone since I'd last I'd been round and I found myself nodding. The place looked great, genuinely classy.

I turned back to face her only to find her lips on mine. Her hands held my face, squeezing my still aching features and for a moment I tried to pull away. She tasted too good however and in a heartbeat I'd slipped my arms round her waist and sunk into it. Her shape still felt great and so did her tits as they crushed in against me. Seconds ticked by until she pulled away. I fought through the haze to open my eyes and found hers sparkling back at me, wicked as ever.

"Hello gorgeous," she grinned then slipped out of my arms with a wink and disappeared through a curtain of beads to bang about in the kitchen.

I licked my lips absently, not entirely sure what had just happened, then sat slow on the sofa. It looked expensive but in an understated way and damn was it comfortable.

"Do you want ice?" she called through the beads. I was gingerly poking at my nose and wincing each time then wincing again when I swallowed. Ice seemed like a good idea.

"Sure," I called back.

She slipped back through the beads pinching two glasses of bourbon between finger and thumb. In her other hand a damp flannel hung limp.

"There you go," she said, offering me one of the glasses, ice cubes clinking. I accepted it and smiled to myself, she always did have her priorities straight. I took a sip and the cold fire felt good on my throat. I was surprised by the smoothness, this was expensive too. She took a sip herself before kneeling down in front of me and placing her glass carefully on the floor beside her.

"Now then," she said, leaning in an applying the corner of the flannel to my face. "What have you gotten yourself into this time?"

"Nothing," I said defensively. "This was just a misunderstanding. Wrong place, wrong time."

"Aren't you always?" she asked with a smile, folding the flannel over and starting again on the other side of my face.

I watched her in silence as she frowned her concentration, the tip of her tongue just visible at the corner of her mouth. She looked older than I remembered. The little lines at the corner of her eyes were new to me and her chin seemed a little less defined. The extra years suited her though, as if she'd become more of herself.

Even roused from sleep in the middle of the night and with no make up, she was still stunning. The delicate cheekbones, that long slender neck and those eyes, still burning with danger and cunning. We'd met back in the day when I was dealing.

We'd had a kind of a thing for while but her work had always got in the way, or at least I'd never been able to get past it. In the end we'd gone our separate ways. It had been a shame but she hadn't seemed to fussed at the time so I'd just left it at that.

As she moved the flannel up to the bridge of my nose I closed my eyes and realised I could smell her. The scent brought back memories, not so much pictures as textures and sounds, long forgotten moments of pleasure. Just as these things began to light a fire in me however she applied a little more pressure so that I winced and caught her hand.

"Oh don't be a little bitch," she said, slapping my hand away. I took another sip from my glass then let her finish up.

She stepped back to beads and slipped through

into the kitchen while I watched how her robe slipped back and forth over her arse. Another subtle rattle and she was back in the room minus the flannel. She scooped up her glass from the floor and curled up in the matching armchair opposite me, saying nothing all the while but smiling just a little and looking right into me with those eyes.

"So," I began, to break the breathless silence if nothing else. "You not working tonight?" I looked around the room again and couldn't help but be impressed. She'd been skint for as long as I'd known her but as it turned out money seemed to suit her. She smiled more broadly as if I'd cracked a joke.

"Not tonight, no. I'm taking a little time off." Back to staring into me, expectant and in control.

Not to be outcooled I relaxed back into the sofa and took another sip of what really was some damn good bourbon. I met her gaze and returned the smile, trying to keep my head in the game and my eyes off the rest of her.

"Right, and how does Harvey feel about that?" It was an obvious question to ask but the mention of her pimp's name seemed to stiffen her. She didn't say anything for a few seconds, then took another sip of her drink.

"Oh darling," she said with mock pity, looking down into her glass as she swirled the ice. "Didn't you hear?" Those eyes came back up to hold me. "Harvey's dead."

The surprise lifted my eyebrows and she giggled at my expression, the tension from a moment before melting away in an instant. She moved forward to sit on the edge of the chair before continuing conspiratorially.

"Someone kicked him to death in his kitchen. They pinned his hand to the floor with that little blade he always used to carry and then quite literally kicked his head in. Everyone was talking about it, where've you been?" She talked as if she were discussing a TV soap rather than an actual murder but then Harvey had always been a total shit.

"I've been.." I thought about it again but still couldn't think of anything better. "Busy," I said.

We lapsed back into silence and she continued to watch me, openly amused but there was kindness too. Outside her front door my job was still waiting and out the back of my mind the seconds were ticking by. Before that however, I just had to know.

"So you're doing ok then?" I asked, looking around the room once more.

"Oh I'm doing just fine baby," she cooed. "As you can see."

"So you're not..." I started but couldn't finish the question. For some reason the words caught in my throat.

"Sometimes," she said with just a touch of defiance. "Just a few regulars, strictly by appointment. No middle man, no bullshit."

"Is that safe?" I asked. It felt like another natural question but again I felt as if I'd crossed some invisible line. I watched as her expression cooled again, just a little. Then she spoke, her voice a touch lower than before.

"They know the rules," she said, chin up. "And they know that I know who they are, who their wives are. Besides.." The kindness in her eyes stiffened into sadness though I couldn't understand why. "..I can take care of myself."

"I've never doubted that love!" I said with a chuckle, trying to regain the mood of a moment before but then quickly shut it down again when she didn't join in. She just looked sad again as if I'd said something to hurt her though I couldn't for the life of me think what. It was like trying to compete in a sport without knowing the rules. I'd never felt so out of my depth.

"All this though," I gestured vaguely at the rest of the room, trying again. "I mean how much do these regulars..." I stopped myself, determined not to let either of my feet back into my mouth.

"It's nice love, really nice. How did you manage it?" I asked instead.

She seemed to appreciate the effort and rewarded me by allowing her eyes to smoulder once more. The air became thick with delicious tension again and she curled back into the armchair.

"Oh I was ripping Harvey off for years." she said casually. "Whoever put their boot into him really did me a favour. Meant I could start spending what I'd saved without having to leave town. Also saved me having to hit him with a car or something."

I almost gasped out loud but managed to keep it together.

"That what you had in mind for me?" I joked, smiling without but feeling shitty within.

How many times had she told me? How many times had she said she had a plan to get out? Not once had I believed her, not once had I even heard her. All I'd ever heard were self deluded promises, empty and full of tomorrows. He'd been in charge, she'd been the victim, helpless, hopeless and foolish.

I wondered what else I'd got wrong about her.

"Oh I don't need to run over you," she said. Her lips returned to the flirty grin but her eyes told me she knew exactly what I was thinking. Surprisingly there was a lot less of the fuck you in them than I deserved, just more of the strange sadness from before.

We stared at each other for a few seconds, more words hanging unspoken than had been said. Again though, the ticking clock. There'd be time tomorrow, time for... well, there'd be time. I decided to change the subject, still curious about the classy make over.

"So what do you do when you're not working?" I asked but realised this didn't sound like as much of a change of subject as I'd intended. Panic must have flashed across my face as I fumbled for more words to dig myself out but she laughed and took pity on me.

"Interior design," she said. "That's my main thing these days. I've got a website and I usually get a couple of jobs a month. Another year or so and I should be able to go full time, maybe even get a new place."

"Well," I said, looking round the room again. "You certainly have the knack for it. I mean this is really..."

"Nice?" she said.

We looked at one another again and laughed, genuinely, comfortably. I realised I'd never wanted her more and for a moment nothing else mattered. Shitty things happened every night in this city, what was one more? Why shouldn't I just stay here, with her?

But then the ticking returned along with the world beyond her door and all the things that had happened since the last time I'd been here. I broke our gaze and sighed, finished the last of the bourbon and held the still chilled glass to my face.

"So," she said, finishing her own drink and placing the glass carefully on the small, stylish table at her side.

"Yeah," I said, rubbing the top of my head with my free hand and lowering my glass to the floor. "I'm looking for someone." She nodded, those blazing eyes narrowing just a little.

"A girl?" she said, her voice straining weirdly. I shook my head.

"Couple of guys, they'll have been with some girls earlier tonight. I need to find them and quick."

"And why's that then?" she asked. I hesitated, she didn't need to know and I didn't want her any closer to this than she already was but the look on her face told me it was a deal breaker.

"They have something that belongs to a friend of mine. I'm getting it back for him." And that was as much as she was getting. I wasn't going to give her a single scrap more.

"Friend?" She said incredulously. "Oh you mean that lad with one eye?" Ok, so she could have that bit as well.

"Yeah, look," I said hastily. "I just need to know who to talk to. They're from round here but they're new to the scene. Who would they go to for girls if they didn't know anyone?" She seemed pissed at me all of a sudden, reluctant to help.

"How would I know?" she shrugged.

"Come on," I said. "You must have an idea. It's important."

"Is this about the hit?" she asked.

"You know about that?" I asked, surprised.

"Is it?!" she snapped. I paused. Yet again she had caught me completely off guard. I had no idea why she was suddenly so pissed off. I tried instead to think of a way to avoid answering but eventually had to give in.

112

"Yeah," I said but then, seeing her eyes flash, quickly tried to explain. "Kind of. Not really."

She leapt out of the chair and walked lightly to the mantle across the chimney breast that dominated the far side of the room and stood there with her back to me. Confused I sat for a few seconds, briefly distracted again by tracing the lines of her through her robe. Then I stood and moved into the middle of the room.

"I'm not involved in all that," I said quietly. "They just took the lad's car to do the job and I need to get it back for him."

Still nothing.

"It's important," I tried again.

Suddenly she span around, a shine in her eyes that threatened to spill over.

"I don't want you to," she said fiercely.

"I don't understand," I said, though my confusion just seemed to enrage her more which just made me even more confused.

"I don't want you to," she said again, as if explaining. "And I won't help you."

She pushed past me to sit back in the chair and seemed to sulk.

I ran both my hands up from my brow over my head to land at the back of my neck before turning to approach her, crouching at her feet.

"Look," I said carefully. "I'm not doing this for kicks and I'm not getting paid alright? I have to do this, I have to help him." She had been staring over my shoulder resolutely but glanced down at me after this.

"You know why," I added quietly, the words dry in my ever sore throat. She shook her head and traced her fingers down the side of my face. A single tear made a break for it and mirrored her fingers trail down over her elegant cheek.

I couldn't for the life of me understand why she had suddenly become so upset. All I knew was that I'd already spent longer here than I'd intended and that I desperately needed her to point me in the right direction.

"Leon," she said simply, retrieving her hand and refusing to look at me again.

113

"Jimmy's enforcer Leon?" I asked, surprised. She nodded.

"After Harvey," she started but then paused and took a deep breath. "After Harvey, Jimmy took over his patch. Most of Harvey's girls stuck around so Jimmy got Leon to run them for him."

This made sense though it was a bit close to the bone for my liking. The unexpected involvement of Jimmy the Jack changed things. It upped the stakes significantly but it couldn't be helped. I nodded absently as I stood, the next step of my plan appearing out of the fog ahead of me. I moved to the front door but paused as my hand hit the handle.

"Thanks love," I said over my shoulder, "thanks a lot, I appreciate it and.." I turned to face her. She was still sat in the chair, more tears on her face now. "..I'm sorry if I," but I still couldn't work it out so settled instead for, "I'm sorry."

I turned back to open the door but in a second she was across the room and on me. Another passionate kiss, the door handle jammed in my back. I responded more quickly this time, pulling her against me only to find her pulling away again almost immediately.

"Just," she said, her voice wavering as she wiped her face and steadied herself. "Just be careful, alright?"

"I always am baby," I quipped with a grin and turned to go but she grabbed my arm.

"I mean it!" she said hotly, then cooling quiet, "and if you wanted to come round again, maybe tomorrow afternoon.." she looked at me weirdly, kind of determined but sad, "..that might be ok."

I tried to keep the total confusion from my face, reaching up to cup hers gently.

"Sounds good," I said with a quiet smile and meant it. Then I turned and opened the door, stepping back out into the dark and the cool.

Heading back up the street I shook my head. I still didn't understand most of what had just happened but decided there'd be time enough for all that tomorrow. I fished my phone from my jacket and watched as my thumb began to skip through the list of numbers.

Jimmy's number came into view, glowing electric

in the yellow street gloom. I looked at it for a while as my feet walked on, dithering about making the call. Jimmy the Jack was a bit of a legend in this part of the city and was definitely not someone you fucked about. Officially he was the owner of a string of legit nightclubs but anyone who was anyone knew he ran a lot more than that.

Everyone had their own stories about Jimmy but the one I'd heard most often was about how he'd got his name. Years ago there'd been a guy who'd had a skinful in one of Jimmy's clubs. He'd kicked off with the staff like a typical drunken arse but unfortunately for him Jimmy had happened to be there. Even more unfortunately, when Jimmy and his lads had approached this guy, he'd thrown his drink in Jimmy's face.

Moments later he'd been out the back taking a severe kicking as was to be expected. Meanwhile however, Jimmy had taken a jack from his own car and cranked the thing up as high as it would go before telling his guys to drag the poor bastard over and put his leg underneath the wheel.

Of course it had been way too late for pleading, though the guy had no doubt tried anyway, and so Jimmy had shoved his car off the jack so that it landed on the guy's leg, crushing it beyond repair. He then repeated the process with the other leg, and of course this time the guy knew what was coming.

Without a moment of hesitation or mercy however Jimmy dropped his car on the guy's other leg too before taking the jack to the guy's head. Supposedly the guy did survive but had lost both his legs, not to mention his good looks.

Subsequently I was a little hesitant about making the call. I'd never been on the wrong side of Jimmy and if anything he seemed to quite like me. I'd always known however that his affection, such as it was, would only stretch as far as killing me quick rather then slow if I ever fucked up.

I swallowed hard, winced and cursed then made the call. Raising the phone to my ear I half hoped he wouldn't answer though in truth I knew that I needed to speak to him first if I was going to get anywhere with

Leon. After a second or two of agonising silence the phone began to ring, shrill and insistent.

Just a couple of rings and then came that voice. He sounded drunk and happy.

"Now then!" he roared. "Kaz! How the fuck are you lad? I've not seen you in ages."

"I'm alright thanks Jimmy, yourself?" I kept my voice calm and friendly but always, always respectful.

"I am fucking brilliant lad! Do you know my little lass is getting married tomorrow?" There was music and laughter in the background.

"I do, I do," I said. "Can't believe it, seems like only the other day she were born. I'm sure she'll have a great day."

"She better fucking had do lad, I've spent enough on it! I tell you what though, I can guarantee you that lass of mine is going to have the best fucking day of her life, and do you know why?"

"Why's that?" I asked obediently.

"Because I will fucking kill anyone or anything that gets in the way, that's why!" More roaring laughter. I tried to join in as best I could even though I didn't find it funny at all.

"And what if it rains?" I asked, just about managing jovial but then wondering if I'd crossed the line.

"Eh now," he said, suddenly serious. "If it rains then that's down to God himself and I can't very well kill the Almighty can I?"

There was a pause during which I gulped.

"So I'll just have to break the Cunt's legs instead!" he added finally, roaring hysterically again so that this time I actually had to hold the phone away from my ear.

"Anyway lad, what you after?" he asked once he'd calmed back down again.

"Yeah right," I began. "I'm after a word with Leon, that's all. Just need a lead on a job I'm working, thought I'd best run that past you first."

"Of course lad! Of course. You tell that fat bastard I sent you and if he gives you any shit you just let me know, alright?"

"Cheers Jimmy, appreciate it," I said, almost

keeping the relief out of my voice.

"Yeah," he said absently then, after a pause, his voice suddenly dropped again. "You still dealing son?" Jimmy was never one to miss a business opportunity.

"No, not my thing any more," I said. "Not for a long time," I added with careful insistence.

"Mm," I could hear his frown.

"I thought you had a lad for that anyway," I added, trying to steer him away from offering me work which I'd have no choice but to accept.

"Yeah I did, got himself blown in half with a shotgun though didn't he." He was still mulling something over I could tell.

"Shit," I said thoughtfully.

"His ex's brother or something, right fucking mess it was," his mind was still elsewhere.

Another pause.

"I'll bet," I took a chance and broke the silence. "Well, thanks again Jimmy and all the best for tomorrow and that."

"Aye, cheers lad," he was back in the present, back to pissed up and happy. "Mind how you go," he chimed and the line was dead. Nodding to myself I slipped my phone back into my jacket.

"Thank fuck for that," I whispered to the night, reaching the end of the street and turning left.

Leon was one of those guys I was aware of but had never actually encountered. When he wasn't cracking heads for Jimmy he was usually hanging around in a dingy little cafe that sat down a forgotten side street out of the North end of town.

If you didn't know it was there you'd never find it. It wasn't a prime location for cafe reliant on passing trade but of course the chipped mugs of tea and occasional slices of burnt toast were really just a front for the illegal bookies upstairs.

It was fair old walk but I was less than a couple of hours in so I had the time. I plodded past a few more rows of front doors with occasional corners in between then cut down a tight, dark alley to emerge on the edge of the main road than ran out the top of the city.

There was a sparse but steady flow of traffic in

both directions, at least half of it taxis, so that as I strode I pondered against a constant backdrop of engines and lights. As ever, a moment of neglect and my mind was back to flicking through the menu.

The taste and the smell of her came back straight away, dragging a tangle of confusion behind it. I batted that away, that wasn't for tonight. Maybe I really would take her up on her offer of popping round tomorrow. I had no idea where that would lead, never did with her, but I wasn't up myself so far as to think it'd be up the stairs where my rampant imagination was now so keen to stray.

No I focused on a mental picture of Leon instead and found him to be just the bucket of cold water I needed. He was a mountain of man and almost as much of a local legend as Jimmy. Some people insisted that he'd once crushed a guy's head with his bare hands though I had no idea if that was actually true or not. Obviously it was in the interests of guys like Leon for rumours like that to spread but there was one story about him that I knew for a fact to be true.

The reason I knew it had happened was that I'd been one of the few people to see the CCTV footage. That night some young dickhead had tried to turn over the bookies with a shotgun, the end of a long and complicated story, the details of which I had no desire to revisit.

I could remember the black and white climactic scene though, as if it were laid out on the pavement before me. It had been well after hours, even for them, and the huge mass that was Leon had been squeezed into a hopelessly inadequate chair behind the desk on the right.

He'd been thumbing through numerous stacks of cash lined up neatly before him when suddenly another figure had come into view from the left. The lad had been skinny and masked up, the long black shape of his shotgun extending out before him. There'd been no sound on the CCTV and the lad's face was covered, but from the gesturing of the shotgun it it had been fairly obvious what he was saying.

Leon had just sat there as if painted onto the

screen, a mountain immovable just staring up at the would-be robber without a flicker of anything. The young lad had begun to wave the shotgun around even more, clearly rattled and had then taken a step forward to thrust the muzzle to within a few inches of Leon's face.

Still nothing, no response, just glaring. Finally the lad had stepped right up to the desk, raising the stock of the shotgun to his shoulder as if to put his whole weight behind as he'd pointed it downwards to almost touch Leon's forehead. Then, in one single fluid motion, Leo had done just about the most amazing thing I've ever seen on a TV screen.

It had happened so fast we'd had to rewind the tape and play it back in slow motion. Leon had suddenly stood, catching up the chair he'd been sat in with his right hand as he'd done so and then swung it up and over his head before bringing it crashing down into the robber. As the would wannabe robber had crumpled under the blow the muzzle of the shotgun had flashed upwards and a small shower of what had been the ceiling had drifted down into shot from above.

I don't know how many times we played that part back but it never ceased to be literally jaw dropping. Afterwards Leon had made his way round the counter, in no rush whatsoever, retrieved the shotgun and laid it on the desk amongst the cash. Then he'd taken a fistful of the guy's jacket and dragged him out of shot. Nobody needed to know what happened to the lad after that.

The grainy grey images flickered out leaving just the bear screen of rolling pavement. This was the guy I was heading for. Utterly fearless and lethal with just about anything that came to hand. Of course I had Jimmy's name in my pocket now so he'd have to give me what I wanted whether he liked it or not, but long term I knew it wouldn't be in my interests to make an enemy of him.

I'd have to appear confident but not cocky, fearless but respectful. It was going to be a bit of a tightrope but I'd walked worse in my time. The key now was to stop thinking about it, too much pondering of what could go wrong and my nerve would begin to waver.

I still had a long walk ahead of me and as I gradually made my way along the monotony of the roadside I thought about the route ahead. In another five or ten minutes the road would broaden out into double lanes and swing round to the left as it began to climb up out of the city. Then, gradually, houses would return to the roadside, building into dense estates stretching back and away from either side. Eventually the road would narrow again and once a row of shops came into view I'd know I was nearly there.

In the meantime however there was nothing to do but keep putting one foot in front of the other. A chilled breeze picked up, lacing my face with the same pain from before. I tried to ignore it, cursing the flat faced little wanker who'd clocked me.

I couldn't think about him either though, somehow that made my face hurt even more. I couldn't think about her, that just clouded my judgement and made me doubt myself. And I mustn't think about what was coming either. Just had to keep on walking, not thinking of anything, ignore the pain in my throat and my face, just be quiet and empty and cold. There'd be time to think later, in fact later would be nothing but thinking. Back in flat, sat still and silent, I knew that thinking was probably all I would do.

As I watched my feet do their thing I let the sounds of the traffic roll over and through me until one engine in particular coughed its way above the rest. I glanced up just in time to see the piece of crap rattle by. Made mostly of rust and belching smoke from the back, it was a wonder that it was running at all. A couple of steps more and I caught a blast of the fumes, lingering in the cool night air.

Fucking hell that's grim.

I'm standing in Billy's garage and the car he's working on has just belched a great cloud of black, foul smelling smoke out onto the street before shuddering into silence. I cover my face and turn away coughing.

"Jesus Billy," I wheeze. "Just fucking scrap it, it's had it."

Billy emerges from under the bonnet and

steps out of the shadows, leaning in through the driver's window to restart the engine. Grubby and grinning he moves out into the pale autumn sunlight to stand next to me. He's wiping his hands on a rag from his belt and admiring what is clearly a piece of shit.

"You give me a week lad," he says chuckling, "and she'll look like she just rolled off the line."

"Yeah," I say, incredulous. "I'll believe it when I see it. So what have you got for me today?"

Billy fishes around in his overalls for a second before throwing a key at me which I juggle then catch.

"That one," he says, pointing out into the street. I follow his filthy finger until my eyes land on tiny, bright yellow box with wheels.

"Ah come on," I whinge. "Really? You've nothing better?"

"I've got what I've got lad. Take it or leave it," he says, heading into his office. I remember he's doing me a favour.

"Aye go on then," I say. "When do you need it back?"

"Couple of days is fine," he calls but as I turn to approach the ugly little thing he comes back out.

"Look lad," he says quietly, pausing so that I move back into the gloom, curious. "It's none of my business what you do, long as you bring the cars back, just.."

I look at him expectant with no idea where he's going.

"Just watch your arse alright?" he says eventually.

We stand in silence for a second and he can see the question in my eyes. He sighs.

"City's changing lad, it's not how it used to be round here, not how I remember it anyway." He stops fidgeting with the rag and puts it back on his belt before plunging his hands into his pockets.

"I mean," he continues, looking genuinely grave. "Did you hear about that kiddy a few weeks back? Gunned down in the street, in broad daylight!"

Hearing the words is like a punch in the gut. My mouth is suddenly dry and the shadows of the garage seem darker and colder than before. I lick my lips but the words aren't coming. I just nod and make a sympathetic noise instead.

" 'kin disgusting. And that's what I'm talking about, there're no rules any more lad, d'you see what I mean?" He shakes his head, eyes shifting focus into the distance. "There used to be rules, there were some things no-one did, they just weren't done. But now..."

I keep on nodding, my stomach clenching, desperate for this to be over now but he's not done.

"I know you're a good lad," he says, returning to the garage and raising his eyes to mine. "Just, whatever is it you're doing, be careful alright? I wouldn't want to see anything happen to you."

I try to talk, to give the expected response but the words are caught in my throat like scratchy little crumbs. I cough them up hard, turning away to clear my throat and swallow a big deep breath. Finally I turn back to Billy and manage a gentle smile.

"Cheers," I say, slapping him on the shoulder. "I appreciate it and don't worry, I'm always careful." I walk away, out into the sun and try to ignore the feeling of his eyes on my back. As I get into the car I see him turn away and disappear back into his office.

For a moment I sit there, fending off bad thoughts and examining the interior of my new ride instead. It's not actually as bad as I first thought, despite the colour. I adjust the seat and mirrors, turn the key and pull away from the garage.

Somehow time has moved on since that summer afternoon, though for me it's as if it never ended. The trees and the bushes that were overflowing with colour are now browning and thinning to nothing, slow death under a bright clear sky.

I turn and start to climb, the little engine straining against the hill, slowly dragging itself up towards the park. This is what I do now, ever since that morning when I woke up in the alley with what felt like a genuinely terminal hangover, my gun just sat in my lap for all to see. I'd shambled home, fearful, ashamed and above all dying, before collapsing into bed. A couple of days later however I found I hadn't died after all and as my head began to clear I recalled the idea.

The idea was sound even my first attempt had not been. So here I was, borrowing another string of anonymous little cars from Billy and stalking my prey, learning his routine, biding my time.

I turn left at the park and glance across the open green. No throngs of bodies today, they've long since gone, just a stiff, cool breeze and damp, chilled grass. The towering tree lines are just starting to drop their shade and in a few weeks more they'll be standing sharp and proud, baring their nakedness to the sky.

I find it makes me feel angry, this change happening all round. It's as if nothing has happened, as if time can just flow right along, when in fact I alone know that the world ended on that day a few weeks before. Well, me alone with his mum anyway, poor cow.

But no! That's just another way back, another way back to those images. Today is another day of work, another step towards getting it done. I pull over by the park across the road from the end of a familiar looking alleyway. I check the clock on the dashboard, should be any minute now.

And sure enough a figure emerges from the alley, a young lad on a bike, a plastic carrier bag swinging from the handlebars. He glances around before pushing off, pedalling hard along the pavement back the way I've just come.

I drum my fingers on the wheel and realise I'm gritting my teeth. I twist my neck to the side until it clicks then take a deep breath and try to calm down. A few cars drive past, a couple of joggers bounce by and then, yes, as expected. Another young lad, another bike, another bag. This one heads off in the opposite direction to his predecessor, also pedalling hard then disappearing from view at the first corner.

The clock tells me I don't wait as long this time and soon the front of the great black SUV rolls into view. It pauses, jutting it's mighty nose out into the road before lazily rolling out and turning. It trundles past me without a care in the world, driver and passengers obscured behind panes of black. I don't need to see him to know he's in there though and my hands tighten on the wheel as I watch the back of the SUV grow smaller.

"Soon you bastard, you cunt," I hiss, filling the tiny car's interior with my venom. "Soon we'll see. You'll see, you fucking bastard, you fucking cunt..."

I could still hear myself cursing as the long awaited row of shops finally came into view. Just a couple of takeaways were still open, gaudy signs defying the night. A small cluster of bodies spilled out of one of these onto the pavement, their drunken chatter floating down to me as I approached.

It was all "..did you see that.." and "..I tell you what.." Shoulder to shoulder stumbles and sharing chips from a tray. I drifted across the pavement towards the shop fronts as they passed me by, all happy and without a care in the world. As their chatter receded behind me I glanced back, one of them pausing to cackle at something, doubled up funny before trotting back after the crowd.

I wondered what it must feel like to be in that place. Relaxed with friends and at ease with the world. As the dark mouth of the side street came into view I supposed that I must have had times like that once, back in the day, before.. well, everything, but no specific memories came to mind.

I reached the corner and stepped off the main street, out of the yellow and into the dark. Suddenly there was a siren approaching from further up the main road, howling its importance and urgency. I took a step to the wall and leant against the brick, just a shadow among shadows unseen. I had nothing specific to fear from the pigs but in my world that sound was almost never a good thing.

The howl reached an almost painful volume but then dropped again as the car flashed past sleek and white. I heard the crowd I'd met moments before, whooping and cheering as it passed them, offering their energies up to the sky and then giggling off into the distance.

I moved further into the dark, stepping careful around anonymous debris in the street. At first I was flanked by the back yards of the shops on the main road but these soon gave way to brief terraces of boarded up units on either side. Eventually glinting glass replaced nailed up wood and I approached the front of Leon's cafe.

The sign said CLOSED but to me the time said different and sure enough the door wasn't locked. I slipped inside and glanced about. The shabby tables and chairs all sat silent in the dark as if caught stealing and now holding their breath.

I moved silently through them, past the counter towards the back, pausing at the door in the corner. This sign said TOILET and underneath OUT OF ORDER. I smiled, acknowledging the partial truth and opened the door safe in the knowledge that I definitely would not find functioning toilet on the other side.

The flight of stairs that was revealed instead was narrow and shabby. It led up steeply from the dark into light, smoke and low level chatter. I began to ascend, pulling the door closed carefully behind me. Before I was even half way however, a tall, thin shape blocked the light from above. This was to be expected however so I plodded on up, towards the skinny silhouette.

By the time I paused two steps below him I could make out more of his face. The guy looked like he was built out of sticks, tall and gangling, hands flopping from his wrists, all topped off with a shock of blond hair. He was wearing a well cut casual suit with an expensive looking shirt, open at the collar though both hung on him as if still on the hanger. He was without a doubt the campest guy I had ever seen in a place like this.

He was a good head taller than me anyway but from his vantage at the top of the stairs he towered over me like an anorexic giant. His face was a mask, unimpressed and uninterested as he scanned me, head to toe and back again. He didn't need to ask the question.

"Here to see Leon," I said, looking up and holding his gaze.

"Who?" he replied, flat, dull and still not fussed but clearly ready to try and shove me back down the stairs in a heartbeat.

"Leon," I repeated, adding, "Jimmy said it'd be ok."

At the mention of Jimmy's name he looked me up and down again, his gaunt features twisting from rockface to dubious.

"Don't know anyone called.." he began but then stopped, tilting his head a little to the left. For the first time I realised he was wearing an earpiece and a second later he took step back and to the left.

"Go on," he said simply, staring past me as I finally bested the stairs and turned right.

The bookies wasn't much to look at. There was a counter that stretched almost wall to wall across the far end of the room, stopping just short to the left so as to allow room for a heavy looking door. Otherwise it was basically still just a cold, dingy room over a cafe. A couple of bare, swinging bulbs were painting the place gloomy.

Off to the right dirty windows looked back down onto the street, or at least would have done if not for the heavy blackout curtains. Hanging from ceiling above the windows were four small TV screens while the wall on my left was dominated by a huge whiteboard upon which dozens of odds had been scrawled.

I ran my eyes over the numbers but recognised only a few of the labels and titles. You could bet on just about anything up here, long as you knew it existed of course. The rest of the room was a scattering of tired looking punters and tall little tables. One or two were watching a fight on one of the TV's, slips clutched in their hand, each urging on their pick, while another was swaying at the counter.

The rest were just hanging about, some muttering to one another but all counting what was left of their money and looking desperately at the big white board. Most losers had long since given up for the night while the few winners had moved on to spend what they'd won, most likely giving it all straight back to Jimmy in one of his clubs. That just left those who'd lost but hadn't yet come to accept it, still believing they could make it all back.

I received a couple of furtive glances as I moved across the room but for the most part everyone in was too busy worrying about either their next bet or their last to pay me any attention. As I approached the counter I noticed the guy ahead of me raise his voice.

"But I never.." there was a pause followed by a long, low belch and then a sigh, "..'kin hell, said that though did I? You know I never.."

For the first time I caught sight of the tired looking woman behind the counter. She was sitting on a rickety looking swivel chair, smoking a cigarette and staring up at the drunk with open contempt. Her eyes sagged under the weight of heavy black bags and the feeble light made her skin appear papery and grey. Beneath her habitual fatigue however was an intimidating stony resolve. As the drunk rambled on she just smoked, pointing her chin at him and glaring.

"Right then!" the drunk announced, his raised voice earning him not even a flicker of expression from her. "You listen to me, 'cos I'm telling you.." here he tried to point at her with his left hand but almost immediately found himself falling forward and so had to land the offending hand on the counter to steady himself. He took a second and then pointed at her with his right hand instead.

"I'm telling," he slurred, "telling you, that I want my fucking money back. You've fucking robbed me you have, you fucking..." but the rest was lost in mumbles.

"I've already told you," she said finally, her voice long smoked and husky. "You placed your bet. You lost. That's it."

The drunk made a strange squealing sound that gradually condensed into recognisable speech.

"A'no, no, no. You said," he stood away from the counter again, straightening up to sway. "You fucking said.." but she interrupted him, her voice irritated but flat.

"Do you want to place another bet?" she asked.

"With what?!" he exclaimed, his voice breaking high with indignation. He flapped his arms at his pockets and turned around to look at the rest of the room. His eyes were wide, his lips pursed, ready to address the crowd but then deflated a little as he realised that no-one was listening, sinking in on himself until noticing me. He blinked and shook his head attempting to focus.

"They've fucking robbed me y'know!" he shouted at me before spinning back to face the counter again, stumbling so that he had to grab at it again to stay upright. "You've fucking robbed me! You've had it all, I've got nowt now, nowt! What am I going to tell.."

"So you don't want to place another bet?" she interrupted again, still unmoved.

"No, I don't want to place another bet," he mocked, impersonating her voice and hopping his fury from one foot to the other in a little dance while he did so before pitching forward to lean against the counter again.

"Right. Fuck off then," she said, nodding towards the far end of the room. For a moment he was speechless but a second more and he exploded.

"Fuck off?!" he screeched. "Fuck off is it?! You're going to fucking fuck off when I'm done with you you fucking bitch." He lunged over the counter but before I could react the skinny lad from the stairs was stepping past me.

He reached forward with an impossibly thin arm and gripped the raging drunk by the scruff of the neck. Then, with quite astonishing strength, he wrenched the guy back away from the counter and sent him tumbling

128

down onto the floor.

I realised I was staring at the skinny lad with my mouth open and so closed it and turned to look at the drunk instead. He was sat up, blinking, looking angry and confused, clearly having no idea what had just happened. He wobbled to his feet, fixed his bleary eyes on his assailant, then lunged screeching behind a wild left hook.

Everything seemed to slow down so that although the whole thing took just a second or two, I saw it all in perfect detail. The lad's face was calm, bored even, as he leaned just a little to his right and avoided the drunk's fist. At the same time, his right hand darted forwards landing a jab, vicious and precise just under the drunk's armpit.

The drunk's momentum carried him forwards but his body crumpled sideways, recoiling from the blow and folding in on itself in pain. Still leaning to his right, the lad brought his sharply pointed left knee up hard so that it disappeared deep into the drunk's gut. The guy folded again, a neat, forward facing right angle this time.

The lad's knee came back down and the drunk began to follow it falling, down towards the floor. The lad's bony right fist fell faster however, blasting the drunk's jaw and firing him into the threadbare carpet with a great, dull slap.

The three blows had been delivered in such quick succession that they'd sounded like knocks on a door. By the time I'd processed it all the lad was already dragging the drunk away, back across the floor towards the top of the stairs.

I watched and winced as he shoved the guy off the top step with his foot. A brief series of ugly sounds followed, painting a picture of what I was glad I couldn't see. Then the lad began his own controlled descent, presumably to clear up the mess.

Turning back to the counter I realised that the rest of the punters didn't seem to have noticed the floor show and were just as they had been. Hoping against hope or wallowing in despair, they had no time for anyone else. I stepped up and made eye contact with the long suffering woman. She looked unimpressed.

"Placing a bet?" she asked, her voice still flat and annoyed.

"No," I said, giving her a smile which she ignored. "Just need a quick word with Leon actually."

She looked me up and down but didn't seem convinced. I drew breath to try and convince her but she was looking past me. I turned to follow her gaze to find that the skinny lad had resumed his post at the top of the stairs and was now nodding to her in confirmation.

Without looking at me she shrugged and leaned forward, pressing some unseen button before settling back into her chair. I took a step towards the slab of a door that stood to the left of the counter but then paused, glancing back at her unsure.

"Well go on then!" she snapped before looking away again, shaking her head.

Whipped on by her barb I pushed at the heavy door and found that it swung inward with surprising ease. The room was small and even more dimly lit than the main room outside but I couldn't miss Leon's bulk, looming behind a desk straight ahead of me.

On the desk in front of him stood several piles of cash while another was split between his hands, the notes busy being counted from one to the other. The sight of the money jogged my memory and I looked up to the far right corner of the ceiling.

Sure enough there hung a small CCTV camera and as I took a couple more steps forward I realised that I was right in the heart of the grainy black and white image I'd seen so many times. The lad with the shotgun had been standing right here when Leon had lamped him with his chair.

"What," he rumbled. I glanced at the visible edges of the chair he was sat on and marvelled yet again at that scene, now appreciating it as never before. Suddenly I realised he had stopped counting and was looking at me.

"Oh right," I said, smiling in vain once more. "I spoke to Jimmy earlier, he said it'd be ok if we had a chat."

"Yeah," Leon growled. "He said."

I nodded and licked my lips.

"I'm on a job and I need some information," I said.

"Yeah," he growled again. "He said."

"Ok," I said, dropping the cheery tone. If he wanted to get down to it that was fine by me. "So I heard you took on Harvey's girls for Jimmy when Harvey bought it," I began.

"Did you," said Leon resuming his counting. It wasn't a question.

"I'm looking for a couple of lads who'll have been partying earlier tonight. Locals but new to the scene. They'll have been after a couple of girls, probably at a hotel in town."

"Couple of lads," he repeated.

"Aye," I replied, unsure.

"Couple of lads hit that big meet earlier," he said, voice still flat, fingers still counting. I cursed silently and tried again.

"Don't know about that mate. These lads that I'm after took something from a friend of mine, I just need to get it back off them, that's all." I waited for a response.

The seconds ticked by.

"As I say," I continued, trying to keep the irritation from my voice. "They're new to the scene, don't really know anyone. I'd heard they might have ended up being hooked up with some of Harvey's.." he paused and looked up from his counting. "..your girls." I corrected myself.

Leon put the wad of notes on the table and scooped up another.

"Dick," he said. I waited but there was no more.

"What?" I asked eventually. Leon sighed.

"Dick," he said. "Shitty arse rich kid, wannabe dealer. They'll know him,"

"Right.." I said slowly, still not getting it.

"Dick knew Harvey, knows some of the girls, he'll have hooked them up," he said.

"Got it," I said. That made much more sense. "So where.." but he cut me off, ceasing his counting again to eye me hard.

"So how long you known Jimmy then?" he asked,

bristling. The air suddenly thickened and my thoughts were drawn back to the chair.

"Jimmy?" I asked, force cooling the word to maintain the facade. "Oh we go way back, known him half my life." Leon thought about this for a bit, staring at me all the while. Finally he seemed satisfied and went back to counting.

"Katie. Woodvale Heights. Number 12." And that was that. We were done.

I thanked Leon for his time but apparently I'd become invisible so I slipped back through the door. There were just three punters left now, the two cringing under the screens and one looking utterly desolate in the far corner.

As I headed for the top of the stairs I turned back and nodded a smile to the woman behind the counter but she just scoffed and turned away. The lad at the top of the stairs stared straight through me and so I trotted down them without a word.

At the bottom I slipped on something while reaching for the door, almost falling right on my arse. Peering down I could just about make out a small dark puddle but decided not to pay it too much mind and moved out into the cafe quickly, pulling the 'TOILET' door closed behind me.

A quick weave through the furniture and I was back out on the street, breathing a few good sighs. I was glad that was over and feeling pretty good. I now had a name and an address and with a bit of luck this lass would be able to point me straight to the two, now infamous dickheads and more importantly to the lad's car.

I knew the Woodvale estate, Heights, Towers and Court. The three blocks stood back down the way on the edge of the city centre. I moved back along the dingy side street to emerge onto the main road.

The street was slightly darker now that all but one of the takeaways had closed and turned off their signs for the night. The last one standing, chicken legs and wings, was empty apart from the sleepy young guy propping up the counter. Out on the street there wasn't another body in sight.

I carried my new found warmth of feeling down the road, smiling at the dark, my throat even felt a little better. This was going to work out just fine. The lad would be ok, he'd get his car back in plenty of time thereby avoiding being tortured to death and then maybe I wouldn't have to feel so fucking guilty every time I saw him.

Having left the still shops behind me I began to walk past sleeping homes instead. The walk was easier this way as the broad road swept down the hill into the city. The incline carried me in, towards my next stop and towards success. Just then however a bitter wind rose up from the brooding mass of the city below, sliding up the road to engulf me. I retreated into my jacket as much as possible, collar up, hands in pockets, but the chill cut right on through me as if I were as if I were naked in the street.

The wind flowed past and was gone but my smile had frozen and fallen. Getting cocky wasn't a good idea I realised. There was no telling what waited ahead, what Flat 12, Woodvale Heights might contain. The more I thought about it the more my chances seemed to fade and harden.

Things rarely went as you expected round here, the city seemed to have a knack for unexpected brutality. I tried to regain the confidence of moments before, the positive outlook, making your own luck and all that but nasty surprises were a local speciality. I'd learned that from bitter experience.

The trees are bare now. Over the road they rise from the park, hard black lines fracturing a grey sky behind. A vicious wind is trying to cut through me but I'm ignoring it and listening hard. The cold doesn't touch me, such is the blazing fury I'm hiding under my shirt. My eyes are fixed on the end of the alleyway.

I'm constantly aware of the weight and the edges of the gun in the back of my belt. My trigger finger twitches in anticipation. After weeks of watching I've chosen my spot well. No car today, don't need one, they're all back with Billy safe and sound.

Of course it'd be nice to be able to pay the old bastard back for all the help he's given me over the last few months. I cut him in on my fee for watching the kid but all the cars he's given me since have been free. Thing is that I know after this goes down I'm probably not going to see tomorrow so I won't get the chance to sort him out.

It's not as if I've got a will or any of that shit, or anything to leave to anyone if I did come to that. No, after today I'll be gone and the world won't look much different. It'll all just roll on as it always does as if I'd never been here. There will be one difference though, the world won't be quite the same because although I might be leaving, I'm not going alone. And here it is, the sound I've been waiting for.

It's on.

I fall back a little, turning away from the alley. This is how it begins.

I can hear the bicycle coming, the mild squeak of each turning wheel, it's right behind me now. I glance over my shoulder and sure enough there he is, a skinny young lad without a coat. Emerging from the alley onto the road, he looks around, ignores me and sets off. He stands up on his pedals and races away from me, white plastic bag swinging from the handle bars.

I take a breath and crack my neck before moving up to the corner, setting my feet.

I'm ready.

Can't hear anything yet.

Fuck me he's taking his time.

Maybe there's only one runner today, maybe I've missed my chance. I can't wait another week to do this again, I haven't slept in days as it is, I'm...

No, here it is, the sound of the second bike. This kid is going to turn the other way, right into me. The sounds grows closer, and now closer. I hear the swish of the plastic bag, the creak of the pedals. I breathe out real slow.

"Sorry kid," I say under my breath.

Just as he reaches the end of the alley I step round the corner and slam my palm into his chest. My feet are set, my swing is true and the poor little bastard doesn't know what's hit him. At the moment of impact I know I've broken his ribs, I feel them go and regret it immediately. That wasn't part of the plan.

He flies backwards off the bike and lands in a wheezing heap. Beyond him, at the other end of the alley, the black SUV suddenly doubles in width as both front doors burst open, releasing two great leather clad slabs of men. The kid's crying on the floor but at least he's conscious and I'm in this now, too late to pull out.

I turn to chase the bike, which has rolled on straight out into the middle of the street, not yet aware that it's lost its rider. Another second however and it seems to notice. It slows with a wobble then finally gives up and swoons dramatically down onto its side.

I dash over to it, ignoring the screech of tires and a blaring horn while my fingers frantically untangle the plastic bag from the handlebars. Bag in hand I being to sprint. The heavy footsteps behind me mean I don't need to look over my shoulder.

They're big and they're scary but they're just hired help. I'm faster and I'm doing this for free. I tear at the bag as I run so that the tiny wraps, the little twists of plastic containing Tall James' product, begin to tumble onto the pavement behind me. I hear a breathless curse and just as I'd planned, one of them falls back to gather up the wraps.

I skid round a corner, almost falling, sheer grit keeping me upright. I chance a glance back and see I'm down to one guy, we've left his mate well behind us by now. His face is bright red and damn he looks pissed. If I let him catch me he'll probably kill me just for making him run.

I skip into a front garden and hop the fence

to the next while he stays on the pavement chasing parallel. Two gardens more and there's a serious wall but I throw everything I am right at it. Momentum at my back, I scramble right up and over, landing in a narrow alley and dumping what's left of the bag.

I'm out of sight but he'll know where I am. Now he'll have to go all the way round. Meanwhile I'm climbing another, much easier wall, and now he's lost me completely. I pause to let the breath tear in and out of me, picturing his face as he makes the end of the alley only to find it empty.

No time to lose though and so it's back to a sprint. I weave between bins and skip over piles of rubbish, fast approaching my final destination. Up another old wall and along it, then a climb onto a low roof and hasty balancing over the tiles.

A long drop that I feel in my knees but now I'm here and so out comes the gun. I'm in a broad empty alley, no one else around. I wipe my face, still breathing hard, and approach the corner slowly. Reaching the edge I take quick look and sure enough there it is just there, the back end of the black SUV.

The doors are still open though I have no idea how much time I have before the big lads return. I'm hoping they'll be scared enough of their employer to want to make a good show of retrieving his gear and at least trying to catch me.

I round the corner and remember that day in the summer, hell I've thought about little else since. I move over to the far side of the alley, sliding my back along the brick as I approach. I'm banking on him being in there but I've no way of knowing if he's seen me and is sat ready.

Now I'm crouching against the rear wheel, eyes fixed on the door handle. I knock the safety off and pull back the hammer, the gun weighing reassuringly heavy. I close my eyes and I see the kid, limp in his mother's arms. I realise I'm baring my teeth and that the moment has arrived at last. In a single fluid motion, I stand and turn, whipping open the door and pointing the gun.

"Thought that was you," says Tall James. He's looking at his phone in his hand, a huge joint burning idle in the other. "Get in," he adds.

I snarl and feel my finger tighten on the trigger, but the chilled wind reminds I'm outside and in full view. Probably better to do it in the car, plus I need to tell him what a piece of shit he is first. I look around warily then climb in, leaving the door open and keeping the gun on his gut.

"And here's me thinking you liked kids," he says, still not looking up. The rage in my blood flares even hotter and I raise the gun to point at his face.

"You bust that lad up pretty bad out there," he continues before actually yawning. "And you've lost him his job. He's no good to me like that."

I'm actually trembling I'm so angry now and I notice dull lines of light down the barrel shuddering in turn. I try to speak but I choke on my rage and have to swallow before I can start.

"Why?" I rasp.

"Hmm?" he says, unruffled, distracted.

"The kid," I manage, fighting the urge to cough.

"Oh," he says, as if the thought hadn't even occurred to him. "Right, that."

"Yeah," I say, words coming more easily now. "That. Your own son, you fucker..."

He smiles. He actually smiles and my finger tightens even more at the sight of it. I want to do it now. I should just do it now.

"He wasn't my kid," he says, amused. "As if I'd ever touch that nasty bitch."

I'm confused. I don't get it. I can't think.

"No, no," he continues. "I just needed to send a message to his dad. All that stuff about restraining orders and that, that was all just bullshit to make sure you didn't pussy out."

I realise my mouth is open. I close it.

He still hasn't looked at me. His thumb's still tapping away at the phone and now he finally takes a drag on the joint.

"You piece of shit," I hear myself whisper but he just laughs to himself at the sound of it. I clear my throat.

"Well I hope it was worth it," I say in a firmer tone. "Because now I'm going to fucking kill you."

He laughs again and takes another drag before blowing a gentle plume in my direction.

"Nah," he says without hesitation. "You're not."

I push the gun even closer to his face, infuriated that he won't look up. I'm thinking I should have pulled the trigger straight away, as soon as I opened the door. This isn't what I expected and as each second ticks by I feel like I'm slipping further from that optimum moment.

"You don't have it in you," he says in a matter-of-fact tone. "Oh you've got some balls I'll give you that, and you're a clever bastard with it," he concedes. "That's why I gave you the job. But you think about stuff too much."

I can't think of anything to say.

"You came here to kill me and you could have popped me when you opened the door but now you're sat here having a chat instead and all those little doubts are starting to creep in." He shakes his head with a smile.

I can feel it all slipping away from me. It had seemed so clear before but now, here, actually looking at the guy, hearing him speak, suddenly it doesn't seem so straight forward. I want to hurt him so much, I even call on that worst of all images, his limp little body swinging in her arms, but now all I can see is the heartache, the senseless pain. My finger slackens away from the trigger, my arm sags a little too.

"You piece of shit," I whisper again.

A world in which I don't do this comes into view, a world where I hate myself every day, where I'm never free of this day and life is just a flat grey forever.

"Yeah you said that," he says again. "If you're not going to shoot me you'd best do one, the lads'll be back any second."

A thought occurs and suddenly my fires flare up again. My hand tightens on the gun and I narrow my eyes.

I have to do it.

I have to.

"But I have to kill you now," I say, my voice suddenly hard and calm. "If I don't you'll come after me. It's self preservation." I get a chill from hearing my own words as I realise they're true. I'm in this now, I've crossed the line and there's no way out except pulling this trigger.

But Tall James is laughing again.

"Nah mate," he chuckles. "You're fine."

Confusion derails me again. This is taking too long. They should have been back by now. I'm way overdue.

"Do you know why?" Finally he lays the phone to rest in his lap and actually looks me in the eye, looks right inside me. "Because you're not a threat."

And from those eyes I can see that he means it. He has nothing to fear to from me. I'm a joke, I'm not even worth killing.

I'm nothing.

I'm less than nothing.

"Now fuck off," he says and returns his attention to his phone. "And close the door behind you."

I can't think. There's nothing in my head, it's all grey. The gun's in my lap and now I'm sliding out of the car. I push the door closed and stumble away from it, blinking while my feet carry me on. I'm round the corner, I'm out of sight and now the autopilot kicks in and aims me for home.

The gun is still in my hand I notice. Something in me knows enough to put it away. I helped him kill that kid, I was too stupid to see what was happening and now he's played me all over again. Suddenly I'm puking, my whole body

heaving as if trying to turn itself inside out.
What have I done?

Finally the Woodvales were towering over me and I was feeling sick to my stomach. I could feel heat on my face at the memories and even a tear in my eye. Approaching the main door of the Heights, I retrieved my key card and pushed the thoughts back down, way back down.

Flat 12 was on the third floor so I headed for the stairs. The double doors groaned as they swung closed behind me. I paused and glanced up as the sound raced past me, leading my gaze up through the void about which the stairs snapped back and forth, all the way to the top.

Bringing my attention back to ground level I started up the steps, trying to retain some perspective by reminding myself that there were a dozen higher floors that could each have hosted the flat instead. With a hint of deja vu I found myself preparing doorstep opening lines for the lady in question and hoping not to find her at work.

I bested the second flight of stairs and was just passing the double doors onto the first floor landing when a noise from above caught my attention. The voices had been low and hushed and had now disappeared altogether but they had definitely been there, at least three of them.

Without pausing or looking up I continued up the next flight as if I hadn't noticed, holding myself from flinching even when the cluster of dark shapes on the landing above edged into my peripheral vision. I trotted up the last few steps and acted surprised to find my path blocked.

"Alright mate," said the first kid standing directly in front of me. There were five of them altogether, not a one out of school by the look of them. They were all wearing scarves with caps or hoods. The one extending the welcome was clearly the alpha but the others looked like they could be mean enough in a group.

"Lend us twenty quid," he said and I noticed that he was chewing.

The rest moved up behind him a little, completely blocking the way now. I watched the first lad's jaw for a second more, there was no gum in there, he was chewing at his own cheek.

So these little buggers were on the uppers tonight, or at least this one was, which meant right about now he probably felt pretty much indestructible, especially on his home turf with his crew at his back. He wouldn't be in the mood to listen to anything I had to say in that state. As much as he wanted my wallet and my phone he almost certainly wanted the easy thrill of some one sided violence even more.

I looked him in the eye and smiled.

"Fuck off lad," I said calmly. "I've somewhere to be." I took another step to stand level with them on the landing, suddenly realising that I was taller than three of them, including their front man.

"Nah mate," he replied, his hand coming up from his side to reveal a short but solid looking blade. "You're not hearing me. You want to get where you're going it's going to cost you fifty." His jaw worked on while the blade glistened lazily in the gloom.

"I thought it was twenty," I said, still keeping it calm and holding his eye.

"Shut the fuck up!" he squeaked, apparently done with the foreplay. "Wallet and phone! Do it! Do it now motherfucker! Wallet and phone." His other hand came up, palm out stretched awaiting the spoils.

I looked away from him for a moment, eyeing each of his friends in turn before returning to settle my gaze on him. I sniffed and cleared my throat.

"Or what?" I said, slowly taking my hands out of my jacket pockets but keeping them at my sides.

"You fucking stupid or something?" he screeched, waving the blade about in front of me. "Give me your fucking wallet and your fucking phone or I'll fucking cut you!"

I made a show of looking him up and down, taking my time and finishing back at the eyes without a trace of being impressed by him or his too hard talk.

"Alright," I said, cracking my neck.

"You what?!" he said, practically vibrating. Uppers and youthful exuberance were clearly a heady combo.

"Well, I'm not giving you shit lad," I said. "So you go ahead and do whatever you have to do, you're getting nowt off me."

For just a second he blinked, mild confusion playing across his non stop features. He glanced over each shoulder, his friends mumbling and muttering at each turn, urging him on. I set my feet shoulder width apart and bent my knees just a little.

"You stupid fucking..." he began but then, glancing at my side, he lunged, the blade flashing up. The thrust was wild, a great ugly swing with everything ounce of him on the back of it. The tip of the blade darted straight for my ribs but I easily had time to avoid it, turning side on and catching his wrist as I went.

Continuing the motion I whipped his arm forwards, pulling him along the path that all that momentum had set for him, before whipping him round. The small of his back hit the barrier but thanks to his vigour there was such force behind him that he went right up over it.

I snatched at the front of his hoodie just below his chin, stopping him mid flight and pausing his way along the quickest route back down to the ground floor. His knees were bent over the barrier so that his shins were still technically safe, but his arse and all the rest of him was dangling over the void.

My other hand still had his wrist though of course

143

it had twisted right over so that his arm ran a slow, painful spiral from wrist to shoulder. With his free hand he was clinging desperately to my arm while his eyes goggled glassy.

The whole thing had been a flash, sudden motion to a sudden halt. A heartbeat more and his friends finally caught up and reacted, shouting and rushing forward. I shoved him a little further out so that he squealed and they stopped unsure.

I applied a little more pressure to his wrist and he winced before releasing the blade. It bounced off the hard floor and clattered through the railings before tumbling down and down to break on the equally hard floor way below. I released his wrist and it flew instantly to join his other, both his hands gripping steel on my forearm.

"Now then," I said, still calm, looking initially at the gang but then turning to face him. "You listening?"

His eyes were clearing now, his brain had caught up while the fear driven adrenaline had washed his system of the best of the pills. He nodded, swallowing hard.

"That's no way to use a blade," I said. "You were being all he-man about it, saw you coming a mile off. If you're going to cut someone you need to be quick and loose and for fuck's sake don't lead with your eyes."

He was still nodding while his friends bristled behind me. My arm was really starting to hurt but I didn't let that show and cast them all another hard glance instead.

"More important than that though, and this goes for all of you," I continued. "Pick your battles. You look at what they're wearing, think about what they're doing, why are they here at this time of night? You weigh it up. You don't just jump any random who comes along because, well," I looked at him, my eyes softening, "where does that you get you eh?"

My arm was through the pain and starting to lose feeling. Much more of this and I wouldn't be able to hold onto the kid even if I wanted to.

"So how about I put you back on your landing and you chill the fuck out?" I asked him.

144

He nodded frantically.

"What's that?" I asked.

"Yeah," he choked. "Fucking yes! Yes!"

I yanked him back towards me and turned so that his feet hit the ground. He stumbled backwards into his friends but stood tall quickly, pushing away their hands and glaring. The shame in his eyes condensed to anger almost instantly. He tensed up again but I held his eye, my eyebrows asking him, really? His shoulders sagged slightly and he dropped his eyes to the floor, stepping back into the crowd to make a path. I walked through them but stopped at the double doors.

"Listen," I said, fishing out my wallet and removing a twenty. "There are some real heavy people about tonight, the kind you don't want to be fucking with and there's chance they might find their way here."

My friend the dangler was listening, his eyes narrowing not sure where I was going. The others were all fixed on the twenty.

"Now I've some business in one these flats and if you are lot are going to be hanging around here anyway perhaps you can be of some use. Anyone heavy looking starts coming up these stairs of yours while I'm in there you make a shitload of noise and then you do one right?"

I offered the note and after a moment's thought he stepped forward and took it, slipping it straight into his pocket and falling back to the group. The moment of danger having past and a bit of distance between us they all went back to eyeballing me insolently. I turned away, smiling to myself and opened the door but paused before stepping through.

"And oh yeah," I said, regaining their attention. "If they do show up, don't try and mug them. They'll not be as polite as me."

I stepped through the door, letting it swing closed behind me and listening to the groan, apparently the signature sound for all doors in the block. Out of sight of the kids, I rubbed some life back into my hollow arm and swallowed through the throat thorns waiting for my heart to slow down.

From behind I could hear the door dulled sounds of the kids reliving the most exciting thing that had

145

happened to them this week. I took a moment to hope that they didn't meet any other players in tonight's apocalyptic shitstorm.

The four doors before me, two to the left, two to the right, were all standard timber with small brass numbers. The landing was clean, tidy and unassuming. It certainly didn't look like a hotbed of vice. A few quick steps brought me to the door of Flat 12 but I paused before knocking, stepping in a little closer and listening hard. There was no light spilling from beneath the door and no sound coming from beyond it. That ruled out a few possibilities but left a long list of other options still in play.

I decided not to knock after all and very carefully gripped the handle, applying some gentle pressure. Sure enough it turned willingly and in a moment more, the door popped inwards with a tiny click. I paused again, listening hard, but as the silence continued I slipped inside and pushed the door carefully closed.

It was almost pitch black inside. Shapes of slightly darker or lighter grey told me something of the hallway but I still found myself reaching out into the darkness as I went. With each step I landed my feet in slow motion, feeling them sink slightly against the carpet beneath.

A pale door loomed out of the darkness on the right but a black mass ahead told me that the hall opened out onto the living room and I decided to head for that. As I approached the open space the blackness began to condense in places, taking on vague textures and hinting at shapes like furniture.

Reaching the threshold I paused. My ears were straining ahead of me so that I cocked my head to listen. Still nothing and yet the prickles in my skin told me I was not alone. I squinted hopelessly into the dark but what lines there were blurred together, shifting and teasing. I glanced back over my shoulder, unsure how to proceed, and noticed a fine line of yellow underlining the front door.

As dark as it was there was a little light and it was coming in from behind me. That meant that while it did me no good in my looking ahead, if there was anyone in the room before me they'd probably be able to make out my silhouette, making me a nice big target for

I hit the floor just in time to see the muzzle flash and hear the shot. It had come from about waist height on the far side of the room. I scrambled round the corner, into the room and out of the slightly backlit hallway, keeping my arse on the floor.

I could hear breathing now, apparently deepened by the act of firing the shot. They'd no doubt heard me hit the floor but now I stayed perfectly still. I knew they'd missed but they couldn't be sure. I was as hidden by the darkness as they were now but I was only safe for as long as I was silent. That meant moving and speaking were out of the question which would make taking things forward a little tricky.

My heart was pounding I realised, the blood throbbing through my ears. My lungs wanted to gasp but I held them tight, allowing only low, controlled breaths. At the same time I could hear panicked huffing from across the room.

While my body recovered from the hot flash panic, my mind cooled sharp and quick. The breaths were feminine but also laboured, a slight rasp tagging on the end of each. There were muffled sounds of motion now too, the abrupt creaking of what could be an old sofa or chair along with the shifting of fabrics. This was almost certainly her, the girl I'd come looking for, but she was clearly in no mood for visitors and seemed to have decided on a zero tolerance approach.

I thought about the time. Clearly I wasn't about to check my phone but I guessed it had been more than four, perhaps even knocking on five hours since the lad had called me. That still left almost the same again until our 9am deadline. If I stayed where I was long enough she'd probably relent. Once the curiosity built to an unbearable level she'd switch on the lights to check the fruits of her trigger finger's labour.

Hell, the sun would start to come up in a bit and that would probably put enough through the curtains to let us see one another. That said, her floor wasn't exactly comfortable and I wasn't sure that waiting for my arse to go numb would be the best use of my time. I needed to move things on a bit.

147

I shuffled a little, purposefully going nowhere just to make her aware I was still here. Sure enough I heard the expected gasp and shuffle. She probably had the gun pointed pretty much right at me now and while she managed to keep almost all of a faint little whimper inside her I heard enough of it to know she was shitting herself.

"Hey," I said, quietly, gently, cringing despite myself and waiting for the shot. "Katie?"

It didn't come.

"One shot's a firework," I continued, keeping my words soft, "or maybe a car backfiring. Any more's armed police kicking your door down."

Still no shot. I could still hear her breathing but she'd levelled out again, getting a grip on herself and probably now realising that if I'd had a piece I'd have fired back. She was in control here.

"Fine by me," came a young woman's voice. There was a hint of a quaver but she held it well. What struck me more was the slight slurring, a mumbled edge to her words. "They can have you, you fucker," she added with a husky rasp.

"You're the one holding the piece love," I said, still keeping it calm.

No reply. She was thinking, trying to decide what to do next.

"Tell you what," I said, each bullet free second that passed building my confidence a little more. "How about you put the light on and we go from there?"

"I'm not scared of you," she said. There was a new edge to her tone and I realised it was true. Sure there some panic in at her at the situation, but the primary current in her voice was anger, pure, old school fury.

"Fair enough," I said, licking my suddenly dry lips. "You won't mind switching the lights on then will you?"

She seemed to think about this for a moment, then came the shuffles and creaks of her standing from the furniture. I could hear her moving across the room, could almost make out her form, but I was distracted again by the sounds coming from her. She wheezed and winced her way, taking what felt like several minutes, before pausing back into silence.

"You stay where you are," she said, sounding knackered but resolute. "You do exactly what I say or I'll shoot the shit out of you. Fuck the police."

"Ok," seemed like the only response I could give.

There was subtle click and then blind. She was moving back across the room but I couldn't see anything past the complaints of my seared eyes as they struggled to catch up and adjust. Gradually the white bled out and in came colours and lines.

The flat was nothing special. Old furniture but in good nick, the place was tidy and particularly clean. There were a few art prints on the wall. Cheap frames but well placed, giving an overall impression of dignified poverty. Skint but classy.

Still blinking heavy just a little, I settled my attention on the girl with gun. She was sitting on a sofa across the room from me, wrapped in a blanket with only her head and one foot on display. The muzzle of the gun peeked out of the folds, still trained on me just right. From the barrel I could see it was a revolver and a hefty one too, not one of the usual little nines you saw knocking about. If she wanted it to, that thing would punch a great big hole right through me.

Despite all of it however, the furnishings, the potential explosive death, I couldn't help but linger on her face. In patches it looked like she might actually be quite pretty but it was hard to tell given that most of it was bloated and purple.

Her left eye was swollen shut completely, an unreal balloon. Here and there dark little lines of vicious little cuts nestled amid the valleys of bruising where sometimes purple had turned to black. She shifted a little under her blanket and the way she moved made my guts twist as I realised the rest of her probably looked just as bad.

"Fucking hell," I whispered, feeling my face twist in horror and sympathy.

"Sit," she said simply and from the corner of her mouth so that I finally understood the weird ragged edge to her voice. The gun jerked a little, directing me to an armchair opposite her. I stood slow and I moved slow, keeping my arms down, hands open and visible, before easing down into the chair.

"Who are you," she said, but then had to pause to take what looked like a painful breath. "And what do you want?" I winced just watching her.

"Look," I said, ignoring her questions. "You need to go to the hospital love. Let me call you an ambulance." I started to reach for my phone but another inch of the gun leapt from under the blanket so that I froze and then melted back to sit perfectly still.

"I said," she began again, though clearly the effort hurt her.

"Ok, ok," I interrupted. "I'm looking for a car," There seemed little point in being anything but honest here.

"Right," she said, drawing another deep breath to summon the effort. "And this looks like a fucking dealership to you does it?!" Her good eye blazed at me.

"I'm looking for a car," I tried again, "that was nicked earlier tonight. Nicked by a couple of lads I think you might have met." I relayed the descriptions I'd received in the pub.

Her eye continued to bore into me, searching for tells and other flickers of bullshit. After a couple of seconds she seemed satisfied and relaxed just a little, sagging slightly under the blanket.

"Oh," she said. "Nicked your car did he? Sounds about right, fucker that he is."

"So you were with them?" I started to ask but then scrapped that and went back. "He?" I asked instead. "Were there not two of them?"

"Yeah but," she began but then had to stop, the pain overwhelming her.

"Look, if you won't let me call you an ambulance at least let me give you something. I'm going to reach in my pocket ok?" I waited for a response.

Her eye shone wide distrustful out of the mess of her face but she managed a sharp little nod. I retrieved the half joint I'd docked before going into the pub earlier as well as a lighter and held the pair out for her to see.

"Yeah?" I asked. Another tiny nod.

I stood and approached her, moving slowly round the coffee table between us, the gun following me all the way. I crouched down in front of her and held the roach end just before her terribly swollen lips. She leaned forward, neither her eye nor the gun ever breaking their stare, and nipped the joint out of my fingers with the good side of her mouth.

I lit it for her then, looking round, scooped up an ashtray from the coffee table and rested it in her lap. I moved back to the armchair while she took a couple of tokes. She stared at me hard again for a few seconds then the gun disappeared into the blanket.

A slender hand appeared from the folds to take the joint from her lips and knock it against the ashtray. She blew smoke out over the table so that it floated between us, tendrils drifting carefree, then appeared to tune back in and carried on.

"Yeah there were two of them but the little one, the blonde one? Didn't have much about him. It was the other one that booked us, me and Suzanne, the tall one. Bradley." She this last word as if it tasted like puke but I seized upon it anyway. Now the tall one had a name.

"And is he the one who..." but I didn't need to finish the sentence. She nodded and smoked and seethed.

"Yeah, this was him, that fucker," she said.

"But why?" I asked. There was something I was missing here. Why would these lads risk pissing off some girl's pimp on their big night?

"They were partying," she explained. "Big hotel suite, booze, gear, us. They were banging on about how they were about to make it big. One big score then they'd leave town and go off somewhere to live the life."

She seemed to have got herself into a relatively comfortable flow that I didn't want to interrupt but I as she spoke I made a list of questions.

"We were all drinking and smoking, mucking about, it was ok, it was a laugh. Then they burnt a load of stuff in the bin, papers and that, bills I think. They seemed really excited about that bit."

She paused for a smoke and a rest while I tried to piece it all together. Burning bills? That was definitely something worth coming back to later.

"Then we got down to it," she continued, pulling

me out of my reflection. "Only the blonde one, he wasn't really up for it, wouldn't even let Suzanne touch him. He said he had a girlfriend, just wanted to hang out. She didn't care, easy money for her.

"Anyway, Bradley and I went into the big bedroom and I started doing my thing. He was rough right from the start but you get that sometimes. If they like it like that they usually finish pretty quickly so as long as they're not over the line you just let them get on with it."

My mind flashed back to earlier on, the same old house with brand new furnishings. For a moment I wondered if those regulars were rough with her and if she just let them get on with it but the thought made something squirm inside me so I slapped it away.

"So he finished up and I went into the en suite to clean up and get dressed only he followed me in and closed the door behind him. He was off his face, still banging on about how he was going to be a big noise and how he must have been the best I'd ever had and how lucky I was to have been with him on tonight of all nights."

She pulled a face, or at least tried to, and finished off the joint. She stubbed it out in the ashtray and then started again only this time her voice was lower, a fine vein of spite running through it.

"I agreed with him, gave him all the usual shite. It's easier if you don't bruise their egos, but he didn't buy it. He said I was laughing at him and started getting all riled up. Started with all this nasty shit about how many guys I must've been with and how I was filthy and all that, winding himself up more and more.

"I could see it coming and I tried to talk him down but he had me trapped in there. The others were still back through in the lounge listening to music and both the doors were closed so they couldn't hear him. He just got angrier and angrier and wouldn't listen, even when I offered to go again, for free since I 'liked' him so much, anything to calm him down you know?"

"And then, this," I said, gesturing toward her.

"Yeah," she said bitterly. "This. He was raging away and then just started hitting me, out of the blue, I wasn't even saying anything by that point. The floor was all tiles and I banged my head when I fell, the rest of it is just a blur. The next thing I remember was Suzanne screaming and the little one arguing with Bradley. He got us downstairs and into a cab and that was the last I saw of them."

I nodded, pondering which of my noted questions to start with but opting for a new one that had just occurred instead.

"So why not go straight to the hospital?" I asked.

"That's what Suzanne wanted, she was all crying and stuff, but I made her bring me back here and told her not to talk to Leon until I did." She looked at me and guessed my next question.

"For this," she said, her hand disappearing beneath the blanket to reappear with the gun a moment later. "Before he knocked me down I managed to cut his face pretty bad and I thought he might come looking for me. He seemed like the type."

"How would he know where you lived?" I asked.

"You found me didn't you?" she answered quickly. I nodded at what was a fair point.

"So you left the door unlocked and sat here waiting in the dark? Why not just tell Leon? He'd have sorted the guy out for you." I said.

"No," she said firmly. "I'll deal with him myself. I want him to creep in here just like you did then I'm going to shoot him in his guts and legs so that I can get the lights on and he can see me standing over him and beg for his life before I put one right in his ugly fucking face." Breathing heavily she sat there and bristled, beaten but not broken.

We sat quietly for a moment, letting the venom fade around us and I found I was impressed despite myself.

"Ok," I said slowly after a while. "So, which hotel?" I asked the first question from my list.

"The George, suite 213," she replied.

"And the stuff they were burning?" was the second.

"Credit card bills and stuff like that I think. They were talking about clearing their debts but..." she

153

paused and I could almost see the new memory rising up before her mind's eye.

"That was weird, I'd forgotten about that," she said. "They were both talking as if they were skint. The blonde one said he was off the Oakfield estate and that he'd had to use the credit cards because he couldn't live off the dole." That all fitted the picture I'd built up of the guys so far.

"Then Bradley," she continued almost to herself, thinking as she went. "He said he was just the same, skint all his life and that the only difference between was that he'd grown up over here instead of on the Oakfield."

I waited for the but.

"But if he was from around here I'd know him, or at least I'd know his name. I remember thinking that was bullshit when he said it but I didn't think owt else of it at the time." She lapsed into thoughtful silence and I joined her.

If the Bradley had lied about that to his friend then that meant they weren't that tight after all. It also meant he had something to hide. I'd been working on the assumption that they were two lads looking to break out of life on the dole who had blundered way out of their depth. Maybe that wasn't right though, at least not as far as Bradley was concerned.

"What about the car?" I asked eventually. "Did they mention that? Or maybe where they were going after the hit?"

She shook her head then winced.

"No, they never spoke about any of that. It was all just about what they were going to do with the money." She slumped a little further under the blanket, obviously weary.

She hadn't given me the lead on the car I'd been hoping for, but the hotel was good enough for a next step, I knew people who worked over there. I stood, cracking my neck and straightening my jacket. She looked like she'd fallen asleep.

"Hey," I said firmly so that her eye flickered open. "I don't think Bradley's coming for you love, though if it's any consolation there are a whole bunch of tooled up, pissed off people looking for him so I reckon he's going

154

to get it one way or another." She managed half a satisfied smile. I rubbed the top of my head and looked at her ruined state.

"So why don't I call you that ambulance now, yeah?" but she was going again, slipping sideways a little to lean against the arm of the sofa, her head lolling back. I moved quickly to the phone mounted on the wall and dialled 999.

In as few words as possible I gave the address and described the state she was in, hung up, gently removed the gun from her hand and slid under the sofa, then walked straight out the front door. I paused just once to look back at her poor wrecked face and wished her luck in finding a new profession. If she didn't she was going to have to drop her prices.

Back out on the landing only a couple of kids remained, including the mouthy one who'd pulled the blade. I stared my question into him and eventually received a quick shake of the head in return. No other strange faces had been hanging about tonight, so far anyway. I said nothing but gave him a nod on the way past which he grudgingly mirrored. I trotted down the stairs still wincing at the image of the battered girl seared into my mind's eye.

As I pushed through the double doors to step back out into the car park I tried to leave the image behind me. The George Hotel was in the centre of the city, just outside the train station and only about a ten minute walk.

I was thankful for this since even though the sky overhead was still deep as pitch, I was becoming increasingly aware of the the time ticking away. The new day would be on me soon enough and by the time it was I had to have that car back or the lad would be toast. Brutally tortured toast.

In the distance I could hear a siren and hoped that it was Katie's ambulance but then shook myself and set off toward town at a solid pace. This Bradley kid sounded like a classic arsehole though the burning bills and the lies about his past did intrigue me.

"What's your game Bradley?" I said to myself as I approached the edge of the city centre.

The city was incredibly still and even relatively quiet as I moved through the shopping streets. At this time on a weekend there'd still be scattered knots of bodies moving to and fro between clubs and late night bars. Tonight however the place was a morgue.

The familiar sight of these streets, littered tight with bustling bodies and stalls, cafe's tables and chairs, not to mention the actual litter, was nowhere to be found now. The streets felt incredibly broad and open, great dark expanses of stone.

As time slipped by and I closed on the hotel, the persistent silence began to make me feel small and exposed, an ant on an elephant's back. There was still time for this to work out. My man at the hotel might very well point me straight at the lads and subsequently the car. Then again he might not.

If this turned out to be a dead end I'd have to start again from scratch, maybe follow the gear angle after all, only I wouldn't have much time left. For a few minutes I walked and thought of nothing, managing to keep the details of letting the lad down, of what would happen to him, at bay.

The feelings that dripped from those details however, they leaked through. Nameless, faceless, senseless, just raw emotions. Something like shame and regret and fear all blended into a thick heady cocktail that, once it was in me, held the door for those memories to all come tumbling through.

I've got nothing.

I've smoked it all, drunk it all, spent it all. I've nothing left. Right now the driller killer headache, the puking, the sweats, they're all off in the distance, spreading slow like the dawn, the unavoidable glare of sobriety.

For now though I'm sat in the armchair in my flat, head spinning full of the last of my gear, the knowledge that there's no more left just biding its time, waiting patiently to be recognised as a full blown disaster.

I haven't left the flat since confronting Tall James, hell I've barely left this chair. I've been thinking about how I was before, all that

apocalyptic rage. That felt like rock bottom, like the lowest I could get, it never occurred to me there could be anything worse.

All that heat is gone now though, the blistering white hot fury, everything's just cold, I'm cold, cold and numb and dead. There's a kind of nausea, a deep rooted self loathing sickness, that never stops but it seems pretty distant at the moment. Everything seems distant right now, as if the whole world is behind glass.

A few hours more though and that glass is going to shatter. Shards of cold, hard reality are going to cut me to ribbons and I don't think I'll be able to take it. There's no way I can make it our and round to my dealer mate's to score so now my hands are moving, searching my pockets of their own accord and now they have my phone.

My thumb finds my new dealer on its own, the keystrokes hardwired into the muscles. The phone is against my ear now, this is happening, I'm going to have to talk to another human being. I shake my head to try and clear it, licking my lips and blinking.

"Hello?" says the familiar voice.

"Alright mate," I respond with someone else's voice, all croaky and far away. "Just wondered if you could pop round."

"Yeah sure," he says. "Be about an hour."

"Thing is..." I catch him before he hangs up. "I'm a bit short mate, thought you might be able to help me out." There's a pause long enough to make me worry. When he speaks again his voice is harder than before.

"When," he says simply.

"What's that?" I hear myself mumble, confused.

"If I sort you out tonight when are you going to settle up?" he doesn't sound impressed, not even a little bit.

"Erm," is the best I can manage.

"Exactly," he says. Another long, horrible silence.

"Alright look," he says eventually. "I've got something needs taking care of. How about you sort that out and we'll call it even?"

He's doing me a favour, I know that. By rights he should have just told me to go fuck myself but leaving the flat feels impossible. That world out there may as well be at the top of a mountain.

"So?" The irritation in his voice is turning to anger. What else am I going to do? The only thing worse than going outside is going to be sobering up. No-one else is going to give me a chance like this.

"Yeah," I say, my mouth dry. "Ok."

"I'll pick you up in ten," he says sharply and is gone.

I look at my phone blankly for a while then my hand puts it back in my pocket. I stare at the wall opposite, my eyes following the cracks and cobwebs though I'm not really seeing any of it.

Suddenly I wonder how much time has passed and my stomach knots. If I just do this one thing, get it out of the way quick, then I can get back in here and shut the door. Just me, the bottle and the smoke, then nothing else will matter again, it'll all fuck off away again.

I realise I'm on my feet, apparently I must have stood up. I move towards the bathroom but my legs feel soft and fuzzy and I stumble a bit along the way. I make it to the sink and run the hot tap but the water is sharply chilled.

The image of the gas meter, silent and perfectly still out in the hallway, flashes before my mind's eye for a second but I dismiss it. Wet's wet, who cares. I splash my face and the bite of the cold happens to someone else, someone far away from me. My phone trills from my jacket's inside pocket, shuddering against my chest before falling silent again almost instantly.

He's here.

I move back through the flat, stumbling still but reaching the front door eventually. My hand is on the handle but my gut wants me to stay. The world beyond this door is too big for me, too heavy and too hard, but without more of what I need that world will get in here. Either way it will have me.

I swallow bile flavoured fear and open the door. I stagger out into the hall and pass the spitefully static gas meter on my way to the front door. The light is fading with the evening but it's still enough to hurt my eyes so I keep them mostly closed as I head out to the street.

His car is there in the usual place, engine running. I straighten my back a little and try to let my shoulders drop, forcing myself into the appearance of calm. I walk up slow then slip into the passenger seat, pulling the door in beside me. I turn to say hello but he's just staring at me, openly appalled.

"Jesus Christ Kaz!" he says. "You look like shit. The fuck is wrong with you?"

Deep in my brain, small sparks stutter, a conversational autopilot kicks in while I hide inside my head, peeking out through bleary eyes and listening to my voice do its thing.

"You know how it is," it says to him. "Been partying a lot lately, just a bit tired."

"Whatever," he says, unconvinced and disgusted as he moves us away from the curb. We pull up the hill towards the park and as he waits at the junction he begins to tell me the tale. Some new guy who's been selling for him hasn't come up with the money he owes. The guy needs a reminder and perhaps even a little encouragement.

"No problem," someone says.

I realise it's me.

We drive the rest of the way in silence and I sink down into the seat a little, starting to feel cosy behind the glass, watching the world slip by. We turn another corner and pull over. He's pointing out a house further down the street.

Fear clings to my guts, squeezing and twisting so that I don't want to leave the car but he's waiting. I remind myself why I'm doing this and push myself out onto the street. My legs are shaky but I'm doing it, I'm walking towards the door.

I knock and wait, panicking that my blows were too heavy. Nothing happens for second after second and so I panic that they were too light instead. My fist is coming up to try again but muffled sounds of motion are bleeding through the door now.

A moment more and it opens, a skinny young lad in hippy scruffs blinking out at me. I realise I have no idea what to say. My mind freezes up, my jaw works empty, sweat runs cool down my back. He just waves me inside and turns away though, thinks I've come to score.

"What're you after?" he says with an easy drawl, dropping onto a battered old sofa.

"Nothing," I say absently, looking around the hazy room. His expression turns from easy to confused to cold. He sits up slow, ready to move.

"You what?" he asks quiet and hard so that I remember why I'm here. The rapidly cooling atmosphere finally cuts through to reach me. I clear my throat and squint at him, focussing and trying to stand tall.

"You need to pay what you owe," I say. I try in vain to sound heavy and serious but he just scoffs, looking me up and down.

"You tell him he'll get it when I give it him," he spits at me. "And sending his fucked up, loser customers round to bug me isn't going make any difference right? You tell him that. Now fuck off." His hand slips down the side of the sofa cushion then he stands and takes a step towards me. I notice that his slipping hand is out of sight now, hiding behind his back.

"I don't think..." I begin, unsure of myself, but he takes another step forward and interrupts me.

"I said," he snarls, the hidden hand appearing now holding short length of metal pipe. "Get the fuck out of my house." I look at the pipe.

160

It looks heavy and hard. I look at his face. It looks mean and hateful.

"But he said..." I try again, struggling to keep up with what's happening. It feels serious and bad but I can't quite connect. He steps up again, almost landing on my toes.

"I'm going to count to three and then I am going to fuck you up," he says, his eyes gleaming with excitement. "One," he says.

I take a step backwards through the palpable tension but I still can't cut through the fog.

"Two," he says, matching my step to stay right in my face. I step back again, I think the front door is right behind me now. I don't know what to do.

"Three," and with this he lunges, swinging the bar over and high to hurtle down towards the left side of my face.

Things feel wrong, slow and unreal. I'm on the floor. My left forearm is hurting, bad. It must have leapt up at the last minute to take the blow which knocked me down here. He's standing over me now. He's saying things but I don't know what they are. My arm really hurts, the pain is real and persistent, sharp and clean.

I don't like it. I don't want it. He's going to do it again.

The bar falls again. Again my left arm takes the hit. The pain screams at me now, white and blinding. My blood is rushing through me, cool to every bit of me, bringing weight, bringing strength. Suddenly my limbs feel solid and real.

I'm here. I'm really here and this is really happening.

"Don't." I think I hear myself say.

He swings again. This time I turn and the bar eats into my back. New pain, new fuel, something is happening to me, I can feel it.

"No," I say but I don't think he hears. He's still shouting his words, eyes on fire.

"No!" I scream, eyes scrunched, neck taught. Suddenly my legs feel like they're full of explosives and I rocket up from the floor, teeth bared, elbows back. I land both palms flat in his stomach and put everything I am and everything I have ever been into the push as my arms extend out before me.

He flies away from me, literally leaving the floor. His pipe and I tumble down but I find myself standing again in a second. The pipe is at my feet so I stoop on down to scoop it up. It feels heavy in my hand. It feels good.

He's on his arse a few feet away, rubbing his head where he banged it. He looks dazed but this is fading into fury as he glares up at me. He's cursing and scrambling back to his feet but as he rushes at me I swing the bar.

It connects with his face and he crashes back down. I stand over him and he raises a hand to ward me away, his other cradling his newly red face. I put my shoe in his ribs so that the defending arm snaps back down then land more blows with the pipe. The swinging feels good, I'm roaring inside.

I'm alive. I'm real. This is real. I swing and I kick and somewhere there's laughter that may well be mine. I tell him to get the money and he scrambles away. I follow him across the room, through a door up some stairs.

He's still talking but the sounds are different now. I think he's apologising, begging even, but I can't hear him. My head is spinning at the action and I feel drunk on the feeling of the sticky dripping pipe in my hand.

We're in a bedroom now and he's rooting through a cupboard, throwing clothes out onto the floor behind him. I watch as he drags out a rucksack and heaves it onto the bed before pulling out a bundle of cash. He's counting cash off the bundle onto the bed, his hands are shaking.

I feel myself sway a little, but manage to hold still and suddenly I'm thinking of my flat. I look at the money and think of my flat and I tell him to stop counting. He looks up at me, his face different now with new colours and shapes.

I hear myself tell him that I'm taking it all, the money the gear, all of it, everything. His face can't seem to decide between fear and anger but eventually fear seems to win. He pushes the cash back into the back and then returns to the cupboard.

After a few struggling seconds he extracts a clear heavy plastic sack, filled fat with dense green bundles. I look at all the green and I think about my flat. I think I'm smiling. I turn my eyes back on him, watching his lips move.

I wonder if this is all there is.

"Get the rest," I say and this time serious weight comes easy.

He's babbling on but I'm just look at him dreamily, my head cocked to one side. I take a step forward and raise the bar over my head with both hands but he squeals from behind his own raised up hands and so I let him scramble out of the room.

I follow the sounds of his desperate journey through the house as more bags appear from dark corners. Another large bag of green, another bag of cash and finally a small sack full of tiny bags packed with white. We pause back in the bedroom, the collected pile of vice on the bed in between us.

"In bin bags," I say, waving the pipe at the pile. He gathers it all up awkwardly in his arms, wincing as he goes at his new found pains. I follow him down the stairs and wait by the front door while he disappears into the kitchen.

The seconds tick by as I listen to the familiar rip roar of big bags being whipped out and then the rustling of them being filled. He reappears and hands me two large, anonymous bin bags. I take them both in one hand, holding them by their twisted scruffs.

I look at him for a second, reflecting on how different we had both been just minutes before, standing right here like this. There's something in his eyes though and it make me wonder if there are still more bags elsewhere.

Then he lunges and I feel a dull blow to my gut. I drop the bags and the pipe and look down, catching his hand. He's holding a knife, a small one from the kitchen only it looks even smaller now that part of the blade is inside me. He struggles against my grip, trying to pull away but I hold his hand vice tight, still staring at the exposed part of blade, nestling between our hands and my stomach.

Slowly I raise my head and look into him. He's standing very close, closer than he wants to be and is leaning away. Confusion and fear twist his features under all the quick drying blood. My free hand comes up to seize his throat. His own free hand grabs at my arm, trying to loosen my grip on his breathing.

His eyes are bulging, he's now riddled with panic, his body fighting for itself while he goggles. I'm moving the knife now, slowly slipping it out, still crushing his hand within mine. It hurts as it moves but somehow it doesn't seem to matter and once its out the pain retreats to ache dull.

I move his hand and his knife up between us now, pushing hard and slow against his desperate resistance. As the blade comes up between our eyes I can see my blood all over its tip. He splutters and chokes as I twist his hand so that the bloody tip now points right at him.

Quivering to overcome his efforts, I do not relent and drive the blade, inch by inch, towards his face. His eyes are locked on it now and he's frozen still, cringing in on himself as the distance closes. I land the tip just under his right eye and marvel as the skin dips in before eventually yielding.

His scream comes slow, through grumble to roar, as best as he can with my grip on his throat anyway. Blood spills out around the blade now as I draw it downwards and it slips sharp through the rubbery skin. I cut him for two good inches towards the edge of his mouth and then release him. He drops to the floor. From above he looks a

164

lot smaller now, curled up at me feet and mewling.

"Fuck you," I whisper and it makes me smile. Everything feels woozy now and I feel giddy to the point of being sick. "Fuck you," I say again a little louder. "Fuck! you," I repeat, this time matching the first word with a kick.

"Fuck you. Fuck you. Fuck you." I'm saying, kicking and stamping and panting. The pipe's in my hands again though I don't recall picking it up, and I'm landing it on him over and over, always in time with the word.

"Fuck you James!" I'm screaming. "Fuck you Tall James. Fuck you! Am I a threat now eh? Am I? Am I?!" There are tears on my face.

Suddenly my arm and my stomach are hurting and I'm covered in freezing sweat. The room seems too small and too dark and I can't breath right, I can't breath. The guy from before, the guy I was talking to, he's on the floor at my feet. There's a lot of blood and he's not moving. I don't understand what I've done, why I'm here or even where this place is.

The guy groans below me and I think I'm relieved. I turn to leave but stumble over something between me and the door. Two large bin bags. I remember the car outside now and the guy sat in it waiting for me. I snatch up the bags and fumble with door before stumbling out into the street. I set off towards the car but then go back to close the door, tangling the bags around myself in the process.

The houses drift past me like sounds but then I see the guy in the car, staring at me, mouth open, from within. I swallow hard and open the back door, throwing the bags in onto the back seat. Then I'm back inside, sat next to him, staring back up the street at the house. It's just sat there as if nothing has happened. The guy next to me is reaching into the back, rifling through the bags I've brought him.

"Fucking hell," he says, slow with genuine shock before continuing as if to himself. "That little bastard. This is my gear but this, this isn't mine, he's been dealing for someone else as well."

I continue to stare, out through the glass. What just happened? What did I do?

"And what's this? Coke! He's been dealing coke on top of the weed, he must be coining it in, so what's..." he drifts off into silence, before twisting back to sit in his seat, a rucksack in his lap. He pulls a bundle of cash out of the bag, then another and peers in afterwards. Finally his face comes up, jaw lagging below, to stare at me.

"Holy shit Kaz," he says quietly. "What did you do?"

I turn to face him but I have nothing. I am empty.

"Well," he continues after a silence that I think he finds awkward. "You've done me a massive favour here man, that bastard's clearly been ripping me off for months. I never knew you had it in you!" His mouth is smiling but his eyes are curious and amazed.

Silence returns and I go back to staring out front while the guy rifles further through the rucksack. Eventually a thought seems to occur to him and he stops still, looking at me again.

"He can't have given this up easy," he says. "What happened in there?"

Something is wet in my lap. I look down.

"I think he cut me," I hear myself say, peeling away my gummy shirt to reveal a dark ugly mark. More blood oozes out as we watch.

"Shit," he says, throwing the rucksack back between us and starting the engine quickly.

"Don't worry mate, I know someone who can stitch that for you. And I'll see you right for this mate, I will see you right for this."

I feel myself being thrown about as the car rattles over patchwork tarmac though I've no idea where we are.

"Was his name James?" I ask, staring blankly at the glove compartment.

"No," he says, sounding confused. "That was

166

Marty."

"Oh," I say.

I don't speak for a while after that.

Moving on, as I headed back into town I wondered when was the last time I'd spoken to Danny at the George Hotel. I'd known him a long time and used to help him out selling a little gear to colleagues and guests until there'd been a ruck in one of the suites.

The daughter of someone big had been snatched and taken there so that the whole place had been turned over by that same someone's lads. That had been enough for us at the time and we'd just never got back into it since. I jingled the mass of change from the pub in my pocket absently, suddenly aware of its weight.

The huddled bulk of the train station rose up over the street to my left as I moved down the street, dark and brooding it showed minimal signs of life at this time of night. Just next door however, the front of the George Hotel was all lit up.

I continued down the street, my eyes searching the grand frontage. There were plenty of people looking for these lads and the hotel was an obvious place to come for information. There were also plenty of people who knew Danny as a hotel man in the know, plenty of people to give him up.

Everything appeared normal from out here, business as usual. I slowed a little, unsure what I was waiting for, there was nothing else to do but get in there, but still I kept on ambling down the street. At one point I became aware of a figure hunched in a doorway ahead of me. Still focussed on the hotel I removed a good chunk of the irritating coinage from my pocket and dropped it into the guy's lap without looking as I passed.

Finally, after several minutes of slow walking watching I decided the time was right and crossed the street, following the great walls of the place round the side to the back where a far less impressive alleyway, complete with filthy skip, lurked behind.

I'd actually taken my phone from my jacket and was in the process of texting Danny when the door opened to reveal the man himself. His face opened in surprise before melting into a hearty smile, an unlit fag dangling from the corner of his mouth. I put my phone away.

"I was just texting you mate," I laughed, returning the smile and following my extended hand towards him.

"I always did have a knack for timing Kaz, you know that," he grinned, taking the cigarette from his mouth and then moving it to his other hand so as to meet mine and shake it.

Danny lit his fag while we stood in the stink and the shadows, talking about the old days with sad smiles and laughter. He looked almost exactly the same as I remembered I realised, as if he hadn't aged a day, though it occurred to me that the same old uniform and poor lighting probably had something to with that.

"So," he said eventually, as our reminiscences reached a natural lull. "What's occurring?"

I caught him up with descriptions of the two lads and a mention of suite 213. He nodded as I spoke, dragging hard on the fag so that it glowed livid in the back alley gloom.

"Yeah I've seen them tonight," he said, frowning involuntarily as he blew another plume toward the slimy brickwork. "Bradley and his little mate. Had a couple of lasses with them."

"You know them?" I asked, surprised.

"I know him from school, never seen his mate before though. What's he to you?" he said.

"They did a job tonight, stole my mate's car to do it. Now he needs it back, urgent like." I hesitated, looking at my old friend before adding, "I'm not the only one looking for them either. They pissed a lot of people off tonight."

Danny's eyes narrowed as he listened before widening them again as the penny dropped.

"Fucking hell," he said slowly, genuinely shocked. "That was them? That was Bradley?"

I just nodded.

"Shit," he said, his eyes slipping focus as he thought about it. "Never thought he'd have had it in him."

"Can we check out the suite?" I asked, snapping him back to the present.

"Aye, no probs," he said. He stubbed out what was left of his cigarette and flicked the butt into the skip. "There'll not be owt left in there now though, cleaners'll have been in."

I followed him back to the door and then through into a cramped, ugly corridor. We moved through more of the same, the spindly, never seen skeleton of the hotel, until we reached a rickety looking service lift. We stepped inside and I felt the thing sway a little under our weight. Danny slid both the cage doors shut in front of us and hit the button for one of the many floors above.

"So is this Bradley an old mate then or what?" I asked as the lift wheezed it's way upwards.

"Not fucking likely," Danny replied and with real venom. "I hate him, always have done. He was the year below me at school. Always was up his own arse. Me and some of the lads used to let him hang around with us because he could always get cash out his mum, plenty."

"They were well off then," I said, thinking back to poor battered Katie and what she'd said about Bradley lying about his background.

"Oh aye, they did alright. Posh semi down a cul-de-sac, second home in the South of France, all of that. And his mum was a right soft touch, give him anything he asked for she would. Once he turned up with all this cash and asked us to buy a load of booze for him, said his parents were going away and he was going to throw this big party.

"Then he gets caught with it all and starts crying, saying that we'd threatened him into getting the cash for us and that we'd been bullying him for months. Almost got me kicked out of school for that. Little shit." The lift shuddered to a halt just as Danny finished speaking, underlining the violence of his tone.

I followed him along another hard floored, poorly lit corridor to a heavy door. Beyond it we were suddenly onto plush carpets, walking past art on the walls, lit rich from expensive fittings. We turned corner after identical corner, passing door after identical door in silence as the thick pile swallowed our footsteps. Soon I'd completely lost track of where we were.

Finally yet another door came into view except this

169

time the numbers 213 gleamed brightly and we stopped outside. Danny produced a key card and slipped it in and out of the lock. A green light, a beep, a click and we were in.

I had to admit, I was impressed. The lounge area alone was bigger than most hotel rooms I'd ever stayed in with its vast L shaped leather sofa and matching arm chairs, elegant glass coffee table and gigantic flat screen TV.

Danny made straight for the sleek little fridge that squatted just beside the floor to ceiling windows. He straightened up holding four golden miniatures, his face a question. I nodded and he tossed two of the tiny bottles across to me.

I dropped into one of the armchairs, sinking immediately deep into exquisite comfort. Danny lolled on the sofa. I twisted the neck of one of the bottle until it cracked, releasing the lid and a familiar smell.

"We alright taking these?" I asked. "Will they not notice?"

"Be right," he said, taking a swig. "I'll just make it look like that dick scammed us and housekeeping missed it."

I nodded my respect and took a drink myself, enjoying the feel of it on my ever complaining throat. He'd been right about the cleaners, the suite looked perfect, brand new and sterile. On the far side of the room sat an impressively heavy looking desk and I eyed the bin sat beneath it. From where I was sat I couldn't see any trace of the scorching the lads' bill bonfire must surely have left. The cleaners must have swapped it for a fresh one.

"So you saw them come in then?" I asked, braking the contemplative silence that had sprung from the opened bottles.

"Yeah, checked them in didn't I," he said.

"Did Bradley not recognise you, from school and that?" I asked.

"Nah," his face twisted with spite. "Twat didn't see past the uniform did he. They never do, his sort."

I settled even further down into the leather, making short work of the short bottle.

"He's been telling people he grew up on the Woodvales, never had a pot to piss in, all that," I said. Danny frowned, thinking about it.

"No, that's bollocks. He's never wanted for owt in his life. He was always good at talking people into doing what he wanted though. It'll be some kind of scam," he said. He drained his first bottle and twisted the cap off the second, clearly still thinking.

"I was surprised to see him though," he added finally.

"Why's that?" I asked, making a start on my own second bottle.

"Far as I knew he'd gone off to uni somewhere down South. Oxford or Cambridge, one of those," he said.

It seemed like the more I found out about this kid the less I knew. Clearly a total shit, he'd had every chance in life, including place at a top university. If it was money, or even other people's money, that he was into then surely sticking out the degree would have been ideal.

Why come back here to risk his life ripping off a few hundred thousand when in a few years he could have been fleecing people out of millions as a lawyer or a banker? There had to be something else, something with a stronger pull.

"Like I said, I'm really just after the car he took. I can't see him waking mummy and daddy with a hot car, a sack of cash and a scruffy partner in tow. Where else might he go?" I felt like I was piling it onto Danny a bit but I'd been banking on him being able to point me to it and so far I wasn't even a little bit further on.

"Couldn't tell you mate, sorry," Danny shrugged. "I haven't seen him for years, not since school even. Like I say, I didn't even know he was back in town until he walked in here tonight."

We lapsed back into a comfortable silence again as I went back over everything I'd heard so far, desperately looking for something, anything that might point me towards the next lead. I couldn't see it though. I couldn't see it at all.

"You know anything else about him? Interests,

habits, anything that might help?" I was starting to get desperate and tired, I could hear it in my voice.

"I don't know," he said, obviously trying to help but genuinely having nothing to give me. I could feel myself teetering on the edge of panic and despair. It had already been a long night and much as I knew I'd have no choice if it came to it, I couldn't bear the thought of starting again.

"Except," he began, suddenly rousing me back from the brink. "There was this lass, Victoria I think. Man, he was mental about her, absolutely nuts."

I sat forward, listening intently.

"I don't know where he met her, I mean she didn't go to our school or anything, her dad was a duke or an earl or something. No she went to some boarding school somewhere but she was about one summer and I remember hearing that he just lost his mind over her," he said, his eyes losing focus again as if he were watching the memories inside.

My heart quickened a little as a single spark of hope flared back into life. I seized upon this latest angle, picking at its edges and letting questions flow by, waiting to grab the right ones.

"Was she from round here?" I asked.

"God no," Danny smiled. "No, they were from down South somewhere. Her dad was up here on business and she'd come along. I reckon she wanted to see how the other half lived you know? Mingle with the plebs."

"And what was her father's business?" This was going to be it, I was sure of it.

"Oh he built that apartment block down the bottom end of town. You know the one, that massive glass thing, you can see it from the motorway when you're coming into town. They only sold about half the apartments in the end, so I heard, right disaster. Kept the penthouse for himself I think, somewhere for the family to stay when they're up this way."

"Nice one," I said, nodding to myself more than anything.

"What, you reckon he's there?" Danny asked, incredulous. "Bit of a stretch isn't it?"

172

But it was all falling together in my head, randomly tumbling pieces suddenly twisting into alignment.

"Mate," I said, finishing the second bottle with a flourish. "I will give you odds that he and this Victoria lass are together but that she makes him keep it a secret so that daddy doesn't find out."

"You mean she's been stringing him along for all these years?" asked Danny, clearly not sold on the idea but wanting to be out of sheer spite.

"Yep," I said, my imagination laying it all out in front of me. "He'll have done something stupid at uni too, something to try and impress her that got him kicked out. He's trying to convince her to go public about the two of them or even, yeah that's it, to run away with him."

"Even if you're right, she's never going to walk away from the family fortune though is she?" Danny said.

"True," I agreed. "But he doesn't see it, he's convinced that she's as into him as he is into her and that he just needs a big enough gesture. That's what tonight was all about. He knew exactly who they were hitting, I bet he's ripped off the other lad too."

"Now that bit, I can believe," Danny nodded.

"And I tell you what else," I said standing to pace, excited now. "I'll double up that she's in that penthouse tonight and that's where he headed with the money."

"And the car?" Danny reminded me.

"Maybe, maybe," I said, rubbing my hands together distractedly. "He might have dumped it on the way but those bags will be heavy. Either way, if I find him I can find out where the car is." Danny was grinning up at me.

"You always did have a vivid imagination mate. Seems like a bit of a long shot to me but I guess you could be right. So what's next?" he asked.

"Next?" I said. "Next I need a piss."

I moved across the room towards the door of the larger bedroom, each step sinking into the deep pile of the carpet. Stepping inside I found the room dominated by the largest bed I'd ever seen, low and broad enough that you could have shared it between four and still had plenty of room to spread out. I stared at the fine linen expanse for a moment, picturing the scene as I crossed to the en suite bathroom.

The bathroom was all tiles and as I felt the floor firm up under my feet I remembered Katie's account of what had happened in here just a few hours earlier. I ran my eyes around the place as I pissed, looking for any tiny red dots to tell of the horrific violence I knew had taken place here.

The place was spotless, one continuous sheen of clean and I was just reflecting how good the housekeeping lot were I heard the door to the room open back in the lounge. Finishing up I didn't flush but stood perfectly still, listening hard.

I could hear voices but not words, a low, menacing sound that crept through the walls. I hoped it was just some of Danny's colleagues, even if it was his boss bollocking him for slacking off, that'd be better than the alternative.

Then came a heavy sound, something big, like a body, hitting the floor hard. Even through the inch thick carpet the impact made its way through into the bathroom. That was enough to convince me that while Danny was not alone in the lounge, he was the only hotel employee in there.

I went back through the bedroom to stop at the door to the lounge. The voices were clearer now, definitely menacing, not the kind to respond well to surprises. I was pretty confident that Danny would be claiming to be alone in the room, not wanting to give me up but that particular lie wouldn't last long if they decided to search the bedrooms, which they almost certainly would.

Besides, even if they didn't and I just hid in the bathroom until they left, they'd take Danny with them to ask him harder question in a less luxurious setting and this wasn't his fault or his problem. I had to try and get him out of this though sacrificing myself to save him wasn't an option either, at least not until after I'd found that fucking car and beaten the ever ticking clock.

My mind raced as I considered various entrances

but failed to find any that satisfied. More sounds of violence slipped under the door and I could hear Danny cursing breathlessly. The feeling of desperate frustration, of drawing a panicked blank at a vital moment, was sickeningly familiar to me.

As ever at such moments, a cold spark of irritation flared, wiping away all the fragments of possible plans and leaving the same old stubborn core concept: Fuck it, just wing it and see what happens. I rested my hand on the door handle, took a breath then strolled on through bearing a mildly drunken smile.

"Damn man! How big are the beds in this..." I feigned shock at the presence of three men in suits, looking back and forth between them and Danny. He was in a tightly curled ball on the floor, slowly staining the carpet red at their feet. For a moment we all froze, the three of them staring at me with a mixture of surprise and vehement aggression.

Their suits were matching, grey and expensive. The one standing over Danny and nearest to me had longish floppy hair, designer stubble and a vivid green tie. Even if he hadn't been in the process of beating a friend of mine I would have taken an instant dislike to his high maintenance trendy good looks.

Beside him stood the next suit, broader but slightly shorter and sporting an ugly yellow tie. This guy appeared disappointed not to be involved in the action and gave the impression that were it not for the neck collar and arm in a sling he'd be elbowing his way to the front of the queue to hand out beatings for his boss.

Speaking of which, the third suit was a much older guy and though I'd never seen his face before I quickly put two and two together and recognised him with dread. Tall and lithe he looked like he kept the years at bay by drinking the blood of newborn children, it was either that or the perpetual stick up his arse. He wore a purple and tie and was clearly in charge, having not the slightest intention of getting hands dirty despite looking quite insanely pissed off.

Green Tie was the first to react, lunging towards me, throwing a low punch to crack my ribs. I managed to turn to avoid most of the force of the blow but realised too late that it wasn't a punch. The stun gun caught me just briefly but enough for me to feel a stiffening cage of pain run right through every last bit of me.

Suddenly my face was in the carpet and I was a wheezing coil just like Danny. I heard murmurings above then felt a steely hand gripping my upper arm and the carpet was falling away from me. I was on my feet again, swaying beside Green Tie while Yellow Tie loomed over Danny. I caught Danny's eye but was relieved to see him looked angry rather than scared.

"Now," said Purple Tie, moving a little further into the room but apparently unwilling to stray too far from the door. "One of you is going to inform me of the whereabouts of the two young men who interrupted our business dealings earlier this evening. That person is going to live. Do I make myself clear?"

"Look, mate," I wheezed, trying to blink away the pain and fuzz. "This has got nowt to do with the lad. I'm looking for the same lads you are and I heard they'd stayed here. He's and old friend and he were just doing me a favour by showing me the room alright? He doesn't know anything about any of this."

Purple Tie didn't seem impressed by this and even went to take a step forward, perhaps to dirty his hands after all. He stopped himself however, his sharp eyes flitting past me only to bounce back from the bedroom door. For a moment I couldn't understand why he was holding back. What there was in the world that could hold him of all people back?

Then I worked it out and suddenly everything felt very cold.

"Oh shit," I whispered despite myself. "Was it here? Is this where they..." but looking at him I daren't finish the sentence. "I mean, your son..." but again I stopped short. Purple Tie's nostrils were flaring now, his eyes ablaze.

I looked away, no longer willing to hold his gaze but catching Danny's eye instead. From my reaction he'd also worked out who this guy was and now he didn't look angry any more, just scared, really scared.

And with good reason.

This was a man who could make you disappear on a whim. Everyone knew his name but no-one ever said it out loud. If you lived in this city then he owned you, whether you knew it or not. Tall James, even Jimmy the Jack, they were just small time bastards compared to this guy. He certainly owned us, for the moment anyway, and here I was, standing in either the very same hotel room in which his only son had been brutally murdered or at least one very much like it.

"Take them," said Purple Tie eventually, having composed himself. "We'll do this elsewhere."

Yellow Tie reached down with his good arm and grabbed Danny by the hair, dragging him up to his feet and then holding him fast by his arm. He marched him to the door of the room, opened it and disappeared out into the corridor. Green Tie and I followed, his fingers digging deep into my arm as if he were aiming to hold the bone itself, while Purple Tie followed on behind.

Out in the corridor Danny and I walked side by side with Yellow Tie and Green Tie following close behind, occasionally shoving us along. Once we were in their car our chances of survival would drop significantly. If we were going to get away from these guys we had to make our move before we left the hotel. Green Tie and his toy were the biggest immediate threat which meant we'd have to get the drop on them and put him down first, hard and quick.

I looked over at Danny and waited until he noticed. I widened my eyes a little and nodded almost imperceptibly, asking him if he was up for this, if he was ready. His expression was grim, fully aware of what awaited him if we didn't get away. I saw him swallow hard and return the nearly invisible nod. I took a deep breath and then began to mutter.

"You fucking idiot," I hissed. "This is supposed to be your patch, how'd you let these guys just walk up on us like this?"

"Fuck you man!" Danny replied. "You brought this shit in here with you. I didn't ask you to come here tonight."

"Quiet!" barked Yellow Tie, giving Danny a little jab in the back for good measure. We turned a corner and continued down another identical stretch of corridor, the only sound our collective footsteps.

"You've always been like this," I muttered again. "You're a fucking flake, do you know that? A fucking flake. I've never been able to trust you with anything. All you do is slow me down."

"Get bent, no mark," Danny threw back. "You walk around this city like you own it, but you're a fucking nobody. You live in a shitty little bedsit. You smoke all your money. You're a loser."

"You little shit!" I said, my voice raising with temper.

"Wanker!" Danny matched my volume.

We took a few more seething steps and then Danny was on me, throwing punches wildly and missing so that we crashed into the wall. I grappled with him, snarling and got in what looked like a headbutt while managing to not quite connect. I managed to shove away from the wall but he got his shoulder into my chest so that I fell backwards, taking him with me.

For a few seconds the suits just let us go at it, watching unimpressed, until Purple Tie gave the nod. Green Tie and Yellow Tie stepped in, reaching down to pull us apart but just as their hands landed Danny and I both erupted from the floor in unison, tumbled them backwards.

I landed three sharp, heavy punches just beside Green Tie's left eye so that he slumped back dazed. I glanced over and saw Danny rip off Yellow Tie's collar before clocking him. Yellow Tie howled in pain, his good arm coming up to his neck, his eyes tight with the pain.

Danny stood up and back from Yellow Tie, glaring and panting but then froze. Green Tie was still murmuring under me, trying to flop about, but I followed Danny's gaze to find Purple Tie stood stock still, his long arm extended in front of him, a quite enormous pistol pointed right at Danny.

Just as it seemed too late I sprang up from Green Tie's chest, batting Purple Tie's arm up towards the ceiling and knocking him backwards and down. I scrambled back to my feet and sprinted after Danny who had already bolted. I prayed that the gun was an empty threat, that even he wouldn't start shooting in the middle of busy city centre hotel, but I couldn't quite believe it for sure.

I followed Danny round corner after corner, through a heavy door and then along more of the dingy little staff rat runs. We got to the service lift that had carried us up earlier I slammed the cage doors closed behind us while Danny stabbed frantically at the buttons. As the lift shuddered around us we both lent against the walls. Danny was sheet white and trembling. I suspected I didn't look much better myself.

"Jesus!" he panted. "That was.."

"I know," I said, panting too. "I know."

The lift trundled us down and down, taking so long it was as if twenty extra floors had been added to the hotel since we'd come up.

"What the hell am I going to do now?" said Danny quietly, more thinking out loud than asking.

"We do one," I said definitely. "We walk straight out the back door and keep going. You're probably best off leaving town for a bit."

"What? I'm at work man, this is my job, this is how I pay my rent. I can't just leg it!" The colour was returning to his face but seemingly in exchange for his reason.

"Mate, what do you think's going to happen if they get hold of you again now? Your job's the least of your worries, believe me." I tried to catch his eye and emphasise my point but he was staring at the floor, lost in thought.

His expression flickered slightly as he tried to deny what was happening and call it rationalisation, rewriting the last ten minutes in his head and trying to convince himself that things weren't as bad as they appeared.

"Seriously man," I tried again. "There's no other choice, we have to get out of here right now."

"I know," he was nodding slowly, his eyes slowly focussing back within the lift before finally rising up to meet me. "You're right, you're right. It's got to be out the front though, I've got to at least go past reception and give them some bullshit about feeling ill or something."

"Danny mate..." I began but he cut me off. Enough time had passed now for his fear to condense into anger.

"Fuck you man!" he snapped. "This is a good gig and I'm not throwing it away. It's alright for you, when was the last time you tried to make a straight living? You any idea what it's like looking for a job these days? There's nowt out there, certainly nowt that pays as good as this. No man, I'm going out the front."

Seeing as I was the one who'd brought this down on him I was finding it hard to argue but he still wasn't seeing the bigger picture, namely the picture of the two of us in a lock up somewhere being brutally tortured to death for information we didn't have. I drew breath to try again but he heard me coming and got in first.

"It's fine," he said, calmer, more confident. "Really, it's fine. I'll go out the front, you go out the back. It makes sense for us to split up anyway and besides, they're not going to grip me in front of witnesses are they?" He tried a smile but couldn't quite make it.

"I don't think they give a shit about..." I began but was interrupted by the lift shuddering to a halt. Danny whipped the cage doors open and set off while I trotted behind, my mind racing to find some way to change his mind. A heavy door containing a small thin window came up on the right and he paused.

"Alright man, this is me," he said. I squinted past him, through the little window and saw the plush lobby of the hotel beyond. "Just follow this corridor round to the right and you'll end up back at the back door."

And then he was gone without giving me chance to say another word. I glanced back and forth along the corridor, but everything was still and silent. Everything in me was pushing to leave but I made myself stay, peering through the door as Danny approached the reception desk.

I could see his hand at his stomach as he span his tale to the mean looking woman behind the desk. She didn't look impressed but eventually she shrugged and said something that apparently released him. He turned and began moving slowly, as if in great discomfort, but

180

steadily toward the grand front doors.

There was still no sign of anyone else on my side of the door or his and for a second I wondered if I had been overreacting after all. Just as the thought crossed my mind however, the backs of three familiar figures came into view.

Without breaking stride, Green Tie and Yellow Tie caught up with him, one on either side, catching his elbows and marching him on towards the doors. Purple Tie strolled along behind, glancing over at the sour faced woman behind reception who paled a little before turning away to busy herself with some paperwork. A second more and all four were gone, out the front doors, into the night and off to who knew where.

I stayed at the window for a few seconds more, cursing inside and point blank refusing to accept that it was too late. I stared at the door through which they had disappeared. There had to be a way, a way I could save him, get him away from them before the hard questions began.

Eventually however I compromised with myself, accepting that even if I could devise some genius stroke to save Danny and still retrieve the car, step one had to be getting out of the hotel. I followed the corridor round and just as Danny had described, the back door came into view.

I slipped out into the alley and moved quickly through the shadows. Now that I'd made the break it made sense to put as much distance between me and the hotel as possible. My feet carried me on, sticking to back alleys whenever possible and turning as many corners as they could find, the thought of the suited bastards cruising the area looking for me spurring me on.

After a while I realised I was heading towards the bottom end of town. I spat, trying to rid myself of the bitter taste my thoughts were leaving. There was no point going after Danny, I'd finally come to accept. I had no idea where they'd taken him and no time to find out.

I realised too that even if I did know where they were, it was highly unlikely that I'd be able to bust in there, take on the three of them, plus whoever else they may have with them by that point, and then get out again, with Danny, and get clear and still find the car.

Up ahead the shadows fell back as the latest alleyway gave out onto the brightly lit street. I moved out into the jaundice light and began to think properly again, cool, sharp, no longer blurred by anger or guilt.

At the end of the day they were business men, or at least old Purple Tie was anyway. If I tried to take him head on he'd swat me like a bug, but if I had something he wanted, something he really wanted, then we could do a deal. And of course in order for me to find that sodding car I'd also need to find exactly what the old man wanted.

I pulled my eyes up from the pavement for a second, looking up at the vaulted blackness overhead. A little way off a great structure erupted from the skyline to pierce the sky. Occasional yellow rectangles betrayed signs of life within while a tiny red light sat like a cherry at the pinnacle.

My feet quickened their pace a little, the fuel of purpose igniting. All I had to do was find Bradley, that had been the plan all along anyway. I'd find the bastard, get him to tell me where he'd dumped the car then, on my way to picking it up, get in touch with Purple Tie and his goons and trade Bradley's location for Danny's life. Nothing to it, piece of piss.

What could possibly go wrong?

Look mate," my dealer says. "What could possibly go wrong?"

I'm sat in the back of his car on some quiet street I don't know. We're parked up in the shade of a wildly overgrown hedge that's spilling out from its home to eat up the pavement. There's another man in the passenger seat, twisted around and looking right at me, mirroring my dealer. We've just been introduced but I'm so battered that his name slipped right through me and now I'm too embarrassed to ask.

"Well yeah," I mumble. My tongue feels too thick. "I guess. I just don't want bring any heat down on him, you know? He's a mate."

My dealer and the other guy look at one another. The other guy looks impatient and annoyed so that the car feels cold and dangerous.

"Really?" the guy says as if I'm not even here. "This guy? He's like a fucking smackhead!"

"Hey, I," I try to sound offended but stumble over the words. "I don't do that," I manage.

Both of them ignore me.

"Come on man," my dealer urges his friend. "You saw what he did to Marty. He's solid, seriously."

We drive for a while and the new guy turns back to stare at me. His eyes cut right through me so even within the heavy haze I can feel him scrutinising the very core of me. He doesn't look impressed. My dealer parks up again and then turns his attention back on me too. The pleading in his voice is starting to harden up a little as he repeats himself yet again.

"You just get a car from the old bastard like you have done a million times before. Then we do the job and you take it back. Easy," he says.

I twist around and look out through the back windscreen. Billy's garage is just over the road behind us. He's in there right now, probably whistling tunelessly or cursing some engine part. The lines of the garage are so familiar, they line up through the fog to frame memories of my teenage years, long summers, happy days, no hassle. Before all this, before, everything. I turn back to face them.

"I don't know guys," I say, my mouth dry.

I'm trying to think, trying to get a handle on what's happening but I'm too tired, too confused. I can't remember when we started, my dealer turned up at the flat with this guy, a big bundle of gear and a few bottles. Was that yesterday? The day before? I feel sick and I don't like the fact that I can't remember this guy's name.

"For fuck's sake," hisses the nameless man, turning away to fume forwards.

"Alright, alright," whines my dealer to the guy. "Chill your boots."

Now he turns back to me, a new and unpleasant look on his face.

"Listen, you remember the money and the gear we gave you after Marty?" he says.

I do remember. I remember waking up in my flat feeling like I'd had the worst nightmare of my life and finding a large bundle of green and a solid stack of cash on the floor next to my bed. It was payment he'd told me later, payment for my "sorting the Marty situation," and compensation for the blade I'd taken. I hadn't wanted to remember any of that but I'd needed the cash and I'd wanted the gear so I'd taken it.

"Hey!" my dealer snaps, reaching back to shake me out of my daydream. "Come on man, focus! You remember the money and the gear right? Well there's going to be a lot more of that this time and you'll get a share. It'll be way more than last time."

I keep squirming. I know this isn't right but how else am I going to buy gear and booze or make my rent? I can barely get myself out of bed now, I feel so shitty all the time. If I don't have anything to smoke or drink it'll all catch up with me and I'll go crazy. I need this.

"But Billy..." I try one last time.

"Fuck him!" snaps the other guy, still not looking at me. The dealer shows his palms to the guy and tries talking soft to me again.

"Ok," he begins again with a sigh. "He's a mate, I get that. But if you're that worried, why don't you just split your share of the cash with him? There'll be plenty, then everyone wins yeah?"

Somewhere in me I know that's wrong too, Billy would rather do without the hassle than have the cash. It's a good excuse though, a more comfortable road towards being able to agree with these guys and getting out of this car.

"Alright," I say, and though the word immediately relieves the tension in the car, it tastes sour on my tongue and turns my stomach.

The car doors open and we're out on the street. The sun hurts my eyes and my head feels light, too light as if it might float off my shoulders. I steady myself against the car and feel cold sweat break out under my clothes as I fight back the urge to puke.

The guys are talking about me.

I can't make out the words but the sounds are dark and I just know it's about me. I look over and they're both staring at me, their eyes cold and hard. I nod, maybe too much, and wave them away, swaying a little.

I stumble out into the road, concentrating hard on getting my feet in line. The far kerb is a tricky one and it nearly catches me out, but I best it and cross the pavement to enter the garage. Billy emerges from his office and smiles when he sees me.

"Y'alright lad? Not seen you for a..."

As he gets closer though his smile crumbles and falls. His eyes run up me and down me and sharpen with concern.

"Jesus Kaz," he says quietly. "What's happened to you?"

"Alright Billy!" I say, my voice booming back at me from the back of the garage so that I frown and carefully lower my voice. "I'm alright mate, are, are you alright? Are you? I'm alright."

"You don't look it." Billy says. "You look like shite. What have you been doing to yourself?"

I laugh but it comes out wrong. The tension strung all through me vibrates feverishly, building to a frenzy so that my laughter sounds manic and empty.

"No no," I say, getting something like a grip on myself. "It's all good, it's all good. Just need..." but I think better of it and take a couple more steps into the garage towards him, dropping my voice to a thick, wet whisper.

"Just need a car Billy, a car. Just for a little bit," I wink at him and nod.

Billy wipes his hands thoughtfully.

"When?" he asks eventually.

"Now man, now," I say, still nodding but Billy shakes his head.

"You think I'm letting you drive in that state? You must be even further gone than you look lad," he says firmly.

"No no no," I say. "No no no, it's fine, it's right. I'm not driving, not me, not. No, it's them."

My arms flails out wildly to point behind me over the street.

"They's going to do it, the driving, all the driving, them, they are."

Billy leans to one side a little, peering out past me at the two figures stood by the car.

"They've got a car," he says simply.

"Yeah," I say, finding words increasingly difficult to come by and feeling my frustration building as a result. "Yeah they have, they have got car, but we need another one, a different one, just for a bit, just for a little tiny bit."

"And they're your friends are they?" he asks. There's disappointment in his eyes and it hurts me, making me angry.

"They are my best mates Billy, my best mates in the world," I say, frowning my irritation. "You know me, you know who, what I am. I have never. When have I ever, ever? Have I? Let you down eh? Eh? Never, that's when. Just want a car, just a little car for a little while, little bit that's all. Come on, I've never, have I? Ever, eh?"

"Fine," he says at last. "But if you take one today that's it. Last time. Never again."

"Aww," I say, trying to land my hand on his shoulder but missing and so fumbling it into my pocket instead. "Don't be that way Billy. Billy, Billy, Billy. Come on man, you're, you're my Billy."

But he's not listening. He disappears back into his office for a second before returning with a set of keys.

"The Honda. Back by the end of the day. Then you don't come around here again. Not like this. Right?" He offers me the keys but doesn't let go when I try to take them.

"Right?!" he asks again, harder.

"Alright!" I say, straining the sound like a petulant child.

"Fucking hell…" I mumble to myself in mock indignation as he releases the keys and I turn away, stumbling back out to the street. The guys are watching me so I wave the keys at them and point to small, red Honda parked a little way up the street.

187

My dealer opens his boot and the other guy takes out a large black hold all. Then my dealer shuts the boot and the two of them walk quickly over the road to meet me at the car. I'm stood at the driver's door out of habit but my dealer takes the keys out of my hand and pushes past me to climb in.

The other guy gets into the passenger seat. Neither of them say anything. I glance over at the garage where Billy is still watching, arms folded, his face hard and cold. My stomach turns and somewhere inside me something screams but I'm too tired to look at it so I just climb in the back.

We drive in silence for what may be twenty minutes. I recognise the part of town we're in but not the tight, terraced streets we're weaving through. Eventually we pull up outside a particularly battered looking house and now the guy in the passenger seat is rifling through the big black bag in his lap.

He throws something soft and black at me over his shoulder. I fumble with for a moment, utterly confused by its woollen texture. Then I find two small holes and a bigger one and I realise it's a balaclava. Now he's thrusting something else at me, a gun, a small nine, pushing it into my hand.

I look at the piece, it's lines and textures. It feels very heavy, heavier than it should. The guy has pulled another balaclava over the top of his head, wearing it like hat and now he's inspecting another, much larger handgun. A feeling takes me, as if I'm falling, tumbling down and down, grasping desperately at thin air. Again I fight back the urge to puke and look to my dealer, the fear no doubt shining in my eyes.

What am I dong?

"Come on Kaz," my dealer says. "It's just like with Marty again. Just get in there, get the gear and the cash and get out."

My mouth opens but no sounds emerge. I look down again, my jaw still slack, the balaclava in my right hand, the gun in my left.

188

"The fuck are you waiting for?" snarls the other guy.

I want to be back at the flat. Doors locked, curtains drawn, just smoking on my own with everything else far away but I realise I'm trapped here. There's no other way out of this car or back to the flat. This has to happen.

Slowly, hands trembling a little, I drag the balaclava onto my head. It itches against my sweating brow. I push the gun into my pocket and can actually feel the colour draining cool from my face.

Now he's getting out of the car, my partner whose name I've forgotten, and I'm following him. Through the garden gate, up the garden path. He's knocking on the front door. I'm looking all around us, up and down the street. So many blank windows, grey net curtains hiding what? Empty rooms? Prying eyes?

I realise that he's pulled his balaclava down over his face now so I do the same, a feeling of clammy claustrophobia slipping over me with it. The door opens and now it's happening. He's barging in, knocking a young guy to the floor. I'm in behind him, pulling the rickety door shut behind us. He's shouting at the guy on the floor now, kicking him and I realise there are other people in the room.

A girl in her early twenties is sat on a ruined arm chair, hers eyes wide now, her body frozen. Closer, on a sofa that doesn't match the chair but is equally wrecked, a second young guy is half standing half sitting. He looks angry, like he wants to help his friend. I draw my gun and point it at him, slowly shaking my head.

I glance down at the floor. The first young guy is a mess already, blood and teeth everywhere. He burbles to the girl to fetch the stuff but she doesn't move until my partner points his gun at her. Then she starts nodding and slowly stands, eyes fixed on the two of us.

She moves to a door in the corner of the

189

room and then disappears. My partner lowers his gun to point back at the first young guy's broken face. We listen to her footsteps rise above us. I keep my gun trained on the second young guy, waving the muzzle slightly so that he sits back down slowly.

I lick my lips as the seconds tick by. Dull sounds of motion come from above and then sharpen as the footsteps descend. The girl reappears, struggling to drag several large bags through the narrow doorway with her.

My partner trains his gun on her, motioning her toward him then reaching out with his free hand to take the bags. I watch her as she shakes violently, weeping, handing him the bags in slow motion.

Suddenly the young lad of the sofa is lunging over the back of it towards the bags and I realise I wasn't watching him. He leaps right across in front of me, slapping at my partners gun out of his hand. I hear it fall to the floor with a heavy sound but then a loud, ugly crack snaps through the room and the gun in my hand twitches violently.

The young lad's head flicks sideways, away from me and he falls, slumping down next to his friend, utterly limp. I don't understand what's happening but the girl is now covered in a fine spray of blood and she's screaming.

My partner turns to look at me but I can't move. I'm just staring at the screaming girl, my own mouth hanging open, a silent reflection of hers. I see him stoop down and then come back up, his arm outstretched ending in his gun.

He shoots once and the screaming stops instantly. The girl sits down hard and stares at me with an ugly dark circle in the middle of her forehead. He lowers the gun and I hear it fire again but before I can see the lad on the floor he's pushing bags into my arms and me towards the door.

Somehow I open it and now I'm moving down the path towards the gate, my partner shoving me in the small of my back all the way. The car engine is running and I fall onto the back seat. I hear the doors close and then we're moving. I claw the balaclava off my head but still find it hard to breathe. By the time I sit up again the guys in front are whooping and celebrating.

We drive for a while but their constant excited chatter sounds a long way away. I realise the gun is still in my hand. I look at it for a while, remembering how it twitched as I watch the lad's head flicking sideways over and over.

Finally I realise we've stopped and now my dealer is taking the gun and the balaclava out of my hands. The other guy is gathering up the bags. An object hits me, then another but both tumble into my lap and then onto the floor.

"He'll be fine man," my dealer is saying as the other guy gets out of the car. I watch as my hands reach down to collect the large bundles of notes and of green, pulling them close to me. I know they're important, that I need to hold on to them, but right now I can't see any value in anything.

"Hey," my dealer is talking to me now. "Hey, come on. It's all done now, all finished. You did well. He says one of them tried to jump him and you plugged them. That's good man, you did good."

I can hear the words but I don't understand them. What did I do? It doesn't feel good. The other guy is getting back in the car now. He slams the door shut beside him and it makes me jump. Suddenly I feel like I need to be outside, I need to feel open air on my face and not be around anyone but the car's moving again.

They're talking again but all I know is that something is very wrong and that I need to be somewhere else. I need to be back in the flat, safe and alone. I think one of them says something to me, maybe asks me a question, but I don't even look at them. There's nothing in me that can respond.

We stop again and now they're getting out. The door beside me opens and so now I'm getting out too. The air on my face feels ok but it doesn't change the tight lace of dread that has wrapped itself around me, cutting down into my flesh, into my soul.

I stumbling along between them now and we're walking into Billy's garage. My dealer puts the car keys in my hand and gives me a little nudge. I take a few more steps forward and Billy appears. I offer him the keys and he takes them in silence. I can't look him in the eye. The others are mumbling to one another behind me. Billy is turns to take the keys back into the office but now my dealer is at my side, talking.

"Hey," he says. Billy stops and turn back, eyeing him unkindly. "So look, we were thinking this is a pretty sweet set up. Maybe we could get another car off you, say next week? Same as today, less than a hour. What do you say?"

Billy takes a couple of steps back towards us. The guys are stood either side of me now and Billy looks them both up and down slowly.

"I told him," he says eventually, nodding at me. "This was his last. No more cars. Not from me."

"Aw come on old man," my dealer says, extracting a thick wad of bank notes from his pocket. "It's in your interest. Here look, this is for today and you can expect the same again next time."

Billy looks at the money, then at me and then finally at my dealer.

"I don't want your money," he says in a low voice I've never heard before. "So piss off, all of you."

"Ok, ok," my dealer says, thumbing a few more notes off the roll then extending them with the rest. "How about now, eh? Yeah?"

"Get out of my garage," Billy says. "Now."

The other guy steps forward now, his voice low and thick.

192

"Listen you old bastard," he growls. "He's trying to be nice about this yeah? If we want a car we'll fucking take it right, so you'd best take that money and count yourself lucky."

Billy looks up at the guy with not a hint of a flinch, then slowly draws a heavy looking wrench from somewhere round the back of his belt.

"Get out," he says. " 'fore I knock you out."

The guy smiles, turns away from Billy to look at my dealer and the pair of them laugh. Billy's eyes him hard, wrench ready. Still laughing the guy turns back suddenly, swinging a heavy punch. Billy leans back a little and dodges the blow before bringing the wrench up and cracking the guy across the face.

The guy staggers backwards, cursing, but then launches himself onto Billy and the pair tumble back onto the oily concrete. I start forward only to find my dealer's hand in my chest. He grips me and turns me, marching me back out onto the street.

The last thing I can see, straining over my shoulder, is the familiar sight of the bottoms of Billy's boots only this time he's under the guy instead of a car. The guy's raining blows down into Billy and cursing breathlessly but then we're up the street and I can't see anymore.

What have I done?

I couldn't see anything.

For the first few seconds in the lobby of the city's biggest and most exclusive apartment block, I couldn't see a thing. Then, gradually, my eyes adjusted to the light and I found myself surrounded by gleaming marble and steel.

A huge curved counter rose up out of the floor and presumably usually had someone behind it. When I walked in however the lobby was deserted. The echoes of my footsteps rebounded around the countless surfaces, all perfectly flat and perfectly, making the place feel even bigger.

A quick glance up made me aware of several security cameras yet the imposing glass doors to the street, ten feet tall with a frosted logo, were open and there wasn't a soul in sight. I moved cautiously towards the desk expecting to hear footsteps at any moment, expecting at least one heavy man in an ill fitting security uniform to appear, hastily tucking in his shirt and asking me just what the hell I thought I was doing.

And yet, nothing.

I reached the counter, a single, chest high piece of marble than ran down flush into the floor. Casting a glance around the sterile room one more time I ran my tongue over my teeth, thought about what I'd heard of Bradley and wondered.

There wasn't much I could do about the cameras but I didn't have to make it too easy for them. Resting my forearms rather than my hands on the top of the counter, I lifted myself off the ground a few inches and peered over the counter to the floor on the other side. I dropped back to my feet and turning away, nodding to myself.

Just as I'd expected. An overweight guy in a stupid uniform, dead on the floor behind the counter. He was laid on his back in a perfectly symmetrical pool of red. His face bore a now permanently surprised expression, punctuated by two ugly, oozing holes, one in the forehead, one in the cheek.

The fact that the holes were still oozing told me Bradley hadn't been here long. Why he'd felt the need to off the guy at the counter however was a mystery to me. Perhaps his rich bitch girlfriend had decided she didn't want to see him after all. Maybe she'd told the guy not to let Bradley up and he'd struggled with taking no for an answer. There was only one way to find out.

I crossed the lobby, chased each step of the way by echoes, and jabbed at the call button for the lift with my elbow. The doors parted smoothly to reveal a lift that had thicker carpet than my flat and was almost as big. I stepped inside, trying to focus on the job at hand and inspected the exquisitely crafted buttons.

Following the numbers all the way up I found that the penthouse didn't have a button but rather a keyhole. Luckily for me however, the back half of a small silver key was jutting out. I stared at it, this small, simple and yet inexplicably convenient object then pulled my hand back into the sleeve of my jacket and pinched the key using my cuff.

A sharp turn to the right and the lift doors slid closed. There was the slightest hint of a noise but otherwise nothing seemed to be happening. Then I noticed the numbers ticking up on the digital display above the door and realised that the lift was indeed moving, just incredibly smoothly.

As the numbers continued to rise with the lift, I recalled the rickety cage lift Danny and I had used back at the George. I hoped he was ok, I hoped something had delayed the onset of the heavy asking. Above all however, I hoped that whatever was waiting for me at the top of this tower meant that I could get him out of wherever he was quickly. And then there was the car of course. Another young lad in line to fall victim to horrific violence unless I could save him. No pressure.

Finally the ticking up digits were replaced by a steady letter P and after a smooth pause the doors eased open lazily and I stepped out. The lift opened right into the penthouse apartment, a vast lounge area rolling away from me. The room was littered throughout with low, stylish furniture and flanked on the right by floor to ceiling windows, mostly black but for the million tiny lights of life the twinkled down below and off to the horizon.

Looking over to the East I noticed faint stains of pale were seeping gradually over the horizon now, tainting the edges of rich deep darkness above. The lightening sky seemed to trigger something inside me, a new energy unfolding, straightening my back and widening my eyes.

The lift doors oozed closed behind me, bringing me back to the moment. I took a long deep breath and tried to soak up the invigorating feeling of the oncoming dawn, drinking it in in preparation for what trials remained. Then it was right back to it, enough dicking about, there was job to be done.

I drove my eyes around the room again, eating up the details this time. It really was quite spectacular, putting even the luxury suite back at the George to shame, a whole other league. Hell, this place made that place look like my place.

Bradley was in here somewhere though, I was sure of it and he might not be the only one. There was an almost imperceptible thickness to the air, a subtle tension that whispered to me that I was not alone. I was prepared to put money on him having ditched his partner but only in exchange for his girlfriend which meant I was still expecting to be outnumbered.

The lounge area appeared untouched. No drained glasses on the low glass tables, ashtrays all empty and clean. The furniture was all neatly aligned, nothing pushed back or twisted on a whim of personal comfort. I moved silently over the lush carpets, my eyes constantly flicking back and forth, checking on the various tall heavy doors that lead deeper into the apartment. Nothing moved. Everything was silent still.

Looking more closely now I realised that the penthouse had been empty for some time. Despite its exquisite decor, a perfectly thin layer of dust was draped across everything. I smiled to myself as I followed that lines of the furniture, inspecting everything carefully. They might live in the sky and drink champagne for breakfast but it was satisfying to see that even the super rich got their tables dusty like the rest of us.

The harder I looked the less I found however. It was as if the apartment really had remained untouched for months. I reminded myself of the dead man in the lobby and of the key in the lift, clear evidence that someone was here, or at least had been here.

For a moment my eyes locked once more on the Eastern view. Even the great rising slopes of the city were flattened out from up here, everything, high or low, was now simply below. It took me a moment to adjust to the novel perspective but I quickly began to pick out landmarks.

I found a particular cluster of distant streetlights, yellow pin pricks, and was fairly sure the building that sat on top of my bedsit was in amongst them somewhere. I followed another, slightly more defined line of lights as it rolled up the hill and was confident that Jimmy's secret bookies was up there.   Finally I eyed a huddle of shapes much closer to home, the three blocks of the Woodvale estate rising up against the sky, stood hip deep in the rest of the city. I tried to work out which block was which and wondered which of the almost invisibly small dark squares I could make out opened onto that room in which I'd sat with poor, battered Katie.

A sound snapped me back to the right side of the glass and then round to face the room. My skin seemed to tighten around me as my senses sharpened. I couldn't tell what I'd heard but there had definitely been something, some subtle sound of motion from somewhere nearby.

I began to consider the choice of doors, still desperately trying to squeeze information from the memory of the sound. It didn't come however so that I just had to go with my gut. The door in the far corner seemed to have something about it the others lacked, though I couldn't for the life of me have said what it was.

Crossing the room towards my choice I passed one last low glass table, glancing at it as I went. I'd actually walked past it before I stopped, something tugging at my eye, begging for another look. Turning back I moved to stand over the table, then crouched to look at it from more shallow an angle.

The dust had been disturbed. Two great oblongs had sat on this table recently. The lines were not perfectly straight and I got the impression of fabric crumpling in the corners. I stood again, my eyes locked on the empty space while I tried to rebuild the objects from their half shadow remnants.

Bags.

The thought clicked into place so firmly that they could never have been anything else. Two huge canvas holdalls, no doubt black and filled to their brims with cash. Bradley had walked in here with the bags, the fruits of his insane labours and dumped them on this table.

I looked back to the lift and traced his path across the carpet to where I was stood. For a moment I half closed my eyes, leaving my mind's eye to do the seeing.

197

If the bags were too heavy and he was dumping them for a rest why carry them to the table? He'd have dumped them right outside the lift. If he were coming in to settle in he'd have stashed the bags somewhere less obvious, somewhere where they wouldn't be in immediate line of sight coming out of the lift.

No, he'd dumped them onto this table in a rush, on his way across the room, on his way towards the very same door I'd been approaching just moments before. There was something, no, of course, someone more important than the cash beyond that door who he couldn't wait to see. He'd rushed through there and been reunited with his beloved before coming back in here to retrieve his spoils later.

It worked, it felt right. I was still certain that they hadn't left yet which meant he, she and the money were all just beyond that door. She was an unknown quantity, rarely a good thing, while he was armed and a dickhead, always a bad thing.

If I made my presence known he, or they, would almost certainly assume the worst, prepare themselves and plug me the moment I opened the door. That left bursting in on them and trying to use the moment of surprise to convince them I wasn't a threat. Tricky but the Eastern sky was lightening a little more every moment and no alternatives sprang to mind.

I continued my approach, reaching the door and then leaning against it. I strained my ears, desperately trying to reach through the door and find any hints of sound beyond. Nothing. The place was silent still. Maybe they were asleep, maybe they'd celebrated and fallen asleep. Pretty reckless considering the mess downstairs but then caution didn't exactly seem to be Bradley's style.

My hand found the handle and I gripped the cool, still listening hard. A second more waiting then there was nothing else for it, I took a good deep breath and stepped through the door. My eyes were cringed half closed, expecting the worst, but the silence rolled on, and then on so that I relaxed again. i frowned at the scene before me.

The bedroom was enormous, almost as big as the

lounge and yet the bed still dominated it. I wasn't exactly sure how big a king sized bed looked but this was god sized at least. The entire left wall of the room was a closet, dozens and dozens of dresses all hanging neatly in rows, endless pairs of shoes lined up beneath.

Interrupting the rainbow flow however, there were dark ugly gaps in the ranks where great armfuls of the designer attire had been torn from their hangers and dumped on the bed. A great, uneven heap of the stuff sat in the middle of the silken plain. Here and there a heel or strap poked out of the fabrics showing that not even shoes had been spared unruly eviction from their perfectly ordered home.

Something wasn't right. No matter how spoilt she may be, I was certain that Bradley's billionaire squeeze wouldn't treat her own wardrobe like this, if only due to the significant physical effort involved. This wasn't hurried packing, this was violence against fashion, an expression of rage.

Stepping closer to the bed I noticed the smell. Perfume, probably expensive, not that I could tell the difference, I just assumed it would be in keeping with everything else in the place. Another step and the smell was overpowering, way too much of a very good thing.

My hand moved to my face of its own accord, covering my nose and mouth but offering little defence against the dry, clawing tang. Sure enough, on closer inspection I could see the remnants of what had been a spectacularly ornate engraved glass flask. It had been smashed open and it's contents poured over the the heap of clothes.

I moved all the way round to the side of the bed until my attention was drawn from the stink soaked pile to the floor. Nestling amid the plush of the carpet was a cheap disposable lighter. For a moment I felt an affinity for it, a familiar object from my world thrown into this alien place where the very best was the least expected and the money just went on forever.

Clearly the lighter was Bradley's, but why go to all the trouble of piling up the clothes, soaking them with perfume and then not light them? And more to the point, why burn all her clothes in the first place? The second question was too big, I wasn't there yet so back to the first question. Perhaps he'd been interrupted, perhaps it had been a threat and she'd talked him out of it.

I scooped the lighter up while I thought about it, trying to picture the scene. I couldn't get it though, I couldn't see past him coming into the bedroom after dumping the bags. My thumb stroked the lighter's wheel absently, turning it slow so that the flint grated cold. Finally irritation won out however and I thumbed the lighter hard, annoyed at my lack of progress.

It didn't light.

I looked down at it in my hand. The transparent red plastic showed nothing but vacuum inside. I gave it shake and looked closer, holding it up to the light. Two thin chambers of nothing. I struck the wheel a couple more times but the flint sparked lonely, a brief flash each time never catching.

So maybe he wasn't interrupted, maybe he wasn't talked out of it, maybe he just didn't have the tools for the job. It made sense, it fitted, it just didn't really help. It didn't tell me where Bradley was, what he was doing or most important of all, why.

I turned my attention away from the bed now, looking at the rest of the room while my fingers flicked the lighter away from me. It fell into the carpet to land silent and still, heavy pile absorbing all motion and sound.

The same floor to ceiling windows from the lounge continued through the bedroom and again my eyes were drawn out and down. Before I was able to sink back into distant mapping however something caught my eye. The carpet rolled away from me to meet the base of the vast windows but just at that join was a line, a wavy line of purple.

I padded towards the window warily, the continued silence unnerving me more with each empty minute that passed. At first I couldn't understand what I was looking at. Somehow emerging from between the frames of two of the mighty panes of glass just an inch above the floor, the delicate little strand curled around on itself, laying out livid purple curves to taint the perfect cream of the carpet beneath.

Crouching down I slowly grasped the strand between finger and thumb, finding it to be silk. I tugged on it a little, straightening out the curves and pulling it taught form the window frames. Peering through the very bottom of the window I could make out something larger but equally purple lurking in the shadows beyond.

I followed the line between the windows frames up and up, standing to follow my gaze, until about half way up I noticed a strange bulge in the frame. I ran my fingertips over it, flicking my glance out through the glass and back in again, feeling understanding spill over the brink just like the sun now creeping over the distant horizon.

These weren't windows.

They were doors.

I gripped the bulge, the super stylised handle, and applied a little sideways pressure. Sure enough the enormous pane slid effortlessly to the side. As it went it revealed the rest of the purple silk camisole that had been pinched in the closing as well as a low terrace outside.

The distant hum of the city washed over me, filling the former silence with familiar low level static. The wind thrashed about a little, twisting this way then that, warping the city sound with bulges and falls. I leaned forward, offering just my head to the fresh air and glanced left and right.

There he was.

Off to my right stood a figure, tall, thin, dark haired and mean looking, leaning against the low wall that enclosed the terrace. He was knee deep in a smaller version of the pile on the bed and every few seconds would snatch up another handful of varied fabrics and hurl them over the edge. He watched them float away and down and down then reached for another handful. Just beyond him, huddling in the shadows at his knees, sat two huge black holdalls.

I stood back inside, licked my lips and just remained for a moment, my fingers cool on the smooth metal. He almost certainly still had a gun and was clearly in the middle of some kind of raging, lovelorn tantrum, not the best set up when taking someone by surprise.

But then what else was there to do?

Nodding to myself, I took a breath and stepped out onto the terrace.

"Alright mate," I said, firm enough to be heard over the wind but no more.

Bradley reacted as if he'd been stung, leaping back from the wall and twisting to face me, eyes wide. I saw his hand go into his jacket and braced myself to dive back into the bedroom but his feet were tangled in the heap of clothing and as he tried to step back he found the holdalls, tripping backwards and falling heavily.

Dim light seeped through the windows from the lounge, bathing him in a low glow. I saw the gun come up with his feet as he landed heavily on his back. He began to scrabble around, desperately trying to get himself right so as to take a shot but fumbling in his tangles.

"Woah, woah, woah," I said, keeping the mild amusement I felt out of my voice. "Chill your boots lad, you've nowt to fear from me."

He finally managed to drag himself to his feet, raising the gun to chest height with both hands while trying to kick away a particularly affectionate strappy cocktail dress that clung to his leg like a hysterical drunk. I eyed the little black spot on the tip of the gun then moved to Bradley himself.

He was flushed, his eyes were red and his face was wet. A dark, heavy gash ran down his left cheek, crusted but still glistening and making him appear even paler. Elbows at my side I raised my hands and showed him my palms.

"You're alright mate," I cooed. "You're alright. I'm not here for the money and I don't work for any of the people you've pissed off tonight. I just want a chat. That's all."

I heard him sniff as he eyed me manic. He blinked frantically, regaining his composure as his face calmed towards a more normal colour. After a few seconds more I saw his shoulders relax and he seemed to stand a little taller. His expression hardened.

"Who are you?" he asked icily, holding the gun steady now.

"Name's Kaz," I said calmly, lowering my hands but holding his gaze.

"Kaz who?" he asked.

"Just Kaz," I shrugged.

"What do you want?" he asked, adjusting his feet to stand a little more solid.

"Like I said, I just want a chat," I replied.

"Yeah?" he said, taking a determined step forward and clicking back the hammer. "Well maybe I don't want to chat with you, fucker. Maybe I just feel like shooting someone in the face. Eh?"

I nodded thoughtfully, glancing at the clothes around his feet.

"I can dig that," I said, still calm. "Nothing like a woman to screw with your head. I can see you had your fun though..."

"Shut up!" he screamed, taking another step forward. "Shut the fuck up! You don't know. You don't know what this is. What she's..." but his eyes were wet again, rage choking off the the rest.

"You robbed those guys for her," I said. He said nothing but stayed where he was and didn't fire so I continued.

"You knew exactly who you were hitting, Dick tipped you off. You got yourself a partner who knew the scene, hit the meet, ditched him, then brought the money here, to show her. Only..."

I noted that the tip of the gun had dipped a little and the look on his face told me I'd been bang on with everything up that point but things got a little fuzzy after that. I took a punt.

"Only she wasn't impressed. Said she'd changed her mind. You had a ruck. She left. So now, all this?" I gestured to the clothes at his feet but knew I didn't have it. There was something else in his eyes.

If she'd walked out she wouldn't have left the key in the lift, plus she'd had almost certainly seen the dead security guard and called it in. That meant she was still here but if he was tearing up her wardrobe where was she? Unless...

Fuck.

The attention the pigs gave a dead body at home

was directly proportional to the value of the home in question. If this crazy bastard had offed the daughter of some titled billionaire in his own penthouse apartment it'd be national news and the pigs would be all over this whole thing like flies on shit. For all I knew they were already on their way.

"Bradley, mate. Did you kill her?" I asked.

"No I didn't fucking kill her!" he snapped, the gun coming back up. I took a step back, raising my palms once more.

"She wasn't here," he said then, in a much smaller voice.

He looked distracted now, pushing past it for a moment to check my face one last time, then giving in to it, lowering the gun and turning to lean back against the wall. Slowly he slid down to sit amongst the clothes, the gun still in his hand but now resting across his knees.

"You were right about the rest of it though," he said.

I lowered my hands again and moved carefully to mirror his position, sitting down slow, finding the sharp cool of the wall for my back.

"We were going to go away," he said, more to himself than to me. "It's all her dad's money you see. She gets whatever she wants but it all has to go through him, it's always been like that. I thought if I could get hold of some money, some real money, we could leave, be together and it wouldn't matter what her parents thought."

I made understanding noises and waited for more. He seemed to be struggling with something, he fidgeted with the gun, as if not wanting to carry on but knowing that he would.

"But it was all just bullshit," he said eventually, his voice wavering just a fraction. "All the stuff about her parents not approving, her dad controlling her money, it was all just an excuse. She never really cared about me, she never..." but whatever the last word was it was a step too far and he lapsed into a bitter, seething silence.

Minutes ticked by as I watched him say nothing, the distant sounds of the city rolling all about us. Eventually I decided to give him a nudge.

"So then when you got here..." I said, leaving a gap for him to fill. He seemed to shake himself from one pain to another, grimacing as he continued.

"When I got here? When I got here that fucker downstairs wouldn't let me in, said she'd told him not to. I rang her but she didn't answer so I left her a message saying, you know, what the fuck's going on. Then..." again he choked, his eyes bulging this time.

"Then," he managed, his voice thick. "Then she sends me a text, a fucking text! Telling me she's not here, she's in Monaco..." His jaw fell slack and he closed his eyes, racked with pain and shame, "...with her fiancé."

And so fell the final piece of the puzzle. She'd played him. She'd let him think they were star crossed lovers and then watched amused as he'd found himself ever greater hoops to jump through for her. For his part he'd loved it, thrown himself into it, lurching from one wild romantic gesture to another at the expense of any and everything else.

I looked at him, heartbreak, shame and fury tearing him apart as they competed for dominance and for a moment I felt genuinely sorry for him. Then I thought about the lad and his car and Katie's battered body and his idiot partner and suddenly that sympathy was nowhere to be found.

Here he was, trying to hurt her, this distant mysterious woman, by lashing out at her stuff. She wouldn't give a shit of course, she'd just buy it all again and he knew it, but he had no other way of touching her. So he'd tried to burn her clothes and then when he hadn't even been able to manage that he'd started chucking them off the terrace instead, just waiting for the police to come and find the dead guy downstairs.

Well if he wanted to wallow and just wait around to get gripped then that was fine by me. Given the people he'd crossed tonight he wouldn't last long in prison anyway and then that would be that. In the meantime however there was the small matter of the lad's car.

"Yeah," I sighed, trying to sound like I gave a shit. "Been there mate. LIke I say, there's nothing like a woman to mess you up."

I nodded. He nodded. We sat quiet and still.

"Thing is mate," I began again, all calm and friendly like. "I really need your help."

He glanced over at me, suspicious.

"I'm not giving the money back," he said, sullen and stubborn.

"No," I laughed. "It's nothing like that mate. I just need the car."

His suspicion gave way to confusion and I could see he had no idea what I meant.

"The car you nicked from outside the pub," I tried again. "I've got to get it back man so I just need to know where you ditched it, that's all."

"That's all?" he echoed, still confused.

I nodded.

"But it was a piece of shit," he said, sharpening up now, his part tantrum part breakdown fading away. "Who cares?"

"It belongs to a friend of mine," I said, feeling my dislike for the lad building even further by the second. "He needs it back."

"Fuck him," said Bradley firmly, getting to his feet again through savage, irritated movements. "He'll just have to buy another one, or nick one. What's the big deal."

"Got to be that car," I said simply, standing too.

"Why?" he said, eyes gleaming now. "What's so special about it?"

"Nothing special," I said, carefree as you like. "He just wants his car back. No hassle. If you just tell me where you left it, I'll go get it. Simple as that."

"Nah man," he said, kicking his way out of the clothes and moving to stand by the bags. "You've come all this way for that piece of shit car? I stuck a gun in your face!"

"Yeah," I shrugged, "but I get that a lot."

"No," he said licking his lips and now I could see it, the only thing in him stronger than his unrequited love. His greed. It was so obvious once I'd seen it, it was probably at least half the reason he'd fallen for the rich bitch in the first place.

"No, there's something about that car isn't there? It's worth something, but why?"

I said nothing, holding his gaze, aware that my expression had cooled. His features crumpled with the effort of thought until his eyes flashed and he began to grin.

"It's not the car is it," he said. "There's something in the car. Yeah? Am I right?"

"Just tell me where it is," I said. He laughed.

"Fuck you man! I'm the one with the gun. I'm the one who knows where the car is. What's to stop me shooting you dead right here then going and getting the car and keeping whatever's in it for myself?" He raised the gun once more so that we were right back where we'd started.

"Look," I said, ignoring both question and gun. "It's of no value to to you."

"So there is something in the car," he said, triumphant. "It's in the boot isn't it? We never opened it, just chucked everything on the back seat. What is it?"

"Look, you can't sell it," I continued as if he hadn't spoken. "You can't use it. It's worthless to you, just needs to be back before 9 o'clock. That's all."

"Otherwise your mate's for it," he said, still smirking.

I said nothing.

"Ok then," he said after a moment's thought. "How much is your mate worth to you?"

I opened my mouth to ask the question but he was ahead of me.

"How much," he said slowly, as if explaining himself to a small child. "Is your mate's life worth to you? What will you give me to tell you where the car is?"

I hated this kid so much and as hard as I tried to keep my face blank I knew he could see it in my eyes and loved it. My mind raced against what little time there was left. I needed to strike some kind of deal with the little shit, something, anything that would convince him to give up the car's location. Once I had it back I'd work the rest out from there, but giving him up to Danny's captors still seemed like the best way, even more so now I'd actually met him.

"What do you want?" I grated at him, glancing down at the bags at his feet.

"What have you got?" he grinned.

I thought about it, actually thought about it honestly for a second.

"Nowt," I said eventually and felt the truth of it. "Not a fucking thing."

"Well then I guess you and your mate are shit out luck then aren't you?" he laughed, tightening his grip on the gun and closing one eye to aim. I knew in that moment that I was fucked.

But the bullet didn't come.

He opened his eye and looked down, as if listening until suddenly his head snapped sideways, staring into the lounge through the window, eyes widening, mouth opening. From where I was stood I couldn't see into the lounge but I guessed we had company.

Sure enough, seconds later, two frankly enormous guys, both in black leather coats, were piling through the bedroom and heading straight for me. The first one had an arm in a sling and a hideous little scar that cut right through one of his eyes. His good eye locked on me, first in surprise then apparently in satisfied recognition that settled into a genuinely terrifying smile.

"Remember me?" he rumbled in a thick Southern accent, stepping out onto the terrace.

I pushed the panic to the back of my mind. If I was going to survive this I had to leave all that sweating and shaking to the hind brain, get the frontal lobes focussing on the facts. I had never seen this guy before in my life, I was sure of that. There was no way I'd forget that face.

Just for a second I wondered why Bradley hadn't just opened fire on both of us. I glanced his way and saw him crouched with his bags, fumbling frantically. Meanwhile the other newcomer, basically an undamaged but slightly stretched version of the first guy, stepped past us and made straight for Bradley.

"Who's the dick now?" was the one eyed nightmare's nonsensical question. Before I could even begin to think of a response however, he'd hit me full in the face, knocking me flat on my back.

The world went quiet for a second or two as everything blurred together to form a heavy grey sludge. Then, gradually, little pieces of real started to slip back through, joining up with one another to paint a picture of the world, sucking me back in.

Bradley was talking, fast.

"It's just clothes," he was saying. I managed to sit and focus. Both the visitors were stood over Bradley now, I could see him through their legs, crouched between the hold alls and clutching his newly bloodied face. At the mention of clothes I suddenly realised that there weren't any strewn about the terrace anymore. He'd obviously stuffed them all into the two bags, hoping to hide the money.

"They're my girlfriend's. I'm just here to get some of her stuff then I'm supposed to meet her so we can leave," he said. I cringed.

"Do me a favour!" barked the taller one, who I now noticed was also holding Bradley's gun. "They're our fucking bags you cheeky little cunt! Did you think we wouldn't recognise them?!" He gave Bradley a flat foot stomp to the middle of his chest so as to underline his point.

Bradley fell back before curling into a small wheezing ball.

"You. Are. Fucked." said the tall one, crouching down to lean over Bradley now.

"We're going take you and your gay uncle over there and your," he paused here to share a smile with his one eyed friend, "girlfriend's clothes, to see our boss. You remember him don't you? He's the guy you thought it would be a good idea to do over."

Bradley just whimpered while the guy straightened up. The pair murmured between themselves for a moment before turning to look at me. Cold sweat ran down my back and I fought the urge to shudder.

"Alright guys," I said with a grin. "You know, it's a funny thing..."

"You sure that's him?" the taller one said to the other, both completely ignoring my attempt at an ice breaker.

"Oh that's him alright," said the one with the sling.

"Stitched us right up didn't he."

Clearly someone had been shooting their mouth off and had dropped me right in it with these two. I had no idea what they'd been told I'd done to them but whatever it was they clearly had a serious axe to grind though hopefully, and I hoped really hard, not literally.

"We don't really need him though," the taller one was saying. "Maybe I'll just do him here," and for the second time in five minutes I found myself staring down the barrel of Bradley's gun.

"Nah," said the one with the sling. "I'll do him myself, make sure he knows he's dead." He began lumbering towards me. His good hand emerged from his jacket with a solid looking carpet knife while his good eye blazed with vicious anticipation.

"Look," I began, "guys. Whoever you think I am, whatever you think I did, well, I'm not, I didn't. Wasn't me yeah?" But he kept on coming.

In the background I could hear the taller one asking Bradley questions and putting his boot back in in between. "Where's your mate? Eh? Where's the other one? Eh?"

And just like that I saw it.

"He ditched him," I called out, past the bulk of my impending, bloody demise. "He ripped him off, took the money for himself and his mrs."

"You what?" barked the tall one, turning away from Bradley to catch up with his friend, Bradley's gun still hanging from his slab of meat fist. I looked up at the pair of them, Tweedle Gun and Tweedle Going-To-Kill-Me. Both were literally bristling with rage, having clearly had a long and frustrating night but if I was right all I needed to do was hold their attention for a few seconds more.

"Guys," I said, moving to stand but seeing their response leaning back on my elbow instead. "We're in the same boat here, you and me. I've spent the whole night tracking this little shit down as well. Now, if I got in your way earlier tonight then you know, I apologise, no disrespect intended, I was just doing my job same as you."

"His mate," growled the one with the carpet knife.

"Right," I said quickly, not allowing myself to glance past them but switching instead from the pair of eyes ready to kill me in an instant to the single eye that wanted to do it slow.

"His mate," I continued. "Well like I said, he ditched him. Lad probably didn't even know who he was hitting, young Bradley here just used him, local knowledge and all that, then as soon as they were done, he jumps the lad and takes all the money for himself."

It was total guesswork but it fitted what I knew about Bradley and if I was wrong then we were both fucked. It had to be true, it had to be. Bradley hadn't just taken his friend's share of the money and run, he'd battered his so called friend, left him for dead and then taken his money.

And his gun.

"So where is..." the one with the knife began only to be cut short by the sound of loud, metallic crack. The tall guy's face seemed to smudge as I looked at him, his right cheekbone breaking outwards so that his eye and nose suddenly raced apart, all amid a shower of blood.

He fell forwards, perfectly straight like a fresh felled tree and I just managed to scramble out of the way before he hit the concrete. A dark puddle immediately began to spread out from under his head. The guy with the sling swung round, raising his carpet knife helplessly and growling.

Through the space that had been occupied by the dead guy, I could now see Bradley again. He was back on his feet, if a little unsteady, and sure enough was holding a second gun. I could see it all, the sudden beating just like with Katie, then him snatching up his mate's piece and throwing it in the bag with the cash.

For a few seconds everything was silent. Our one eyed friend clearly wasn't the type to beg or even to flinch at the sight of a gun. He just stood there, knife up, waiting for Bradley to make a move. It came soon enough, a single shot that span the guy round and sent him tumbling down towards me. I scrambled backwards this time, again just managing to avoid the human timber, before slowly getting to my feet and dusting off my jacket.

"Well then," I said. Bradley still had the gun up but his eyes were fixed on the bodies at my feet.   "How did you know?" His voice seemed to come from a long way away.

"What's that?" I asked, eyeing the swaying gun warily.

"How did you know I had another gun in the bag?" he asked.

"Oh," I said. "Just a guess."

"Good guess," he said blankly.

"Yeah," I agreed.

"So," I tried after a few more seconds of silence had slipped by. "Seeing as how I just saved your arse, how about you tell me where you left the car and we both get the hell out of here."

Nothing.

"Those shots are going to bring a whole host of trouble our way," I tried again. "Not much time, so..."

Still nothing.

"Bradley!" I barked at him. He jumped a little, before his eyes finally seemed to come back into focus and he looked at me.

"What?" he said.

"The car lad! Fucking hell!" I snapped. Somewhere in the distance the sound of sirens rode the breeze. They weren't necessarily for us but if they weren't others soon would be.

"Right," he said, brightening with each word. "Right, yeah, the car!" He was still pointing the gun at me.

"So how about it?" I asked, licking my lips.

"Nothing's changed," said Bradley, the smile returning to his sheet white face, bringing a little colour with it.

"You what?!" I said, genuinely shocked. "I just saved your life you little shit!"

"More fool you," he said with a grin and pulled the trigger.

I was on my back. There'd been a blow, like a punch in the throat and now I was on my back. I couldn't breathe properly, it was all wet and I felt like I was choking. I was choking. I couldn't swallow, my mouth kept filling with a thick, hot coppery liquid, spilling over my lips as I coughed.

Somewhere above me Bradley was moving. I had the impression of him stepping over me, carrying the bags but then there was no-one. I was alone on the concrete, the two great dead lumps laid by my feet, the wind flowing over me like I was nothing.

I couldn't move, it was as if my legs were already dead. One of the piles at my feet groaned. I tried to lift my head but found all the muscles in my neck had been removed. I settled for looking down and could just about make out some motion. It was the one with the carpet knife, maybe Bradley had just winged him.

My right arm was still there, I could feel it and so tried lifting it. It flopped about a bit but the guy was too far away and still lost in his own problems. I could feel the texture of my coat under my hand and with a little effort I managed to get my fingers into my pocket and onto my phone. They dragged it out and then somehow I convinced my elbow to bend, drawing my hand up into the air before it flopped down again, phone and all, against my shoulder.

That little shit!

My right hand managed to make it up to my throat, my fingertips moving as carefully as they could. Yeah there was a hole there, running free with more red stuff. He's killed me, I realised, the truth cold and clear through the ever heavier drowsiness, he's fucking killed me. I stared blankly at the phone in my hand.

He could still get out.

The thought staggered through the fog, fuzzed out but there. If I could just warn him he could still make it, still run. I watched as my thumb moved uncertain across the keypad, dabbing red all over as it went. Eventually I could hear ringing and let my hand drop against the side of my face.

"Hello?!" came the familiar voice, all confusion and terror.

My mouth opened but there came no sound. It was as if my voice had leaked out onto the floor along with all the blood now spreading out around me.

"Hello?!" the voice continued but all of a sudden

the phone and my arm seemed way too heavy and both fell away from my face to the side, landing in the sticky spreading puddle. I looked up and saw that the sky overhead was now much lighter than it had seemed just minutes before and yet everything seemed to be getting darker around me.

I lay there, feeling nothing but cold now and reflecting in the pool around me that I hadn't been a very good friend to him after all. I thought about Danny too, I hadn't been a very good friend to him either in the end. Finally I thought about her, about her invitation to go and see her this afternoon. I wondered what she had wanted and felt sad that I'd never find out.

Then a weird head rush took me and just for a moment everything was bright white silence

In the pub, on the way off the back of my stool.

I snatched at the bar and managed to steady myself, quickly glancing around to see if she, or anyone else, had noticed. Shaking the fuzz from my brow I focussed. Neither gear nor girls were the way after all, at some point I seemed to have decided that.

I thought about it a little more and realised that there were only three things I was really sure about. Firstly, a couple of amateurs had taken the lad's car to do a job. Secondly, wherever they were now, they almost certainly didn't have the car any more, they'd be bound to have dumped it right after the job. Thirdly, and this was the important one, depending on the job, there would probably be some people I didn't want to meet looking for them.

Putting these all together it seemed pretty obvious

that chasing down the lads themselves in the hope of finding out where they'd dumped the car would inevitably involve a variety of dangerous situations with no guarantee of actually finding the it. No, there was another way and now I'd seen it I knew what I needed to do next. I rose from my stool as the barmaid returned and smiled as she took my glass.

"Mind how you go won't you," she said, a stock phrase but now with additional meaning, genuine concern peeking from behind her professional smile. Damn she's great, I thought and returned the smile.

"Just before I go," I said leaning in and lowering my voice to hold her attention. "Anything else happening tonight?"

"Besides the obvious?" she asked.

"The obvious?" I glanced around but no-one seemed to be paying any attention to us.

"Bloody hell Kaz," she said laughing. "You really have been busy haven't you."

I smiled sourly, much to her amusement.

"There was big sit down earlier tonight, you-know-who and that Southern lot. Well somebody hit it, stormed in, took the money and ran. Now both sides are going crazy looking for them. Everyone's talking about it." she said finally.

"Where was it?" I asked, trying not to make the obvious connection. My night had just become significantly darker.

"Maggie's," she said.

"On poker night?" I asked, picturing the place. From the outside it was an dingy little antiques shop but if you knew the right people and turned up on the right night you could find something else entirely.

In the back room of that dingy little shop, Old Maggie had played host to some of the longest, highest stakes card games I'd ever heard about. I'd had a couple of good nights in that back room myself over the years but in the long run I'd lost more than I'd won, just like everyone else.

"Exactly," she said with a knowing look. "It was supposed to be a secret. Those lads probably thought they were ripping off a game and got more than they

216

bargained for."

I nodded, picturing first the place itself and then the route from here to there.

"Cheers love. You're very good to me you know." I said with a smile.

Her face stiffened slightly before twisting into kind but weary disapproval.

"Hey, no," I said quickly. "I just meant you're a good friend to me, god knows why you are but you are and I really appreciated it."

Surprise opened her expression back up and a faint hint of red rose in her cheeks. Then she smiled, curiosity tightening her eyes.

"Are you alright Kaz?" she asked kindly, landing her hand on mine.

"Me?" I said with a grin, removing my hand and standing away from the bar. "Never."

She laughed a little and nodded but it was all tinged with sadness, pity that made me cringe. I turned away and headed for the door.

Back out on the street, I rubbed my hands together, trying absently to work the pain out of my right with my left and thinking about the next stop on my trip. Turning right out of the door and then right again, I followed the wall of the pub round into the car park, it was time for a bit of lateral thinking.

I looked around me but there was no-one else about, just me, a few cars and the dark. The two cars parked nearest were pretty new looking so I dismissed them immediately, opting instead for a battered old piece of crap parked further back. The front bumper was hanging off on the passenger side and the driver's door was a different colour to the rest of the severely rusted bodywork. It would do.

Looking around again, I moved past the car to a small wall at the back that was gradually collapsing into the car park. I scooped up half a brick and returned to my chosen vehicle. The chunk of masonry went through the back passenger side window surprisingly quietly, the breaking glass hissing rather than screaming into the right.

I reached in carefully, popped up the lock on the

217

passenger door and I was in, clambering over into the drivers seat. A little gentle persuasion and the plastic casing flopped down from under the steering wheel, revealing a tangle of wires. I let my hands do their thing while I scanned the car park and the pavement beyond for sings of life.

It had been many years since my misspent youth but there were some things you never forgot, it was like stealing a bicycle. As I peered through the windscreen, grimacing at my fumbling fingers, I reflected that I was practising a dying art.

My eyes followed the sleek lines of the modern cars parked nearby. It was pretty much impossible to break into new cars these days, not even worth trying. Of course that didn't stop people nicking them, it just meant if you wanted to be a car thief today you need to up your game to include a bit of breaking and entering too.

A particularly vicious spike of pain shot through my hand so that I dropped what I was certain was one of the right wires and cursed, having to glance down for a second to retrieve it. Returning my gaze to the car park I thought about how things had changed. Ten years ago the little bastards would just twoc your car from outside your house. Today the little shits break in while you're sleeping to look for the keys.

"Progress," I said to myself as the engine spluttered to life.

I found the windscreen wipers then the indicators and then finally, cursing some more, the lights. I knocked them on before crawling slowly across the car park towards the street, pausing before pulling out.

So I'd just stolen a car and was now on my way to Maggie's, imagining that I was going to rob the regular poker game there. The most direct route would be to turn right out of the car park and get on the main road down towards town. My finger tapped on the wheel, waiting for my me to make my mind up.

Obviously I was hoping that the owner wasn't going to notice the car missing until the morning but to be safe I'd have to act as if they'd realise and report it immediately. Since the last thing I wanted on my to or from a robbery was to be pulled over by the pigs it'd be best to avoid the main roads. Also, although the lads in question didn't seem well known they obviously had some local knowledge or they wouldn't have known about the game in the first place.

My mind made up I turned left out the car park and then right at the pub. Weaving my way through the dense web of terraced streets would take longer but there was far less chance of my encountering any unwanted attention from uniforms or cameras.

I began to make my way through the rows upon rows of now quiet red brick houses. I tried to imagine the feeling, the rising tension, the tightness in the stomach. The lad in the passenger seat had probably been fiddling with the guns, checking and rechecking while the lad driving had been trying to concentrate, trying not to think about what was coming.

There was one particular corner coming up on the left that I knew would catch my attention, taking me away from the pressure cooker scene and back to a time long before. I'd known a lass who lived round here, probably still did. We'd had a bit of a thing for a while but her work had got in the way, or at least I'd never been able to get past it.

She rose up before my mind's eye, the look on her face, the smell of her, but the image was shattered as I hit an especially bad pothole. Stealing an old banger to ride in their shoes had made perfect sense back at the pub but I quickly realised there was at least one fairly serious drawback, namely the lack of any real suspension.

Between the continuous rash of potholes and the seemingly endless speed bumps I found myself being constantly bounced about, the top of my head occasionally actually meeting the roof. I drove as slowly as I could stand but may as well have been driving a horse and cart down a country lane.

I was so busy cursing the urban rollercoaster that I didn't see the young asian lad until he was literally on the bonnet. He'd dashed headlong into the street from the left and my hand had found the horn before I really knew what was happening. Despite crawling along at a snails pace I'd still somehow managed to make the tires squeal as I brought the wreck to an almost immediate halt.

For a couple of pounding heartbeats the lad lay on the bonnet, then he looked at me. His eyes were wide with a terror that went beyond the shock of being hit by a car. The moment he saw me however his expression changed.

He stared in at me, his fear seemingly put to one side for a moment as confusion and disbelief came to the fore. Slowly he turned to look back at the tight little knot of bodies on the pavement he'd come from before turning back to stare at me again. Then, catching himself in the midst of an almost terminally foolish act, he shook himself, leapt off the right side of the car and sprinted away into the night.

I glanced over at the pavement and realised that beneath the small but energetic crowd someone was taking a right shoeing. I cringed my sympathy but drove on. I was certainly no-one's knight in shining armour and besides, wasn't I already helping someone out?

Driving on, I wove my way back and forth past more and more rows of terraces, trying to put the violent scene from my mind and focus on the job at hand. Eventually the sleeping homes gave way to small warehouses and workshops and I knew that beyond these lay a small run of shops, including the locally infamous M.Thwaite's Antiques. I turned off before reaching the corner, leaving the car in the shadows of an electrical outfitters place, and walked the rest of the way.

Turning the corner I paused, taken aback by what appeared to be a traffic jam straight up ahead. Usually the street would be dead at this time, silent and empty so that you would never guess that in a little back room behind one of these dark windows, people were drinking and cursing and occasionally winning, but for the most part losing, large piles of dirty banknotes.

Tonight however the street was alive with bodies. Whole motorcades of high end cars, SUVs and occasional vans flanked each side of the street while among them angry looking men spoke angrily into mobiles and at one another. Further down and on the far side of the street, the entrance to Maggie's itself was completely obscured behind a particularly large van and it was immediately obvious that I wasn't getting anywhere near the place.

The near side of the street was less crowded so I wandered along, sticking to the shadows of the doorways and keeping my head down. I ambled down the street, casting occasional glances over towards Maggie's and straining my ears to catch an odd word here or there. Then I noticed a figure hunched in a doorway up ahead.

"Alright mate," I said, settling onto the cold step next to the figure.

"Alright Kaz," said Sid, quietly but with a smile.

We sat for a while watching people come and go. One group of guys, mostly heavy set with black leather coats, was gathered round a map one of them had spread out on the bonnet of a nearby Bentley. They were taking in turns to stab at the map with thick fingers and murmur to one another in dark tones.

"Bit of a circus all this innit?" I said eventually, retrieving the half done joint from my pocket and lighting it.

"Aye," Sid replied and then yawned. "Someone's stirred up a right shitstorm in there tonight."

I hid the joint in my palm and we lapsed into heads down silence as two men in suits strode past us. I looked at Sid's hand as it rested on his knee. You wouldn't always know Sid was on the streets to look at him. He seemed to know where to get a free shave and haircut now and then and even fresh clothes every so often too. It was his hands that gave him away.

Looking at them in the yellowed shadows, I could see that his hands were swollen and darkened and I knew that in the plain light of day they would have a faint purple tinge to them too. They'd been too cold for too long too often and now looked like latex gloves that had been filled to bulging with plaster and then painted. I thought about how close I'd come to having hands like his in the past and returned my gaze to the pavement at our feet.

"So how long you been here then?" I asked,

passing him the joint once the pair were a bit further up the street.

"Oh all night," he said happily, taking a drag. "Just sat down for a bit of a rest earlier then all this kicked off and I've been enjoying the show ever since."

"So you saw the whole thing then," I said as if making idle conversation.

"You know me Kaz," he said, returning the joint. "I see a lot of things."

I smiled and holding the joint in my mouth, retrieved a twenty from my wallet, folding it thin and palming it to him without looking. Then I passed him the lad's description of his car and the barmaid's description of the pair.

"Yeah I saw them," he said. "Didn't see any of the usual faces going in for the card game, just some of this lot, all serious like. Then about ten minutes later your lads pulled up in that car. They left the engine running and went inside then, seemed like no time at all, they came dashing out again, carrying these big black bags and off they went. Been like this," he waved vaguely at the circus before us, "ever since."

I nodded as he spoke then kept nodding when he'd finished, passing the joint back automatically while I stared at nothing. I just wanted the lad's car back but those stupid little bastards had gone and used it to rip off the two most dangerous organisations in the city, potentially sparking an apocalyptic gang war in the process.

"Made a right mess of the street too," Sid added, suddenly sounding bitterly annoyed. "Right old piece of crap, leaking oil everywhere."

I nodded but didn't say anything. This was going to be more difficult than I'd thought.

"How come there was a sit down anyway?" I asked.

It wasn't strictly relevant but the thought had occurred to me and wouldn't leave. "This Southern lot kidnapped his daughter then offed his son didn't they? Surely he'd just be looking to wipe them out."

"You'd think wouldn't you," said Sid. "Lot of rumours flying about. Some people reckon he took the

Southern boss's wife, real nasty, old school retribution like." Sid pulled a face which I mirrored.

"One guy told me it had all got too much though," he continued. "It was affecting business and that, so they agreed to sit down and straighten it out." He leaned towards me a little so as to lower his voice.

"But that's not the question, is it," he added mysteriously offering the joint.

"Is it not?" I asked, bemused. Sid just looked at me, eyebrows up, waiting.

I took a long toke and thought about it, the whole situation, looking for the obvious gap.

Then I saw it.

"Why are they up here in the first place?" I tried.

"Exactly," said Sid leaning back again, apparently satisfied.

"Just expanding?" I offered, but knew that wasn't right. I was seeing the gap but not the piece that fit it. Sid shook his head and continued to wait, watching as two cars set off back up the street, tyres screeching. I thought hard, my eyes scouring the dark pavement as if the answer was hidden between the slabs.

"Third party," I said finally, feeling it fit.

"There you go," said Sid happily, accepting the joint back again. "There's something happening down South, someone new, Eastern European or something. This lot were being pushed out so decided to try and move in up here."

"Only the North was a bit harder than they expected," I picked up the thread and ran with it. "So instead of a neat little invasion they end up fighting on two fronts, sandwiched between this new lot down there and him up here."

"You've got it," Sid confirmed. I continued, more to myself than to Sid.

"So now they don't just want to settle up with him, they want him on side to help them take back their turf. They'll have told him if they go under then he'll be next which means the meet tonight was..." I started.

"...a big fucking deal," Sid finished, passing the joint.

"Fuck," I whispered, accepting what was left of it

223

without looking and letting it smoulder between my fingers.

"Yep," said Sid.

It was too big to look at, too big and too scary. I pushed it away, ignoring the horizon to concentrate on the next step instead.

"Anyway, this car," I said, trying to picture the scene. "So they come out, jump in, then screw it around, presumably with lots of revs and tire squeal, then speed off back up the street right?"

"Well, more or less," said Sid but I wasn't listening. The joint was down to the roach now, I could feel its heat against my fingers.

"But where," I said, snatching one last toke and thinking hard. I had no way of knowing where they'd gone next. After all, I didn't know anything about them or even why they'd hit the meet in the first place.

"What do you reckon?" I asked Sid desperately, flicking the roach away from us and running my now empty hand over my head.

"Couldn't tell you mate, didn't recognise the lads myself, wouldn't know where they'd go," Sid said simply.

We sat in silence for a while longer, watching the footsoldiers of two regional crime gangs dashing about and bumping into one another. So much for lateral thinking, I'd barely started and here I was at a total dead end.

I stood up, stretching the cold out of my legs and arse and rubbing my face with both hands. I could feel the gear on my brain like a warm, thick blanket. It took the edge off the clawing panic and let me think more calmly which was great, except that I didn't have any more leads to think about.

"Alright mate, well thanks for that, see you around yeah?" I shook Sid's swollen hand, holding back a wince and set off back up the street the way I'd come.

"See you later," Sid called merrily, slipping further into the shadows with each step I took until he became invisible once more. Except that then I turned and hurried back to him so that his shape faded back into focus again.

He looked up at me mildly questioning.

"More or less?" I said.

"What's that?" he said.

"You said more or less. I asked you if that was how it went down and you said more or less. What did you mean?" I had to fight against rabid hope to keep my voice down.

"Oh," said Sid, understanding. "You said they turned round. They didn't."

"You mean they carried on up the street when they left?" I asked.

"Aye, straight on," he said.

"You Sid," I said, retrieving another twenty and slipping it to him via an enthusiastic handshake, "are a fucking lifesaver!"

Bemused but happy enough Sid took the second twenty and the handshake then gave me a nod and a wave as I hurried off back towards the car. I'd assumed that the lads must have turned the car round since the road didn't really go anywhere in that direction.

Technically it wasn't actually a dead end but rather one end of a huge horseshoe that ran into the Oakfield estate and then out again. If you were trying to put a lot of distance between you and Maggie's quick though, there's no way you'd drive straight on since the road would just bring you more or less back where you started ten minutes later, albeit a couple of streets over.

If they'd known enough to find Maggie's on poker night then surely they knew where that road led too. If they were based there though, if they were holed up there right now, then they were insane. Ripping off two gangs like that then hiding out next door? It was suicide.

Of course that would mean that the car would be there too. Climbing back into my own piece of hot shit I considered how great it would be to drive into the Oakfields carpark and see my mate's car just parked there, waiting for me.

Starting the engine however I knew I'd never be so lucky. The hit had been hours ago so they'd either been and gone or, if they were mental enough to stay and mental enough not to have ditched the car, then they'd be there for the night and intending to use the car again tomorrow.

Either way I didn't need to rush over there right now. I paused, listening to the engine run rough, clearing its throat every few seconds. No, better to seek out a little more information first, try and find out who I was dealing with. If I ended up meeting them and having to try and convince them to part with the car, any information could prove vital.

Also, though it wasn't the most important thing on my mind, I really did fancy another smoke and maybe a brew. I pulled away from the kerb and headed back towards the pub beyond which lay a block of flats and a guy I knew.

The road rattling returned but I tried not to think about it, taking it easy over the bumps and dips back the way I'd come. As I passed the pub I was reminded of the thoughts I'd carried in there earlier on. That day in the park, the skinny lad with the summons. Without getting into the detail, it was safe to say that it hadn't gone well, that thing with Tall James, in fact it had turned out really bad.

Even after that things had just kept on going downhill and some other really bad things had happened too, things I wasn't proud of. I thought about this for a moment, as one yellow streetlight sheet after another slid silently over me.

I tried to think of anything I'd ever done that I was proud of.

I'm useless. I'm hopeless. I'm done.

I'm sat in the flat, staring at nothing, vaguely aware of the weight of the revolver in my lap. I don't know how long I've been sat here. I went for a piss a while back, I don't know how long ago that was but it was dark. Now determined lines of light are pushing round the edges of the curtains, trying to force life and vitality into my place but I won't rise to it.

My body's complaining, I'm vaguely aware of that too. My lower back aches from sitting for so long and my throat is all dry barbs from not drinking. Next to the gun in my lap, my hand complains of a painful stiffness, who knows what that's about. It's good though, the pain. It feels

right that I should suffer after all that I've done. Every twinge, every throb, every bite and wince, feels like penance, like paying my due.

There's a bottle of bourbon on the table. It's two thirds full and I could reach it without getting up, but I'm not interested any more. I'm not interested in the little gripper bag of green nestled amongst rolling papers either, not now.

Getting blasted, getting wrecked, arseholed, wasted, destroyed, it wasn't helping, it didn't stop it, it was just making me weaker, less able to cope. Sleeping was worse, sleep just meant dreams, dreams that made it all real all over again and again and again. So I stopped drinking, stopped smoking, stopped sleeping, got my gun then sat in this chair and waited.

Eventually I'll do it, I know I will. Eventually the point will come when my aching hand will grip my gun and raise it to my head, then I'll pull the trigger and all this will stop, finally, all this relentless bullshit will just stop.

It's like it's all painted on the walls around me so that wherever I look it's all I can see. To the left there's the kid, playing in the garden, grubby, pudgy fists and bright, innocent eyes. But now they're dead those eyes, cold and empty, his arm so limp as it swings, again and again, mum snatching him close and it's as if I pulled the trigger myself. I did that, I caused that, I made it happen, me.

I can't bear it, I turn away but straight ahead there's Tall James, doesn't even need to look at me, laughs at me. Even with my gun, I'm not a threat, I'm nothing. All that apocalyptic anger, that cold, furious rage, even that is nothing before him. I did nothing, had no effect, made no difference, me.

I can't stand it, I turn away but off to the right there're the bottoms of Billy's boots. Sticking out from under a car, asking for this tool or that one, telling me stories, making me laugh. But now those boots are still, not moving, he'll never move again. I brought that down on him and he knew it, he saw it, and I saw it when he looked at me that last time, betrayed and disappointed.

It's too much, I turn away, back to the left, but now I'm back to the kid and around and around it goes. There's no rest, no hope, no escape and right inside me I know that's how it should be. No-one ever made me do anything. I chose all of it of my own free will.

I could have grabbed the kid and his mum, taken them somewhere safe, but I made a choice to to just watch as they shot him to death. I could have killed Tall James, just blown him away, but I made a choice to let him make me his bitch. I could have stopped those guys at Billy's, got in the way, taken the punch for him, but I made a choice to just let him die.

There was no-one else to blame, no excuses, no reasons. I've done nothing but bring pain and death to good people and suck the dick of all the evil I could find. I never wanted any of it to happen, I didn't mean to, I didn't plan it, it had just happened, it all just happened around me and even now I can't understand why.

The only explanation, the only thing that makes sense, is that I must be flawed, tainted, diseased. No matter what I want or how hard I try, all I'll ever do is make things worse for everyone else. The only thing I can do, the only good thing I'll ever do, is to take this gun and end myself, remove myself and all the pain I would have caused from the world.

And yet I'm still here. I've been waiting for hours but it still hasn't happened. I move my hand in my lap, onto the gun and the handle feels cool in my palm. This is it, this is happening, it's going to be now, I'll just do it and then it'll be done.

I lift the gun from my lap and tilt the barrel to the ceiling. I sit forward a bit and relax my shoulders then take a breath and place the muzzle under my chin. I think about the angle and move my wrist back and forth until I'm sure that I have it just right.

Do it.

My finger tightens on the trigger, I can feel its slender line against my skin.

Do it.

I close my eyes so that those same old images begin to flash past.

Do it.

Every muscle in my body is tensing up. I apply a little more pressure to trigger and feel myself cringe, my head desperate to pull away.

Do it.

My heart is pounding and there's icy sweat running down my back. I'm gritting my teeth.

Do it.

A little more pressure on the trigger, it's now, it's here, this is it.

Do it.

I'm crying and growling and wheezing. My finger doesn't want to tighten any more, it keeps asking are you sure? are you sure? are you sure?

Do it.

Do it!

DO IT!

I scream and snatch the trigger tight.

There's an explosion.

My left ear is ringing, so loud it hurts. My chin is buried into my right shoulder. Slowly I force my eyes open. Everything is exactly the same. The flat is just sat there as if nothing has happened. Nothing has moved, nothing has changed.

I can smell the acrid tang of the tiny explosive wafting from the end of the barrel. I collapse back into the chair, dropping the gun back into my lap so that my body jumps. I come back to myself a little more, the pain in my ear coming larger and closer. The ringing throbs over and over as if a screwdriver is being jabbed into my ear.

My face is wet and I remember that I'm crying. The sobs grow now, shuddering through me. I feel my stomach plunge down through the

floor as I realise that I can't do it, can't end it, can't escape. I am empty and broken, lifeless and limp and now I realise that my legs and my arse are warm and wet because I've pissed myself like a frightened kitten.

I try to throw the gun away from me with a childlike squeal but it doesn't go far, clattering bluntly across the threadbare carpet. The pain and the shame and the guilt and sadness, it all rolls through me now, unrestrained in great, drowning waves.

And so I sit and I drown in tears and piss and the absolute, certain knowledge that this is my life, forever.

I swallowed hard, feeling the heat of shame rise to my face then forcing the memory back down. A great angular mass rose up out of the night ahead, a low block of flats, one of which might just be the place for me to get some smoke, a brew and a bit of a chat. Somehow the thought of seeing my friend made me even more ashamed of the memories, as if he might see their stains on me despite my efforts to slap them aside.

Determined to leave all that crap in the car, I parked up and stepped out. I headed towards the block and soon I was making my way up the stone stairway, hard, dark and cold, pushing through the echoes of my footsteps to the third floor. Strolling along the landing, I held my chin to my chest against the unrestrained chill and listened hard for sounds of company but found nothing more than distant TV mumbles.

Pausing at the familiar door, I pounded on it and tried the handle. To my surprise the door was locked. I frowned, confused and knocked again, checking back and forth along the landing as I waited. I supposed he wasn't always in, though thinking on I found I couldn't remember him ever being out before. It occurred to me to wonder if he was ok.

Just as I was beginning to give up however, I heard movement inside. A few seconds more and still nothing happened. I checked back and forth along the landing again then slowly moved against the door, pressing my ear to the cool wood. I was sure there was someone in there, as if I could sense a sound just beyond hearing from the other side of door.

Time was ticking by and I was annoyed at myself for having wasted so much of it coming over here only to find an empty flat. I frowned my irritation and headed back to the stairwell. Trotting down through the dark I continued to chastise myself. I'd never liked cul-de-sacs and here I'd just driven myself straight into one.

By the time I reached the car I'd set my jaw and firmly decided, no more dicking about. The old wreck gave me a bit of a scare when it wouldn't start, but half a dozen turns of the key and a steady stream of swearing did the trick and then I was back on my way.

Row after row of dead grey buildings slipped by, each rushing up to the fill the windscreen only to shrink down to nothing in the rear view moments later. As I ate up the streets I found myself imaging that the shop fronts and factory sides were just cardboard cut outs. Perhaps the whole city was just an empty prop and all the bad vibes and danger were just fiction for fun.

I thought about what it would be like if, when all this finally went down, wherever and however that happened, someone just yelled "Cut!" and the lights came on. Not a sleeping city at night after all, just a large brightly lit room full of cameras and people in costume.

A red light brought me to a shuddering halt but the scene played on in my mind. We'd all go home then, walk out into bright sunshine and go back to our real lives. All of this, all of the shit and the pain and the guilt, it was all just acting, read from a script, none of it real. My real life was waiting for me out there, fresh and clean, filled with hope.

The blaring of a car horn shattered the dream and I found myself sat still in a glow of green. I raised my hand in apology to the car behind and continued on my way. A little further on and the road opened up into two lanes for a stretch.

The car behind overtook me, pissed off and pausing alongside to make sure I knew it. The guy was all angry face and fingers but then he was gone, two red dots shrinking in the distance. As brief and meaningless as the encounter had been it had left a sour taste in my mouth. I turned off onto a smaller road and rolled along past more stale grey facades, except they were real again now, it all was. I took a breath and dragged myself back to the present.

I'd messed up and wasted time, it was now more important than ever that I be sharp and focused, ready to pounce on anything, no matter how insignificant, that might point the way. Shaking the last of the incident from my brow I leaned forward over the wheel and squinted up. The towers of the Oakfield estate were looming over me now and I returned my gaze to ground level as I crawled into the car park.

I pulled into the first space I found and hopped back out into the chill night air. Occasional yellow oblongs floated above me and faint strains of music wafted down here and there but for the most part the estate appeared to be sleeping.

Hunching my shoulders up to my ears I began to move slowly through the cars while trying to ignore the cold. My instinct still told me the car wouldn't still be here but I couldn't take the chance. I looked at every vehicle in turn, discounting them one by one, even checking the reg when I encountered a similar model.

Each of the three blocks had its own parking area around its base and it took what seemed like an age to check them all. Eventually however, I closed the circle and my own hot-but-not wheels came back into view. I sat back onto the front end of the car and looked through the night, thinking hard. With no direction from me, my hands began to idly search through my jacket for a second joint which I knew wasn't there.

The staring and fumbling stopped however, the moment movement hooked my eyes. Off to my left, among the first huddle of cars I'd searched through, a husky figure was stooping in the shadows. For a moment it disappeared from view, apparently crouching, but a moment later it straightened back into my eye line, turning one way then the other.

I ran my tongue over my teeth and grimaced. I was stuck, the trail had gone cold and I was struggling to think of alternative options. Still, approaching some random shifty stranger in a dark car park in the early hours of the morning seemed just too desperate.

As it happened the guy made the decision for me. After a bit more skulking about he began moving with a purpose, emerging from the clustered cars and headed straight for me. I knew he'd seen me and was closing in but for some reason he seemed determined to pretend that he hadn't and wasn't.

He moved awkwardly, as only someone who is trying hard to appear casual can, and threw his eyes wildly, looking up and down and away, anywhere but at me. Finally he stopped a few feet in front of me but continued his performance.

Keeping my arse planted firmly on the bonnet of my car, I watched, openly confused and unimpressed as he thrust his hands into his pockets. He sniffed loudly and then let out a long sigh, riding up onto his toes and then down again to rock to and fro on his heels as he looked back and forth, back and forth. Then, suddenly, his shoulders dropped along all with the pretence and walked straight at me.

"Alright," he hissed dramatically.

I eyed him hard but nodded once both to return the greeting and invite an explanation. He licked his lips and cast yet another gaze all about us before speaking again.

"You don't know where I could score do you mate?" he asked, his words quick and sharp. I frowned as all my natural defences shot up.

Even though he was right in front of me, the gloom of the car park meant I couldn't make him out in detail. He seemed out of place and deeply uncomfortable, but without seeing more of him I couldn't even guess as to why.

For all I knew he could be a smackhead caught short, desperate to the point of madness and ready to explode in an instant. Or, just as easily, some undercover pig on a bust gone wrong, hungry for a trophy however small to cover at least some of his shame.

I glanced once at his shoes before locking straight back onto his face. Ragged ruins would have said smackhead while bright shiny black with glaring white socks would have screamed narc. His showed neither however, they were decent but dull, scuffed but respectable. Determined to be neither put down nor picked up I chose my words carefully and made sure I was ready to move.

"Score what?" I asked flatly, giving nothing away.

For a moment he seemed genuinely confused until his eyes widened and he spoke again, his voice a little higher than before.

"No! No, no, just weed. I just meant weed, I don't, I mean..." he closed his eyes, apparently cursing himself internally, cringing at his own lack of cool. He took a deep breath, opened his eyes and tried again, his voice calmer.

"Look," he said, sounding tired. "I'm just looking to score some weed. My usual guy has let me down and I could really do with a smoke."

I thought about about my own failed attempt to score and my hopeless hands searching my jacket just moments before. I relaxed a bit.

"It's funny..." I began but was cut short as his face fell, collapsing into an expression of misery and despair.

"Ok," I conceded, "it's not."

"Sorry," he said, now taking his turn to examine his shoes. "I've had a right shitter of a night."

"Erm..." I heard myself say, though apparently he didn't and ploughed right on with his story regardless.

"It's this girl," he continued, still staring down at the ground. "I just... I mean she's just so... I can't... you know?"

He looked up at me, eyes pleading for understanding. Faces flashed behind my eyes, the barmaid, the lass who's neighbourhood I'd driven through, others from before. I felt twinges in and amongst but nothing on a par with what was sat in those wobbly eyes. Somehow that made me feel sad and while distracted I realised I had nodded.

"She's a bit younger than me and I know she's out of my league but I can't help it, I can't get her out of my head. I talk to her down the pub every so often but I've never had the balls to ask her out." He was staring through me now, pouring his heart out all over me. I glanced around us, looking for an escape but finding nothing more than shadows and concrete.

"Then the other day I mentioned I sometimes smoke a bit of dope and suddenly she invited herself and her mates round to mine." He smiled at the memory. It didn't last.

"Only then my guy rips me off, leaves me with no cash and no gear and then she turns up with her mates and they're all pissed off at me. Now they're back there in my flat, waiting for me to come back with some gear only I don't know anyone else who deals." Once more his eyes returned to mine, pain welling up in the corners. I winced my compassion for him, genuinely this time as it occurred to me that the girl in question was probably fucking someone else in his bed right now.

"Sorry buddy," I said to the pale face before me. "Just not your night."

He nodded and sniffed, dragging the back of his hand across his face. A few seconds of silence slipped between us. He blinked and took a breath.

"Someone," he began again, his voice suddenly different, steadier. "Someone told me there's a lass called Lindsay P deals round here. You know where she hangs out?"

My eyes narrowed a little.

I'd known Lindsay P for years. She was a mate, not to mention a force to be reckoned with. She'd got where she was by being smart and hard. She didn't throw her name about like some dick new kid, playing at being a gangster, she kept it all low key, only worked with people she knew she could trust.

How did this guy, this apparently poor, lost and helpless guy, how did he know the name Lindsay P? Something smelt bad. I shook my head.

"Never heard of her mate, sorry. I'm not from round here," I said.

He glanced up at me a little too sharply, his eyes glinting hard as if within all the soft and the wet there lay hard, little balls of steel.

"You sure about that?" He continued to whine pathetically, but I could hear an edge under it now. "You don't know anyone who might know her do you?"

"No," I said firmly. "As I say, I don't live round here, don't know anyone."

The guy blinked a couple of times in rapid succession and just for a second I saw frustration elbow its way to the fore of his expression. A second more however and he pushed it back down, settling back behind his mask, shoulders drooping.

"Oh, ok then," he said, his broken little voice completely convincing once again. "Thanks anyway," and he began to shuffle away.

I watched him shuffle until he faded to black then hopped off the car. I shifted my weight from one foot to the other, trying to flex some feeling back into my well numbed arse. Glancing back over in the direction the guy had left, I slipped my phone out of my pocket and thumbed my way to one of Lindsay's numbers.

As I jabbed the phone into dialling and raised it to my ear, I suddenly remembered what I'd seen when I first noticed the guy. The call connected and began to ring as I strolled over towards the dark corner I'd seen the guy inspecting.

After just enough rings to make me frown, the call connected and a young male voice answered.

"What?" was his curt and surly opener.

"She there?" I asked, squinting down into the dark now as I stood in the empty parking space the other guy had found so interesting.

"Who is this?" he snapped.

I sighed my irritation at him and then drew breath to snap back but caught it. The shadows at my feet seemed to shift before my eyes as a shape came into focus.

"Just tell her to be careful answering the door tonight," I said quickly. "She's got people she doesn't know asking after her."

Without giving him chance to reply I killed the call, dropped my phone in my pocket and myself to my knees. Crouching there still more shapes revealed themselves, dark stains on the concrete, their freshness shining but slightly beneath the black of the night. I peered closer still, sniffing a little too.

Oil.

I was looking at two fairly large, fresh oil spots on the concrete. The larger one was a long tear drop shape while the smaller sat a few inches away and was an almost perfect circle. I rested back on my heels, a hand rising to massage my face as I thought about it.

Sid's words floated back to me.

"Made a right mess of the street too," he'd said and as I recalled he'd sounded bitterly annoyed about it too.

"Right old piece of crap, leaking oil everywhere," he'd added.

The shot was long but it was also the only one I had. The more I thought about it, the more I wanted it to be true, the more likely it seemed. The car I was hunting, the car I absolutely had to find, had been parked right where I was stood just a few hours earlier. I was now certain of it.

Remaining crouched I stretched my neck up to take a quick scout around me. Satisfied I was still alone I returned my eyes to the floor and looked deeper into the shadows. Sure enough, further back sat another stain, this one framing a single, tiny object.

This third sticky pool wasn't oil, it was duller and smelled faintly of copper. The tiny object was angular and pale and for the life of me I couldn't work out what I was looking at. Tilting my head one way then the other didn't help so eventually I relented and reached out, pinching the sharp little thing between finger and thumb and holding it up before the end of my nose.

The liquid was thick, tacky and familiar while the object itself was almost perfectly smooth and rounded, like a weird little stone, except for single, vicious, jagged edge. I rolled it back and forth between my fingers, searching my brain for a match. And then it came. And I knew what it was.

A tooth.

It was a broken tooth lying in a pool of blood.

I cringed for moment, staring at the suddenly grotesque thing while my face folded in on itself in disgust. Then my hand took over, no longer willing to wait, and flicked the tooth away from me, skittering into the shadows. I wiped my finger and thumb on the cold concrete beneath me, twisting my wrist this way and that so as to scrape as much of the blood off as possible.

I lurched upwards and backwards to return to my feet. Staggering a little before righting myself and heading back to the car to think. Just as my hand landed on the handle however I paused and looked back over to the darkness into which the stranger from before had vanished.

"You cheeky bastard," I said quietly.

I thought about the stains I'd just inspected and how he'd been inspecting them too. The guy had put on quite a performance, all that nervous, desperate crap. I popped the door and dropped into the driver's seat, sliding down low and absently wiping my hand again, this time on the passenger seat beside me.

Glancing into the wing and rear view mirrors, I reflected with satisfaction that he'd need a lot more than that to get anywhere near Lindsay P. I wondered what she'd say to him when he tried that shit with her, assuming he got that far. I spent a few seconds amusing myself by picturing various possibilities.

Shaking off the indulgence I returned my focus to the matter at hand, pondering the stains once more. That was a lot of blood and relatively fresh too. Someone had taken a serious beating and it seemed almost inconceivable that it hadn't happened right next to the car I was after. The car around me and the car park beyond faded a little, smudging themselves dark to make way for my train of thought.

The blood had been concentrated in that one place, there hadn't been any other big pools. That said to me that it was a single, surprise beating rather than a drawn out scrap. I thought about where exactly where the stain was and where the car would have been when parked. It lined up in my head to show just one guy, jumped while getting out of the driver's seat, knocked down quick then stomped badly right there.

It had to be one of the lads but who had stomped him and why? I pushed on through the tangle of doubt and confusion, craving a quick toke more than ever. So either the second guy, the passenger, had stomped his driver friend, or some third party did.

If it was someone else though, the passenger hadn't intervened since the beating must have lasted long enough for the driver to bleed that whole puddle out of himself. Perhaps there'd been more than one outsider, a second guy holding a gun on the passenger, making him watch the beating then marching him away after.

Somehow that didn't sit right though. Nobody anywhere seemed to know anything about these lads so who would know to jump them? Equally, if they had been working for someone else surely someone would know about that by now, the city just wasn't that big. Finally, if someone wanted to hire a couple of lads to do a job like this, there was no end of up and comers to choose from. Why go for two such total no marks?

No, the most obvious and compelling explanation was simply that the passenger had double crossed the driver. I followed this a little further, watching it all unfold in front of me. There was no body but neither was there any sign of dragging, the pool of blood had been particularly neat.

Through this I thought I could see the passenger getting straight back in the car after stomping his former friend, actually stepping over him to get into the driving seat, and then leaving him for dead. I doubted the driver would have been able to walk on his own though, and the absence of a dragging smudge was also the absence of a crawling smudge.

Now I could see the lad on the floor phoning a friend, someone nearby, someone in one of these blocks who had come down, picked him up and propped him up, then walked him away from the scene. A local link explained the local knowledge, knowing about Maggie's and all that. It also explained the apparent madness of visiting the estate after the job.

The further I followed the thread the thinner it got but just before I felt myself slip over the line into total guesswork it occurred to me that maybe the driver was the driver because he had the local knowledge. Maybe the passenger, the double crossing beat down bastard, was an outsider and a cold one at that. As soon as they got back to the estate he'd no longer needed the driver and so had ditched him to keep the cash for himself.

What a shit.

I straightened up in my seat and pulled my seatbelt on distractedly. It felt right, it felt solid, it felt like progress. As I turned the engine over however I realised that for all my heavy thinking, I still didn't know where to go next. I focused in my original plan and tried to put myself into the shit's shoes.

I imagined that I'd just ripped off the two biggest gangs in town to the tune of several, heavy hundreds of thousands. I thought about how my heart would be racing as we sped away from the scene, not just with the rush of what had just happened but also the knowledge of what was to come, of what I was about to do.

We'd twist and turn and finally pull up in the car park, my partner expecting some brief drop off or hook up, some bullshit I'd told him. I'd have jumped out of the car to get round to his side and get the drop on him before he had chance to get out.

I'd've clenched my fist at my side, breathing hard and fast, ready to strike. Then, just as he stepped out to stand, I'd've crossed that line forever and cracked him from the side, just behind his ear. He'd've gone down hard, maybe catching his head on the way.

At first he'd've just lolled there, dazed and it'd've been onto that stunned expression that I'd've first dropped my boot. My heart would've been pounding in my throat and I'd've probably felt a massive rush, a kind of trembling ecstasy as I smashed his face.

I might have even heard the sickening crack as his tooth broke sending a thrilled chill right through me. There'd've been a brief window during which he'd've realised what was happening and looked up at me through the violence with heartbreak and fear.

I'd've stomped harder then, smashing that accusing look right out of him until I'd suddenly noticed he'd become limp and defenceless. Then there'd've been a few long moments as I'd've stood over him, panting hard and looking at what I'd done. Finally I'd've stepped over him and climbed into the car. I'd've known I needed to get out fast and that I couldn't go back the way we'd come in.

With that I pulled out of the space and drove quickly through the car park to the far end, before pulling out onto the road and rapidly leaving the estate behind me. Whoever he was he hadn't needed any more local knowledge at this point. He knew where he was going now and as low sleeping houses on either side rolled by a sudden dread gripped me.

He was an outsider but from just how far outside had he come? What if he'd just kept on driving? Ditched town and done one back to wherever he'd come from?

If he'd fled the city I was fucked, or rather the lad was. I quickly tried to think of reasons that made this less likely. If he was from out of town how did he know the other guy well enough to convince him to take such a risk? I could think of lots of ways. I cursed.

Up ahead was a crossroads where the small residential street that led to the estate strayed across the big main road coming up out of the city centre. The was a petrol station on the near right corner, a beacon of harsh artificial light fending off the natural night.

I pulled over to the side of the road. Once I reached the crossroads I'd have to make a decision and at that point I knew I'd just be rolling the dice. I killed the engine and sat quiet in the dark, catching a glimpse of my own grim expression in the rear view.

I was out of options again.

Stuck.

Trapped.

Fucked.

I'm totally fucked. Every time I wake up I have a couple of blissful seconds where I don't remember my life, or their lives. Then I open my eyes and it's there at the end of my bed, leering at me, reminding me of all the shit I've done and I can't stand it. I sit up in bed and look across the chaos of the room. From beneath a grubby T-shirt I spot the muzzle of the gun, still laying on the floor where I threw it after

I shake my head, rattling the too familiar torturous images against one another. I dig around in the bed for a bit but can't find what I'm looking

for. Finally I heave myself out from under the covers and wade across the room. I place my feet carefully among the drifts of crap, occasionally encountering the actual carpet but mostly not.

Reaching the far end of the room near the door I pick some clingy plastic off the sole of one of my feet and begin to look for my jacket. I search feebly, vaguely moving this or that just a bit and fighting hard to summon even this little effort.

Eventually I find it and drag it out from all the crap I've thrown on top of it over the last few days. Shaking it free I search the pockets and finally find my phone, a lighter and a third of a joint. I fall back into the armchair but then immediately have to arch my back and lift my arse.

With curses and groans I drag a cracked, dirty plate out from under me and frisbee it at a nearby pile of clothes and menus. I raise what's left of the joint to my lips and notice that my hand is shaking. Ignoring it I bring the lighter up next and suck on the wobbling flame.

As I puff the joint back to life I focus on the lighter and without any real interest, note that I don't recognise it. I place the strange light on the arm of the chair very carefully then settle back and close my eyes, taking my first deep and proper drag.

After a moment I sigh the smoke out in a plume and squint down at my phone. It takes a second for the digits to come into focus but eventually I notice that it's late afternoon and am relieved since the pub will be open.

I take a few more drags, feeling the heat against my fingers grow as the joint burns down and down. I can feel the delicate fog of sleep being gradually replaced by the heavier fuzz of the gear as I try to hold on the feeling of detachment, fending off those same old pictures and feelings.

The joint's just about gone now and I know I don't have any more gear in the flat. I'm not as high as I need to be though and it's all crowding in on me already. I know that soon the guilt and the despair will set in and rot me from the inside out. For now though I'm just angry, seething at being so helpless and useless and lost.

The idea occurs quickly and I act in an instant, plunging the almost dead joint down into my thigh. I feel the heat straight away but it's not until it's burnt through my shorts that I feel the red glow really stab, biting into my flesh, sharp, precise and livid.

The pain courses white right through all of me and for a moment there is nothing else at all. There is no past and no future, in that moment there is only now, a perfect, single place containing nothing but that rush.

And then it's gone, and I'm just me in my flat with all that I've done and my leg is fucking killing me. I groan my frustration but refuse to acknowledge it fully, even dragging my jeans on with purposeful roughness past the wound just to show myself how little I care.

Then I'm up, slipping on my jacket and walking out the door. I don't even close let alone lock it these days. There's nothing in there worth taking and if there was I wouldn't give a shit. I stumble a little on the street and nearly fall, the world seeming to spin and sway all around me. I take a moment to steady myself against a nearby wall however and then I'm off again, up the hill and round the corner.

The whole front of my thigh is aching now, a broad, thick pain that demands attention. I just limp on regardless however, it's not much further to the pub. I pass the park and cross the road, heading down the hill on the other side.

The pub's in sight now and I lock my eyes onto the sign, clinging to it from afar and using it to reel myself in. Just as I'm crossing the road to reach those heavy double doors however, faint sounds of anger float round the corner from the car park.

I lick my lips and think of drink but once seeded the curiosity grows. I don't have any money anyway so I know I'm going to have to cadge drinks from the barmaid and one or two regulars. Whatever's going on in the car park might be an opportunity to score some funds or freebies.

Keeping one hand on the wall of the pub I follow it round to the car park. As the small scattering of cars comes into view, so does a group of five or six big lads. There all clustered together with their backs to me in the far corner. Their shirts appear almost violently colourful in the fading glow of the afternoon sun and their jeering and growling seems to come slow through the thick, lazy air.

I move away from the wall and use the cars to steady myself and I approach the group. As I get closer I begin to get flashes of someone beyond the group, trapped in the corner, hands up, eyes wide. He's a skinny lad, tall and pale with a shock of jet black hair. His clothes are dirt cheap and ill fitting and the fear in his eyes speaks of knowing from experience what the beating he's about to take will feel like.

The lads have pint glasses in their hands and are all broad shouldered and towering. I don't recognise any of them but they look like sporty types, they might even play for a local rugby team, I wouldn't know. Either way they're not regulars or locals and all that fear in the lads eyes stirs something inside me.

They're pretending to throw punches now, roaring with laughter as the lad flinches. He's not saying anything though, no pleading, no whimpering. He's clearly shitting himself but his jaw is set, he's ready to take the beating when it comes.

I move in a little closer and my foot catches something. I look down and find an empty bottle spinning slowly to a halt. A sharp slap catches my ear so that I look back up but not soon enough to see the first punch.

I just see the lad holding his face and

stumbling back against the wall before sliding down onto his arse. A couple more of them lunge in to stamp on his face and chest. The rest are ready now too. It's so brutal, so unfair, their harsh laughter enrages me. I can't understand why we have to be like this. I can't stand it!

"Oi you, you bunch o' cunts!" I hear myself screech quite wildly, and am surprised to find the empty bottle from the floor in my hand.

I fling it with everything I've got just as lads turn to face me. In a quite spectacular fluke the bottle catches one of them right between the eyes, exploding to spray glass and blood all over his friends. He crashes down onto his back, squealing and clutching his face.

The rest of them stand there for a second, stunned and stupid, unable to understand what has just happened. It's plenty of time for me to close the gap and literally fling myself into them. The guy I collide with grapples with me but I've completely lost control now and bite rabidly at his face. By the time several huge hands drag me off him I can taste hot, thick copper on my tongue and now that guy's squealing too.

They're holding me up by my arms while another one comes at me front on, but this just lets me flail a huge kick right up into his balls. He crumples and I manage to get my other knee up into his face before he falls away. I think I'm laughing but then something heavy explodes over the back of my head. They drop me and I tumble forward, ending up on all fours, dazed by the pain.

I reach back to where it hurts and find the back of my skull studded with weird little alien objects, strange little hard things bitten into my scalp. I run my fingertips over the strange texture, confused, but their edges bite into fingertips. I bring my hand back to examine it and find little gaping red mouths slashed across my fingers.

Just as I realise I've been glassed another glass hits me, this time knocking me sideways and down and almost but not quite unconscious. I cut my hands even more as I can't help but cradle the new wound and then it goes dark and I look up.

They're crowded in over me now and before I can grab a leg or do any more damage the stomping begins. Blunt, heavy blows rain down over and over all over me. I feel bones break and other things burst and tear inside me.

I feel it all slipping away and now I think I might be smiling. I stop trying to protect myself and relax, welcoming each boot into me. It feels right to be under these feet, they're going to kill me and then I'll be done. I'm waving goodbye to all those memories now and thinking that I did it, I escaped it all in the end.

But now they've stopped and people are shouting. I think I hear John the landlord roaring about calling the police. I imagine him waving his bat. There are other voices too but they're all blurred together. In and amongst I can pick out shocked questions and sympathy and the word ambulance throbs in and out.

Now there's a voice much closer than the rest. It's young and male and wavering but I don't recognise it.

"Don't worry mate," trembles the voice with thinly restrained hysteria. A kindly hand lands on my shoulder. "You'll be right, we'll get you to hospital. You'll be right, you'll be right"

His hand on me feels warm and strange. Everything is sliding in and out blackness now, strange snapshots sickly and drunken. The hand and the voice are always there though, every time, even as the pubhubbub fades to be replaced by distant sirens.

I know I'm going to die, I can feel that I'm broken inside, but the hand and the voice are still hopeful and somehow that makes me a little hopeful too. The siren grows ever louder but now I can feel the final slip. This time the blackness will be forever and as I slide willingly, happily under, the voice comes closer still until it's whispering tearful right in my ear.

"Thank you," it says.

The intensity of the memory made the world seem suddenly dull and pretend. I sighed as it left me, waving it off by absently running my sore hand over my head, noting as always the bumpy little scars under my hair. The temptation to wallow, to actively dredge up more scenes like that was powerful but remembering the lad and his car I pulled back from it and took a long, deep breath.

I told myself I just needed a little time and a little faith, that I'd work it out in another minute or two, that it would come. In the meantime a change of scene seemed like a good idea so I stepped back out into the night, this time relishing the sudden nip of the air as a welcome distraction.

Pointing my feet at the near distant glow of the petrol station, I let them do their thing and was quickly lost in thought. As I ambled along I went back over all the connections and assumptions from the car park and began to realise that all the dead ends looked similar. It all fell down on the same point, the passenger. I didn't know enough about him yet in that I didn't really know anything at all. I stalled and returned to the night.

The petrol station was close enough now for me to be able to make out the details of the forecourt. At the nearest pump was a tired looking, middle aged woman, jaundice under the fluorescent lights and leaning against her car as it sucked greedily at the station's teat. She was staring blankly and in that moment looked utterly broken within. It was as if somewhere along the line she'd stopped being a person and become a shuddering series of drab mechanical moments instead.

Sadness elbowed its way into the moment and I found myself hoping hard that she was just having a rough night. I wished that her blank stare, her slumped, defeated shoulders, weren't her whole life and realised in my wishing, that behind that hope lay fear.

I realised that looking at her terrified me. It was the thought of total defeat and the zombie life that came after, of drowning without death. It was unbearable, unthinkable, but a distant voice behind me whispered the incessant truth. No-one can run forever.

247

Shivering with what I preferred to believe was the cold, I squinted and stepped onto the brightly lit petrol station forecourt. Over at the window a small, round man, almost as wide as he was tall, was talking to the cashier while the tired looking woman had finished wearily pumping and was now wearily standing behind him. I crossed the forecourt to stand behind her and the three of us became a queue.

Somehow she even looked depressed from behind.

I turned on the spot, running my eyes over everything around me, the pumps, the cars, the signs, the floor. Occasionally a car would slide pass and the low rolling sound of the tyres on the road would throb in and then out of the station. They all ran straight along the main road, none turning onto the smaller road, none even slowing down.

I looked back at the route I'd taken along the pavement and could just about make out my car in the distant shadows. My eyes rested on the spot where my thoughts had stalled, where I'd become distracted by the tired woman and fallen back towards the fear.

Another deep breath, I closed my eyes. I did know some things about the passenger. He was a young white guy who was probably an arsehole and probably wasn't from in this part of town. It wasn't a lot but it felt different now. I suddenly felt like there was now something else, an additional piece that I'd missed and would spot if only I could look at it right.

The guy at the front of the queue appeared in the corner of my eye as he turned from the window and set off back to his car with an arm full of confectionery. I looked at him as he wheezed and rolled as if limping with both legs.

His trousers were just a little too long so that the hems caught the floor at the back as he walked. I was reminded of the belt at my middle, made necessary by the fact that the only jeans I could ever find long enough were always far too big in the waist.

This guy clearly had the opposite problem and subsequently small semicircles of grime had spread upwards from the back of the hem of his trousers, dragged into the fabric from dirty pavements and grimy,

248

oil stained petrol station forecourts. The woman stepped up to the window and I absently shuffled after her, still distracted by the feeling of missing something obvious.

Turning back to face front, I looked over the woman's shoulder and drove my eye into and around the store beyond. By day petrol stations were drab and sterile, pale imitations of cosy newsagents or mighty supermarkets. After dark however, once those miniature aisles were all lit up and locked away, unavailable but on display, then suddenly they became magical caves of brightly coloured treasures.

I began to wonder if I wanted a drink, maybe some crisps and sandwich or something but then stopped again, stopped everything and slowly turned back away from all the gaudy treats. The concrete at my feet was littered with smooth dark stains and occasional flashes of texture from tyres.

Two pumps over from where I was standing however, in an amongst the rash of smudges, lay a long tear drop and a smaller but perfect circle, glistening a little more than the rest. He'd come here, the passenger come driver, he'd stopped here after leaving his partner for dead back in the car park. From the way the tell tale shapes were arranged I could even see which way the car had been parked.

The woman had finished paying and looked miserable about it as she passed me heading back to her car. I stepped up to the window, all thoughts of additional treats now forgotten. "Ten B&H and some silver Rizlas please," I said into the little grill and smiled at the surly young lad beyond the glass.

With the slightest of nods he turned away, utterly disinterested, and moved along the counter to retrieve the fags and skins. I retrieved a few banknotes from my wallet and waited for him to return. Behind me I heard the woman's car rumble to life then drift out and away into the night. Taking just as long as he felt like, the lad made his way back to the window and casually cast my purchases down in front of him.

"Any fuel?" he asked robotically. I glanced over my shoulder and then looked at him, there wasn't a single car on the forecourt. He wasn't even looking at me.

"No," I said. "No fuel."

"Anything else?" was next, again without even a hint of presence.

"Yeah actually," I said. I described the car and pointed out where it had been parked, asked him what he remembered about the driver. He looked at me for a moment with cold, dead eyes and then simply told me how much I owed as if I'd never asked him anything.

I held a couple of twenties and a ten over the sliding tray. "Keep the change?" I asked.

His eyes locked on the notes and suddenly his face came to life. He licked his lips while his eyes darted about over my shoulders. He leaned towards the window a little so as to talk quietly through the grill.

"He was a cock," he hissed. I nodded then raised my eyebrows at the pause that followed. That was not worth half a ton and we both knew it. Eventually he sighed and whispered again.

"Quite tall, dark hair, ring on his little finger," he stood back from the grill again, still flat and reserved but looking at little hopeful too. It still wasn't enough.

"How much fuel did he buy?" I asked, glancing back over to the spots that marked the spot.

"Not much, hardly any in fact, just topping it up probably, piece of shit that it was," he said. "He'd probably get more for it in scrap than he spent on the fuel."

I nodded past his opinions and pushed on to more facts.

"He buy anything else?" I asked. The lad's face hardened.

"Nope," he said, suddenly becoming almost animated. "Wanker, he had me bring him like every box of chocolates and every stuffed toy we've got so he could look at them and then didn't buy any of them. Said none of them were good enough and why didn't we sell classier shit."

"Sounds like a dick," I agreed. "Which way did he go?"

The lad pointed over his shoulder to tell me the wanker had turned right at the crossroads. I dropped the notes into the tray and watched as the lad quickly pulled it through. He swapped the notes for my fags and skins then returned the tray to my side of the glass and his attention to a tiny TV under the counter. We were done.

Satisfied I gathered up the supplies and dropped them into my pockets before setting off back towards the car. With each step I picked through what the lad had told me, adding it to the pile and seeing where it led me.

Not a lot of fuel, what did that say? Short of cash maybe? Except for the heavy bags obviously but he wouldn't've wanted to break into that, so short of cash in pocket? But no, he'd intended to buy other stuff, the most expensive stuff in the place in fact.

Topping up the tank the lad had said but that didn't make sense either. This guy was on the run from an almost suicidal job and had just screwed over his only ally. He was doing one with an almost full tank but took the time and the risk to stop and and top it up?

The glow of the petrol station was fading again now as I moved deeper into the shadows. Maybe he'd stopped for those other items not the fuel but then why put any in at all? As my own ride slowly faded into full view it occurred to me to wonder how much I had in that tank. I decided there was probably enough, I wasn't going far and then I just ditch it anyway.

And there it was.

His car, the lad's car actually, was nearly dry so he'd had to stop. He hadn't put much in though because he knew he'd be dumping it somewhere he wouldn't need much to get to, somewhere relatively close by. The thought sat well with me and made me smile, partly because it seemed to make the most sense but mostly because it suggested that he hadn't left town and that I still had a chance.

Reaching the car, I put this minor success to one side and considered what else had been said. The car door clicked open then clunked shut and I drummed my fingers on the wheel as I pondered, ignoring the pain in my palm. The gifts, the not good enough gifts, who were they for? Girl, boy, didn't matter, it was someone who was hard to impress, someone he was desperate to impress.

And after all, what's more desperately impressive than hundreds of thousands of pounds in violently stolen cash? I sat back in the driver's seat and landed my palms on my brow before running them over my head. What else could be so all consuming as to drive someone to take such insane risks and burn such valuable bridges? What else but love?

No, not love, not quite. If it were love would he have taken such risks? The job had been and continued to be suicidal, with large numbers of very heavy people now out for his blood and probably that of anyone close to him. It was too desperate a move.

It was unrequited love, that was it.

As soon as he'd jumped the driver and left the car park he'd've made a beeline to ditch the car and present his beloved with several hundred thousand gifts, all stuffed into two heavy black holdalls. It would be enough money elevate them from their lives, to overcome all those obstacles he thought were keeping them apart. Of course the only real obstacle was the one to which he was blind, the fact that they just weren't that into him.

I pulled on my seatbelt and started the engine, feeling nice and relaxed as it all unfolded in front of me. Whoever the object of the lad's affections was, their expensive tastes probably extended to their home. Since he was now on his own and unlikely to be able to carry both of those heavy bags very far, he was probably going to ditch the car within short walking distance.

Slowly rolling out onto the road I straightened up and crept back towards the petrol station, one hand on the wheel the other on the gear stick as the crossroads approached. The lad in the station had said the guy had turned right. To me that said waterfront penthouse out the bottom end of town rather than plush hotel in the centre and there weren't all that many of them.

I slowed even further as I rolled up to the junction, mechanically checking each way but really thinking about the odd alleys and yards that hid in the shadows of the apartment blocks down on the river. It was just a case of working my way through them systematically until I found where he had left the car.

Suddenly I felt something cold, something wrong, a hole. What if he didn't just ditch the car, what if he torched it? For a moment I sat there, indicating right but going nowhere. I thought about the contents of the boot of that car and then another chill ran through me.

There was something else, something worse.

My jaw dropped, my eyes widened.

I'd been a fool, a ridiculous, disastrous fool! I should have thought of it in the pub, before gear or girls or walking in their shoes, it should have been the very first thing to occur to me. It was obvious, painfully obvious, but was it too late?

Flicking the indicator the other way I tore the rickety old bucket of shit I'd stolen round to the left, pushing the poor old thing so hard that for a few seconds its arse wiggled manically. I straightened it out as I climbed through the gears though, blurring the streets on either side and cursing every second between me and my destination.

Never underestimate your own potential to fuck things up. I'd been so set on taking things easy, so convinced that cool and calm would win the race that I'd missed the most obvious place to start. I kept my foot down for a few uneventful miles more while the buildings began to thin out until there was nothing but a few boarded up husks and the odd scrawny tree.

Up ahead I could make out the large low buildings of the Blackroyd Industrial Estate, huddled in the gloom and soon after came the right turn I'd been waiting for. Just for a second I noted how quickly I had managed to make it all the way across the city on the empty streets with no crosstown traffic to slow me down.

I wound through the estate, twisting and turning between warehouses and old factories before finally drawing up at the gates of a chicken wire fence.

Killing the engine but leaving the lights on, I lurched out of the car and made straight for the gates, rattling them and calling out desperately. The cold night swallowed my voice and for minute after agonising minute it felt as if I was the only person left in the world. The wind whipped cruel about me, mocking me with its chill and gently rattling the huge tin sign that hung precariously a few feet above my head.

Though faded and dented, the sign still valiantly proclaimed, " eve's reckers Y rd" and I knew that in broad daylight faint outlines of the missing letters would be just about visible. I kicked at the gate and called out again, squinting hopelessly through the wire at the mighty piles of long ruined vehicles that reached up to the sky, obviously unable to spot that car I was looking for and yet trying anyway.

Eventually a tiny shaft of light appeared within the compound, bouncing and flickering as it approached. I continued to rattle the gates impatiently as a dumpy figure emerged from the gloom, coming slow and cautious as the thin beam of torchlight bounced excitedly ahead.

"C'mon Evey," I called again, irritated. "It's an emergency love, I'm on a fucking clock here..." But as the figure finally reached the gates the torch in her hand illuminated puffy, tear stained features and a shotgun in the crook of her arm. I shut the hell up and felt my heart sink in silence instead.

Evey's name wasn't actually Evey, it was Jane or Joan or something like that, I'd never been quite sure. Her husband Steve had owned the wreckers yard originally but had died many year's before and she'd run the place ever since. It was the missing letters from the sign that had christened her Eve and somehow it had stuck so that now anyone who knew anyone round here called her Evey.

Steve had been a big burly bloke but Evey had made him look like a wimp. Arms as thick as my thighs and a face like the bottom of an old fashioned kettle, she could be the warmest, kindest person you'd ever meet but get on the wrong side of her and she'd knock you out soon as look at you.

256

"Have you got her?" she asked, quietly but with a quaver that betrayed the hysteria bubbling just below the surface. I felt the confusion play across my face and opened my mouth but before I had chance to speak she asked me again.

"Have you got her? Do you know where she is? Have they hurt her?" The quaver grew stronger and fresh tears began to flow.

"Evey love," I said carefully, eyeing the shotgun all the while. "I don't know what you're on about. Is it Lucy?" From her reaction I saw that Lucy was exactly what it was and immediately began to put the the pieces together, cursing myself yet again. I wasn't Evey's first visitor of the night.

"They took her," she said before falling forwards against the gate to sob, her knees apparently giving way.

"Ah Christ," I said, rubbing my forehead and wincing at her pain. "Look," I tried, "just..." but in a moment she had composed herself, straightened up and moved the shotgun into both hands, clasping the torch alongside the barrel so that it glared in my eyes.

"What the fuck do you want Kaz?" her voice was perfectly steady now, perfectly steady and fucking furious. I licked my lips, trying not to look directly into the torch while wondering what to say.

"I'm looking for a car," I said simply. "It was used in a job earlier tonight and I need to get it back."

"You bastard," she breathed and I heard the shotgun's hammers click back. I immediately took a step back from the gate, raising my hands as I did so.

"You fucking bastard," she continued. "They sent you didn't they? Told them I'd listen to you didn't you? Well I've already told them everything I know so they can just give her back. Give her back!"

This last was screeched and for a second I cringed, honestly expecting the roar of the shotgun to follow. It didn't come however, she just stood there, blinding me with the torch and fuming. I lowered my hands and took a breath, my mind racing ahead.

The lads had local knowledge, so where else would they have brought the car so as to dispose of the evidence? Unfortunately I'd taken too long to come to this most obvious conclusion and if Evey had already crushed it for them then my the lad really was proper fucked.

In the meantime one, the other or both of the gangs had beaten me to it. Evey hadn't told them what they'd wanted to hear, either because she genuinely didn't know or for reasons of her own, and by the sounds of it they'd taken Evey's teenage daughter Lucy with them in order to loosen her tongue.

"Ok, Evey, look," I began, keeping my voice low and level. "You know me yeah? I'm not working for anyone alright. The lads that pulled that job, they nicked my mate's car to do it. I don't give a shit about them, I just have to get his car back, have to Evey, otherwise he's dead."

I paused for breath but she said nothing. We stood in silence as the seconds ticked by, the blinding glare of the torch, and the shotgun it contained, wavered just a little.

"Please Evey," I said, feeling my heart quicken. "Just tell me, have you crushed that car tonight?" I clenched everything I had and waited.

"You're not with them?" she asked quietly after a while.

"I swear down," I said as the tension crushed me from within.

"And it's just the car you're after?" she asked again.

"Just the car, that's all I need," I said quickly. We lapsed back into silence as she apparently thought about it.

"I'm sorry Kaz," she said eventually and my stomach dropped, but then, "I can't say."

As my rollercoaster guts swung back up I felt anger flare inside me.

"What?" I said, failing to keep the edge from my voice.

"Look, I haven't crushed that car tonight alright, that's all I'm saying, nothing else." She lowered the torch and the shotgun. Red shadows still blinded me but as they faded her face came back into view.

"So you do have it?" I asked desperately.

"I'm saying nowt more about it Kaz," she said, sad but defiant.

"Evey," I began. "What the fuck..."

"They took our Lucy!" she yelled, suddenly furious again. "They took her and now they've got her and god knows what they're doing to her!" Just for a second a sob broke through the words but almost instantly she pushed it back down and continued.

"Go and get her Kaz," she said quietly. "You get her and bring her back here and I'll tell you everything I know about that car."

"But Evey," I tried. "How am I..."

"The club," she snapped, before settling calm again. "I heard one of them say something about taking her to the club." It occurred to me immediately that this would be the lap dancing club down near Jimmy's bookies. I sighed.

"Right, but y'know love," I could hear the pleading tone in my voice and didn't much like it. "There's one of me and a shitload of them and they're all pissed off and..." Despite all the fury her eyes were still wet.

"Please Kaz," she said. "I don't know what else to do."

I closed my eyes for a second. How could I possibly rock up to a club full of tooled up, pissed off gangsters and single handedly take back Evey's daughter without getting one or both of us killed? I opened my eyes and looked at her again.

How could I not try?

Fuck.

"Alright," I said quietly. "I'll go and have a look." Her eyes lit up and she drew breath to speak but I beat her to it.

"No promises mind," I said and then, muttering to myself as I moved back to the car, "probably get myself fucking killed in the process but whatever."

I slammed the car door in beside me and cursed wildly as the engine decided it needed three attempts at ignition before turning over. Evey and the yard quickly faded in my rear view as I weaved my way back through the industrial estate towards town.

I didn't need this, the night was slipping by too quickly now and with it the lad's chances of survival. A heavy tension laid itself across my shoulders and brow and began the long, slow process of crushing me under its weight and to top it all off my hand was killing me too.

As shapes and shadows flashed past outside, something within me recoiled, resenting the sense of compulsion. This is what happens when you get involved in the lives of others instead of just keeping to yourself. Reaching the edge of town I paused absently at a red light and thought about how great it would feel just to be in bed, full of drugs, nice and cosy and fuck the world.

I'm in bed and that's all I know. I can feel a pillow under my head and sheets on top of me. I open my eyes and see a high, light coloured ceiling that I don't recognise. The rest of my body is starting the wake up and now I realise there's pain, quite a lot of it but it's somehow distant. My brain feels like a lagged pipe, sat snug within a thick, fuzzy layer of insulation from the horrors beyond.

It's difficult to think, but as I realise that it's difficult to think that in turn helps me to recognise this strange sensation. I am high, really high, but it's a strange buzz. Everything seems soft and distant but there's no warm glow, no sleepy smudging here. The fuzz around my mind is cold, as if some of the rooms in my head are empty and bare.

I've closed my eyes again now though I've no clue for how long. Opening them, I'm staring blankly up at the same alien ceiling. I'm unable to move and my thoughts are coming slow and heavy, thick tongued and bleary eyed. This kind of high, that's what one of them is saying, I know this kind of high, rare but remembered. The words 'prescription' and 'painkillers' are here now, having floated up from somewhere, but I'm not really sure what they mean.

A little more life flows through me and I think I might even be able to move my head a bit

now. It lolls to one side and I squint out at the world. There are other beds here, other people and everything is coloured cream or pale green.

I flop my head the other way and noticed that my jaw is a little slack. Here is a figure, a skinny young lad sprawled across a chair, snoring quietly to himself. He looks familiar but I know it's beyond me to recall who he is. My eyes are closing again, I can feel myself slipping down into a cool, deep blackness.

And now I'm awake again.

I don't know how much time has passed but I feel somehow closer to my body this time, more connected to my limbs and to the pain. It sits within all of me, aching relentlessly like a growling beast. When I try to move it lashes out with spiteful bites, shards of it cutting through me.

I'm aware of it now, it's on me and so there's no escape back into the black. I open my eyes and find the young lad from before only now he's reading a magazine. His eyes flick over the top of the page and meet mine for a second before widening. He drops the magazine and leans forward.

"Hey!" he says grinning a lot, too much for my liking, especially for someone I don't know. "You're awake!"

I'm trying to ask a question but the sounds trip in my throat so that gibberish collapses off the end of my tongue. I lick my lips and realise that my mouth tastes foul.

"Don't worry," he's saying to me, leaning forward so close that I can smell the stale coffee on his breath.

"You're ok, you're in hospital. I'll go and get someone." He scampers away, clearly happy and excited about something.

I watch him go with a complete lack of comprehension. What the fuck is going on? With each second that passes the pain is building, braking over me in waves. I don't like this, I don't like this one bit. The lad is coming back now, behind him I can see a woman dressed like a nurse. Perhaps she is, did he say hospital? Here she is, standing over me, looking into me. She can see that I don't understand, she knows what's happening in my head and that worries me.

Her hands are cool and soft on my face but have a firm grip now that they've moved to my wrist. She's looking at a little upside down watch hanging from her uniform and now she's talking to the lad, talking about me I think, as if I'm not even here though I'm fairly certain that I am.

She slips one of her cool, soft hands alongside my face now, cupping my cheek. Even though it feels nice I want to resist, to push her away but my body is too complex a machine. She's leaning over me now, peering right down into me, right inside me through my eyes.

"Kaz?" she's saying, I can hear her saying it. "Kaz, do you know where you are love?"

My mouth moves a little and I wait to see if it's going to say something.

It doesn't.

"Ok Kaz," she's still saying. "It's ok, you're in hospital, we're taking care of you. Your son's here, he's been with you all the time this one, never left your side. You just rest while I go and get the doctor."

Son? But now she's gone. The skinny lad is still here though, he's watching her go and now he's moving in close. I don't understand what's happening but the pain is starting to push everything else to the side.

"Sorry about that," he's hissing at me. "I had to say you were my dad or they wouldn't let me stay. My name's John and I just had to see you were alright. Thank you so much..." but I can't listen anymore. I can see his mouth moving and I know there are sounds coming from it but this is all too much. I'm closing my eyes on all of it.

And now I'm awake again and everything makes sense, cold, empty, sickly sense. Christ I hurt, I mean every part of me hurts so that I think

I'm going to puke. Desperate for distraction I open my eyes and look around.

The ward is quiet, there's one bed over there with the curtain drawn all the way round it but otherwise people are dozing or reading. The lad, the lad from the pub carpark obviously, I know that now, is here and he's still looking happy and excited like a fucking puppy. Even just sitting there, his energy irritates me.

"Hey!" he says again. "How're you doing?"

I frown at him and lick at my brittle lips.

"...the fuck is..." I manage but as he begins to speak it's all coming back to me anyway. I'd thought they were going to kill me, in fact no, scratch that, I'd hoped they were going to kill me. But no, on it goes.

Fuck.

"...believe you did that!" he's saying. "I mean you don't even know me man! Who would do that for someone they don't even know these days? I should be lying in that bed mate, not you, I don't know what to say..."

I just about manage to lift my hand from the bed covers and wave it a little, frowning with the effort and hoping he'll take the hint.

"What's that?" he's asking earnestly, leaning in close again. "Do you need something? Shall I get the doctor?" I take a deep breath and work my jaw a little before choking out three little syllables into his ear.

"Stop. Talking." I croak.

"Oh," he says. He sits back into his chair but apparently isn't even a little offended. "Right, sorry," he continues before pressing his lips together hard but still fucking smiling.

The next few weeks pass just like this. The pain racks me day and night, the more I come back to the world the worse it gets. There's occasional oblivion when I can convince them to pound me with the hard stuff but for the most part it's just long hours of lying here, stiff and sore while this kid chatters on and on at me.

263

I'm regularly tempted to tell them that he's not my son, that I don't even know the lad but for some reason he genuinely seems to give a shit and that's not an entirely bad feeling, weird but not unpleasant. Besides, I've done a lot of things but I'm not a grass.

The novelty of being able to shit and piss in bed, wears off very quickly and as soon as I think I'm able I insist on trying for the gents. The first time I go the lad just about carries me there and back. I still don't understand his angle but I am grateful and grudgingly tell him so.

Finally the day comes when they kick me out. I get a letter about some future appointments, a few boxes of pills in a little plastic bag and off we go. The sunlight hurts my eyes as we step out on the street and the sights and sounds of the traffic are almost overwhelming.

As ever, the kid is at my elbow, flagging down a taxi and helping me inside. The world flits past the windows unchanged and I realise it has all just carried on without me as if nothing has happened. For some reason that stings.

We pull up on my street and I realise I don't have a penny on me but before I can say or do anything the lad's already paid and is opening the door to help me out. I resent having to lean on him but I know I won't be able to get to my door without him and so let him take me inside.

He eases me down into the armchair and then disappears into the kitchen and starts rattling around. The sound is irritating but I'm too tired to complain and before I know he's back again, brandishing mugs of black tea.

"No milk," he says apologetically as he hands it to me. I say nothing but take the brew and sit with it. All I want now is to be alone, to draw the curtains, lock the door, maybe find some gear and roll one and just let everything else fuck off.

"So," I say eventually when he's finished his brew, letting the word hang between us ominously.

"Oh," he says, getting to his feet immediately. "Right," but he doesn't leave.

"Look," I say with difficulty. "I really appreciate..." but I don't even know where to begin so I just say, "...everything, but I mean you must have, y'know, stuff to do...?"

He licks his lips and squirms a bit, he won't look at me. I can feel myself frowning as I watch his hands clasp at one another. He draws breath to speak but doesn't, just loiters there instead.

"You got something to say lad?" I ask eventually, the pain adding an unintentionally hard edge to my tone.

"Thing is..." he cringes and tales off, moving from one foot to the other until I being to wonder if he's desperate for a piss or something.

"What," I say, feeling genuinely tired and annoyed now. "What's the thing?"

Finally he looks at me. His eyes are wet with shame.

"I don't have anywhere to go," he says but my patience has gone.

"Ah give over," I say, my eyes closing on their own. "You must have mates or something. Get yourself to B&B for the night, I don't know..."

"Yeah," he agrees, enthusiastically at first before dropping into a smaller, quieter voice. "Yeah, I was staying with a mate actually but then his mrs wanted the sofa back so I had to leave there and then, well, that's when I asked those lads at the pub for some change and then..."

I force my eyes open to frown at him for a few seconds.

"Well since then I've just been at the hospital and I mean, yeah, a B&B, obviously, except I kind of..." he pauses and swallows. "The pills and the taxi and all that so I don't really have any..."

Something cold cuts through the growing fog and I look at him again, as if for the first time. He's younger than I'd thought and now that I really look at him I can see it all over him, bleeding through all that enthusiasm and optimism.

He's absolutely terrified.

"Fine," I say, waving a heavy hand across the room. "Sofa," I say and then blackness.

I was standing in total darkness, trying not to laugh out loud.

I'd parked the car on the narrow street that ran behind the strip club and made my way along the even narrower alley way that ran up its side, tracing my right hand along the wall to find my way through the clutter. It was more than twenty years since I had last stood in the pitch darkness in that particular alleyway, stroking the walls looking for that special spot.

There'd been girls at this club for as long as I could remember. Back when I was a lad it had been a members only gentlemen's club and the girls had done their thing in rooms in the back. These days it was a legit pole dancing club with everything up front, there was even a girl on the sign, but it was the same old game.

My fingers had run a little smoother as I passed a heavy metal fire door, before a brief return to rough brick. And then there it was. I had found what felt like exactly the same old vent cover that had become the stuff of legends when I was a kid.

I had run my fingertips underneath, thrilled by the tacky metal texture that matched my memory so well. Without having to even think about it I'd moved fingers to the middle of the base, then back out just a touch and finally up and back towards me, hard.

Sure enough the whole thing popped off the wall and leapt into my hand. Stifling the laugh, I slowly lowered the vent cover to the floor and placed it quietly on the floor. Straightening up I leaned in grinning and peered inside.

Back in the day, this had been the vent into one of the back rooms where the girls did their thing and therefore always our favourite. These days the action was all up front so that the vent now appeared to show the inside of the girls' dressing room instead.

Directly opposite I could see a row of mirrors behind chairs running left to right to a door. To the right of the door were racks of costumes. Looking to the left I

266

caught my breath. I couldn't see any more than a skinny pair of legs, but there was definitely someone sat on the tired looking sofa at the front end of the room. Judging from the patterned leggings and battered bunny slippers I was fairly sure it was a teenage girl, and therefore almost certain that it was Lucy.

I stood back from the vent and listened carefully. Lucy wasn't making a sound but I could hear voices from somewhere inside, faint but aggressive. Determined not to give myself away I groped my painfully slow way further into the alley until I found the second vent. The same procedure as before liberated this vent cover too although it was a lot less willing to leave the wall. Given that this vent had always used to show the main room of the club and therefore generally just guys sat around drinking however, this didn't really surprise me.

The moment I prised the vent cover away from the wall the voices sharpened up and sprang closer. I stared into the vent and saw that other than adding some stages and poles, the interior of the club hadn't changed much. Directly in front of me I could see a guy tied to a chair. I couldn't make out his face as he lolled away from me in a daze, but he was wearing some kind of uniform.

To my right four young guys stood in front of him arguing. Two of the lads were wearing crappy looking suits and had local accents. The taller of the two was wearing an orange tie and seemed to be trying to calm the situation down while his shorter, more aggressive partner wore a pink tie and was clearly deeply pissed off about something.

The others had their backs to me. One was wearing a white and blue shell suit that made me cringe while the other wore a leather coat that looked way too big for him. The lad in the shell suit was clutching his left ear and I noticed a vivid dark stain across his left shoulder.

"What, are you a puff or something?!" yelled The Bleeder in a strong Southern accent. Pink Tie almost exploded at this and would have stepped to The Bleeder but for Orange Tie blocking him.

"It's called being a fucking professional dickhead!"

screeched Pink Tie, his face grey with fury.

"Nah mate," crowed The Bleeder, trying to shake off his own restraint in the too Big Jacket. "You just ain't man enough to have a go, you're a fucking pussy!"

"Yeah," scoffed Pink Tie. "So says the man who's just had his fucking ear ripped off by a teenage girl."

"She hasn't ripped it off!" snapped The Bleeder, self consciously leaving his ear alone for a moment. "Little cunt just bit me a bit. It's nothing, it's a fucking scratch."

"No lad," said Pink Tie before actually spitting on the floor, his eyes wild. "Those great fucking slashes on the other side of your face are scratches. They're going to scar up right nice and all, a permanent reminder for you of the night you a little girl tore you up eh?"

"You Northern twat!" raged The Bleeder lunging at Pink Tie.

"You Southern cunt!" raged Pink Tie lunging right back at him.

The four of them wrestled for a good two minutes, their shoes squeaking on the hard floor, occasionally cutting through the grunts and curses. The guy tied to the chair appeared to have passed out and just hung limp and oblivious beside the scuffle. Eventually Orange Tie and Big Jacket were able to restrain their partners and all four fell back to pant and glare.

Orange Tie spoke first.

"Alright look," he said, still breathing heavily. "We might be here all night for all we know so let's just settle it down yeah? Why don't we get some food in and just try to chill out a bit? "

None of the others spoke but all nodded or grunted their agreement. There was a bit of back and forth about who would go get the food as it seemed neither pair wanted to leave the other with either the guy in the chair or the girl in the back. Eventually they all agreed that The Bleeder was too conspicuous to go out so Pink Tie and Big Jacket left together while Orange Tie and The Bleeder stayed behind.

Orange Tie moved to perch himself on a stool at the bar while The Bleeder returned to the guy in the chair. He looked bored, mean and pissed off as he began to slap the lad in the chair awake. I cringed for him but knew I wouldn't get a better opportunity than this. Moving quickly through the darkness I began to tap gently on the fire door.

"Lucy," I hissed, tapping a little harder. "Lucy, come on." Almost straight away I heard soft, padding footsteps and then a pause before the fire door popped open to reveal a sharp, scowling face.

"Who the fuck are you?" she asked and wrinkled her nose as if she could smell dog shit.

"Your mum sent me here to get you. Come on," I said, moving back from the door and waving to her to move past me.

"You what?" she snapped. Framed in the door, she folded her arms and set her jaw.

"We need to go," I said firmly. "Now."

She raised her eyebrows at my tone and pouted, looking utterly unimpressed.

"I don't know you," she said sourly and turned back into the room, pulling the door closed behind her.

I just managed to catch the door in time. I yanked it back open and followed her into the dressing room, blinking at the harsh strip light flickering overhead. Lucy was back on the sofa, arms folded, legs crossed at the knee and glaring at me with total contempt. For the first time I noticed her left cheek was swollen and glowing an angry red.

"What are you doing?!" I spluttered at her. "We've got to go, right now!"

"I don't have to go anywhere with you you pervy old cunt. Fuck off!" she snapped quickly, her head bobbling about. I stared at her in disbelief. Her face looked sore as hell so that I winced for her. There wasn't a hint of pain in her expression though, nothing in her eyes but rage.

"I don't even fucking know you right?" she continued, pointing at me accusingly. "And I have had enough shit off dirty bastards like you tonight to last me a fucking lifetime and I'm not having any more of it so if you think I'm running off out of here into that dark alley way with you you'd best think again."

The tirade washed over me relentlessly while my

mind reeled. At no point during the drive over as I'd considered all my options and chances, had it occurred to me that Lucy herself would be the problem. I'd expected to find a tearful, terrified child.

"You should see the last guy who tried to cop a feel of me, I bit his fucking ear off and I'll do worse to you and all, you old bastard," she was still going. "And don't you be chatting shit about my mum either. You know my mum?! I don't fucking think so!"

"I do know your mum," I interrupted, hissing and desperately trying to re-enter the conversation. "And will you keep you fucking voice down!"

"Oh do you now? Do you? Do you really?" she said, maintaining her volume and smiling spitefully with it. "Well if you know my mum so well you'll know her name then won't you."

"Evey," I replied immediately. "Your mum's name's Evey, now come with me, quickly before..."

"No, no, no, no, no," she said loudly. "Everyone who knows my mum knows that's not her real name. What's her real name eh? Eh? If you know her so well, what's her real name?"

My mouth moved but nothing came out.

I knew it was Jane or Joan or maybe Jenny, certainly a J name. "Erm," I said for bit, thinking desperately but hopelessly, secure in the knowledge that I definitely did not know. Lucy's spiteful lips tightened in triumph as she watched me struggle.

Before I could venture a guess however, I heard the door behind me and knew I was out of time. I turned to find Orange Tie standing in the now open doorway already reaching into his jacket.

"Who the fuck are you?" he said darkly. It was time for Plan B, the same Plan B as always.

Just wing it.

"Who the fuck am I?!" I roared, redirecting my irritation with Lucy and widening my eyes so that they blazed. "Who the fuck are you more like! And what the fuck are you doing?!" He paused, his hand still inside his jacket, his fierce, knitted brows loosening just a little with confusion.

"The bosses sent me to check on you lot, make

270

sure you weren't cocking things up and what do I find when I get here?" Orange Tie seemed unsure whether I expected him to answer or not but I didn't give him the chance.

"I find this lass, this lass who you're supposed to be holding here, completely unguarded. And what the fuck happened to her face? Who told you you could do that?!" He bobbed like a goldfish as I drew breath for another blast.

"I just walked in through the fucking fire door! I could have popped her, could have taken her, whatever I wanted and you dickheads wouldn't have even known I was here!" I glared at Orange Tie venomously until a voice came from behind me.

"You weren't taking nowt. I wasn't going anywhere with you," Lucy taunted, defiant. I looked back at her over my shoulder for a second with despairing questions for eyes. She just shrugged and refolded her arms.

"Erm," tried Orange Tie, frowning from Lucy to me but I cut him off. Shouting even louder and angrier than before.

"I asked you a question! What the fuck.." I screamed. "..has happened to her face?!" Any suspicions Orange Tie had been nurturing were instantly trampled by the guilt splashed across his features.

"That was one of their lot," he said, his voice suddenly smaller. "We didn't know what he was doing. We stopped him though, before..."

"Did you fuck," came the shrill heckle from behind. "You stopped nowt. By the time you lot got in here he was already on his arse crying about his ear!"

Orange Tie made to protest but then seemed to think better of it and looked down at the floor instead. I worked hard to suppress a smirk. Lucy's mockery was actually quite funny I realised, as long as you weren't on the receiving end of it.

"And what about the other lad?" I asked, maintaining the outrage. "What's happening there?"

"He's not said owt yet," said Orange Tie, still looking at the floor.

"What?!" I exclaimed as if I knew what he was talking about but couldn't believe it. "How long have you had him 'ere?"

Orange Tie actually checked his watch and swallowed before answering. "Few hours now. He's a right tough bastard, won't give us anything about the other guy he was with or what they were doing."

"A few hours!" I spluttered. "You've had that lad tied to a chair for hours and you've got nowt out of him at all?!" Orange Tie just shook his head.

"For fuck's sake," I seethed, taking a step towards him.

"Go on then," I snapped, waving a hand at him so that he backed away and then turned towards the door. "Let's see this tough guy then."

I turned to fire one last furiously pleading look at Lucy as I followed him through the door. She just raised her eyebrows and pouted again, still spitefully unimpressed.

As Orange Tie led me through into the front of the club my mind raced. I had no idea where this was going or for how long I could maintain my bluff. I just needed an edge, something I could turn to my advantage, a gap I could prise open just long enough to do one, somehow with Lucy in tow.

We stepped out onto the floor of the club just in time to see The Bleeder land a heavy, wet sounding blow on the lad tied to the chair. Hearing us arrive he turned and frowned upon seeing me.

"Who's this?" he said, still breathless from the beating he'd just delivered.

"From the bosses," said Orange Tie, hovering off to my right now as I looked The Bleeder up and down and made a show of looking unimpressed.

The Bleeder looked surprised but seemed to accept it and moved away from the lad in the chair to take a seat of his own. For the first time I got a good look at the lad and though it was hard to make out his features under all the blood and the swelling, the moment I saw his face I knew exactly what to do.

"So you've been battering this lad for hours and he's given you nowt right?" I looked from The Bleeder to Orange Tie and back again. Both nodded their heads.

"Fucking hell," I said in a low, disgusted voice.

"You really don't know owt about owt do you?"

I looked over the lad in the chair in more detail. Despite my display of derision, it seemed as if they had worked him pretty hard. His face was bloated and bruised almost beyond recognition and all but one of the fingers on his left hand were badly broken. I had no idea who the lad was protecting but I was impressed.

"Right then," I said, tilting my head to one side until my neck cracked. "You two, come and sit here, watch how a professional does it." I waited until they grudgingly dragged chairs across the floor and sat on either side of me, facing the lad.

I stepped in and took his chin in my hand. His eyes were glassy and rolling so I slapped him a couple of times until they sharpened and finally focussed on me. Then I leant right in until my lips were almost touching his ear and began to to whisper. I spoke to him for a good half a minute and then took a couple of steps backwards so that I was stood back between The Bleeder and Orange Tie.

The lad's eyes were wide and trembling now, or at least as wide as they could be, and still locked on me. For a moment he said nothing and a thick silence lay across all four of us. Then came a quiet dripping sound that grew to a trickle.

"Ah Christ!" said The Bleeder. "He's pissing himself!"

Sure enough, a small puddle was growing on the floor beneath lad's chair. Orange Tie looked from the lad to stare at me with a mixture of awe and fear. Before he could say anything though, the lad in the chair had started talking, talking fast as if he couldn't get the words out quick enough.

"Urgh, urgh, ok, ok, alright. I'll tell you, I'll tell you, just don't, don't let him, ergh, ergh..." he looked over at me for a second before dropped his eyes back to the floor and continuing desperately.

"Two lads, two lads, known one of them for years, never met the other, argh. It were them, it were them who robbed you..." he paused for breath, panting and dripping.

The Bleeder and Orange Tie were transfixed, both

sitting open mouthed as they listened to the lad spill his guts. I moved quietly away from them to lean against the bar behind them and watch the show.

"First one, oh, oh fuck, first one, called Bradley, went to school with him, urgh fuck," he spat on the floor and groaned. "He went to uni down South, I didn't even know he were back until I saw him at work earlier tonight. His parents still live here, little detached place on some cul-de-sac somewhere, I don't remember it exactly, but he's, ooh..." the lad paused to gasp and sigh.

I watched him go and smiled a little. What I'd said to him had clearly had the desired effect and I was impressed with the effort he was making, the level of detail was great.

"He's probably with his mrs, some posh bird lives in one of them luxury apartments down the bottom end of town." The lad slumped and for a moment it looked like he'd passed out.

"Oi!" snapped The Bleeder, rousing the lad again. "And the rest of it," he added, his eyes locked on the lad's now quivering form.

As the lad drew breath to carry on with his confession I eased myself off the bar stool, picked it up and then carried it and an empty pint glass from the bar very carefully, silently even, towards the door that led through into the back.

"The other lad, don't know him, never met him. Local I think, I heard he either lives on the Oaklands Estate or he's got friends there, grargh..." he thrashed against his bonds for a second in frustration at the pain.

"If he's still in town he's probably there. The first lad will have screwed him over, probably just stomped him in the car park and left with the money. Someone on the estate will know him."

Again the lad slumped to hang limp against his restraints. This time it was Orange Tie who pressed him while I very carefully placed the stool on the floor and opened the door nice and wide.

"What about the guy you were with when you got gripped? Who's he?" Orange Tie was leaning forwards in his chair now, fully focussed and deadly serious.

274

"Oh him," wheezed the lad. "He's no-one, just some old pisshead I've known for years, think's he's fucking clever."

"Who's he working for?" Orange Tie snapped back instantly while The Bleeder bristled.

"He doesn't work for anyone," said the lad with disdain. "Thinks he's a freelancer but really he's just a nosy bastard, sticking his oar into everything. He's no-one, he's not part of it."

From the silence that followed I guessed that The Bleeder and Orange Tie were both thinking hard, desperate to find the right question, the question their bosses would want asking, now that their prisoner was being so obliging. It was The Bleeder who spoke up first.

"Why are you telling us all this? What did he say to you?" he said. The silence thickened and I could almost see the two of them leaning forward in their chairs, curiosity holding their breath.

"He said," the lad just about managed, clearly broken and exhausted from his ordeal. "He said I should be afraid, more afraid than I've ever been in my life. And he said I should tell you everything, all of it, much as I knew and then some, and that I should take my time doing it too."

"But why? What did he say he'd do if you didn't?" Orange Tie was just as desperate to know the secret.

"Nowt," replied the lad cryptically before pausing dramatically. "He just said I should keep you dickheads distracted long enough for him to get away with that lass out of the back."

For a second there was no sound but the rasping chuckle of the lad in the chair. I could just imagine The Bleeder and Orange Tie starting, snapping their necks round to look for me at the empty bar, then at wide open door and finally at one another.

They dashed for the door, one of them even knocking over his chair in the process. I waited for their footsteps to thunder past then, from my hiding place behind the door, quickly pushed it closed and wedged the stool under the handle. I broke the pint glass against the door and turned to face my friend Danny with a grin.

"Fancy a stroll?" I said.

"Just get me out here," he wheezed. "That'll not hold 'em for long."

Sure enough, by the time I'd used what was left of the pint glass to cut through his bonds, the door through to the back of the club was taking a pounding. I could hear The Bleeder and Orange Tie raging on the other side and knew that in a few minutes more the safety barrier I'd created would be no more than splinters.

"Great job mate," I said as I untangled the mess of thin rope. "All that stuff about knowing one of them from school? And pissing yourself was nice touch too. How did you manage that?"

"You kidding?" he wheezed, rubbing his red raw wrists. "They've had me tied to this chair for hours. I were absolutely busting!"

I got one of Danny's arms over my shoulder and heaved him to his feet. He'd taken a fairly serious beating but thankfully it had all been from the waist up so that he was able to lope alongside me pretty well as we made for the front door. Out on the street I made a call and pushed some banknotes into Danny's hand.

"There'll be a taxi round the corner by the takeaway in a couple of minutes. Take it and get out of town till this all calms down yeah?" I laid my hand on his shoulder and grimaced my sympathy.

" 'kin hell Kaz," he wheezed while trying to smile. "You are something else, you know that?"

"We don't have time for this mate, just get yourself in that cab. We'll catch up some other time." I retrieved my hand and glanced down at my phone, looking for the next number I needed to call.

"Alright mate but look," he grabbed hold of my wrist so that I stopped what I was doing and stared at him. "It wasn't your fault."

My expression must have shown him that I had no idea what the hell he was talking about so he took another breath and tried again.

"Back at the hotel, me getting gripped, you had to leg it, it wasn't your fault. You didn't have to do this," he squeezed my wrist and his eyes shone.

"The hotel?" I asked, confused. "I've been nowhere near The George tonight lad. They must have hit you harder than I thought."

Danny just grinned, releasing my wrist and turning to leave with a wink.

"Course you haven't," he called back to me as he went. "My mistake."

I returned my attention to my phone, shaking my head to dismiss his weirdness and making it to the corner of the street just as I heard footsteps and curses spill out behind me. My thumb jabbed the call to life as I raced around the next corner so that my excuse for a car came back into view.

Plunging back into the alley way I told the worried voice on the end of the line to wait a minute before wrenching the fire door open and stepped back into the dressing room, thrusting my phone at Lucy. Scowling all the while, she accepted the phone cautiously and raised it to her ear, never taking her eyes off me.

"...but mum!" she hissed, her voice suddenly softer and smaller. "I didn't know did I? He didn't even know your... yeah alright."

She handed me the phone and glared at me.

"Well?" she snapped. "Go on then!"

I raced back out of the fire door, down the alley and across the street to the car. Leaping inside I turned the key before Lucy had even opened her door and sent us lurching forward before she had chance to close it again.

As we sped through the night I tried to slow my pounding heart while Lucy slumped down in her seat and sulked behind folded arms. For the first few miles I checked my rear view every few seconds but as I put more and more corners and distance between us and the club I gradually began to relax.

"You alright?" I asked eventually as we headed back towards the Blackroyd Estate. "How's your face?"

"Fuck off, pervert!" Lucy snapped, shifting in her seat to look away from me out of her window.

"Fair enough," I said and returned my full focus to the road, trying to ignore the paling colours of the Eastern sky.

As I pulled up to the yard gates Evey was was already unlocking them. By the time I stepped out of the car they were already hugging. Evey inspected the welt on Lucy's face before weeping into her daughter's hair while Lucy mumbled and squeaked into the bulk of her mother's shoulder.

It was touching and everything but the lad's life was still dangling in the balance and the clock was ticking ever louder. Evey finally glanced up at me from within the hug and I raised my eyebrows expectantly. She whispered something to Lucy who seemed to initially object but after another second of hissing and a little poke from her mother she eventually turned to look at me.

"Thanks and that," she said flatly, still managing to scowl. "For, y'know.." and with that she turned and walked into the yard. Evey watched her go with wet, adoring eyes. I waited until Lucy was well inside and out of ear shot before stepping closer to Evey but she was on me with a bear hug before I could open my mouth.

"Oh thank you Kaz!" she said. Her voice wavered in a way I'd never heard so that she sounded like someone else. "Thank you so much! I don't what I do if I ever lost her. Oh god I was so scared, so scared..."

I attempted to break free but it was like being bound in rolls of carpet so I just waited instead.

"I can't ever repay you Kaz, bringing her back to me..." she was still teary but to my relief the emotions seemed to have peaked.

"Oh I think you can love," I said, determined as she finally released me and I took a step back. "You can give me that car."

Evey began to say something but then stopped, staring down at the floor like a child chastised. My stomach clenched. This wasn't good.

"Evey..." I said, half asking, half warning.

"I'm so sorry Kaz," she said, looking me right in the eye now so that I could see she meant it. "I didn't know what to do, I just had to get her back." I found I was shaking my head as my jaw went slack and tiny prickles ran up my arms and neck.

"I didn't exactly lie to you love," she continued, cringing her guilt. "I haven't crushed that car tonight..." she paused to look wretched. I strained my expression of disbelief a little further to nudge her on.

"In fact, I haven't even seen it," said finished.

"Fuck!" I roared, turning to land a couple of heavy kicks on my wreck's back bumper. "Fucking fuck!"

"They never came here, I've not seem 'em," she wittered on while I pinched the bridge of my nose and thought hard behind closed eyes. "I told those bastards, over and over I told them, they just didn't believe me, that's why they took Lucy. I'm so sorry love, what can I do? Can I get you another one? I bet I've one just the same in the yard somewhere..."

"Forget it," I snapped, moving back round the car and opening the door.

"But Kaz!" Evey pleaded. "What could I do? She's my daughter."

I paused and took a breath before looking at her.

"You're alright Evey love," I said more gently. "It's ok, I get it. It's not your fault."

I dropped back into the driver's seat and pulled the door in beside me, my heart racing. Of course I still had the original plan, searching through likely dumping sites down the bottom end of town, I just no longer had the time to check them all. Now I needed to be lucky and somehow that didn't feel like a good place to be. I started the engine and rolled down the window.

"You know they're going to come back here," I said to Evey. "I left them a bit confused but sooner or later they're going to get their shit together and then they're probably going to come back for both of you. You need to get out of town, sharpish."

"I know," Evey nodded. "I told her to go and pack a bag, we're going. And I am sorry Kaz, I..."

"I'll see you later Evey," I cut her off. "Be lucky," I said and managed to force a smile before swinging the car round and heading back into town, again.

I drove as fast as I dared, ever vigilant for unwanted, blue lit attention. At the same time I tried desperately to explore in my mind's eye all the various dark corners and dead end alleyways towards which I was racing.

A thought occurred again and again, the idea that I should just call the lad right now, call him and tell him

279

to run. Every time it came around however I had to face the reality that the idea was not a solution. It might buy him some time but it would mean a life on the run, tearing up the few fragile roots he'd managed to put down and forever looking over his shoulder. Well, not forever obviously, eventually they'd find him.

I had to fix this.

I had to get his car back for him so that we could deliver what was in the boot on time, so that the people he was involved with would never know, so that his new found life could continue. So that he could continue, I had to. I owed him that much, in fact I owed him much more.

Eventually he left. I'm sat in my bedsit drinking hard, smoking hard and enjoying the silence. After months of him hanging about the place, trying to wait on me hand and foot, chatting shit day in, day out, the lad has finally gone.

I have to admit that it was handy to have him around for those first few weeks after I got home. He helped me in and out of bed, even took me to the toilet for the first few days for fuck's sake. He picked up my prescriptions, cooked meals whether I asked him to or not, even when I told him not to actually.

He kept us stocked with booze and gear, poured the drinks, rolled the joints. He even had a go at tidying the place up a bit and all the while he would talk and talk. He'd had a shitty life by all accounts, always battered or neglected then passed on and passed on and yet he just laughed and joked all the time.

It did my fucking head in.

Once I was back on my feet I had a word with some people and got him a bit of work with Jimmy the Jack's crew. Nothing hairy, just running and fetching. He wanted to pay rent but I knew the kind of cash he'd be making and if I'd taken rent out of it he'd've ended up living here forever. Last week I managed to get him a room in a house with some other lads I knew. It's just a mile down the road and yesterday he moved in and I finally got my place back.

I felt good to back in the black, sat here in the darkness, slowly wrecking myself. It's easy and safe and comfortable. It's home. The lad's relentless positivity had just been starting to drag me out, back into all that hassle, all that fake bullshit the world has to offer.

It feels good sometimes, but ultimately it's a con. It's always a con and you always end up back here, back in the hole, cursing yourself for letting it happen. Better to just stay here from the start. No expectations. No disappointment.

I find myself hoping he's having a good time. He seemed to get on with those lads and they're all decent enough. It's better that he has some mates his own age, it was starting to get a bit weird him hanging around me all the time, not knowing anyone else.

I realise that I am glad I could help him on, help him get himself a life to live. He can move on now, meet some lasses, or lads, whatever he likes, make some solid friends and stop bugging me. He said he'd back round to hang out later in the week but that'll soon go. Now he's safe and settled he's no reason to spend time with me any more.

And that's good, really it is.

It's good to be alone. I can rest, I can breathe, I can just be. I can get back to where I was before. Funny that, I hadn't thought of the gun hidden in this chair for months now. It's sat there right now, just a few inches below my arse, waiting for me.

My face twists into disgust at the thought of it, of how I fucked it up last time. I couldn't do it, I wussed out like a little bitch. It'd've been better if I hadn't've woken up after those lads in the car park, then it would have just been done with. Over. Though I suppose it had worked out like that then I wouldn't have been here to help the lad out.

But someone else would've. There're better people in the world than me for fuck's sake. He'd've been right. Besides, he's sorted now anyway, settled and safe and moving on, so what's keeping me here now?

I move to pour myself another drink but find the bottle's empty. I check my pockets and find that I'm almost out of gear again as well. I decide to take a stroll down to the local and see who fancies buying me a pint or two or even front me a bit of gear. I don't realise just how wasted I am until I stand up and the room lurches about around me. I take a breath and widen my eyes, trying to clear my head just a little.

It doesn't work.

I stumble about a bit, gathering up my jacket and keys. I leave my phone on the bed, deciding I don't need it. There's no-one I particularly want to talk to and who's going to ring me? I close the door behind me but the key decides to be awkward when I try to lock it. In the end I give up and wander outside, stroking my keys against my jacket a few times before finally getting them into my pocket. They just don't seem to want to go in anywhere tonight.

It's the same old walk to the local, I don't even really remember it by the time I get there, except for a graze on my face where a wall jumped into me on my way down the hill. It's not very busy and it doesn't take me long to do the rounds of the regular faces.

I end up with a pint so I'm happy enough. I sit in the corner and nurse it, unsure where the next one will come from. Somewhere inside me something is burning sick, it's a long way down under all the blurring fog but I can still feels hints of it niggling.

It was their faces, those regular faces, when they saw me coming, when I slapped them on the back and part joking, but mostly serious, asked if they were going to get me a drink. They didn't scowl, none of them, there were no hating looks, it was all just soft eyes and pity.

As if they give a shit!

I can see some of them talking about me now, occasionally glancing over as I sip my way through my freebie. That burning turns sour so that I suddenly realise I hate them, all of them, even the pretty lass behind the bar who sometimes forgets to add drinks onto my tab on purpose. In my head I call them all fuckers and suppose it makes them feel good inside to feel sorry for other people.

For the first time, I notice that there's a lot of noise coming from the other room. I drain my glass and stand carefully before tottering through to have a look. I make a point of not meeting anyone's eye and wear what I'm pretty sure is the cool expression of someone who has risen above petty lives such as theirs.

In the other room of the pub is a group of three very loud, very drunk young lads. They're celebrating something and keep ordering rounds of shots which they slam immediately and then cheer about. I steady myself against the wall and scan the room. There's barely anyone else in here, most people having opted to sit in the front room away from these dickheads.

I'm suddenly outraged. Why should the locals, good people most of them, despite what I might have said a minute ago, why shouldn't they be able to sit where they like in their own pub? It's not right. Of course they're scared I realise, they don't want to get hurt, they don't want to risk getting fucked up, they've too much to lose.

It seems to me then, that I am in a unique position. I don't give a shit about getting fucked up and thinking about it I don't have anything to lose either. I wonder if perhaps I can kill two birds with one stone here and repay the regulars for the pint they bought me while getting these lads to finish a job long overdue. I push away from the wall, stagger over to the nearest one of the group and poke at his shoulder with a weaving finger.

"What?" he says, his question gradually shrinking the broad smile on his face.

"You..." I say firmly, poking him again, this time in the chest, "...are a cunt."

He scoffs and turns to his two mates who are laughing before looking back at me, confusion and amusement now joined by just a hint of menace.

"You what mate?" he asks, puffing his chest out just a little.

"I shed, said..." I slur before shaking my head and trying to focus. "I said, you're a cunt. And do you know why you're a cunt?"

"Why's that then?" he asks as the menace in his voice steps to the fore and his friends both step to his side.

" 'cause your mum's a cunt. You're a cunt from a cunt's cunt, ha!" I declare with relish and a grin. I sway and think hard for a moment before adding, "you cunt."

I don't even see him swing, I just feel the impact in my jaw and then find myself on the floor. I can hear laughter, shrill, manic laughter but it's not until I try to get up and fall back down again that I realise I'm the one laughing.

Another second and the lads are on me, kicks and punches raining down. I relax and I think I'm still laughing as I make no attempt to defend myself. There's pain in there somewhere but it's distant, all I can feel is the movement, the power of the blows and my rag doll frame jerking wildly.

But now it's stopped, someone is shouting

and I hear the slap of a heavy punch above me. I push my hand to my face and then look up, everything is swimming so that my stomach wants to turn inside out.

At first I can't make out what's happening. The guy I poked in the chest is sprawled across a table over there, clutching his face while a skinny figure above me is scuffling with the other two. I try to stand again but still can't make it and so try to look harder at who's who.

It's the lad.

It was him who clocked the first one, and now he's grappling with the other two. They're trying to grab hold of him and push him down onto the floor to stomp him but he's flailing like a maniac and landing blows on both of them. He can't half scrap for a skinny lad.

Just for a second I feel something strange inside me, it's soft and warm and it glows in my chest. Then he finally manges to break free of the pair and turning manages to swing his elbow right into one of their ears.

Suddenly, everything slows down, I can see it all happening. I know I have to get in the middle of it but my body is suddenly leaden and it feels like I'm moving through treacle. My lad watches the guy he's just hit as he drops and then turns to meet the last one, but this guy's already swinging.

I see the light catch the guy's hand and I realise it's not a fist but a glass. I try to move, to shout, to stop it but my lad turns just as the guy lands his blow. I think I hear myself scream at the crunching sound of the glass breaking into his face.

It sounds wet.

I watch my lad tumble backwards and down, clutching his face with bright red hands. The three guys scramble to their feet, picking each other up and fleeing while somewhere a woman is screaming and someone else is shouting about an ambulance.

I still can't get up, my legs won't work and so

I start dragging myself towards the moaning heap of my lad. The pretty barmaid rushes to reach him, actually stepping over me on her way. She gets an arm around him and moves him to sit, cooing and trying to calm him.

I sit and watch without comprehension, utterly empty, utterly lost, as others crowd in around us. Hands pull at me, trying to help me up, while concerned voices ask questions, but I can't move, or speak, or think. All I can do is look at him.

His hands are still at his face and I can't believe how much blood there is on them. The barmaid is talking to him, right in his ear and gently pulling at his wrists. He finally moves his hands to let her see and a collective gasp silences the room.

My blood is cold, my stomach implodes. A howl catches and blocks up my throat. The top left part of his face, of my lad's face, it's just red, like an animal that's been torn open by a car. There are just deep, ugly rips and wetness and holes and red and red.

And not even a hint of an eye.

What have I done?

What I'd done so far was check three nasty little dead end pits and found nothing. Strictly speaking, I had found rats, piles of decaying rubbish and finally a couple of smackheads. She was stood leaning forward against a wall with her trousers at her knees while he sat in the floor behind, his face apparently buried in her arse.

I'd initially assumed they were at it until I realise the lad was actually trying to inject the lass in her thigh. I don't think they even noticed I was there. The image had stayed with me but even that didn't have the same impact as the distinct lack of cars in each of the places I tried so far.

While driving down there I'd tried to pick the most likely spots for the guy to dump my lad's car and then begun to check them out in order. By the time I'd been wrong three times over however, I was starting to doubt myself and could feel panic building deep in my stomach.

I returned to my car and tapped my fingers on the steering wheel in irritation, relishing the pain this brought. I could think of at least six or seven more back alleys, dead end yards and shadowy railway arches, all within walking distance of the area.

The problem was, the clock on my phone told me there wasn't time to check them all. I had to choose one, or two close together at the most, I had to get it right and do it right now. Closing my eyes didn't help, nor did swearing under my breath. Each of the options took their turn at the forefront of my mind, one then the next, over and over.

There were a couple of pairs of places, close to one another, close to me. I could probably check one pair or the other in time and checking two would certainly increase my odds. My gut kept pulling me towards the last one though, the one dark little corner furthest from me or any of the others. If I went for it and was wrong, there wouldn't be time to look anywhere else.

I started the engine and headed for the tallest apartment block in town. At its base, round the back and over the road, was a secluded railway arch that had just become my lad's last hope and a basket for all my eggs. My lips were dry as I passed the corner that would have led me to two other, closer spots to check if only I'd decided to take it.

Shifting in my seat I kept on going, trying not to grit my teeth. As the city's biggest and most exclusive apartment block loomed over me I began scanning the area frantically, expecting to see at least some of residents of the high class apartments leaving the underground car park to start their day but didn't see a soul. The place appeared deserted.

Rolling past the glowing lobby entrance I was briefly distracted by a swarm of shapes and colours. Spattered all across the dawn grey pavement were fluttering flashes of colour of motion, glaring unreal. Places like those apartments often charged the residents extra to keep the surrounding areas pristine, which made this sight even stranger.

As I slowed almost to a halt and peered at the

weird, I realised the street was littered with women's clothes. Just as I was wondering where they could have come from, a burgundy thong flopped silently onto my windscreen, followed by a couple more equally flighty pieces of underwear.

"What the fuck?" I asked no-one in particular before nudging the wipers to sweep the smalls from view. Speeding back up I left the crazy rain behind and shook my head. Who knew what the rich got up to up their in their gleaming tower? It was a different world up there.

I left turned once and then again to reach the back of the building and then turned right and away just a little further on to approach the railway bridge that squatted beyond. To get the car under there I'd need to drive all the way around but luckily I knew a more direct way in. Leaving the car I took a deep breath and steeled myself for whatever I would find.

Moving quickly over the grass verge that lay between me and an old, overgrown chicken wire fence, I carefully picked my way through the dense hedge until I reached a hidden hole. I slipped under the fence and then followed it along until I came to a corner that opened onto the black, gaping maw of the dead end arch.

It was empty.

I knew straight away but rushed into the shadows anyway to check. There was nothing, nothing but the stone, the weeds, the litter and the darkness. Precious seconds ticked by while I just stood there, my eyes stinging with the knowledge that I'd fucked him over. Again.

There was no point even ringing him now, he wouldn't have time to get out. I just needed to get over there, to get in between him and what was coming. Maybe I could talk his way out of it and if not that then I'd just lie. I tell them he hadn't lost the car, that I'd taken it, that it was all on me. Then I'd spit in their eye and take the fall for that as well.

It wasn't going to be pleasant and it might not even save him, but it was all I had left now. I sprinted back to the hole in the fence and tried to dive straight through but the fence snagged my jacket and held me. I thrashed and cursed and stumbled free before bursting from the hedge and running straight for the car.

Just as I was about to leap inside however, I glanced over the road at the apartment block where something hooked my eye. The large shutters that led down to the underground car park were open. It was a tiny detail but it bugged me enough to stop me getting in the car.

Those things were always closed. Always. They only ever opened long enough for someone to drive in or out and then closed automatically after them for security. Maybe they were just stuck, some mechanical fault over which some poor bastard was probably going to have his ear chewed off by all the rich bastard tenants.

Still I couldn't get in the car.

Would he? Would really be quite so dense as to rock up in the car he used to do the job and then bust into the car park of his girlfriend's apartment block and leave it in there? It was highly unlikely, in fact it was almost ridiculous, but it was worth a look, a very quick look.

I jogged across the street and glanced about me. Everything was still silent and from the pavement I could see nothing but gloom in the car park below. Nodding to myself I moved down the ramp cautiously, peering into the darkness within. A few seconds inside and my eyes adjusted so that a neatly ordered crowd of high end luxury cars slowly appeared all around me.

Under other circumstances I couldn't have helped but stop and appreciate some of the hardware on display but as it was I just marched on deeper into the belly of the building, scowling at every car that wasn't my lad's beaten up piece of crap.

Until one of them was.

For a second I actually froze, staring at the arse end of the car I'd spent the whole night looking for, reading the reg three times over to be sure. There it was, just sat there all on its own in an empty corner at the back.

He'd even parked it pretty neatly within the thick

white lines. I felt myself grin and sprinted to the car, landing my hands on the boot. Sweat ran cool under my clothes and a fresh rush of clean adrenaline washed through me. First things first, I went to open the boot but immediately froze as the sound of engines thundered off the concrete walls.

I turned around, the car pressing into the small of my back, and watched as a convoy of half a dozen cars filed into view. I recognised all of them and although it had been just a few hours, it now seemed like ages since I'd been sat with Sid across the road from Maggie's Antiques watching an army of guys mill about around these vehicles.

Well now a good chunk of that army was here, emerging from the vehicles as they stopped. An old guy in a sharp grey suit with a purple tie and a short bloke in a polo shirt wearing lots of gold, each appeared from the backs of their cars and began to approach. Both were flanked and followed by footsoldiers who spread out on either side until they all formed a bristling arc in front of me.

For a heartbeat after heartbeat they all just stood there, glaring at me. A suit with stupid, floppy hair and green tie glared particularly hard off to my left. Meanwhile a one eyed monster with his arm in a sling did his best to compete, glaring while being propped up by mates on either side.

Both looked as if they knew me and wanted me dead, while the rest just gave off a general hostility to all things.

"Y'alright?" I said, addressing the crowd and just about managing to sound cheery. Off to my right, Polo Shirt beckoned the propped up cyclops to his side. His wrists were heavy with gold so that he jingled as he moved.

"That him then?" he asked his lieutenant with a harsh Southern twang. The larger man glared at me hard and narrowed his eye.

"Yeah," he growled eventually, still eyeballing me. "That's him. From the dealer's flat earlier and then from upstairs. I thought the kid shot him, but that's definitely him." Polo Shirt took a step forward.

"You been sticking your nose in my business son?" he snapped at me.

"Don't know who you are mate," I said with technical honesty though I was pretty sure I knew who I speaking to. "So I couldn't say."

The small man's eyes were ablaze as he continued.

"So you didn't lock a couple of my lads in a flat earlier on and set off the fire alarm? You didn't get them both shot upstairs?" he asked.

"Ok look..." I began, but then stopped as his words caught up with me.

"Wait," I faltered, utterly lost. "What?"

"Don't play dumb with me son," he continued. "They only just got out of that flat before the old bill turned up, far as I'm concerned that makes you a fucking grass. Then you help that little shit shoot two of my lads?! Well you're mate only did half a job with Dave here. Now I don't know how you conduct your business up here but we don't tolerate that kind of behaviour where I come from."

He took another step forward and this time his troop moved with him.

"You'll excuse me if I interrupt." This was the old guy in the suit with his purple tie. He was flanked by two more suits, the mean looking bastard with a green tie and a tired looking guy with a neck collar and sling, just about sporting a yellow tie.

"We didn't finish our conversation did we?" he said to me.

"Erm," was the best I could manage, now thoroughly confused. I'd worked out who this guy was of course, though I'd never met him face to face before, let alone had a conversation with him.

"Don't try my patience lad," Purple Tie growled, apparently enraged by my confused expression. "You escaped us at the hotel but you must have known we'd catch up with you eventually."

"Right," I tried, licking my lips and holding up my hands. "I'm a bit lost here guys to be honest, can we just back it up a bit.." but I was silenced by the sight of a younger guy I recognised as Orange Tie.

Just behind him was angry little Pink Tie. Both were now furiously whispering with Purple Tie. Meanwhile who else but Big Jacket and The Bleeder should emerge from the other crowd and start muttering with Polo Shirt.

I winced and waited. Eventually, underlings silenced, Purple Tie and Polo Shirt looked at one another. Polo Shirt conceded with a nod and Purple Tie spoke first.

"And apparently it was also you who liberated the young the bellhop and the car crusher's daughter from my club as well. You have had a busy night."

Of course this last part was actually true, but since they seemed to have mistaken me for someone else several times already, I thought I'd push my luck with a bare faced lie.

"I honestly have no idea what any of you are talking about," I said, looking from Purple Tie's watery grey eyes to Polo Shirt's blazing piggies. "I've not locked anyone in anywhere, I've not set off any fire alarms, I've not had anyone shot. I've been to no hotels, no clubs, no bars and I've not liberated anyone either, alright? You've got the wrong guy here, the wrong guy."

Again Purple Tie and Polo Shirt exchanged glances and this time Purple Tie gave way with just a hint of a nod.

"Hit him," said Polo Shirt and in an instant the bulk of one of his lieutenants was on me. A blow to the jaw put me down and I took a couple more to the back of my head before he started kicking me. I felt a couple of my ribs go then Polo Shirt called him off.

On my hands and knees I stared at the pale concrete beneath me, then spat blood and coloured it dark. Slowly I got to my feet to find Purple Tie, Polo Shirt and all their less than merry men still glaring at me. This time I glared back.

"Listen," I said in a low voice, trying hard to stay afloat amid strong currents of anger and fear. "I'm not the guy you're after. I can't be. Think about it!"

I put my hand back on the car boot behind me to steady myself and looked back and forth between Purple Tie and Polo Shirt, staring them right in the eye each time.

"I can't have been in some dealer's flat with your lads and been at the hotel with you and your lads and been at your club and been upstairs here all at the same time can I? Just think about it. Someone's got it wrong." This kept them quiet for a bit and I saw suspicious glances been fired back and forth between the two groups.

"Make sure he doesn't go anywhere," snapped Polo Shirt to his lieutenant.

I glanced up at the enforcer but saw the blade too late and barely even had time to cringe as he brought it down into the back of my hand. The dull thunk it made as it passed first through my hand and then through the boot of the car, conveyed nothing of the blinding pain. It exploded up my arm and brought me to my knees.

The enforcer smirked at me as I wobbled slow, back to my feet, clinging to the car all the way. My shoulder elbow and wrist were all bent ugly, leading me back to my punctured palm. A low murmuring began and then grew as the two kingpins consulted their lieutenants. Eventually however, Purple Tie shook his head and stepped forward. Slowly, carefully, I leaned away from the car to stand taller.

"You were at the hotel," he said, pointing. "I saw you with my own eyes, I spoke to you. I spoke to you again on the estate and that time I gave you a message for these gentlemen here."

He waved a long arm towards Polo Shirt and his crew.

"Now at the time I believed you were working for them and I suspect that somewhere along the line they believed you were working for me. You've played us off against one another very well all night long and now here you are attempting to do so again," he said. "Right to the death."

I swallowed hard. Cold sweat was streaming from my brow but I kept my grey face grim, not dropping the old man's gaze for a moment.

"These gentlemen are guests in my city and you have caused both them and myself a considerable amount of inconvenience tonight. Now as a mark of respect I will give them an opportunity to suggest how you should be dealt with and by whom before taking any action against you myself, but before we get to any of that," he paused and took a deep breath.

"Where. Is. My. Money?!"

"Check his car," said Polo Shirt, and the bastard who'd pinned me just moments before was bearing down on me again.

"Hang on!" I snapped, raising my good palm to the would be investigator. "You don't really think I'd be stupid enough to leave the money in the car they used for the job do you?"

I looked from one murderous crimelord to the other, ignoring the pain and listening with interest to my own unplanned words. My mind raced, desperately searching for fuel for my verbal fire. I wondered what my mouth would say next.

"I'm only here to get rid of the car, cover my tracks. The money's long gone." I heard myself say.

"Gone where?" said Purple Tie.

I asked myself the same question but couldn't come up with a single answer.

"Nah," said Polo Shirt. "He's stalling. Check the car."

Again I stopped the guy in his tracks, this time by shouting.

"My boss!" I yelled. "I've delivered it to my boss haven't I? You don't really think I'm the brains behind all of this do you? I just do what my boss tells me. He's the one who's been playing you and he's the one with your money."

"And who's your boss?" asked Purple Tie, his voice quiet and level which was somehow worse than before. I silently repeated his question to myself and again I found nothing.

"I can't," I said instead, buying time. "He'll kill me."

Purple Tie just raised his eyebrows and stared the obvious question right into me.

"Right yeah," I nodded. "Fair enough."

I dropped my eyes to the concrete floor and thought about the end of the road but to my amazement

I found an idea there. My head snapped back up to meet Purple Tie's steady gaze.

"Thing is," I began, picking my way quickly through the too new thoughts. "I say he's my boss, I don't actually work for him."

"The fuck are you talking about?" snapped Polo Shirt, clearly well out of patience.

"What I mean is, I do what he tells me or he'll kill me. I'm not getting paid here, he's literally got a gun to my head."

"So what?" asked Polo Shirt with venom. "We're going to kill you anyway, why should we give a shit?"

"What I'm saying is, I fucking hate this guy. If I help you take him out then I'm doing myself a favour. Why don't I ring him right now, get him to come down here? Then you don't need me any more."

Polo Shirt started to say something but Purple Tie cut him off.

"Call him," he said simply.

"And then I can go right?" I asked, awkwardly retrieving my phone from my jacket my my free hand.

"Call him and I won't have you shot where you stand," Purple Tie replied.

"Alright," I said, not quite keeping the shake out of my voice. The idea wasn't working quite as I'd hoped but I had no other option but to push on with it. I found the number I was after, hit the button and raised the phone to my ear.

"On speakerphone please," said Purple Tie. I nodded and lowered the phone, holding it out in front of me and hitting another button so that the car park was suddenly filled with electronic ringing. After an agonizing number of trills the phone was finally answered.

"The fuck do you want bitch?" came an unpleasant but familiar voice. "I've just this minute got in from the airport and now I'm chilling with my woman. You better have good cause to be bugging me or the next time I see you you're going to get your neck wet!"

"Y'alright James," I said, keeping my voice steady now. "I've some people here want to meet with you. They're not happy."

"You what?!" Tall James' voice blasting up at the

low concrete ceiling. "You ain't got no people. You ain't got shit. Shut the fuck up! You do what I tell or you get a bullet in the head fucker, that's it."

"I'm serious James. They're not happy about about what you had me do, in fact they're pretty pissed about it. They want to take it up with you in person." I watched Purple Tie and Polo Shirt carefully as I spoke.

"It's my fucking patch! I'll do whatever the fuck I like on my fucking patch and I'll kill any cunt who says otherwise. Where are you you little shit?!" Tall James continued to rant. "What, you got yourself a crew have you? Got yourself some little mates and now you think you can step to me?! You just tell me where you are you little shit, I'm going fuck you up this time, you and your mates!"

I looked at Purple Tie and Polo Shirt and received nods from both. I gave Tall James the address before adding, "I'm not joking James, you're going to fucking get it for what you had me do you short arse cunt."

I cut the crackle of furious expletives almost before it started, just to ensure he was pushed into a total blind rage. I fumbled my phone back into my jacket and looked back to the army before me.

"There you go," I said. "He doesn't give a shit about anything, he's no respect for either of you. Far as he's concerned this is his city. What could I have done?"

Purple Tie narrowed his eyes while Polo Shirt called his lieutenant back to his side and whispered in the big guy's ear.

"He's on his way," I continued to anyone who'd listen. "So you don't really need me, I'll just get out of your way." I turned to grip the handle of the knife that was pinning me to the car.

"Wait," barked Purple Tie, silencing everyone and freezing me solid.

"Yeah?" I asked hopefully.

"Like you said," said Polo Shirt in a dark voice. "We don't need you anymore."

I stared at the car under my hand. I was so fucking close, I actually had the car, I was touching the thing. I couldn't stand it. Suddenly my fear seemed to melt away, it wasn't helping anyway. I'd still fucked it all up, me and my lad were both still going to die. With fear and hope both gone I found that all I had left was anger. My knuckles whitened on the knife handle.

"Right then.." Purple Tie started but I cut him dead, turning back to face the lot of them.

"Do you know what?" I said, tearing the knife back up through my flesh and then flinging it wildly so that it clattered away into the shadows behind me. I glared at every guy I could see in turn while my hand dripped red beside me.

"You do need me. All of you and do you know why? That bastard on the phone is already bragging about what he's done. He's already telling people how he mugged you over, took your money and then had you running in circles all night." I drew a ragged breath and felt the pain in my hand spur me on.

"And yeah, you're going to kill him, make an example, whatever, but the damage has already been done. People in this town know him, they know he's a dickhead and they'll know the only reason he didn't get away with your money is his own big mouth." They were all staring at me now, a few of the younger ones open mouthed.

"They're going to be thinking about that, thinking that if he can do it and almost get away with it then all they have to do is be a little bit smarter and believe you me, there are plenty of nasty bastards smarter than Tall James in this town, enough to drown the fucking lot of you." My heart was rattling in my chest, driving ever more red out of my hand and rage out of my mouth.

"Once word gets around that you're not untouchable any more, every other dickhead who fancies himself a crook is going to be trying it on. You're going to be working morning, noon and night just to keep the peace in your own back yard." I let them hang for a second before dropping the bomb. "And how's that going work for you when you're fighting off an invasion from Eastern Europe at the same time, eh?

"Oh yeah, I know all about that and soon enough they'll know all about this. You think those guys are going to give you enough time to get your alliance sorted out when they hear you're under siege in your own city? No chance, they'll be up the M1 and up your arse before you know what's happening."

Purple Tie's eyes weren't the only part of him looking grey now, he looked downright sick and I knew I was touching a nerve. To give him credit however, he kept his voice steady. "Even if all of that were true, what has it to do with you?" he said quietly.

"What's it to do with me?!" I shouted. I licked my lips and thought hard, running back all the mad shit they'd been talking about before.

"When your lads went to see a local dealer, I was already there. I ran rings round them then fucked off. When you went to the hotel looking for information, I was already there. I got away from you and all. When your lads went upstairs, I was already there. They got shot, I got out. Oh and then I busted out the lad you'd taken from the hotel for a grilling by conning both your lads, not to mention the lass you took for collateral."

"You might own this city mate," I said to Purple Tie, lowering my voice. "But you don't know it, not like I do. How do think I found all those places and people. How do I keep getting there ahead of you and then getting away again? Because I know this city, I know the people who live here, I know the people who hear things and I know who people listen to."

"If I die today you are all fucked, the lot of you." I pointed with my dripping hand, relishing the rush of agony. "Six months from now and every last one of you will be fucking dead. On the other hand, if you take care of Tall James then you'll have done me a favour, one I'll be happy to repay by making sure that everyone in this city knows who's in charge. I can make sure there's not a man, woman or scally bastard kid walking these streets who won't know that this place is locked down and you are the only guys with the keys."

"And then, when those Eastern Europeans who've been giving you so much grief, when they turn up, all quiet at first, asking questions, which they will, well then they'll hear it too won't they. They'll know that this city is a fucking fortress and that now's not the time to try expanding up here. And if you guys get your alliance sorted, well then they might even think twice about fucking with you lot down South 'n all." I could feel my knees shaking beneath me but maintained the glare regardless.

"I can do that for you, I can make that happen. Or we can all die in a fucking ditch. Your choice." I folded my arms and stared right inside Purple Tie before turning it on Polo Shirt. Both of them searched my face, looking for the slightest tremble, the slightest hint of fear.

I gave them nothing.

They looked at one another and eventually I saw the subtlest of nods pass between them. Polo Shirt gave an order and his guys moved back to their cars, arming themselves from the boots and moving the vehicles into position ready for Tall James' arrival. Purple Tie's guys did the same, though Green Tie lingered to glare at me for a while. Purple Tie just stood in the middle of it all and looked at me thoughtfully.

"I'll see you again lad." he said finally.

He turned away and walked back to his car where Yellow Tie was holding the door open for him. I watched them all in their preparations for a moment, stunned and reeling, then slowly made my way to the driver's door of the car.

As I reached for the door handle I noticed my hand was shaking and so got inside quickly. I fumbled with the wires hanging below the steering wheel for long minutes, unable to press my trembling, sticky red fingers into effective service. Finally the engine spluttered to life and I reversed slowly out of the parking space. Weaving carefully through the flurry of military might I expected a bullet at any given moment.

Had I really just done that? Had that really just happened?

I turned one long slow corner and then another and the daylight oblong of the exit came into view. I glanced about but no-one was following, in fact from this end the car park appeared quiet. A bump and a scuff and I was out on the daylit road, the sun having now well and truly risen. There were tears on my face.

I slammed my foot down and drove like a maniac, leaving behind all those dreadful things in favour of

300

better things on the other side of town, at once closing distance with my lad while putting it between me and the car park. Fumbling as I went so that the car veered dangerously to one side for a moment, I managed to retrieve my mobile from my jacket and found my young friend's number. Before I could do anything else however I had to pull over briefly to puke. I wrapped my hand in a rag from the glove compartment and made the call.

"Y'alright mate?" I said, almost managing cheery.

"Fucking 'ell Kaz!" he whimpered. "What's going on? What's with all the silent calls? We've got to be there in like twenty minutes!"

"It's fine lad, it's all..." I said before trailing off.

"What calls?" I asked but then shook myself, not giving him chance to answer. "Never mind, tell me later. I'm on my way to you right now and I'm driving your car," I said.

"Really?" he sounded like he genuinely couldn't believe it.

"Really," I said with a smile. "There isn't time for me to pick you up. Get all the shit you need and head over to the house. I'll meet you on the corner."

Wispy, broken clouds stuttered across the sky which was now a pale and fragile blue. Somewhere in my chest I felt the soft energy of the second wind that comes with the dawn. No matter how hard you've partied or how terribly you've wrecked yourself, there's something about seeing the night pushed back, seeing that first thin blanket of daylight that both stirs and relaxes the soul.

I felt my shoulders drop and my neck seemed to stretch up as I began to climb out of the city through the dense tangle of inner city housing. Past the tower blocks and endless terraces the roads widened and more of their sides became green. Before long I was closing in on the city's most exclusive suburb and as I cruised round one last long, sweeping curve my lad came into view.

He stood nervous, moving from one foot to the other, his hands clasped together. I'd never see him dressed smart before and somehow the full morning dress, tie, tails the lot, made him look taller. On seeing

301

me he stooped to pick up a heavy black holdall and used his other hand to wave vigorously.

I smiled and shook my head, the lad would never learn to play it cool, it just wasn't in him. Everything he was was right there on the surface. I pulled over to the kerb and stepped out onto the street. I kept my bloody hand in my jacket pocket and scanned all about us carefully. We appeared to be alone.

"Thank you so much for this," he began to gush, his one eye shining wet. I silenced him with a look.

"Let's just do this yeah?" I said, trying to be firm but feeling myself soften at the sight of him.

We moved round to the back of the car and I popped the boot. I stood shoulder to shoulder with him as we looked down at the naked figure curled foetal inside. His eyes were closed and he didn't respond to the sudden rush of air and light.

"Fucking hell," the lad's voice wavered. "He's not dead is he?"

I cocked my head to one side, considering the guy in the boot for a second then leaned in to slap his face. He started, blinked, groaned and coughed.

"There you go," I said, slapping my lad on the back and stepping out of the way. I moved round to the side of the car and leant against the driver's door, absently cradling my aching hand. The guy in the boot was moving now, rubbing his hand over his face before shifting to sit. His face was creased and his eyes narrow as he looked about, surveying the scene until he found my friend.

"You bastard!" he said, a broad grin forcing fatigue to the fringes of his face. "You stagged me good mate. I thought you guys were just going to dump me somewhere or chain me to a lamppost or something."

My friend laughed and produced a bottle of water from the holdall, passing it to the yawning stag. He gratefully accepted it and took a long drink before pouring the rest of the water over his head and rubbing his face.

"Time is it?" he asked as water dripped from his nose and he began to shiver in the cold morning air.

"Late," said my lad, passing the stag some

underwear. "All your stuff's in here but we need to get going, we're supposed to be at Jimmy's in like ten minutes."

The stag clambered from the boot wearing nothing but his shorts and began to dress in the street. The pair laughed and joked about the previous night's antics and after impressively few minutes, he was done. Suited, booted and ready.

"Who's this then?" asked the stag, approaching me. I pushed away from the car to meet him.

"This is Kaz. Martin, Kaz. Kaz, Martin." I returned my bloody palm to my pocket and we shook hands.

"Kaz is my.." the lad paused to think before settling on, "..designated driver. We were all a bit too fucked to move the car last night so I asked Kaz to pick it up for us."

I smiled and nodded, impressed by my lad's lie.

"Congratulations," I said. "Jimmy the Jack for a father in law eh?"

Martin smiled and shrugged. "Nah. There's a lot of talk about him but he's always been a gent with me. He's a good bloke."

"Yeah," I said, exchanging a quick glance with my lad. "I know, Jimmy and I go way back. You just take good care of his lass and he'll see you right." I left the 'or else' to the imagination but Martin was oblivious, grinning so much I wondered if he was still pissed. It occurred to me later he was probably just in love. Same difference.

"Come on then," said my lad. "We're going to be late."

I took the empty holdall from him and wished them well but my friend hung back.

"Seriously Kaz," he said. "I owe you one."

"You owe me nowt lad. Get yourself up that road, I'll leave the car back at yours." I opened the drivers door and got in.

"Was it," the lad persisted. "Was it hard, getting the car back I mean. Did it cost you owt?"

"Nah," I said, starting the engine as the events of the night flashed through me. "Piece of piss."

I left the pair making their way up the street to

303

Jimmy's huge detached house. I could just imagine the state of the place. The vast landscaped garden to the rear would be choked with the most decadent decoration imaginable, seething with expensively dressed guests and occasionally punctuated by huge towering men in dark suits and sunglasses. Jimmy never did anything by halves.

My friend's place was quiet, his housemates would all be at the wedding. I left the car outside and walked slowly back to mine. The air was still cool and refreshing but the initial dawn buzz was fading now and a thin veil of weariness had settled over me. My hand throbbed sickeningly.

The walk seemed longer than it should have been and by the time I made it back my legs were beginning to ache, a familiar sign that I'd had enough. Walking back into that same old room I threw my jacket at a pile of crap and dropped into the same old armchair.

The bed was literally just a few feet away but once I was down even that was too far. The chair would do, it would just fine. I sat for a while, staring at nothing and just enjoying the absence of any demands or pressure.

I might have dozed off for a while, I wasn't sure but eventually I managed to drive myself to rummage about in the guts of the chair until I'd retrieved everything I needed and dumped it into my lap. Very slowly and with great care I managed to roll a joint, still enjoying the nothing.

It was a nice shape and I was sure it would smoke well. I stared at it and thought about the whole lifetime of practice that had gone into being able to roll. I was surprised to find how good it felt to know there was at least one thing I was good at, even with my messed up hand.

As I continued to stare at it I thought about a lot of things, about my lad and his new life, about Tall James and what had hopefully been the end of his. None of it balanced out all the darkness from before but it felt a little better at least.

I placed the joint carefully on the arm of the chair and sighed deeply. I smiled to myself, unable to remember the last time I'd felt as peaceful. I lifted the remaining weight from my lap and felt the handle cool in my palm. I didn't turn the revolver back and forth this time but just held it. I already knew all its details, angles and curves.

Tilting the barrel to the ceiling, I eased the hammer back with my thumb. The click sparkled in the soft morning light and then thrilled gently up through my spine. I moved with slow and deliberate care to rest my chin on the upturned muzzle, adjusted the angle to my satisfaction and settled. My finger curled over the trigger and I smiled. I was calm and I was ready.

To take your last breath, knowing that it is indeed your last, is an incredibly powerful experience. I enjoyed it. I closed my eyes and began to tighten my finger. I felt the trigger begin to give under my pressure and didn't even

Printed in Great Britain
by Amazon